NEIGHBORLY

NEIGHBORLY

ELLIE MONAGO

LAKE UNION
PUBLISHING

Text copyright © 2018 by Holly Brown
All rights reserved.

Published by Lake Union Publishing, Seattle

www.apub.com

Amazon, the Amazon logo, and Lake Union Publishing are trademarks of Amazon.com, Inc., or its affiliates.

ISBN-13: 9781542045773 (hardcover)
ISBN-10: 1542045770 (hardcover)
ISBN-13: 9781542048286 (paperback)
ISBN-10: 1542048281 (paperback)

Cover design by Rex Bonomeli

Printed in the United States of America

First edition

NEIGHBORLY

AUGUST 20

Welcome back to GoodNeighbors.net!

You have 8 new messages from your neighbors!

Looking for a reliable landscaper. Any recommendations?

Server at the microbrewery that just opened on Main didn't wash her hands after using the restroom.

Free aquarium.

Thanks for all the nanny referrals! You AVers rock!

You don't want to miss one of the last block parties of the summer.

My three-year-old lost her favorite stuffed bunny (rip in his right ear, answers to the name Carrots). Last seen at Shoreline Park. Reward for its return— Chardonnay at our house!

Lemonade stand now open at 1340 Griffith Street.

AVers, I have some horrifying news. Last night, one of our own was shot. Details are still emerging, but it looks like the perpetrator was another resident of the AV. At a time like this, we need to lean on each other more than ever . . .

CHAPTER 1

WELCOME TO THE AV!

Two Months Earlier

Doug and I grin at each other in surprise and delight. Even Sadie's in on the act: I feel her feet hyperextending joyously as she's suspended against me in the BabyBjörn.

I couldn't have imagined anything like this—who gets welcomed to their new neighborhood with a block party and a ten-foot-tall balloon arch?—and yet, it's exactly why we spent everything we had to live in Aurora Village (AV to the locals). They say it takes a village, and Sadie deserves one.

Our block is a carefully maintained mishmash of architecture that includes Colonials, Mediterraneans, Tudors, Georgians, Victorians, and California Craftsmen. Some are original, meaning they're more than a hundred years old. Our Craftsman is by far the smallest, a bungalow really, but our neighbors don't seem to mind, so I won't, either.

While the houses might appear to be a random assortment, the trees reveal the AV's covert design. Beech, Japanese maple, jacaranda, birch, cherry, and oak all come together to create an ever-changing seasonal kaleidoscope. The tree canopy above dances like a mobile. There's a flowering pear tree in front of our house, and its fluffy white blossoms take on a silver cast as dusk falls. It's stunning, and I mean that literally. We moved in last week, and I'm still stunned that we get to live here.

Good thing I took care of all that move-in trash yesterday. Sure, my methods were unorthodox, but it had to be done. This place is immaculate. It's like that movie *Pleasantville*, only it's already in Technicolor. The sun is high in the sky, radiant yellow against cloudless blue; it's a child's drawing of a day. The air carries the smoke and tang of barbecue.

The neighbors must have been waiting for us. Before we've even descended our front steps, there's a round of applause, whoops, and whistles.

The children below are bubble blowing and Hula-Hooping and playing tag, dogs at their heels. I spy a pogo stick. There's not a handheld device or smartphone in evidence—no video games, no scrolling. It's like we've stepped back in time, except for all the late-model luxury cars, including, in one driveway, matching Porsche Cayenne SUVs. Since it is the San Francisco Bay Area, the landscape is dotted with Priuses. There are some solidly middle-class cars like ours, a Subaru Outback that we bought used before Sadie's arrival and that I now wish we'd thought to wash.

Card tables span the block, piled high with homemade appetizers, salads, innumerable bun options (several of them gluten-free; one made from a blend of ground-up seeds), and desserts. I feel guilty that Doug and I don't have some sort of contribution, though I was explicitly told that we were meant to be empty-handed as the guests of honor. While there are plenty of cut-up vegetables and six kinds of hummus, the buffet could have used some pretzels, popcorn, or chips. Everything seems so well organized, nearly military in its precision, that I imagine the absence of snack food is not an oversight. In the AV, I bet there are no oversights, only a consensual choreography.

"Do you think there's a block-wide ban on chips?" I whisper to Doug.

"Maybe someone once choked on a fat-free, low-carb quinoa crisp," he whispers back. We giggle, loopy with excitement, irrepressibly thrilled to be the newest residents of the 1800 block of Bayberry Lane. Sadie—who, at four months old, is reveling in her new superpower of controlling her head instead of it lolling around on her neck—strains upward, letting out a giggle of her own.

Four high-end grills are lined up, laden with every variety of organic, grass-fed, free-range meat and, of course, meat substitute product imaginable. A man with appropriately fire-colored hair is moving back and forth among them, alternating between tongs and brushes, a study in male dominance and efficiency. It's a martial arts display. The thought that our neighbors have gone to this much trouble for us is nearly dizzying.

Everything we did to get here was 100 percent worth it. It wasn't exactly a devil's bargain, but it was close.

So many people would kill to be in our shoes. Hundreds showed up at the open house for what is now our home, so many that prospective buyers had to enter in shifts, waiting outside like it was an exclusive club, the selling agent acting as bouncer. Now we're on the other side of the velvet ropes. That balloon arch is directly in front of the walkway to our house. The welcome banner is for us.

All morning, I could hear the setup happening outside: "Let's move this table!" and "How about over here?" and "What do you think of this?" accompanied by laughter. A lot of laughter. I just kept thinking, *Our neighbors like each other; please let them like us. Please let them like me.*

Everyone loves Doug everywhere he goes, effortlessly. He's good-looking but not intimidatingly so—tall and well built but not six-packed, with brown hair and brown eyes and a ready smile. His wit is quick yet never scathing. He listens deeply when people talk; he has a gift for making others feel interesting. He engenders goodwill and reminds you there are trustworthy people in the world. I often need that reminder. In large part, I married him for it.

And people go nuts for Sadie, with her golden curls and cerulean blue eyes. Whenever we're out, strangers make references to the Gerber baby. I was a true blonde, too, when I was her age. Now my hair's much darker, wavy rather than curly, and my eyes are hazel. Me, I'm passably pretty, but she's prototypically beautiful. Doug is an extrovert, while I've always been slow to warm up. Yet that's about to change. Moving here wasn't just about a new house to go with our new baby. It was about a whole new life, one I'll do my best to meet unguarded, with open arms.

At that very notion, my smile wobbles. What if I'm marked in some way that I can't see? What if my life before is indelible, the past written in invisible ink? What if the intensity and purity of AV sunlight will bring it out?

As I teeter, our next-door neighbor approaches and hugs me, her arms a wide arc to encompass Sadie, too. Several days ago, she knocked on our door to introduce herself and extend the invitation to today's party. I was so touched by her warmth and kindness that everything flew out of my head, including her name.

Since moving in, I've seen her the most of anyone, through our front window. She and her husband are empty nesters with a pair of golden retrievers they walk three times a day. She's always wearing work-out shorts and microfiber T-shirts. A space-age fanny pack lies extremely flat against a stomach that's also notably flat, but it somehow goes with her look. Her husband is tall and trim, with a shock of silver hair, and I see he's off talking to a cluster of men who I presume to be the block alphas—all dressed neatly in chino shorts and polo shirts—owners of the largest and most renovated houses on the block. These are men who get their lawns serviced professionally rather than simply mown, who work with large sums of other people's money.

I try to listen as the woman I think of as Fanny introduces herself to Doug, but just then, Sadie lets out a peal of excitement. Well, Doug'll tell me later. He's good at remembering names.

"Come with me," Fanny says, taking my hand and leading me forward. "Meet everyone."

There are orange cones at either end of the block, which she tells me were put there by the neighbor across the street, Wyatt, who is a police officer. I don't know if it's legal to arbitrarily cordon off his own block for gatherings, but I'm not about to question the Shangri-La before me.

A huge bounce house is emblazoned with pictures of Mickey Mouse and friends, and Fanny informs me that the Rileys own and inflate it for every gathering. "Just one of the perks of being on this block!"

A face-painting table is set up with a stool and a five-tiered makeup kit, manned (womanned, actually) by a comely brunette. The little girl on the stool is currently half-cat.

"That's Tennyson," Fanny says, indicating the painter. "Isn't that a beautiful name?" I murmur my assent, hoping I sound convincing. "Her parents were English professors. She was almost named Coleridge. She lives in house number 1812. Her husband, Vic, will be dressed up like a clown later, making balloon animals. He's a day trader. He's also the Easter Bunny and Santa Claus."

No response leaps to mind, so I just nod, smile, and wipe at Sadie with the burp cloth that's tucked into the Björn. I'm on constant drool patrol.

A children's soccer game is being organized on an expanse of emerald lawn; meanwhile, chalk is laid out on the sidewalk for the artistically inclined. Younger kids play harmoniously with older ones. It's unclear which are family members and which are simply neighbors, since a deep familiarity exists from the youngest to the oldest, kids and adults alike. People move easily among different clusters, with shoulder pats and laughter. It's so different from our last neighborhood where we'd rented for years, just twenty minutes away in downtown Oakland, with anonymous bustle and bars and nightclubs. That was pre-Sadie, and this, the AV, is very definitely post. This is where I want to be. These people—they're who I want to be.

While I've never been as outgoing as Doug, I'm sure I can hold my own. It's just that I haven't done much socializing since Sadie came along. I'm a little rusty, that's all.

This is going to work out. It has to. We did what was necessary to get here, because that's how it is once you have children. You make sacrifices so they can have the best lives possible. But that feeling in my stomach is more than a pit. It's the whole peach.

I almost wish I still drank. A glass of wine might sand my slightly jagged nerves. I can't help noticing that there's plenty of white wine and champagne on ice in what appear to be expensive silver buckets. Several coolers are full of juice boxes and milk for the kids, while another is yawning open, full of beer.

I haven't had any alcohol in more than a year, not since before I was Sadie's incubator, and now I'm her main food source. For the first time, I seriously consider a pump and dump, but I've always hated the idea of anything going to waste. Doug's already grabbed a Sam Adams and is taking in his surroundings with a huge smile.

I need to find my next someone to talk to. The vibe is incredibly friendly, and I've got my own balloon arch. There's nothing to worry about. I just need to look around and leap.

By and large, the clusters are gender-specific. Doug joins a male minyan, and I scan the quorums of women. I notice how variously dressed they are, yet so easily commingling. This isn't like high school, where social organization is by type—jocks with jocks, brains with brains. Here, I can't tell who the popular kids are.

The vast majority of women appear to be in their thirties through late forties, so in that way, I fit right in at thirty-four. Some are in lululemon; others are outfitted from REI, like they just got done with a hike; there are lots of sundresses; a few women are done up like Real Housewives, in high fashion with perfect coiffures and full makeup and expensive jewelry; there are a couple of pairs of frumpy knee-length shorts; and one woman wears cat's-eye glasses with a retro print romper, an arty tattoo vining along her arm and up her neck. There are different body types, some much more toned than others, but obesity seems to have been outlawed. Two obviously pregnant women are chatting with each other, mirror images, each rubbing her belly in slow concentric circles.

Women spend their lives trying to set up a certain image—through their clothes, their hair, their shoes—that will serve as a dog whistle for other women of similar ilk. Me, I've always been a career-minded quasi-intellectual, taking pride in my work. I'm happy to see the *New Yorker* magazine in the dentist's office but never subscribe; I aim to look reasonably attractive but not like I've spent too much time to get there, with wedge heels and never stilettos, in the requisite cute top and jeans, loath to take any risks with bold accessories. I don't want to call too much attention to myself; I'm just hoping to blend in. It seems like a low bar, but at a glance, it's not at all obvious to me where I fit. That I will fit.

As I'm scanning the crowd anxiously, I'm set upon by two men. They're both tall, but that's where their similarities end. One has a baby face, silky blond hair, a neatly trimmed beard, and is wearing a pair of jeans and a plaid button-down; the other is craggily handsome, his hair dark with filaments of gray, his muscles on full display in a tank top and tight shorts, his arms tattooed from shoulder to wrist in bright colors, like exotic plumage. I'd guess there's at least a fifteen-year age difference between them, maybe even twenty.

"Hey there! I'm Brandon and he's Stone," the older, tattooed man tells me with a broad smile. "Congratulations on the house! Welcome to the 'hood! We're so excited to meet you!" He leans down to get a better look at Sadie. She preens for him prettily, a flirt at four months. "Look at this little one! So gorgeous. We need another, pronto."

Stone's smile says he's happy being background to Brandon's foreground. "She is a beauty."

"Thanks," I say.

"Have you met Oliver yet?" Brandon asks me. I shake my head. "He lives in that perfectly restored Victorian over there. When Stone and I first moved onto the street, I couldn't stop laughing." I must look perplexed because he points to the Victorian: "Oliver," and then to his partner: "Stone." I laugh. "This one," he says, gesturing to Stone again, "calls me Bran. Doesn't Stone Bran sound like a remedy for the worst constipation you ever had?"

"Stone and Bran should have an 'Esquire' at the end," Stone says, mildly corrective.

"I've always felt we're more of a variety show," Brandon counters. "We're like the Mandrell sisters. When I first said that, Stone had no idea who they were. Do you know who they are?" I indicate no, and he does an exaggerated sigh. "You young folk. No sense of history."

I can tell this is a routine they've done before, but I don't mind. I like them.

"Enough about us. I want to hear all about you!" Brandon says. "It's Katrina, right?" He pauses to mug for Sadie, who coos appreciatively.

"Yeah, but I go by Kat."

"I *love* Kat! So spunky."

I want to live up to that billing, but nothing comes to mind. "What do you guys do?" Ugh. Could I have seemed any less spunky and more conventional?

"I'm in one of those finance jobs no one wants to hear about," Stone answers. "And he's creative."

"I've always got a project going on. I've constantly got to beautify myself or Zoe or the house. I'm a fifties housewife trapped in the body of George Clooney." Brandon dimples. "A much younger, more

10

attractive George Clooney." He glances over to where Doug is engaged in energetic conversation. "Speaking of good looks, can I just tell you, that husband of yours . . ." He does a little wolf whistle.

"Thanks. He's a great guy." I wonder if Brandon's thinking that Doug is too handsome for me, suddenly self-conscious about my new size-eight body. Before Sadie, I was a four. Doug and I used to be better matched. Physically, that is.

"Special delivery!" A voluptuous woman in a halter dress walks up, holding the hand of a lovely child, dark-haired and dark-skinned and dark-eyed, Sadie's precise opposite. I'd guess Zoe is between one and two years old, walking semisteadily on plump legs.

"Yolanda!" Brandon plants a kiss on the woman's cheek. "You're a lifesaver. Where was she?"

"In a flower bed."

"Always with the flower beds." He lifts Zoe high in the air as she giggles. Yolanda recedes before I can officially meet her, but I have a feeling I will eventually. "It's all fun and games until somebody loses their tulips!"

Sadie stretches her arms as if to say to Brandon, *"Pick me up, too!"* I do some knee bends to give her a ride of her own. I fear her fussiness. We're trying to make an impression here.

Brandon says, "The thing I love about these parties is the freedom. Everyone watches everyone else's kids. You can just take off and be an adult for a while."

I don't know that I'll ever be able to just take off. I can't picture not knowing that Sadie's in a flower bed. But I love that I'm entering a world where people look after one another and each other's children. It's an enclave of trust and safety. I've never had that before, not even as a kid. Definitely not as a kid.

"There you are!" Tennyson, the sexy face painter, comes up to join us. "Leave it to Branstone to monopolize the guest of honor." Brandon gives her a side hug. She has a beer bottle sweating in her hand, and I eye it enviously. It's not the only thing I envy, since her body is incredible. She's tan and fit, in a short black catsuit that is at once completely ridiculous and entirely flattering on her. Her face isn't traditionally pretty (her eyes are close together and her lips are thin), but she just oozes good health and self-confidence. "I'm Tennyson."

"I'm Kat."

"Love that." She swigs from her bottle and wipes her mouth with the back of her hand. A few stray brown strands escape her carelessly perfect bun. I have the sense that she's at least forty or even forty-five— her sort of confidence feels like it's grown into—but her smooth skin belies this. "How are you settling in?"

"Pretty well."

It's not exactly true. I've done as much unpacking as I can, but there's still so much building and assembly for which I have to rely on Doug. Handiness is not my forte.

Tennyson lowers her head so she's level with Sadie. She strokes Sadie's hair, then closes her eyes rapturously. "I miss this age."

Sadie reaches out and grabs one of Tennyson's complicated dangling earrings. "No," I admonish, trying to sound just the right amount of firm. It has no effect. I work to remove the earring from Sadie's grasp, and she starts crying. "Sorry." I know I shouldn't feel embarrassed; she's just a baby.

Tennyson is laughing. "No worries. I remember this age. She's putting everything in her mouth, right? Dropping things twelve times in a row so you'll pick them up?"

"The world's just one big experiment in cause and effect," I say.

"That's a cool way to put it."

Sadie's stopped crying, thankfully, and is just studying the throng around us in fascination. She hasn't been in a crowd for a long time, not since I fled the moms group.

"You look at that baby girl," Brandon says, "and you know you need another."

"I'm definitely not saying that," Tennyson responds. "My IUD is staying right where it is, thank you."

"You know who I've heard is trying for another?" Brandon looks around and hooks a thumb in the direction of a tall redhead I haven't yet met. "After that labor of hers? Color me shocked."

"You're such a gossip." Tennyson laughs.

"I don't repeat any true secrets. I mean, you were going to find that out sooner or later anyway." Brandon makes a convex motion with his hands to indicate a pregnant belly.

"When it comes to your children," I say, "you forget the pain so fast." They both give me curious looks. "I mean the pain of labor." I have the sense of being out of sync, that they were speaking lightly and I went heavy. I try to paper over it by asking Tennyson, "Which kids are yours?"

A woman must have overheard because she joins our conversation, with a laugh like music. She's short, her brown hair in a low-maintenance pageboy, wearing a plain tank top and jeans and holding a thumb-sucking toddler in her arms. "Which kids aren't hers?" The phrase could seem barbed, yet her delivery is pure honey. She's instantly endearing, with a round, childlike face and simple wire-framed glasses. She even smells innocent, like some sort of throwback soap. Do they still make Ivory? Tennyson has a scent that's a little bit musky and a little bit spicy. Cardamom, maybe? It doesn't even seem like a perfume, more like an emanation.

Tennyson points to the massive Colonial that's directly across the street from my house. I've seen bands of teenagers trooping in and out of there since we arrived but hadn't yet met the parents. "Yeah, we're the Brady Bunch. Vic had four from his marriage, I had three from mine, and we had one together in a bout of total irresponsibility."

"You're the Brady Bunch, and she's the Gerber baby," the other woman says, her soft voice going even softer as she regards Sadie. Then she smiles at me. "I'm Raquel. And this is my little one, Meadow. We

live in 1805. We're the ones who need to take better care of our lawn."
It's a good shorthand: ironically, Meadow lives in the only house with
a patch of cappuccino-colored grass on the entire street.

"Why don't you just spray-paint it? That's what they do at some of
the condo developments," Brandon says. He and Tennyson laugh with
a clear note of superiority. I realize that Stone has slipped away, and a
few minutes later, Brandon does, too.

But their absence is quickly replaced by another woman who joins
us, and another, and another, and another. Throughout the conversation, they take turns fawning over Sadie, and she's in heaven, surrounded by all those admiring eyes. It's like she already relishes the
impact her beauty has on people. Cause and effect indeed.

I instantly forget everyone's names. In response to their questions, I
tell them that I'm an assistant provost at a state college, on an extended
maternity leave. They're all stay-at-home moms, except for one who
works part-time as some sort of consultant, and Tennyson, who owns
a boutique on the AV's main drag. I do a lot of smiling and nodding.
Until a topic comes up that legitimately piques my interest.

"Nils and Ilsa weren't really here that long," Raquel drops. She gestures toward my house. "I was so surprised when they decided to leave.
Their son was only seven. I don't even think they left the Bay Area, did
they?" She seems genuinely confused that they'd want to raise their son
anywhere else.

"I think they just wanted to cash in," Tennyson says quickly, as if
eager to end the speculation. "They bought, what, three years ago? And
they probably turned a massive profit."

I'm surprised that they're so casually discussing Nils and Ilsa's
finances and, by extension, mine. I feel my face reddening.

"But if they really wanted to cash in, why didn't they take the highest offer?" A woman with hair shaped like a mushroom cap—Regina,
I think?—turns to me like I should have the answers. They must have
known Nils and Ilsa better than I did. As far as I was concerned,

the former owners were just names on the paperwork, the people to whom my realtor submitted our offer along with a beseeching letter. The unknown masters of our fate and now, the purveyors of our good fortune.

"You weren't the highest offer?" Tennyson gives me an admiring look.

"No," I say, a little bit proud, and then a little bit embarrassed at my pride.

The whole conversation feels askew somehow, but I think that's just because we're culturally conditioned not to talk about money. In some company, it seems more taboo than sex, more intimate.

As I tip my head back to underscore my confidence in spite of my mild discomfort, my eye catches on a man who is standing apart from everyone, motionless, his face and body tense. He's sinewy, with a receding hairline and ruddy skin. He's staring at our group, his eyes slightly narrowed. I feel my own body tense, a response as involuntary as a bouncing knee reflex from a rubber mallet.

"That's my husband, Bart," Raquel says, like his behavior is nothing out of the ordinary. Maybe he's just an intense guy. Or maybe he is entirely normal, and my subconscious is just sending up flares. She jiggles Meadow in her arms. "You'll meet him at some point."

I'm kind of hoping not.

"So how did you beat out higher offers?" Tennyson brings my attention back with her surprise, as if I've climbed Everest or cracked the double helix.

I force my eyes away from Raquel's husband, though he seems like someone I don't want to turn my back on.

"I wrote a letter to Nils and Ilsa," I say, "and I included a picture of Sadie with a homemade onesie that said 'AV or bust.'" I regret it the second it leaves my mouth. Using Sadie like that just seems so . . . cheap.

Yet the smiling faces before me register complete comprehension. You do what you have to do to get into the AV. We're on our own little island, jutting out into the Bay, just minutes from Oakland and San Francisco. Low crime, every school a ten, and you can smell the brine in the air. What wouldn't you give to raise your kids here?

Regina wrinkles her nose slightly. "Was it really just a letter and a picture? Ilsa and Nils weren't exactly sentimental people."

"They were a little cold," Raquel allows, with the air of someone who doesn't like to speak ill of others.

No, it wasn't just a letter and a picture. It was also an offer $450,000 over asking. The kind of offer we could never have made without Doug's parents; a debt we'll be paying off for the rest of our lives in more ways than one.

"Well, on that note, I guess we have to do it." Tennyson releases a dramatic sigh. "It's the inevitable conversation."

"Real estate." Regina fills in the blank. "The way this place has exploded. New money and old money. The people who've been here forever, the newcomers, the ones who inherited like Wyatt and Yolanda, and everyone in between."

"It's pretty strange," Raquel says, "to suddenly be sitting on a gold mine. It used to just be a house."

"A house on the best block of the best neighborhood," Regina says passionately. "I mean, there's no other place like it. Some people have more money, some people have less, but there's no tension. No conflict. No artifice. No airs. Only community. Where else can you find that?" She pauses to position her soapbox. "The AV isn't quite city, and it's not quite suburban. You can walk to great stores and restaurants and to the beach. You can bike along miles of trails. Yet you can always find parking on your street. It's the best of everything. It's trans-urban." She says it like the term just occurred to her, but then a man passing by (her husband, presumably) outs her:

"Going on again about the whole trans-urban thing?"

She laughs and swats at him.

While I'd never state anything as forcefully as Regina, she's right: the AV is rare. Neighborhoods tend to be homogenous—everyone has great wealth, or no one does. But here you have houses of vastly different sizes on the same block, used Subaru Outbacks beside Porsches, hedge-fund managers next to normal people like Doug and me (he's a senior market analyst, so his field is about as lucrative as mine, which is to say, not terribly).

It's everything I never had growing up. Good schools, a community full of warmth and kindness, and, above all else, safety. I'm going to make sure nothing happens to this little dangling bundle of mine.

But I have to admit, the AV is not diverse in all ways. I'm looking at a sea of white faces, an alabaster undertow.

Meadow says, *"Potty, now!"* and Raquel excuses herself, heading toward her brown-lawned Georgian. I notice that her husband is following, and I feel a tightness in my stomach, like we shouldn't leave them alone together. Which is crazy, because they're married. They're behind closed doors all the time.

"It's not quite the best of everything," Tennyson says, her face suddenly somber. We all look at her expectantly. I'm the most worried of all. A part of me has been waiting for the catch ever since we went into escrow. "You can't park just anywhere on the street." She indicates the open spot in front of a rambling Victorian with peeling green paint, the closest this block has to an eyesore.

I laugh the loudest, the most relieved. "I met her!" I say. "Well, I didn't exactly meet her. She came out to yell at Doug and me about not parking in front of her house, when we'd actually just parked on the opposite side of the street, in front of our house."

"You're Gladys's worst nightmare. A Craftsman couple with two cars and no garage. You're a threat," Tennyson informs me with a grin.

Doug and I had laughed about Gladys (not that we knew her name). We called her "the old crone" and "the local color," the eccentric everyone has to put up with, who's probably lived here forever and who'll undoubtedly die here. The one bad apple, the exception that proves the rule. Gladys keeps this place from being too good to be true.

"She doesn't even own a car," Tennyson says, "but she wants the space available in case someone visits her." She rolls her eyes.

"Which is practically never," Gina says. "It's kind of sad, really."

A handsome man with gelled curls and wolf-blue eyes comes up behind Tennyson, snaking his arm around her waist and whispering in her ear.

"It's too early," Tennyson says. "Wait until after we eat." She looks at the rest of us. "He can't wait to get in his clown suit. It's a shame it's not something plush. Then at least I'd get a little kink out of it."

Vic lets go of Tennyson, a bit reluctantly, it seems, and extends his hand to me. "Good to meet you. Kat, right? I was just talking to your husband. Great guy. We're really glad you're both here."

"Thanks," I say. "We're really glad we're here, too."

He slips back into the crowd. I have a sense the spell has been broken, the inevitable conversation is over, and everyone is considering their next move. If they disperse, where will I go? I look around and see that Doug is headed my way, his plate piled high. He's always the first at a buffet, with utter unselfconsciousness.

"For you," he says. "Do you want to give Sadie to me for a while so you can relax and eat?"

The other women seem impressed by his solicitousness. There are introductions all around. Doug takes Sadie from me, and a new crowd forms around us, all couples. Some of them have plates, but those who don't are happy to accept Sadie, saying that Doug should eat, too, since he's the guest of honor.

It's Sadie's first time crowd surfing, and she clearly loves it. Having all these new people to bewitch by looking into their eyes, touching their faces, and trying to put anything she can into her mouth . . . what more could she ask for? I work to quell the slight anxiety that I feel. After all, this is why we came; this is the Village.

It is nice to actually focus on eating, to not just scarf but to relish. I do that so rarely, and this food is so worthy. The ribs are succulent, alongside an arugula fennel salad with mandarin oranges, some sort of marinated greens, and homemade corn bread. Doug quickly fills a plate for himself, and then between bites of barbecued chicken, deviled eggs, and potato salad, he fields questions about the new house.

"Kat has all these amazing decorating ideas," he says. "Have any of you heard of the tiny house movement?" Heads shake no. "There's this network we call THN—for Tiny House Network—because every show is about building and decorating your tiny house. And most of them are way smaller than ours, like three hundred square feet. We've got nine sixty. We're *huge*!" Everyone laughs.

It's true, I have been pretty obsessed with THN ever since our bid was accepted. It's where I could find a whole spate of shows to validate our decision. On one, an eco-friendly host announces that tiny houses are the next big thing, and I like that. It's not that Doug and I couldn't afford a larger house; it's that we're part of a movement with a shared ethos to pare down to your own personal essentials. It's about figuring out what you truly value, about having less and doing more. It's not about possessions but about living fully. Yet that trash mound in front of our house told a different story. Thankfully, it's gone.

"So Kat DVRed, like, every episode of every show on the THN," Doug continues. "She got really inspired. And she was most excited about stairs. Under the stair storage! Pull-out drawers built *right into the staircase*! Steps turned in bookshelves! Every day, I'd come home and there would be another idea about a flight of stairs."

"I'd never even thought before of how pretty that expression is—a flight of stairs. It's like a flight of fancy, you know?" I say, because I feel like I should be contributing, that Doug and I should be like Stone and Brandon, a variety show, a vaudeville act. But either my timing is off or my tone. I can see that despite my hopeful "you know?" our audience doesn't know. I feel my face growing hot, and I stuff it full of corn bread.

"So you know how it is in this market," Doug continues, and they turn into bobblehead dolls. That, they know. "It's like pandemonium, and there are so many people at the open house, and our agent is like, 'Hurry up, write the offer, bid high, waive your contingencies!' You barely have time to even look around; you're just eyeballing all these people, your competition, and you're in a frenzy. Did you guys see the hordes spilling out onto the sidewalk, frothing at the mouth? It's like we'd all been let out of the zoo or an asylum." He pauses for audience appreciation.

He's flattering them. Who doesn't like to think they have what other people want? Sunday open house was probably like game day, watching the masses with a beer and some chips. Well, maybe not chips. They probably had a vibe about who they liked. Maybe they even saw Doug, Sadie, and me. Were they rooting for us? Did they want us on their team?

Doug smiles at me. "So when we finally get into the house, we're walking around, taking it all in, saying, 'This is it, this is where we live, we made it!' and then I see Kat is standing frozen in front of our stairs, and she just looks crushed. Like, totally defeated. In all our daydreaming, we sort of forgot our house is more like a split-level but with only two levels. We've got five steps, and each one is yea tall." He pantomimes the distance. "No under-the-stair anything for us! Back to the THN drawing board!"

Everyone finds him charming, and he is, but I wish he hadn't spent so long underscoring our mini house and my preoccupation with stair storage. Yes, the houses on the street are of different sizes, it's one of the cool aspects of the AV, but even the next-smallest house to ours is probably double our square footage.

Also, listening to Doug has taken me back to the thud in my chest the day I thought we'd made a big mistake. We'd come out of the purgatorial escrow and gotten our keys. We pushed open the front door, electrified with excitement, and looked around. *Really* looked around.

We had seen the house only that one time, when we had to assume that if everyone wanted it, it was worth having. Then we were in a bidding war, waiving all inspection contingencies and writing sycophantic letters and pimping out our newborn. And then we were exultant. We were winners! Who doesn't want to be a winner? After that, fantasy (and THN) took over.

But staring around at the reality of the unstaged living room, I realized how much I had forgotten, or rather, how much we'd never had the time to register. Like the five crummy little steps. Like the hardwood floors that needed a polish, at a minimum, and the largest space in the house that would encompass our living room at one end and dining room at the other, which featured the galaxy's cheapest aluminum blinds to keep us from looking directly into our neighbors' house. Why were random wires protruding from a floorboard? Was that a loose brick in the nonoperational fireplace? I also realized anew the fact that I'd conveniently overlooked: 960 square feet with two bedrooms was actually smaller than the one bedroom in which we'd been living.

This was, indeed, a tiny house, and a well-worn one at that. No, well loved.

"It's the *Velveteen Rabbit* of houses," I told Doug. We smiled and clasped hands in silent agreement: there would be no looking back.

Sadie's been passed around enough by this point; she's starting to let out little protest cries. I reattach her to me via the Björn, and she immediately starts to fuss in that way that makes me think she could use a diaper change and some milk, maybe some homemade carrot puree. The introvert in me would like a break from all the socializing anyway.

I tell Doug that I'm going inside for a bit, but just as I'm stepping onto the sidewalk in front of our house, I'm nearly run over by the sixteen-year-old Goth girl who lives next door to us with her mother, June. (I can remember June's name because it's the same as the current month, the one in which we moved into our dream house.)

"I'm going out, and you can't stop me!" the teenager yells. June doesn't even notice me, she's so busy giving chase. "Take my car keys, I don't give a fuck! I'll find another way!" They both round the corner, and I see June grabbing her daughter's arm roughly. I avert my eyes, realizing that others are doing the same.

June seems friendly but distracted, like her head is permanently turned around on her neck, seeking out her wayward daughter. Every time I've seen her, she's been racing in and out of the house, giving off the fumes of the desperately late, or maybe just the desperate.

Mother and daughter don't look anything like each other. June has curly auburn hair and blue eyes, and she's in a pair of jeans and a pretty floral top with spaghetti straps. She's no Tennyson, but she's definitely attractive. The daughter's face is covered in white paint, and she has piercings in her lip and nose. She dresses head to toe in black. Her hair is also black, with electric-blue streaks. She has her own Audi and frequently tears out at far too high a speed for a residential street. I've seen June on the sidewalk, shaking with impotence in her daughter's wake. I'm pretty sure there's no husband.

I hadn't noticed June at the party earlier, but I'd seen her contribution: a few store-bought pies. People were joking about it, but in a nice way, like it was one of June's charming peccadilloes.

I take another step toward my house.

"You're not leaving already, are you?" Gina asks.

"Just going inside for a while," I say. "Sadie needs to eat."

"Don't worry," Tennyson sing-songs, "you can just whip 'em out!"

I feel a twinge of shame, caught red-handed. I'm not able to breast-feed. Since Sadie never latched, it's pumping only. I'm not hiding my boobs; I'm hiding the fact that Sadie won't drink from them, which sometimes still feels (irrationally, I know) like a kind of rejection.

I force a laugh. "I'm going to keep some things private just a little while longer."

"There are no secrets in this neighborhood!" Tennyson winks. I realize she's past tipsy, and maybe it's true that there are no secrets, because she's not trying to hide her drunkenness at all.

"See you soon," I tell her and then walk up the porch steps.

That's when I notice the rectangle of cardboard.

It's from the boxes of our new dining room chairs, with their disappointingly wobbly legs, like a colt that hasn't yet matured. I thought I'd gotten rid of all that cardboard yesterday.

But no, a piece of it is right here, in front of our door, positioned like a welcome mat:

THAT WASN'T VERY NEIGHBORLY OF YOU.

CHAPTER 2

What does that mean? What wasn't neighborly?

There's no one I can ask. The note is anonymous.

I shut the front door behind me and lock it, holding Sadie tight. From where I'm standing, I can take in the whole first floor. The living room yields to the dining room, with a corner office nook, and then on through the kitchen, where a door leads to the backyard. We painted every room a different bright color, because this will be a happy place: a yellow kitchen, a red dining room, a blue office nook, a green bedroom for Doug and me, and a purple nursery for Sadie. It's my tiny home. *Our* tiny home.

Happy is the life we're meant to have here, in this neighborhood. And we will, that note notwithstanding.

Someone was probably just drunk; that's all it was. Or kids were playing a prank. Next, they'll toilet paper our house. It's just innocent, throwback fun.

I make my way into the kitchen to get Sadie's bottle from the fridge. In my preoccupation, I slam my shin into a heavy box. That's something they don't highlight on THN, all the bumps and bruises you'll incur while adjusting to your Lilliputian house. Inside the box is my new desk, still awaiting assembly, the one with almost impossibly small dimensions that we bought to fit into my undersize office nook. I wish Doug would hurry up and get this house done. I wish he were here, right now, to give me a hug and tell me we have a block full of awesome neighbors and not to let some silly note give me any pause.

In the living room, there are two striped love seats facing each other because we couldn't fit sofas, and I take a seat on the one facing the door. I cuddle Sadie as she sucks hungrily, obliviously, at her bottle. Some Styrofoam has already found its way onto my skirt, and I try to bat it away, but it clings resolutely.

While Doug and I scraped together enough money to buy essentials like love seats, we had to skimp on some other things. Our house is full of particleboard furniture with nearly impenetrable instructions and bolts, nuts, and screws that get everywhere. Doug's job is building, and mine is trash removal. I scurry in his wake, picking up plastic wrapping, cardboard, and of course that infernal Styrofoam.

I can't wait until this house is fully assembled, until I can sink into the love seat with Sadie and croon in her ear, "We're home, little one." That's what keeps me up at night, fixating on things like the replacement part that's in transit to finish Sadie's dresser. So much depends on delivery schedules and on Doug's marginal building skills. As handy as he's not, I'm worse. He's also a procrastinator. I've definitely got my character flaws, but that's not among them.

On an early date, Doug and I asked each other questions that we had to answer immediately, automatically, with no time to craft an appealing persona. It went like this:

HIM: What are you best at?

ME: Making to-do lists and knocking them out.

HIM: What are you worst at?

ME: Relaxing. What are you best at?

HIM: Reading people and giving them what they want.

ME: What are you worst at?

HIM: Getting anything done before the eleventh hour.

He wasn't kidding.

It's not that I enjoy being in constant motion; it's that what I want most is to relax, and I can't allow myself relaxation until everything's done.

Since Sadie, everything can never be done. In a sense, it's my worst nightmare, this Sisyphean life, yet she offers the greatest reward. She forces me to sit, and rock her, and smell her hair, and for that I am profoundly grateful.

The cheap metal blinds are shut, and the house is cool. I watch Sadie's eyelids droop. I love when she falls asleep on the bottle, in my arms. It's the most complete happiness I've ever felt. Sadie in my arms is incredibly soporific. I begin to drift away.

Then I'm jarred awake by knocking on the front door. I don't know how much time has passed. Sadie's still asleep, deadweight in my arms. I just need to stay quiet and whoever it is will go away. They'll leave us in peace.

The knocking stops, and I let out my breath in a whoosh. I don't need to go back out there. It's a thought that's at first comforting and then sad. I was having fun at the party; I don't want to stay away just because of some lame handwritten note on cardboard. I don't want to have to build my walls up again.

I hear a key turning in the lock, and I freeze.

It's only Doug. My entire body loosens as I see him.

But it's not only Doug. "Hey," he says. "There are some people I really want you to meet."

It takes me a second to realize that he means right then, as in, right behind him.

"I wanted Wyatt to try some of the Talisker," he says, "and Yolanda hasn't gotten a chance to meet you yet."

The three of them step across the threshold. Despite my poor name recall, Yolanda is unforgettable. She was the one who returned Zoe to Stone and Brandon, the one oozing out of her halter dress. Now I bet that woman can breastfeed half the state. She has an absolutely beautiful face, with pale, luminous skin and eyes like emeralds. Her hair is long and blonde, and her blowout is starting to frizz, but it just makes her look softer somehow, more touchable.

"Are you sure it's OK?" she asks, sotto voce because of Sadie.

"Definitely," I say, mustering a smile. "Come in. Sadie can sleep through anything." Sometimes that's true; at other times, just a shaft of light can blow a whole afternoon. But I have a feeling she's going to stay down this time. I wish I'd changed her ripening diaper before giving her the bottle. She teaches me a thousand little lessons a day.

Doug walks in, swaggers really, and I can see that he doesn't need that Talisker. He's pretty buzzed already. Wyatt and Yolanda enter much more tentatively behind him. He goes to raise the blinds, and I gesture toward Sadie so he turns on a lamp instead.

"Pardon our mess!" he yells as he goes into the kitchen. "We're under construction!" I hear the clink of a bottle against a glass. He's clearly not worried about waking Sadie with all that racket, but I don't want to chastise him in front of our new neighbors.

I'm not in the mood for company, still bleary from my nap and a little self-conscious about the state of the house, but Wyatt and Yolanda do seem really lovely. Wyatt has a sweet, *aw shucks* manner that I wouldn't have expected from a police officer. He'd be tall, dark, and handsome except that his features seem a few centimeters off, like he's a poor reproduction of a classic painting.

"Please, have a seat," I say, gesturing to the love seat across from me. There's packing material on the floor and book boxes that I can't empty until Doug bolts the shelves to the wall, since we're in earthquake country. The nonoperational fireplace has become a repository for all sorts of detritus, and the mantel is laden with measuring tape, a hammer, nails, and other random tools. Doug already apologized for our mess, and there's nothing I can do about it now, but still, I'm aware of it.

"I love how colorful it is in here!" Yolanda says. She and Wyatt take the love seat opposite Sadie and me, and she casts an appreciative glance around. "We are surrounded by white walls. It's so sterile, you know?"

"How long have you lived in your house?" I ask.

"Six years," Wyatt says. "It was a gift from Yolanda's parents."

"Not exactly a gift," she corrects. "It's my inheritance."

"Lucky ducks!" Doug calls out. It's a rare social blunder, I think. Doesn't *inheritance* imply both her parents are dead? But neither Yolanda nor Wyatt seem offended. Doug carries in three glasses of whiskey on a plastic cutting board. "Couldn't find a serving tray," he says apologetically. "Kat, do you want an iced tea or anything?"

"No, thanks. I'm good."

After everyone has their drinks, Doug puts the cutting board on the floor and sits down next to me. He leans back, his arm across the width of the cushion, and he looks down at Sadie and up at me with a slow grin. I'm not used to this posture from Doug, his version of a manspread. But then I see that Wyatt is already sitting this way with Yolanda. The phrase *social butterfly* never quite fit Doug. He's always been more of a social chameleon.

"We should paint our house like this," Yolanda says to Wyatt. "Bring in some color."

"Sure," he answers amiably. "Color's good."

Yolanda looks at Sadie. "I don't know if I've ever seen a more beautiful baby."

Then we're off and running. We talk babies, while Wyatt and Doug talk whiskey, followed by the Golden State Warriors and the NBA playoffs. Doug must have given Yolanda a pretty stiff pour because she becomes confidential quickly. She tells me about multiple rounds of IVF before she was able to have their twins, who just turned two a few months ago.

"Bran's watching them now," she says. "We tag team. I wanted to be a stay-at-home mom, but sometimes you just need a break. It can be exhausting, having two." She runs her hand along the shaft of her hair, smoothing it.

"I can only imagine. It's exhausting having one."

"I used to be in pageants, if you can believe it." This seems apropos of nothing except perhaps a sudden bout of insecurity. I've noticed that Wyatt is always touching her back or arm or shoulder like she needs constant validation.

"I believe it."

"I'm talking way too much!" She indicates her empty glass and says, "I'm such a lightweight." Then she laughs self-consciously. "That's one term that doesn't usually apply to me! Not anymore."

"I've put on weight, too, since having Sadie."

"You look great." There's a peculiar note of accusation in it, and I'm glad when she changes the subject. "I think about going back to work sometimes. Do you?"

"I don't just think about it. I am going. In about two months." I feel a rush of sadness, looking down at my beautiful sleeping girl in my arms.

"Part-time?"

"No. Full." To my surprise, I'm on the verge of tears.

"Then don't go!" Yolanda says sympathetically. She's trying to help, but doesn't she get that it's not always a choice? For me, it's a necessity. You'd think she'd realize that, since her husband is a police officer, not a finance guru like some of the other men on the block.

"Kat's a career woman," Doug says. "That's always been true of her." I don't know how long he and Wyatt have been listening. His comment is intended as support, but I feel like there's an undercurrent of him thinking I'm better at work than I am with Sadie. Sometimes I fear that myself.

"Other women on the block work, too," Wyatt says. "Tennyson runs that boutique on Main. It's called Le Jardin. Have you been there?"

At the mention of Tennyson, Yolanda's expression hardens like cement.

"We haven't really been on Main yet," Doug says.

Wyatt rubs Yolanda's arm as if it's a lamp that might contain a genie. She won't look at him.

"We should head outside for dessert," Wyatt says. "Yolanda makes these Nutella squares you won't believe. No one eats just one."

"That does sound killer," Doug says, with an overblown enthusiasm that tells me he's sensed the sea change between Wyatt and Yolanda, too. He stands up. "You want me to handle Sadie's diaper? You know I've got the magic touch. She won't even wake up." I hand her over, feeling suddenly exposed, like I've lost my security blanket.

Yolanda gives me a high-wattage smile. "It's been great getting to know you, Kat."

"You too," I say, returning the smile.

"Thanks for the booze," Wyatt says, "and the talk."

"It's so good to have people like you on the block," Yolanda says, fixing her gaze on Doug and then on me in turn. "You know, normal people."

What were Nils and Ilsa?

Yolanda and Wyatt walk out, and I want to wilt back into the couch. We came, we saw, we conquered. I avoided any major social faux pas. That's enough for one day.

Doug carries Sadie upstairs to the changing table, and though he does have a talent for minimal jostling, she wakes up with a wail anyway. I hear him soothing her expertly. He's just the dad I hoped he would be, and I think I always sensed that and was attracted to it from the first time we got together, even before I knew that I wanted to be a mom myself.

They come back down, and Sadie's in a fresh purple onesie that reads DADDY'S GIRL.

"Seriously, Doug?" I say.

He smiles. "You dressed her for Round One. I get Round Two."

I'd put her in a cute print sundress, not a onesie from the five-pack his mother had given us, which we made fun of when we'd found a pink You Go, Girl! in the mix. But no need to split hairs.

"Should we call it a day?" I ask.

"Did you even see the dessert table? I'm having at least three of those Nutella squares." He lifts Sadie high in the air and then drops and catches her. It's a game she finds endlessly delightful. "Come on, Introvert. It's only one more hour."

I don't know where he gets all his energy. Right now, he's practically vibrating with it. He was recently promoted to senior market research analyst and has been working longer hours, then coming home and still getting in his quality time with Sadie. While the raise couldn't have come at a better time, there's no customized Tesla in our future.

"Are you OK?" His question reminds me that we're in this together, and if it's not OK right this second, it will be soon. "You don't have to go back out if you don't want to. I get that this stuff is hard for you."

I feel a tsunami of love for him, for them. Doug and Sadie. They're my life, and it's good. "Let's go."

When we step outside, the party is still in full swing, though the laughter is more raucous (read: drunken). On the curb across the street, the kids are lined up like a photo op, seemingly according to height, their feet in the street, their knees practically touching, while they eat ice-cream cones. I see that there's an actual silver cart nearby with a pinstriped umbrella, and an adult I haven't met yet is scooping.

The heat seems to have skyrocketed, and I'm feeling a little faint. Maybe I do need to quit while I'm ahead. Doug is wearing Sadie in the Björn, so I could just go inside and let them carry the torch for our family. At parties, Doug likes to outlast everyone. He says you get the best dirt during cleanup.

I'm looking around, trying to decide where to insert myself, when I notice something. Where people were talking in groups earlier, now

31

they're talking in pairs. Cross-gender pairs, for the most part, and no one is with his or her own spouse. They're standing closer than seems customary. Coy smiles, flirtatious laughter, the occasional hand on an arm . . . I've been around the block, so to speak. I know what chemistry looks like.

What is wrong with me? It's daylight. Kids are nearby, and everyone is happy. More than happy. There's no hint of jealousy, no sense that people feel their partners are behaving in an untoward fashion, and indeed, whatever touch is happening is totally PG.

But I think of the note. Is this what it means to be neighborly? If so, maybe I'm not. I don't want anyone looking up at Doug the way, say, Tennyson is looking at Raquel's husband, Bart. Or, for that matter, the way Raquel is looking at Tennyson's husband, Vic.

It's just conversation among neighbors, among friends, I'm sure.

Yet I'm still feeling slightly off-kilter when a petite woman in well-fitting jeans, a white tank top, and a chunky necklace approaches me. I haven't seen her before. She's got thick, straight strawberry-blonde hair that falls a few inches past her shoulders, which are as freckled as her face.

"I hope it's OK that I'm crashing the party!" She has the best smile I've seen all day, and there have been a lot of smiles. "I live over there." She points to the huge—and I mean *huge*—corner Tudor on the 1700 block. It looks new, too, like maybe the owners bought up two houses and knocked them down in order to build it. "I'm Andie Praeger."

"I'm Kat Engells." I don't know what makes me do it, but I lean toward her. "I'm sorry. I'm so tired, I feel like I'm going to fall over."

"It's overwhelming, meeting all these new people. Especially when they're so nice."

Despite the heat, I feel a chill. "Why especially then?"

"Because you can't just put in an appearance. You have to small talk *for hours*. And *that* is the definition of exhausting." She glances back toward her house a bit furtively. "Listen, I can't stay long, and I don't want to hold you up. I just came to invite you over to our place for dinner. What night works for you?"

I can't say no. Not that I want to, exactly, but it's hard to know precisely what I want. I feel disoriented by her directness and by her charisma. It's like I have no choice. "Um, Tuesday?"

"Perfect. My husband, Nolan—he says welcome, too, by the way— works way too many hours, so it's a treat to be able to tell him he has to be home early on Tuesday. And my son, Fisher, is about Sadie's age. I think we'll all get along famously." Another brilliant smile.

Fisher's not with her, so she must have a nanny. Of course she does, with a house like that. She probably has a whole staff. A maid to clean, a butler to answer the door and mix martinis, and a nanny for Fisher. How else could the mother of a four-month-old look so fresh?

"Is six o'clock OK?" she asks, and I nod. "Can't wait for Tuesday!" She sashays back to her house.

Doug comes over, and we're both transfixed by Andie's retreat. It's not like she's the prettiest at the party—that title would go to Tennyson or Yolanda—but she's got a way. Your eyes follow her entrances and her exits. You want to know what she knows.

"That's Andie," I say. "She wants us to come over for dinner on Tuesday." We watch her go inside the Tudor.

"I have to agree with you," he says. I raise an eyebrow questioningly. "About the garbage. Can you imagine a woman like Andie inviting us to dinner with a garbage mountain in front of our house?"

He kisses the top of my head, and I lean into his shoulder. One of the neighbors shouts, "Get a room!" and everyone laughs, myself included. I realize the clusters are back. No more coupling with other people's spouses. Tennyson, Raquel, and their husbands have become a convivial foursome. It's like I'd imagined the earlier configurations, the flirting, the scent of sexual possibility. It's a block party, a perfect summer day, with tipsy neighbors who truly like and trust each other.

The AV is utopia, and so egalitarian that you can even talk about money. No matter what you have, you're good enough. Andie Praeger just sought me out. It's a brave new world.

As Doug and I stand together, surveying, the tide starts to turn. It happens that quickly sometimes. One influential family says their goodbyes, and then everyone's packing up, packing it in, leaving in droves, back to their houses. We're not in party mode anymore; we're in get-shit-done mode, the story of a parent's life. A party is an organism with a natural life span, and this one is expiring quickly.

"Let's go home," Doug says into my hair.

"You don't need to stay till the bloody end?"

He kisses my head again. "Not today."

"You don't want to be part of the cleanup crew? That's when you'll get the best dirt on our new neighbors," I tease.

"Nah. We're the guests of honor. Besides, whatever dirt there is, maybe we don't want to know. Maybe they can all just stay pristine." He calls out, "Thanks, everybody! You throw a hell of a party!"

A chorus of exclamation points comes back: "Thanks for coming!" and "Glad to have you in the neighborhood!" and "See you soon!" and "You've got to come watch a Giants game with us!" and "No, an A's game!" and "No, Giants!"

I behold the street, with all the industrious worker bees cleaning up and then disappearing inside their beautiful houses. I take in the banner they put up in our honor. I'm one of them. I'm home.

A feeling comes over me, starting in my stomach. It tells me that all that light has to have a shadow, that all the camaraderie and the community could just be a mirage, a cover for something darker. That maybe the AV is too good to be true after all. That we've made a colossal mistake, and it's going to cost us a lot more than our life savings.

No. This is just an example of what Dr. Morrison told me, that I have trouble believing I deserve good things. It took me a long time to trust Doug, and look how that turned out.

CHAPTER 3

"Did you meet Tennyson? Really hot and, later in the party, really drunk?" I whisper.

"No. I met her husband, Vic." Doug speaks at normal volume. He says that's one of the benefits of having Sadie down the hall in her own room. I still wish her crib were at the end of our bed like it was in the old apartment. I miss her like a phantom limb.

"I met Vic just for a second," I say. "He seemed like a nice guy. But what's with the clown outfit? And I hear he's the Easter Bunny, too. Oh, and Santa Claus."

Doug laughs, and I fight the urge to shush him.

I'm enjoying the spooning and the talking (we're usually too tired to do much of it), but there's a bit of a disconnect in terms of our moods. Doug is in a state of pure, unadulterated happiness, convinced he did the right thing for his family by moving here, and I want to be where he is, I really do. Yet a tiny but significant part of me remains unsettled.

I'm about to ask Doug if he noticed anything unusual about our neighbors, if they seemed just a little too friendly with one another, when he says, "My dad called." Is it just coincidence that he picks that moment to roll away? "I should probably hop to it and call him back."

"Now?"

"That's the deal, right? He calls, I jump." He adds, "*We* jump."

It's only eight thirty at night, so it might not be that unreasonable for Doug's dad to expect a callback, but it seems that way to me. Meeting all those new people and trying to make a good first impression takes its toll. Any other parent would understand that, but Doug's parents don't have to understand anything. That's part of the deal, too.

I haven't mentioned the note to Doug. I don't normally keep things from him—well, present-day things; the past is a different story.

I just don't want to tell him that I've already managed to piss off one of our neighbors. I'm pretty sure I figured out who wrote the note and why.

First the who: it's got to be Gladys.

Someone who's that territorial about a parking space she doesn't even use obviously has a screw loose. The good news is, she's got to be eighty years old. She's harmless. She's a joke. At the block party, people were literally laughing at her.

But it's my fault that her ire is targeted toward me. Since we moved here, I've been nothing but neighborly, except for that one time, that one lapse in judgment.

Yesterday morning—barely morning, four a.m.—I'd woken up from the chronic sleep deprivation and the stress of the impending party. You could argue I hadn't been of sound mind.

I'd gotten out of bed carefully and creaked into the hall. I had to fight myself because the pull toward Sadie's room was so strong. Yet I knew that opening her door was likely to wake her and trying to catch a glimpse would just be selfish.

Doug says that he and I need to have our intimate space back, that we've been living like roommates since Sadie. But I have so much tactile connection with her that I feel sated. I can't tell him that, though. It would be too hurtful.

Sometimes I can't believe I've inhabited motherhood for only four months, this strange land with its own customs and vocabulary (sippy cups and breast shields and onesies, oh my!). It seems like I've been living in disorientation, exhilaration, and anxiety for much longer. It's such a different love than I feel for Doug. He's fully formed, but I have the power to screw her up totally.

These are four a.m. thoughts.

Once downstairs, I peeked out the window, marveling at the beauty of our neighborhood in the half-light. It was dimmer than that, actually, more like two-thirds dark. No one was out, and I assumed no one was up.

I couldn't help seeing the twelve full garbage bags and untold pounds of cardboard that I'd broken down the day before and that now rested against the front of the house, way too much to fit in the cans that Doug had lined up neatly along the curb. Doug's plan was to let all the garbage accumulate and then schedule a big pickup. "It'll be hauled away in one fell swoop," he'd said, doing an expansive motion with his arm to underscore the point. Wiped clean, all at once. It was an appealing idea. But I was staring at an ugly reality. That's when I thought of the block party, and I went into a true what-would-the-neighbors-think? panic.

On this block where everything is so geometrically neat (every hedge, even the garbage cans along the curb are precisely horizontal), I was gripped with fear. They were throwing us a party, and we were sullying their perfect neighborhood. We stuck out, worse than a sore thumb. We were a *dirty* thumb. All the other houses dwarfed ours, and we had our own trash mountain, like it was Appalachia.

Plus, Doug hadn't even set up the big trash pickup yet. He told me not to worry, he'd handle everything, but how could I not worry? Given his procrastination issues, when I add things to his to-do list, I never really let go of them. The item on my to-do list simply becomes, "Ask Doug if he's done *x* or *y*." That's way worse than just doing *x* or *y*, because it turns me into a nag. I'm not a nag; I'm a doer.

June from next door had happened to mention that she hoped we were early risers because trash pickup was at the crack of dawn. So, by the time everyone woke up, our trash mountain could be gone.

The street was entirely still, with not even a drape twitching. Conditions were perfect. If the neighbors knew, they'd thank me. But I was sure they'd never know.

I put a jacket on to conceal my pajamas and stepped outside. With a surreptitious look around, I walked over to Fanny's cans and lifted the lid. I felt a twinge, like it was a form of theft, that I was taking something that wasn't mine. I should ask permission, no excuses. But who was awake except me? If I waited to ask, I'd miss this week's pickup entirely.

I was just so tired, and I could hear the garbage trucks rumbling, blocks away. There wasn't much time to make a decision. If I was going to do it, I had to do it right then. I thought of the block party in our honor and first impressions. I needed to be good enough, to *appear* good enough. Decision made.

With twelve bags of trash and untold amounts of recycled cardboard, I must have loaded up practically every can on the block. I remembered Tennyson and Vic had extra cans, which made sense given the size of their brood, and I tossed a bag or two in their auxiliaries. Raquel's can, for sure, and Wyatt and Yolanda's, and who else's? Gina's. Brandon and Stone's, but they would never leave a note like that. June's cans were too full, which made me wonder how two people could generate that much refuse in a week.

I stayed on our block. Nothing went in Andie's can.

It had been too easy, and I'd felt light-headed with success. Or maybe that was just sleep deprivation and lack of food. I'd been forgetting to eat lately.

I even came up with a name for it: distributing. It was kind of like being part of the tiny house movement. Ridding the neighborhood of trash and doing as much recycling as I could—in that second, it seemed like I had discharged a civic duty.

"Distributing?" Doug repeated when I told him later. He broke out in a big grin. He clearly thought it was nuts, but in a cute / quirky / Zooey Deschanel way. It made him laugh to imagine the neighbors catching me on my clandestine trash run down the block. "New Mother Skulks through Neighborhood, Clutching Cardboard," he said, his fingers splayed out, like it was a newspaper headline.

Wait. The realization dawns on me. I never used Gladys's cans. Does that mean the note couldn't have come from her?

It had to have. Everyone else on the block is so nice, so welcoming. None of them could be behind such a stunt, even if my stomach just dropped, trying to suggest otherwise.

Anxiety craves a certainty it'll never get, Dr. Morrison once told me. But the majority of the time, the most obvious suspect is the right suspect. If a wife is murdered, chances are the husband did it. Or vice versa.

CHAPTER 4

DO YOU THINK THEY ACTUALLY LIKED YOU?

My eyes roam the street for someone who's lying in wait, watching for the moment I'd find this next note on the windshield of my car.

There's no one around. The street is as silent as it was at four a.m. on trash day.

They've used another square of cardboard from the box containing the dining room chairs. I try to remember which recycling can got that particular piece, without success. I didn't commit that kind of detail to my already overloaded memory. Bandwidth is scarce these days, and it's not like I thought it would turn out to be a clue.

I could understand the first note. It was a rebuke, telling me to keep my trash in my own cans. I assumed it was specific to an action I'd taken, one that I'd make sure never to repeat.

This note is different. More global and yet more personal, it strikes at the heart of my insecurities, where I'm the most vulnerable. It's like this person knows me.

I'm trembling. It's Monday morning. Sadie's already buckled into her car seat in the Outback, and we were going to try out a Mommy and Me class before our trip to the supermarket. I've avoided a lot of activities with "Mommy" in the title since my experience with the moms group in my last town. But this is my fresh start.

I make a snap executive decision to skip the class this week. It's better to go when I'm in the right frame of mind, so I can make the right impression. But there's no avoiding the supermarket.

"Hey! Yoo-hoo! Kat!"

I blink in the sunlight, startled. Tennyson is running across the street toward me, all legs in a pair of white silk hot pants and a short-sleeve silk blouse with a tie at the neck, almost like a cravat. I don't know how she can pull off that outfit or move that fast in three-inch heels.

I drop the cardboard and kick it under the car, hoping she won't see, hoping she won't ask.

"Did you have fun at the party?" she asks.

"Definitely." I try to convey the enthusiasm I felt before I saw that welcome mat. "It was so great of all of you to do that for us."

"Honestly, we were going to have a block party anyway. It's just great to have an excuse. And we are extremely psyched to have the three of you here." Her hair is loose around her shoulders today, and she shakes it back from her face, smiling brilliantly. "Don't you just love when everything comes together like that? That's what life's all about, synchronicity."

I try to agree heartily. I worry that I'm undoing all the good work I did at the party, that I seem awkward and strange, and my awareness of that only enhances it. Best to remove myself from this conversation as quickly as possible. "Sadie's in the car already," I say. "I should probably run."

"Oh, sorry. I'll talk fast. There's a girls' night out on Thursday, and we want you to come." She must see the question in my eyes because she begins to enumerate on her fingers: "Gina, Raquel, June, Yolanda. And Andie. We invited Andie for you."

Whoever wrote the note is wrong. They do actually like me.

"Sorry about the short notice," Tennyson says. "We all thought someone else had already mentioned it to you at the block party and just realized no one had. It's like Kitty Genovese. You know who I mean, right? That woman who got stabbed in her courtyard with, like, thirty people watching from their apartments and no one called the police? The more witnesses, the less likely anyone is to call the police." She must see the WTF in my eyes because she adds, "Bad example. Anyway, once a month or so, we ditch the husbands and the kids. We just get to be *women*, you know?"

"Sounds fun," I say. "Let me check with Doug."

"Check with him? Just tell him." She touches my arm gently. "We really want you there. Make it happen, OK?"

I smile. "OK."

As she starts to cross back to her side of the street, she calls over her shoulder, "Don't forget the rule, though: no talk about kids!"

It's a rule that instantly scares the crap out of me. I'm not sure what else I have to fall back on at the moment. But I'm almost certainly going to find out. If I turn down this invitation, I might never get another.

When she's out of sight, I squat down and retrieve the cardboard. I toss it facedown on the passenger seat and turn the ignition with my shaking hands. This is an opportunity, I tell myself. Tomorrow, it's Andie and Nolan, and Thursday, a bunch of potential new friends. This is why we moved here.

"It's going to be OK," I tell Sadie, using that lilting tone that she likes. But I can't hear any sounds in reply.

I wish car seats weren't rear facing so I could see her right now. She was asleep when I carried her out. It never ceases to amaze me what she can sleep through or what will wake her up. There seems to be no rhyme or reason to it.

I can't stop myself. I reach over the seat and push back the fabric canopy that veils her. Spot-checks make it more likely that she'll wake up prematurely and be fussy when we get to our destination, kind of how every time you change lanes, you increase the odds of an accident. But in my present state of mind, I can't resist. I'm solely responsible for the welfare of this helpless, delightful, occasionally infuriating person. OK, not solely responsible, but primarily. Doug leaves the house at seven thirty and doesn't get home until seven o'clock most nights.

The college generously allowed six full months of maternity leave (and Doug's parents have subsidized it financially, with strings attached, as per usual), but I'm down to the last two, the home stretch. I need to start visiting day cares, figuring out where Sadie will be safe, where she'll be loved, in my stead. It's a painful thought, and maybe that's why I've been dragging my feet, despite the fact that procrastination goes against my nature.

Many times, I've questioned whether I'm equal to the challenge of motherhood. Her continued existence depends on me. How could anyone not be daunted by that, at least a little?

Sadie had been sleeping, but with the sudden increase in light, she startles and cocks her head back to look at me. A spiderweb of drool spins toward her onesie. Then she starts to howl.

"It's OK, sweet girl," I tell her. I move to stroke her hair and her face, but she's having none of it. It's like she knows that this awakening was completely unnecessary, and at my hands. She doesn't want my ministrations.

So, after a few minutes of trying, ineffectually, to soothe her, I reach into the diaper bag, remove the pacifier, and thrust it in her mouth. She sucks as loudly and contentedly as that baby on *The Simpsons*. I just hope she doesn't suck for as long. That show must be pushing thirty seasons by now.

I used to fear that Sadie would become a pacifier addict, wearing one on a chain around her neck at college like she's at a perpetual rave.

At first, I said I wouldn't use them at all, then I said that it was just for when she needed to sleep. Now, all bets are off. It seems like I reverse myself all the time since she was born. When I used to say, "I'll always do this" or "I'll never do that," it was because I didn't yet know how intolerable her distress would be for me, that it would shape my every action and reaction. I had no idea she'd be able to control me with her pleasure and—maybe even more so—her displeasure. The threat of her unhappiness hangs over me all the time, my own sword of Damocles.

Trader Joe's is only a few minutes away, and I drive extra slowly, gathering myself. I manage to find a parking space close to the entrance. I decide that instead of using a cart, I'll snap Sadie's car seat into the stroller and just fill up the mesh bottom underneath. That's the quickest way.

Shit, where's the list? I forgot it, and that was before I found that note. That's just my normal mommy brain.

I hate that expression, *mommy brain*. It's so insulting. But, in my case, accurate.

I remove Sadie's stroller from the trunk and then lift her car seat into it, waiting for the reassuring snap that tells me I've done it right. I wish life had more reassuring snaps, just a split second of limbic soothing: "Correct, now proceed."

I take a few deep breaths and then we cross the parking lot. Sadie's still sucking on that pacifier, a baby crack pipe, but I can't worry about that now. She's a baby. College is almost eighteen years away.

I've got more immediate things to worry about.

No, I don't. It's just a scrawled note on some cardboard.

But it wasn't scrawled at all. It was in a neat, even script, carefully printed rather than written in cursive. The person was taking her time. It wasn't the heat of the moment. It was a considered act—two considered acts—and that makes it much scarier. Twice is a pattern. Someone's holding a grudge.

This is about trash, literally. How seriously can anyone take it? I will not take this seriously. I will not.

The double doors slide open at our approach, and Sadie and I glide inside. I don't have my list, but my brain is working just fine. She's moved past rice cereals and loves the purees I make. I started with a small amount, just an experiment, so I'm ready to make a big batch, frozen in the special ice trays with their eco-friendly green lids, designed for just this purpose. I like having things match their purpose.

I look around at the organic fruits and vegetables, hoping for sweet potatoes, since those are her favorite. I'm trying to smile at all the people who are smiling at Sadie and me—much more at Sadie, really—though it feels so unnatural, so counter to my emotions, that I hope it's not coming across as a pained grimace.

I put my head down and focus on the produce. If I don't see their smiles, then it's not unfriendly when I don't smile back.

I hum "Apron Strings," a song I love and, fortunately, one of Sadie's favorites, based on frequency of leg kicks. I toss a bunch of organic apples in a bag. Just fine, we are just fine.

"Hey, Katrina!"

I nearly jump. When I look up, it's Fanny (dammit, I forgot to ask Doug her name), beaming. Sadie is smiling back, around her pacifier.

"Oh, hi!" I say with an extra-wide smile that I hope appears genuine rather than clownish.

"Did you have fun at the party?"

"It was the most amazing block party I've ever been to. Everyone's so welcoming and so kind."

She nods, like she's heard it many times before but it never gets old. "I knew you and your family would be a great addition." She beams again. "And how are you settling in?"

"It's coming along," I say, trying to act normal. Do you ever seem less normal than when you're trying to act it?

She adopts a sympathetic expression. "Moving is just about the most stressful thing there is. And with a little one? Even one this precious." She's doing sort of a baby-talk thing on the last sentence, directing it at Sadie, which Sadie seems to appreciate.

"Yeah, it's been pretty stressful." Made more so by some neighbor who chooses to remain nameless. Would Fanny have a guess who it is? No, I can't tell her. She might wonder what I did that was so unneighborly to begin with. "Well, I should finish the shopping. I need to get Sadie home and down for her nap."

"That's it," she says with approval. "Stick to a schedule. It's the thing that keeps you sane!" She pauses to cast an adoring look at Sadie. "I raised my girls in this neighborhood and watched it change around me. But only in good ways."

"What ways?"

"The property values have gone through the roof, obviously, but it's just stayed so—accessible, I think that's the right word. If anything, it's only gotten friendlier. People truly want to know each other." Another pause. "Everything about each other." Her face turns so thoughtful it's nearly grave. "The AV is a very special place, Kat. You'll see."

I try to tell my tightening chest: that wasn't a warning; it was a promise that there are good things to come. I've arrived.

Before I can think of a proper response, she's walking away. "See you soon!" she says gaily.

Sadie and I get through the rest of our shopping trip without interference. Once we're home, I decide to take the old advice: nap while your baby naps. But I've never been able to do it when she's in her crib; I need her flush against me.

We lie together on the love seat, my feet dangling just a little off the edge (good to be only five four when you can't fit a full-size couch). Sadie is pancaked to my chest, and we breathe together, slowly, deeply, hypnotically. Doug and I talked about having Sadie nap only in her crib so she's used to being on her own, but I'm just not ready to be on my own at the moment. Doug would understand if I told him about my morning, about getting a second note.

But I'm not going to tell him. Better to let him be my distraction, to let his spirit of optimism and his presumption of a world worth trusting suffuse me.

"Crudité again?" he asks that night as he drops into a kitchen chair, grabbing some of the cheese I've cut up and sticking it on top of a cracker. He doesn't actually mind, or if he does, he's never said it.

I didn't only cut up cheese but some vegetables, too. It's a balanced meal, sort of.

I'm a lot better than I was earlier. After our nap, Sadie and I took a bath together, read books, listened to music, and I don't even know what else we did, but the hours passed and most important, we didn't have to leave the house. It was just the two of us.

Even when it's good with Sadie, even when she's not having any of her outbursts, there's a pressure I feel: to keep things good, for her to remain happy. It's a low-level hum, the pressure, like having a bug burrowing in your ear canal. Listening to that all day can suck the life out of you, though I never want Sadie to feel my lack of energy. If she did, then how could she stay happy?

When Doug comes in, the bug dies, just like that.

Sadie's in her high chair, and I'm feeding her the last of the puree cubes. I'll have to make the new batch tomorrow, no excuses.

My breasts are heavy with milk. I missed my last pump session. It's not that I was sleeping or that I forgot; it's that I just plain didn't want to hook myself up to that god-awful machine. It doesn't hurt anymore—my nipples are inured—but having to occupy Sadie in some way for fifteen whole minutes while I'm indisposed, holding the breast shields to my nipples, seemed especially onerous today.

"How was Mommy and Me?" Doug asks.

"I didn't go."

"Why not?"

I shrug. That's not the same as lying. "I was tired."

"You skipped class for no reason?"

"You say 'skipped class' like I was going for my PhD. It's Mommy and Me. We were going to sing 'Old MacDonald.' I'll go next week. I think I'll be able to catch up."

He pops another cracker in his mouth. "Someone's touchy."

"Just tired."

"You know what might help? Some relaxation." He drawls out the word, and I know he's not thinking what would help me, he's thinking how long it's been since we last had sex.

I play dumb. "After we put Sadie down, you want to start a new show? We could have a Netflix marathon."

"Whatever." His tone is mild.

I want to tell him about the notes.

I can't tell him about the notes.

Because either they're about the trash, in which case I'm to blame, or they're about something else, where the question of blame is much more nebulous.

No, they're just about the trash. I have to believe that. And soon, the writer will get a new hobby and leave me alone, and no one will ever have to know the rest. Not even Doug. Especially not Doug.

Session 1.

"You're a doctor, right? So you can prescribe medication?"

"I have a doctorate in clinical psychology. So yes, I'm a doctor, but no, I can't prescribe medication."

"I was told you're an expert in trauma. Are you?"

"It's one of my specialties, yes."

"What are your other specialties?"

"Would it help you to know that answer, or do you think maybe you're a little uncomfortable being here and you're trying to delay? That's a perfectly normal thing to do in a first session. It's a perfectly normal thing to do, period. No one likes talking about their pain."

"I'm not perfectly normal."

"I imagine you want what we all want. To be valued. To connect. I know you've been through a lot, but you have the same needs and desires as everyone else. It's all about how we fulfill them."

"That sounds profound."

"Are you being sarcastic? It's OK if you are."

"So, everything's OK in this room?"

"Emotions are OK in this room. You just need to learn the healthiest ways to express them. My job is to make this a safe place for you. But I need you to tell me how to do that."

"I can't tell you that. I can't even tell you the whole story."

"I know from your intake form that the trauma happened when you were a child."

"I'm not even sure it's a trauma."

"Let's take a step back. Slow down and start over. What brings you in today?"

"I want to feel better. I need to get over what people have done to me."

"That was then, and this is now. You didn't have control then. You have it now. You just aren't convinced of that yet."

"And your job is to convince me?"

"No. It's to cede control to you. We go at your pace. You pump the brakes when you need to. You tell your story the way you want."

"Why do I feel like you're doing some Jedi mind trick on me?"

"Let's take a step back. Slow down and start over. What brings you in today? Why now?"

"My whole life is a mess. I thought I'd gotten away from my past, but it just keeps shadowing me. If I'm not careful, I'll fail out of school, and I can't seem to be careful. I just can't seem to care."

"Yet you care enough to be here. That's huge."

"It doesn't feel huge."

"How things feel isn't necessarily how they are."

"Are you always going to talk in riddles?"

"That wasn't a riddle. That was as straightforward as it gets."

CHAPTER 5

It's 3:23 a.m. Doug hasn't built my desk yet for the nook, so I'm huddled over the laptop, which is open on the coffee table. I'm studiously ignoring the affront to my sense of order: book boxes that still need unpacking, the pictures and coat hooks and mirror that haven't yet been hung on the walls. And that's just the living room.

Instead, I peer at my screen, where I'm logged into Homestore, and right next to it, our credit card. Homestore received my return three days ago, but the refund hasn't shown up on our Visa yet. We could use that $107.46. I've turned off auto-pay on all our bills because I need to keep a strict eye on what's going out right now. In more than ten years of having a joint checking account with Doug, our balance has never been anywhere close to this low. It frightens me to look at it.

So I stop looking.

I click on my "To Do / To Build / To Install" file, taking note of the satisfying check marks beside what's already done, though I haven't entered a new one in days. I also keep a tally of when backordered items should be arriving, as well as replacement parts. Every time I go into

Sadie's room, my eyes involuntarily travel to the half-built dresser. Doug can't finish it without Part C.

I'm pretty much obsessed with Part C. It's become a running joke with Doug and me. "When's the messiah coming?" he asked the other morning. "You know, Part C?" I laughed, but he could never truly understand what it means to me. He grew up in comfort rather than chaos, in attention instead of disregard. Part C is a repository for all my anxiety, a symbol of my great desire for Sadie to have better than I had—for her to grow up in a home that's childproofed in every sense of the word, with someone thinking of her well-being first, always. Things half-built, haphazard, disorganized, or dirty remind me of how I was raised. Doug certainly doesn't know everything, but he knows that much.

I'd logged out of Visa, but I'm still logged into Homestore, and almost against my will I find myself clicking on my wish lists, room by room (though "Outside" isn't technically a room). For such a small house, our yard is large, and it's in need of mowing and weeding. That's on the TD/TB/TI list, too. Someday, I'd like to be able to buy the child-safe fire pit I've saved to my list, and some furniture to surround it. A bistro table and chairs for the deck, for sure. A hammock. A papasan chair. That's the life we're going to have—where we relax, and we entertain legions, with kids and dogs running around, chasing bubbles until their satisfying pop.

Doug wanted us to have more people over when we still lived in our apartment. He has plenty of friends that he doesn't get to see nearly enough. But I didn't want to entertain; I just wanted to be with him, drinking fifteen-dollar cocktails in ambient bars and restaurants to put me in the mood. I didn't even like the bartenders to recognize us, so we rotated. Not being known is one of the best parts of city life, as far as I'm concerned.

But that was then; this is now. Doug and I are no longer a couple. There are already three of us. So, the more the merrier, that's supposed to be my new motto.

I keep trying to put my anxiety over the notes to rest, but it continues to surface. It's probably because I have so much trouble resting, myself. If only I could sleep, the world would look so different.

I close my eyes, and I see the handwriting. It's so neat. That's a person who means what she says, who could wreak systematic havoc on someone, if she so chose.

There's nothing overtly feminine in the handwriting. Yet I can't help thinking that caring about violated garbage cans and writing catty anonymous messages is something only a woman would do, that it's a particularly female strain of domestic passive-aggression. Maybe it's because the professional world feels a million miles away right now, because I spend my days sweating what I know to be the small stuff, while Doug—i.e. men—is off immersing himself in masculine productivity. At least, that's how it is in the AV, where it seems like Tennyson is the only one with a job outside the home.

Has motherhood paradoxically turned me sexist?

Consciously, I know Doug isn't working harder than me. Being a stay-at-home mom is far more taxing than any other job I've held. And what's more important for society than raising a child well? Somehow, though, my daily life feels insignificant, my tasks like that of a worker ant scurrying back and forth, holding a single crumb aloft.

The truth of it is, sometimes I don't know who I am anymore. Without the accoutrements and accessories of my former life, without all that was automatic and assumed, without the tether of familiar routines, I'm unmoored. I grab on to Sadie and I hold her tight because otherwise, I might just drift off into open water.

I'm so tired of worrying—about being a good mom, about fitting in, about the stupid notes. I'd love to wake Doug up right now and have him reassure me that I'm doing a great job and it'll all turn out fine. Better than fine. We're AVers now.

I tell myself the things he might say, but they ring hollow. I head for the stairs. It's time for me to 'fess up about the notes and be reassured.

But something stops me before I reach the first step. It's an old friend. Shame. I'm ashamed that I brought the notes on myself and ashamed that I'm getting myself so worked up. Doug has always thought I'm a little bit fragile because of my childhood, and he doesn't know the half of it. Doesn't know an eighth of it.

Dr. Morrison heartily disagreed, but a part of me still feels like I brought things on myself with Layton, too. In sessions, she encouraged me to call him Layton. Not Mr. Layton, like I was used to calling him in class. Or Steve, like I called him outside of it. Just Layton, my abuser. "A pedophile," she said. I didn't want to disappoint her, but I couldn't attach that word to him. I still can't.

I do what I always do when thoughts of Layton rise to the surface: I make myself busy.

Settling back on the love seat, I check my e-mail. The top one is from something called GoodNeighbors.net:

Andie Praeger invited you to join!

Andie's up at this hour, too? I would never have guessed, based on her visage at the block party. She looks like a woman who gets her beauty sleep.

I click "Yes" on the invitation. Instantly, another e-mail appears:

Register now to find out what your neighbors are
up to!

We're going to Andie's house tonight, so I feel obligated to start the sign-up process. I don't want to reject her this early in our relationship.

I click around GoodNeighbors, getting a flavor for it. People are talking to strangers—correction: neighbors—about sheds they need built, the best piano teacher for a three-year-old, a free bicycle that just needs a new front tire, how to plant tulips, and where they can find a nontoxic dry cleaner. It's all stuff I would have turned to Google, Yelp, or Craigslist for, but this is about going local and building a community. There are potlucks and more block parties coming up. Girl Scout cookies are being sold on the corner of Vine and Bowdoin. "We're new to town and have a five-year-old. Anyone going to the park today?" is a typical message. People are hungry for connection, in a wholesome, 1950s way. It's not quite city because of how trusting everyone seems and not quite suburbia because people actually walk and know their neighbors, and because Main Street has only local businesses, no chains allowed. It's trans-urban, like Gina said, a high-tech Mayberry.

I haven't even uploaded any kind of profile, and the messages are already pouring in:

> Ty and Linda welcome you to the neighborhood!

> Brandon and Stone welcome you to the neighborhood!

Which one's up, Brandon or Stone?

> June welcomes you to the neighborhood!

June next door? We're a block full of insomniacs. Is there something in the water?

> Garrett and Maya welcome you to the neighborhood!

And of course:

> Andie and Nolan welcome you to the neighborhood!

GoodNeighbors wants me to introduce myself. I should say where I'm from, why I moved here, what my interests are. I'm exhorted to upload a pic.

Since Sadie came along, my photos are of the two of us, and I'm not especially pleased with how I look in any of them. I don't have any recent pictures of Doug and me (who would take them, Sadie?). And I'm not the selfie type.

I think about uploading a picture of Sadie alone, but would that make it seem like I'm uncomfortable with my appearance or obsessed with my daughter or both? It could say that I have no identity outside of her. Besides, it could give potential predators ideas—predators who'd know, vaguely, where we live.

I skip that step and fill in the text bubble. Since Andie's the one who recruited me, I don't want to reflect poorly on her, if anyone can see our linkage.

> Hi, neighbors! My husband, Doug, and I just moved here with our new baby. Can't wait to meet everyone!

It couldn't be more bland and really, two exclamation points in three sentences? But at least it won't give too much away or offend anyone. It's the Hippocratic Oath of the new neighbor: first do no harm.

Immediately, my mind goes to the one person who's not afraid to tell me that I've done harm.

But that's one person, and I've got a whole neighborhood welcoming me with open arms. My generic profile message has already garnered twelve likes. I have girls' night out on Thursday. Andie stopped by the block party just to invite us to dinner.

I wish that last bit soothed me, but I feel the opposite. Andie's overtures make me nervous. She seems like the kind of person who'd already have a life (over)populated with friends. So why is she pursuing me?

CHAPTER 6

I can't believe I'm about to knock on the recessed door of this massive stone Tudor. In grays and browns, with tall, narrow, multipaned windows, it actually has side gables. You could fit five of our house inside, comfortably. But it's not just about the fact that Andie and Nolan have so much more money than we do. It's that they're in a different developmental stage altogether. This is a house where adults live.

We, on the other hand, live in Crayola.

Doug thinks of our new home as a member of the family, and he insisted it should have a name. He likes naming things, in general. So I told him to go for it, and he did, and now . . . Crayola was the obvious choice, given our primary color scheme.

I want to tell him not to call it that in front of Nolan and Andie, but I can just imagine the hurt that would shoot across his face. Besides, there's something incredibly sweet about the pride he takes in saying each morning before he leaves for work, "See you back at Crayola?"

When we first got married, he never just said, "This is Katrina." No, it was, "This is my wife, Kat." He was proud of me, the way I'm proud to present Sadie. It's one of his most endearing aspects.

"What's going on?" he asks, sensing my hesitation.

"We're just such small potatoes."

"The Praegers are big potatoes. King Spuds."

That's a name that will stick, I can tell. "See you at the King Spuds'!" he'll call out. That's if we make it to a second hangout. The night is still young.

Noticing my fidgeting, Doug tells me, "You look great."

I don't know that I believe him, but it gets me to ring the bell. Andie opens the door immediately, like she's been waiting just inside for us.

The whole place is filled with this almost religiously golden light, reflecting off the yellow walls, as if we're entering a monastery. The entryway flows into the living room, and there's mahogany wood everywhere—the floors, the railing, the exposed beams. The living room has an imposing brick fireplace at its center. There are orange velvet wing chairs and a green velvet sofa, heavy draperies and what has to be a real Persian rug. I'm not sure I like it, but you can't help but respect it. This is a serious house.

You wouldn't know that a baby lives here, except in the living room, where I see the same vibrating chair from our house (so they shop at Target, too!). They also have one of those Jumperoos we've been meaning to get. Both look laughably out of place.

I finally realize that Andie's been talking, and fortunately, Doug's been talking back. She ushers us inside.

Andie's even more petite than I remembered, dressed casually in jeans and a brightly patterned button-down shirt. She's holding Fisher in her arms. He's in a striped Sleep & Play that has a touch of Rikers Island to it. She's got some sort of orange puree (carrot? sweet potato?) in her thick strawberry-blonde hair. She's a hands-on parent, apparently, though she doesn't have to be, and that makes me warm up to her and let my guard down. That, and her smile. She's freckled and dimpled and despite her house, there's something down-to-earth about her.

Sadie is gazing at Andie with fascination. I give her chin a wipe with the burp cloth.

Fisher has begun to squirm in Andie's arms. He's a blocky kid, with dark eyes, very little hair, and surprisingly brutish features for a baby, like Andie's got a future schoolyard bully on her hands.

Nolan walks in. He's short, five seven or so, and older than Andie. She looks my age, midthirties, and I'd peg him as midforties at the youngest. He's dressed identically to Doug: North Face fleece, jeans, and high-tech running shoes. They both start laughing. I can't help noticing that Doug is much better looking and a good five inches taller. "Can I get you two anything? Coffee, tea, Perrier, beer, wine?" Nolan offers. "We've got a great Pinot. We bought a case of it on our last trip to Napa."

"No, thanks," I say.

Andie is making faces at Sadie, who is giggling. Sadie never calms down unless something has stopped or started; something has to change. Like when Andie takes her attention off her and she lets out a sudden, windowpane-rattling cry. Her face turns crimson, fast. It's the flip side of that peaches-and-cream complexion.

"She might need to eat," Doug says. He looks at his watch casually. "How long's it been?"

"Can you get the bottle out of her diaper bag, please?" Sadie is screaming, eyes bulging. It's like we've never fed her before. It's that way every time. I shift her in my arms and coo, even as I know it won't work. Only the bottle will do. Still, I want them to see that I'm a loving mother. The first hangout is always an audition.

Doug hands the bottle to me, and Sadie wraps her lips around it, eyelids drooping dramatically. "You're not breastfeeding, either?" Andie asks me.

"She's drinking my milk. But she never latched."

"So you pump all her milk?" As I nod, Andie smiles at me. "Good for you. That takes a lot of discipline. I'd miss my wine too much."

"Not that she has the option," Nolan says. "Fisher's adopted." He looks at Fisher fondly, like an especially good acquisition. I don't know why I thought that. There's nothing overtly objectionable about Nolan. He just reminds me of someone. I can't place who, but it's unsettling. "Why don't we relocate?"

Andie smacks her head. "Sorry about that. I've got you feeding your daughter in the foyer. Follow me."

We trail her to the dining room. It's through a doorway that's limned in mahogany, framed like a picture. There's a casement window and persimmon-colored draperies left open to reveal brighter light than the other parts of the house we've glimpsed. There's a long, narrow antique table with eight chairs upholstered the pale-green color of sea grass.

"Jesus, that's beautiful," I blurt.

Andie grins. "This is actually my favorite room."

"Andie did the decorating herself," Nolan says. "With some consultation." She had an interior designer, is what he probably means. But who cares? It's still Andie's vision that I love.

The table is laid out with a lavish spread, all sorts of crackers, cheeses, olives, and dips, of which I can only recognize hummus. Nolan starts to point and name things like "walnut pomegranate," but I'm transfixed by the kitchen beyond. It's immense, with vintage red-painted cabinets, a random plank wood floor, and an enormous kitchen island, and it has the most amazing ceiling I've ever seen: a series of sunken square panels, each made out of a different species of wood with its own unique patinas.

"What do you call that?" I ask, pointing upward. I suddenly feel the weight of Sadie in my arms. I'm startled to realize I'd forgotten her. I don't even usually care about architecture.

"It's a coffered ceiling, made of reclaimed wood," Andie says. "The dining room is my favorite room, but that ceiling is my favorite thing in the whole house." She smiles at me, and I smile back, like we're kindred spirits. I haven't felt that way about a friend since Ellen, and I was six years old when Ellen and I met. Sometimes I think I would have deeply loved anyone I met at that period of my life, before anything bad had happened to me, when I was so open to the world that I would have imprinted on any child just like ducklings do.

Andie pours the Perrier for me, and she, Doug, and Nolan share the bottle of Napa Pinot. We all settle down at the table. Andie puts a high chair for Fisher at one end and a guest high chair for Sadie at the other.

Never one to hold back, Doug makes it clear that he has just been served the greatest wine that man or nature has ever created. I try not to feel resentful as I sip my water. Sadie is banging her fists on the tray of the high chair with glee, while Fisher sits solemnly in his.

"What was the adoption process like?" Somehow, from Doug, the question doesn't seem invasive.

"Stressful, and then exhilarating," Andie says.

"We flew around the country and got grilled and waited to be chosen." Nolan sounds affable enough on the surface, but I sense an undertone. He isn't used to waiting for anything; he's typically the one asking the questions.

"We got close three different times," Andie says. "We were the runners-up. It makes you wonder, 'What did we do wrong? Why not us?' And then you try to change that the next time, and sometimes you overcorrect. You overcompensate." She looks at Nolan. "Am I saying too much?"

Nolan says to Doug and me, "She tends to talk a lot when she meets new people."

Doug nods with complete understanding. "Kat clams up."

My face ignites. Now I have to speak up and prove him wrong. "You were telling us about the adoption?"

"Oh, right," Andie says, like she's grateful that I kept her on track. "So, it was getting discouraging and tiring, all that flying around the country, trying to impress, and then we met Fisher's parents when we just didn't have it in us to put on a show."

"And that won them over," I say. Now I'm overcorrecting, talking too much. Doug is, as usual, being the consummate listener—leaning in just enough, making Andie feel like she's the most fascinating woman he's ever encountered.

"No," Andie answers. "The other couple fell through, and we got a call from the adoption worker months later, while Fisher's mother was in labor—"

"I pick up the phone," Nolan interjects, "and there's Danielle from New Connections: 'You're about to be a father.' Andie and I had three hours to kiss our old lives goodbye before we got on the plane."

"Wow," Doug says. "If it were me, those three hours would include a lot of sex and alcohol and dancing naked and eating Cheetos." Laughs all around.

"Were you spying on us?" Andie asks. Everyone laughs again.

It occurs to me that we're all just waiting to be chosen for something, all wanting to find out that we're good enough. It's comforting to know that even with all their resources, the King Spuds aren't immune. And then Andie says, "Nine months of that roller coaster. I guess we can't complain. It's the normal gestation period, isn't it?"

It's not the normal gestation period for a domestic adoption, I know that. I've heard people wait years for a white newborn. I think of all those people languishing on the adoption rolls while Nolan and Andie just slid through. But then, it probably wasn't just a rough nine months for them. It was most likely years of trying and maybe infertility treatments. You never know other people's struggles. They can't tell mine, looking at me. At least, I hope they can't.

"Are you a stay-at-home mom, Katrina?" Andie asks.

"Please, call me Kat. And not exactly. I'm still on maternity leave." I look at Sadie, feeling the anticipatory pang of leaving her. I'm grateful that she's so content with her banging, that she's not on the verge of one of her inconsolable outbursts, though it occurs to me that I haven't had anything to eat yet myself. I've been too nervous about how I'm coming off.

I overcorrect again, filling the gold-rimmed plate with far too much of everything.

"What work do you do?" Nolan says.

"I'm an assistant provost."

"What exactly is a provost?" He's smiling at me, and my stomach curdles, though he's being perfectly nice. There's nothing inappropriate in the question or in his manner.

I detail my duties overseeing the admissions process, trying to capture how stimulating it actually can be. There's something about that stage of young people's lives, when they're so full of promise and the thirst of competition—I love it. Well, I used to love it. I don't know how that version of myself will jibe with whoever it is I've become.

Nolan is nodding politely. I'm not getting it across. I was a communicator in my other life, pre-Sadie. In work, I was always so sure of myself. Lately, I falter. But that's why I need to get out more. Nights like this are important before I go back to the office.

"That does sound fascinating," Andie says. "I'm just home with Fisher. And I volunteer. I'm a member of different boards. It sounds so frivolous, doesn't it? But I'm fulfilled, mostly. That's the weirdest part."

"What did you used to do?"

Nolan and Andie exchange a glance so quickly that I think maybe I imagined it. "I was an art history major."

"Then she met me," Nolan says.

There's more of a story there, but neither of them seems eager to tell it, which is notable, since they'd offered up Fisher's adoption tale so readily. But who doesn't have more of a story than they want to tell?

"Where did you two meet?" Andie asks.

"Online," I answer.

"On Tinder?" Andie says, teasing.

"We're old school. Pre-app." Doug smiles at me. "But I would have swiped right for her."

I smile back. On Match.com, I had checked the box for casual dating, wanting companionship, not at all equipped for intimacy, and Doug had checked the box for serious relationship. But he changed my mind. I'd never thought I'd be the marrying kind, let alone the mothering kind, and yet here I am, courtesy of him. He made me want both. No, more than that, he made me believe I could be good at both.

Not that I want to go into any of that. "The walnut pomegranate spread is phenomenal."

Nolan slides the serving platter down. "Please. Have more."

"Gina and Oliver met online, too." Andie sips her wine. "I think he used to be a real player."

"Which people are those?" Doug asks. "I'm not sure I met them."

"He's tall and thin. Graying mustache—"

"He looks exactly like John Waters," Nolan interrupts. "It's uncanny."

"And their house is impeccable."

If Andie is calling someone's house impeccable, I don't even want to imagine. "Gina's the one whose hair is shaped like a mushroom," I say.

Andie lets out a peal of delighted laughter. "It totally is!"

"She's going to girls' night, right?" I query.

"She's a regular."

"Are you a regular?" Doug says to Andie. "I need to know more about this cult that's recruiting my wife."

"Andie's not a regular," Nolan answers. "It's a very—how do I put it?—selective group."

And they haven't selected Andie? I want to know what that says about them, or about her, but there's no tactful way to ask.

"I didn't know we were surrounded by snobs," Doug says. "But you can't tell everything from one block party."

"No, it's not like that." Andie is directing her comments at me. "They're all great. Every last one of them. Tennyson, June, Yolanda, Gina, Raquel—you couldn't ask for better neighbors. We're going to have so much fun on Thursday."

If they're all great, and Andie's clearly great, then why isn't she a regular?

"Which one's Raquel?" Doug says. "Is her hair shaped like a bell pepper?"

Then we're all laughing and talking, like old friends. It's nearly perfect.

Except halfway through the main course, when I finally realize who Nolan reminds me of, and I lose my appetite completely.

CHAPTER 7

You have 15 new posts from your GoodNeighbors!

What's the best weed whacker?

Lost corgi named Bamboo

Free outdoor pizza oven

Never mind, I found Bamboo! Thanks for the
outpouring!

Any recommendations for home day cares?

That last one is me.

It's 1:49 a.m.

I haven't been able to fall asleep. I just keep replaying the dinner in
my mind. I like Andie so much. It's painful to think that I won't be able
to be her friend, just because I can't stomach her husband.

Maybe I can just avoid him. There are girlfriends, and then there are couple friends. Andie and I can be the former.

Unfortunately, though, Doug likes both Nolan and Andie. I don't really see how I can just cut him out of the equation, not without revealing parts of my past that I intend to keep hidden.

And honestly, it's not Nolan's fault. I don't want to hold a vague resemblance against him. It feels bigoted somehow. But I can't have a relationship that's like one long PTSD flashback.

> Hey there! No recommendations, but I can tell you a few horror stories. Places to avoid. The kind where they let the kids fall asleep in car seats and Rock 'n Plays. Total deathtraps.

That response is from Yolanda. I hadn't even realized she was on GoodNeighbors. I never got a welcome message from her.

I asked Andie about childcare, and of course, she has a nanny. She offered information on the agency she used and I took it, even though there's no way we can afford that kind of luxury. We can't even afford a childcare center. It's home day cares all the way for us.

Andie's out of my league. She and Nolan are out of our league, both Doug's and mine. That, I decide, is why we can't take the friendship any further. "Can you picture them eating in Crayola?" I'll say to Doug. "It's ludicrous." We can just stick with our own kind.

Who would that leave, in this neighborhood?

"I hope it's OK that we're just stopping by." Raquel has Meadow in her arms again, just like at the block party, and Meadow has her thumb in her mouth as she regards me with surprisingly dull eyes for a toddler. "I didn't have your number to text you."

"It's fine," I say. "It's good to see you. Do you want to come in?" I'm still in my pajamas and bare feet and, I realize, no bra. I cross my arms over my chest. Sadie is lying on the floor on her play mat, various plastic animals dangling above her along a stuffed nylon arch. She tries to grasp them, but they're out of her reach, which fortunately seems to make her more determined than frustrated.

"What she doing?" Meadow lisps around her thumb.

"Reaching," I say, wondering if there's a better way to explain it. Meadow seems satisfied.

Once they're inside, Raquel doesn't put Meadow down. They remain intertwined as Raquel perches on a love seat.

"It's cute in here," Raquel says.

"It's a work in progress, but I feel like it's going to be really nice. Homey."

She smiles at me. "It already is. Homey."

I smile back. "Thanks."

"We were about to go to the park. Do you and Sadie want to join us?"

I hesitate. Raquel's so nice, but I'm just not really in the mood for getting-to-know-you small talk. It feels like work.

No, it's an investment. If I want a new kind of life, I have to be willing to put in the effort. With her brown lawn, Raquel might make a lot more sense as a friend than Andie does.

"Let me get dressed. I'll just be a minute." I snatch Sadie up off her mat, and she bursts into tears. Meadow's eyes widen in fascination.

We go upstairs, and I grab a pacifier for Sadie. "Sorry," I tell her. "Last-minute change of plans." Her eyes regard me warily as I get her into a fresh diaper and clothes, but at least she's sucking instead of crying. I put on her sunscreen with long, deep strokes, turning it into a baby massage, and her eyes close in pleasure.

I don't really like being in Sadie's room. For one thing, it reminds me that we're more separate than we used to be. For another, even though I chose the color purple, my mother-in-law insisted on choosing everything else, and I couldn't stop her. I can't stop her from doing anything, really. So there are preppy plaids and ginghams, matching curtains and valance and shams and trash can. Doug tells me it's a small price to pay, but sometimes when I'm in here, it still chafes.

I don't normally leave Sadie tethered to the changing table, but it's just this once, while I dash into my room and put on clothes. Still, I forgo washing my face. I decide toothbrushing is a necessity, with a new potential friend, and then I stick a sun hat on in lieu of sunscreen. It has the added benefit of covering my messy hair.

I bring Sadie back downstairs. Raquel says, "Meadow never got into pacifiers. It's been all thumb her whole life."

"It must be a hard habit to break."

"I don't know. I haven't tried. She's always been young for her age, if you know what I mean. She's going to start half-day preschool in the fall."

"How old is she?"

"Three. Her birthday's in February."

So that means she's almost three and a half. I'm startled, though I hope it doesn't show. It's not just that Meadow's behavior appears to be that of a younger child; it's also that Meadow is so physically underdeveloped.

She's not skinny, with spindly limbs; rather, it's the opposite. Her cheeks are too full, and her belly protrudes in that way of toddlers who've not yet been reduced by movement. She's built like a child at least a full year younger. It's concerning, almost like Meadow has failed to thrive. Yet Raquel seemed so matter-of-fact.

But maybe she's already spoken to her pediatrician, and Meadow's on medication, or in therapy, or whatever they do for kids who are developmentally delayed. Maybe it's just about patiently waiting for Meadow to catch up. I'm glad that Raquel doesn't seem embarrassed by Meadow, that she's not transmitting any sort of shame to her child.

Raquel's matter-of-factness could be a sign that she's highly evolved. She's obviously a very loving mom. Meadow barely leaves her arms.

Besides appearing younger than her age, Meadow is the most physically ordinary child I've ever seen. She has fine brown hair up in a ponytail, brown eyes, medium-toned skin, and undistinguished features. If she stays this way, she'll be well suited to a life of crime. No witness would ever be able to describe her to a sketch artist. Kind of like Raquel, come to think of it, who's also wearing a ponytail and those wire-rimmed frames of hers, like granny glasses.

Raquel puts Meadow on the ground, and Meadow whimpers. Raquel leans in and whispers for a little while, until Meadow brightens. Then they clasp hands, and we all head for the door. I have Sadie's diaper bag slung around me, messenger-style, and I carry her folded-up stroller down the front steps. It used to seem like the biggest production in the world, a deterrent to casual activities, an easy excuse to stay inside where it's cozy and safe. But I'm turning a corner in the AV. Well, trying to.

On the pavement, I get her into the stroller, and we're off. I'm full of an inexplicable joy at this most simple of excursions, perhaps because it's so simple. It's just a trip to the park a few blocks away with a new friend and her little one, the first of many.

The residential streets are built around an emerald quad. There's a baseball diamond, a soccer field, and tennis courts. The playground is a marvel, with different fenced areas for kids of varying ages and equipment ranging from the classic S triumvirate (swings, seesaws, slides) to the high-tech (geometric shapes anchored by complicated ropes and pulleys, a cross between a playground and an art installation). Much of it is under brightly colored canopies to protect the kids from the sun, lending a circus feel to the proceedings, while the parents can sit beneath long stone gazebos with mosaic tile benches.

We head for the sandbox. Raquel removes her shoes and I do the same, wiggling my toes in sand that hasn't yet been warmed by the sun.

I dressed Sadie in layers, in true Bay Area fashion. I'm in just a T-shirt and shorts, and I shiver a little.

"Where did you move from?" Raquel asks.

"We were living in Oakland."

"That's where I grew up. Right off International Boulevard."

I wouldn't have imagined that she'd spent her childhood in one of the more dangerous neighborhoods in Oakland (a city that also has some insanely expensive ones, stratified and gentrified). If I'd grown up off International Boulevard, I might not volunteer it so readily, worrying that it would cause people to revise their opinion of me in some way I couldn't predict or control. I envy her fearlessness, that she can just present the facts of her life so—well, matter-of-factly.

"Yeah, East Oakland's as good as you've heard," she deadpans. "But awesome Mexican food. And the pawn shops?" She mimes an expression of heavenly delight. We both laugh. "Bart grew up there, too. We looked after each other."

Meadow is staring at Raquel, like she's in a trance, while Sadie is ignoring me completely, dredging her arms through the sand in fascination.

"And no," Raquel says, "Bart isn't short for anything. He was actually named after the BART train—as in, Bay Area Rapid Transit—which tells you a little something about his parents." I don't know what it says when you name your kid after transportation, so she explains. "His mom was a drug addict. She was still on heroin when he was born, so she couldn't think all that clearly. It was at Children's Hospital in Oakland, and she looked outside her window and the BART tracks were right there to help her out."

Not sure how to respond, I parrot, "Heroin?"

"She was a trailblazer. I mean, now heroin's an epidemic but back then, in that neighborhood, crack was king."

Raquel is not what I expected. Not at all. When I first met her, I thought she was sweet and childlike. And in her delivery, she is, but there's steel behind it. She's seen a lot, and apparently, so has Bart. But he looks like a guy who's been around, whereas she has a quality that makes you want to protect her. Maybe that's how Bart feels about her, or used to feel about her. It sure didn't look that way at the party.

"What does Bart do?" I say.

"He has a construction business."

Construction. Of course. He could bury all the bodies in the cement foundations. Does he have unusually neat handwriting?

I'm being ridiculous. I haven't received a note in a couple of days. I need to focus on what's ahead of me, not what's behind.

"Did you grow up in Oakland?" Raquel asks.

"No." I prefer not to say more.

"Where, then?"

"Haines."

She furrows her brow, like she's heard the name somewhere. "That sounds familiar."

"It's not far. Just along 880, near Newark and Union City."

The furrow becomes a full ridge. "Haines is famous for something, right?"

"Not really." I hope she doesn't Google it later. "It's a pretty ordinary, middle-class kind of a place." I don't need to mention that there's a poor part of town, which is where my mother and I lived. "By now, though, who knows? The way gentrification's going in the Bay Area, those could be million-dollar houses."

"It's crazy." She shakes her head. "And sad. So many people being driven out."

"Really sad."

"Meadow, why don't you go climb over there?" Raquel gestures toward a metal parabola that's not more than three feet off the ground at its apex. We're in the infant/toddler section. "She loves that."

It's hard to imagine Meadow loving anything, other than Raquel. There's just something so careful about her. Raquel and Bart must have grown up having to watch their backs, and even though they moved to a place where you should never have to look over your shoulder, their only child retains some of that awareness. I'm hoping that won't be true of Sadie. It doesn't look like it so far. She's already more of an explorer than Meadow, examining each grain of sand as it trickles through her fingers. Growing up, I had no real sense of home (unless you count Ellen's), but I want that for Sadie, so much. And I suddenly realize: I want it for me, too, for the little kid I used to be. The one I could have been.

Meadow is shaking her head convulsively.

"Meadow," Raquel says. "Go." The emphatic shaking continues. "I'll walk her over, and then she'll be fine." She takes Meadow's hand, and Meadow obediently accompanies her toward the small climbing structure. Sadie's been sitting between my legs, and I reach to pull her into my lap, wanting a dose of nearness, but she lets out a wail. She values her independence, even if it's only a few inches, and looking at Meadow, I see that I need to encourage that, in any form.

Raquel returns a minute later, and I see that Meadow is now sitting on the top of the structure, watching Raquel retreat.

Raquel says, over her shoulder, "Climb, Meadow!" and Meadow does, but joylessly. Within a few minutes, she's running back. "OK, Momma?" she asks.

"You're OK," Raquel says, though I'm not sure that's what Meadow meant. She might have meant, *Is Momma OK?*

Raquel tells Meadow to go back, to keep climbing, and Meadow does, calling back, "Look at me, Momma!" For the next ten minutes, they reenact that needy little drama, over and over, as if choreographed, and it all just feels so exhausting and heartbreaking that I don't think I can take it much longer. As much as I like Raquel, I'm grateful when Sadie lets out a poop so messy and noxious that I can beg off and head home.

"See you tomorrow night!" Raquel says merrily.

"Good girl," I whisper to Sadie as we hurry off. "Good girl."

Unlike myself, I admire how forthcoming Raquel is about her past. She's just the kind of person I should trust, maybe even aspire to be like. But somehow, all I want to do is run.

Session 16.

"You were going to tell me more about your family."

"No, you asked about my family. That doesn't mean I was going to tell you."

"We can just sit here quietly."

"So you can make an easy hundred bucks?"

"So we can go at your pace. So you have control in here, since I know you don't feel like you have it in other areas of your life."

"Have you heard of Haines? Or Mr. Layton?"

"I don't think so. Should I have?"

"You must not be from around here. Good."

"Let's not talk about the past right now. Let's talk about the present. How you did with resisting some of the behaviors we talked about."

"It wasn't a good week. Let's just leave it at that."

"You don't have to hold back. Nothing you say will shock me or make me reevaluate your worth. I won't abandon you."

"What makes you think I'm afraid of those things?"

"They're normal fears."

"You and your normalcy again."

"You and your sarcasm again."

"I guess we do know each other. But no one else can know me. That's why I drink. I take whatever drugs people hand me, and I have sex with people I shouldn't. People who don't give a shit about me, and I don't give a shit about them. I did it all again this week, even after all we talked about."

"That's OK. We're still early in this process. We'll just keep working at it."

"I just do the same thing over and over. I have—what do you call that?—impulse control problems. Or maybe it's that definition of crazy. The same thing but expecting different results. Expecting to do dirty things but end up feeling clean. Do you think that I'm actually crazy?"

"I don't use that word."

"For anyone? Or just for me?"

"You're finding ways to cope with your pain, that's all."

"All I want is oblivion. To not be me for a while."

"Good. That's a good insight."

"Knowing doesn't change anything. I still do the same thing again and again. You'd think I was programmed."

"Childhood is a template for all that comes later."

"Let's hope you're wrong about that."

CHAPTER 8

"Go get 'em," Doug whispers to me. He's lying in our bed with Sadie in his arms, and she's sucking on a bottle, her eyes closed in absolute peace. The last thing I want is to leave them, but I was supposed to be knocking at Andie's door five minutes ago.

"No," I moan. "Don't make me."

"You're going to have a great time. More important, you're going to *be* great. They're going to get to know you, and they're going to love you."

Is he right? Is it more important to be great than to have a great time? For Doug, the two are interconnected. He enjoys himself because he's sure people are going to love him, and then they do, in a positive feedback loop. I don't have that same confidence, nor do I have the burning need. Doug thinks it's just nerves that make me want to stay here, beside him and Sadie. It's not. Or at least, not only. It's that I can be fulfilled here, loving and loved by Doug and Sadie. That's my positive feedback loop.

"Andie's expecting me," I say. That's what it comes down to—fulfilling my obligation. So I plant a kiss on Doug's cheek and a more lingering one on Sadie's brow, and, with effort, I pull myself away.

Girls' night out is not an appealing concept for me. A cluster of women could feel uncomfortably close to a moms group, with the resultant groupthink. As I recall the rule—don't talk about motherhood—I'm hit with a new fear. What will I talk about? The work I'm afraid to return to? The debt we put ourselves in to get here? The fear that I'll never pass, I'll never belong?

When Andie opens the door, it's confirmed that this is no moms group. She's in a black leather peplum top and matching black leather pants with stilettos, and her strawberry-blonde hair is mostly a smooth curtain but with a slight wave toward her face, like a movie star from years gone by. I feel like I've made a mistake in my usually error-proof cute top and jeans.

"Do I look that bad?" Andie laughs.

"No, no! You look perfect. I just feel like I'm dressed all wrong." Not that I have a couture dominatrix ensemble in my closet for occasions like this.

"I'm probably overdressed. Since I don't always get invited to these things . . ." The way her voice trails off makes me want to throw my arms around her. So she's subject to insecurity, too.

She steps outside and closes the door behind her. I'm surprised she doesn't call back inside to Nolan or need to give Fisher one last kiss. Maybe the nanny is there and they've already said their goodbyes, or maybe Nolan is actually out somewhere with Fisher. We've only just met, and I have no idea about the rhythms, routines, and inner workings of her home. Given my reaction to Nolan, it may be better that way.

My current plan is to keep Andie at arm's length. I'm good at that. I have people to lunch with when I'm at work, there are a few couples who Doug and I socialize with, and that's pretty much it. My world is small and manageable.

Andie's car is a midnight-blue Lexus sedan, almost like an upscale police cruiser. I'm instantly at ease once inside because it's a total mess:

a not-entirely-clean burp cloth on the floor, crumbs everywhere, an inch of dust on the dash. The fact that she offered to drive and then didn't think to tidy up suggests a level of intimacy between us. Either that, or she doesn't care in the slightest about my opinion of her.

I was surprised when Andie offered to drive, since Main Street is a pretty short walk away, but after seeing her stilettos, it makes more sense. Then I realize we're headed in the other direction.

"Where are we going?" I ask.

"A place called Hound. In Oakland."

"We're not going to one of the bars on Main Street?"

Andie gives me an odd look and an even odder response: "You don't shit where you eat."

It's ten minutes of driving with a soundtrack of superficial chatter, and then we cross a steel grate bridge so that we're in one of the industrial areas of Oakland. Metal cranes sit immobile in the middle distance, beside the bay. There are warehouses, some commercially inhabited but many more derelict and emblazoned with graffiti. The streets have a bombed-out look, but stylish people are loping along them. Much younger people than Andie and me. Nonparents.

At least parking is easy. There's only one place anyone's going, it seems like, and it's unmarked. I follow Andie, who is doing her usual confident trot, and we enter a tiny building dwarfed by the warehouses on either side.

I've never seen a bar this dark, though there are paper lanterns hanging from the ceiling every few feet casting the prototypical dive-bar red light. I've also never seen a bar this long and narrow. The bartenders are situated along one wall, and there's a corridor to move back and forth, plus the tables, and it's all about eight feet wide, total. People are dancing on tabletops because where else could you do it? It's not exactly dancing, more like slithering, which makes sense because I've never heard music this slooooooooow. It's a syrupy trance, like you could fall in and never find your way out, a fly eventually hardened in amber.

When we finally reach the back wall, after maneuvering around assorted hipsters with carefully careless outfits, I see a row of retro pinball machines. It's the most illumination in the place. Andie is texting. She reports, "Their ETA is about five minutes. Should we get our drinks now or wait?"

"Let's wait," I say. I haven't yet decided if I'm drinking. Sadie is well stocked in her milk supply. A pump and dump wouldn't hurt her, but I should probably keep my wits about me.

"We can make ourselves useful," Andie says, "and find a few tables we can push together."

We squint our way through the din. Some tables are round, some oblong, and some square. It takes a while to find two squares, but we do it. Andie carries one over, stilettos be damned. Everyone gives her as wide a berth as they can, given the layout. It's actually a reasonably nice crowd, the way people are when they're all laboring under the same poor conditions. There's camaraderie in close quarters.

"Who picked this place?" I ask, once Andie and I are in our uncomfortable mismatched wooden chairs.

She shrugs. "Tenny, I guess? She's the de facto leader. Though Gina's got some pretty strong opinions, too. Have you heard her trans-urban riff?"

I'm considering whether to say something snarky when I look up and see Tennyson, Raquel, Gina, and Yolanda headed straight for us.

Tennyson is wearing black leather, too, her hair in some intricate chignon, and she and Andie laugh in acknowledgment. Yolanda is also in black, showcasing her cleavage in a partially unzipped Lycra top that has a peculiar sort of eighties workout vibe, her blonde hair long and loose with that slight threat of frizz. The three of them are like Charlie's Angels with their vampy outfits and their different hair colors. Meanwhile, Gina, Raquel, and I are matte to their shine, the backdrop that makes them sparkle like diamonds. Like me, Gina and Raquel are in jeans and cute tops—Gina with her mushroom hair (you can't do a thing with that, its only redeeming quality must be how wash-and-wear it is) and Raquel in her ersatz granny glasses and limp brown hair. It's moms versus vixens tonight.

There are hugs all around, and then we settle into chairs. I'm between Andie and Tennyson.

"What's with this music?" Tennyson asks. "It sounds like ice caps melting." Then in case we didn't get it, "Glacial pace."

"You picked this place," Gina says. "Don't complain."

"I wasn't complaining. I was noting. I like that you can actually hear people talk in this bar." She turns her phone outward and makes an exaggerated frown. "June'll be late. It's got to be another Hope emergency, right?" Tennyson looks around at all of us, like someone might have insider information.

"Probably," Raquel says with a sympathetic expression.

"Poor June." This from Yolanda.

"You know June. She doesn't like to bring everyone else down by talking too much about it, but man. That's got to be rough." Tennyson tosses her hair back. Her tone is compassionate, yet there may be a little underlying smugness. After all, she has a houseful of teenagers herself. "Running with the wrong crowd, you know? It can be scary."

We all shake our heads, a prayer, a for-the-grace-of-God. Then Gina drums on the table. "We're getting dangerously close to breaking the rule."

"We're not talking about our own kids!" Raquel protests.

"But it's a slippery slope," Gina says. "If we can't keep to *one rule*, what are we? Animals?"

"Hopefully." Tennyson gives a mischievous grin.

I realize I haven't said anything. Neither has Andie. I'd assumed her self-possession extended to all scenarios. It's comforting to think it doesn't, that she's merely human. Except that when I look at her, I can't see any hint of her earlier nerves. She's just texting on her phone. If it were me, that would be the one rule: no phones. That's going to be my rule someday with Sadie. When we're together as a family, we turn everything else off.

But that's just the kind of thing I'm not supposed to talk about tonight. So what do I say?

"First round's on me," Gina says. She smiles at me. "In honor of our newest member. What are you drinking, Kat?"

She sounds perfectly friendly. Yet it registers somehow as a challenge. I want to have the strength of character to say no. You're not supposed to be subject to peer pressure in your thirties.

"Well, what do they have?" I ask.

"They don't have an actual menu," Tennyson says, "but they do all kinds of stuff with crazy names. Like the Silk Purse and the Velvet Revolver. Dead Man Walking. The Catapult is really good if you like tequila."

It's a dive bar, so those drinks are going to be strong, and I haven't had alcohol in more than a year. And it seems prissy to order a Merlot.

"Do they make a Sow's Ear, too?" Andie asks. "Maybe it would have bacon bourbon. Have you guys ever had that?" Everyone shakes their head. "I'll have you all over soon." She's wooing them, I realize, and her methods sound so much like Doug's. I think of Yolanda and Wyatt drinking Talisker in Crayola the other day, and how Yolanda seemed so sincere about wanting to get to know me better. But she's quiet tonight, almost surly. She's barely looked at me.

Andie's complimenting Tennyson, another of Doug's techniques. Andie admitted the other night that she's not really part of the clique. So am I actually her way in? Is that why she reached out to me? I feel like she's already abandoning me for someone cooler.

Not that it matters. I shouldn't be Andie's friend anyway.

"So, what'll it be?" Gina asks me, with a hint of impatience.

"Just a Coke," I say quietly, feeling like I'm letting them all down. But I can't afford to let go of my inhibitions.

Everyone debates and then places their drink order with Gina, who makes her way over to the bar.

"We're allowed to talk about husbands," Tennyson announces. "Like, can I just say, Doug is awesome?"

The other women nod enthusiastically. I should be grateful that Doug's a hit. Instead, I feel like the weaker part of the duo. "Thanks," I say. "He likes all of you, too."

"What's not to like?" It comes out flirtatious, of course, but then, it's Tennyson. I notice Yolanda stiffening, similar to when Wyatt mentioned Tennyson's name. It brings me back to the end of the block party, all those noncouples seeming to couple, just for a moment. Then it was over so quickly, I thought maybe I'd imagined it.

"The way Doug dotes on you and Sadie is so beautiful," Raquel says. "And he's such a good listener. And a good talker. Really, where did you find him?"

"Online," I say. "It was efficient, but it makes for a crap story." They all smile.

"Wyatt and I met in a bar," Yolanda says. "That's not much better."

"And you all know where I met Vic." Tennyson grins. "Just around the neighborhood."

It feels like an in-joke. For my benefit, she adds, "We used to live around the corner from each other. I was on Overlook, and he was on Tremont. Do you know that intersection?" I indicate no. "So, his marriage was tanking, and mine was, too, and we found each other."

"She means they had an affair." Yolanda's voice is cold. She then turns toward Raquel in a very deliberate manner, engaging her in a low voice. I feel a little frozen out, but I'm thinking I shouldn't take it personally. It's really directed at Tennyson, and Tennyson must think so, too, because she has the sort of bewildered and hurt expression that I'd associate with a much younger woman. A teenager, really, whose friends have just pulled a disappearing act.

"It obviously worked out," Andie says. "I mean, you're the happiest family in the AV." It's such a suck-up move, but she looks like she means it.

"We're pretty happy," Tennyson allows. "But I think Kat, Doug, and Sadie could give us a run for our money. I couldn't get over how cute you all were at the block party."

"Thanks. I worry sometimes how I come off, since I'm not really a big group person." I sound pathetic, even to my own ears: Don't judge me, please! I'm great once you get to know me! I come with a ninety-day warranty!

"I'm more one-on-one, too," Tennyson says. Andie looks dubious. "No, really, I am! You think I'm all fun and games? I've got layers, people. Seriously, I'm a Bermuda onion." We all laugh.

Gina returns with some drinks, and Raquel leaps up to grab the rest. When we each have a glass in front of us, Gina lifts hers. "To girls' night out, with all that it implies!" Everyone drinks.

I learn that while we're not supposed to talk about kids directly, we can laugh at the ridiculous competition for "the best" preschools and the series of tests that two-year-olds are subjected to while their anxious mothers wait outside, like the kids' whole lives hang in the balance.

"It's *American Ninja Warrior*, toddler edition!" Tennyson says.

"I'll e-mail you my research," Gina says to me in a low voice, as a sidebar. "Get Sadie on the list *now!*" I have the sense that Gina is wound a lot more tightly than the others but that no one minds that, including her. I'm touched by her offer.

We all talk about the reality TV shows we're watching when we should be reading books with heft; we admit we don't want to join a book club, unless it's for the wine; we trade harmless and amusing anecdotes about our husbands; the women compete for who's the worst driver (Tennyson wins) and who has the messiest car (Andie); we make faux confessions about biting our toenails, Brazilian waxes gone wrong, and late-night binge eating.

I realize: I'm actually having fun!

June arrives at our table, drink in hand, full of apologies that are immediately dismissed but in the best way. She doesn't need to be forgiven. We're all friends here, and we make allowances for one another.

Everyone starts reminiscing about stupid things they did in college, stupid boys they did in college. I'm laughing, though I still know to keep mum about my own exploits.

"I didn't go to college," Raquel says, "so I had to fuck things up in other ways." She drains her glass. It's her second Silk Purse. She's slurring, just a little bit. While cursing still seems wrong from someone who appears as innocent as she does, I remind myself about East Oakland, crack, the BART train. She's lived, maybe as much as I have.

"My problem is," Tennyson says, and everyone perks up just a little, since Tennyson seems least likely to have problems, "Vic and I have plenty of sex, but he still wants more."

We all look a little disappointed. Her confession is sort of like when you're asked at a job interview about any weaknesses and you say you're too detail-oriented. It's really a strength. I mean, we could have guessed Tennyson and Vic were hot for each other all the time. There's no need to flaunt it in front of us mortals.

"When he wants sex and I don't," Tennyson continues, "he gets all desperate and pushy. Sometimes he sulks. It's like, I've got enough kids."

Raquel laughs loudly. "Yes, you, of all people, have enough kids!"

"Do you have an issue with the size of my family?" Tennyson demands.

We all fall silent. You just don't expect anyone to turn on Raquel.

"You make all these comments," Tennyson says. "What is it, Raquel? You think we should have a one-child policy like China?"

"I don't think China has that policy anymore," June says in a charmingly inept attempt at deflection.

"You want the truth?" Raquel says. She doesn't wait for an answer. "I think it was kind of messed up that your last child was a mistake."

Oh. My. God. Did she actually say that? I don't know if I've ever heard anything as ugly as calling someone else's child a mistake.

No one moves; Andie freezes with her drink halfway to her mouth. Then Tennyson laughs. "I think it's messed up, too!" We all join in, relieved. Fight averted.

I've never witnessed or been a part of friendships that can handle that degree of honesty. These women aren't just drinking buddies. There's a genuine depth to their connection. Part of me wants what they have. Another part is frightened by it.

"Sex is one of our favorite topics on girls' night," June says. "Whatever you do or don't do, there's no judgment."

"For example," Gina tells me, "I'm asexual. I just have no desire. Never have. But it's still fun to listen to my friends talk about it." She must see the expression on my face because she adds, "Oliver's fine. We've worked out an arrangement."

If I were drinking like the rest of them, I might ask exactly what sort of arrangement she's talking about, but instead I just nod, as if I meet people who proudly declare themselves asexual every day. It is pretty cool that someone as overtly sexual as Tennyson has no problem with it, that none of them does.

"I want to want sex," I say. They all look at me, and I'm surprised to find that I spoke it out loud. I must have been lulled by the promise of all that acceptance. I don't desire sex, but I desire reassurance that it's normal not to. They're all looking at me expectantly, so I have to keep going. "I don't want to just become Doug's roommate or just the mother of his child." My tone is full of sadness, and maybe that's why no one speaks for a long moment.

Shame rushes in to fill the void. I can't believe I just told a table full of women—of neighbors—that I have no desire for my husband.

"If I wasn't attracted to Bart anymore," Raquel says, "I'd feel the same way."

"It's not that I'm not attracted to Doug," I say. "It's that I'm not attracted to sex. I'm so tired all the time, and it just seems like a lot of work." I never should have said anything. I'm not just your average new mom with no sex drive. It's a lot more complicated, and it all started much further back than having Sadie. In childhood, actually. But if Doug doesn't even know that, there's no way I'd ever tell a group of women I've just met.

Only I already told them far more than I should have.

"Sex is a lot of work," Gina says. "For not a lot of payoff."

"Your baby's only a few months old," Tennyson says. "Give yourself a break."

"Maybe you have postpartum," Yolanda says. "That can definitely do a number on your sex drive."

"Every relationship ebbs and flows," Raquel chimes in.

I appreciate the chorus of support, but what I really want is to change the subject. Away from reality, back to reality TV. I want them to forget I ever said anything, not become an object of their pity.

"Nolan and I have been married nine years," Andie says. "So I find that lately, I'm horny a lot more."

All the women laugh, except me. June explains, "In California, ten years is the magic number. That's when alimony kicks in."

"Wyatt and I haven't been doing it much lately," Yolanda says, her voice so low I have to lean in. Everyone else does the same. "I can't blame him for not finding me very attractive anymore. I don't find myself very attractive these days."

Everyone tells her how gorgeous she is, and Yolanda seems bolstered. She's clearly a person who can take a compliment.

So, they're not perfect, but Andie was right. They're all great.

I've never been a joiner, but part of me does really want to be a regular. From here on out, I just need to keep my sex life to myself.

CHAPTER 9

Come outside, Kat.

I've got a surprise for you.

Hurry up, OK?

Please?

Pretty please?

It's not even five thirty, which is earlier than Doug's been getting home, and the texts come one after the other, barely a pause between them.

I step onto the front steps, leaving the door open behind me so that I can hear Sadie if she wakes up. A pickup truck is double-parked, and Doug and a grizzled man are lifting two bikes onto the sidewalk, one red and one blue. Crayola colors. They look brand-new.

"That's not all," Doug says. He's practically vibrating with excitement; it's so strong it's seismic. You could measure it with a Geiger counter. He steps back into the bed of the truck with a ta-da motion. The object of his affection has two large bicycle tires on the sides and is encased in bright yellow fabric with mesh inserts. There's a silver hitch. "It's a bike trailer! So Sadie can attach to one of our bikes and we can all go riding together!"

I have to choose my words carefully. "You want to go riding with a newborn?"

"She's not that newly born anymore, Kat." He turns to the other man. "This is Milo. He just happened to be in the bike store when I was there, and he offered to help. Otherwise, I would have had to buy a bike rack to get these babies home. I mean, we'll need one anyway, but still. It was pretty awesome of him. Milo, meet Kat."

"Hi, Milo," I say. "Nice to meet you."

"Congratulations on the move. You're going to love it. You won't believe how many kick-ass trails you can get to from here in, like, five minutes." It's funny to hear "kick-ass" from a fifty-year-old man, but then, he's not a mere man; he's part wildebeest. I've never seen a beard that bushy in person before.

"Thanks," I tell him, "for bringing the bikes home."

"My pleasure. Enjoy them."

I wait until he's back in the truck and has pulled away before I turn to Doug, who is eagerly awaiting my reaction. "What were you thinking?" I hiss.

The hurt on his face is instant, and it pains me to see it, to cause it, but I can't humor him. We're probably skating into overdraft territory. "Can you return all this?" I ask.

He shakes his head, as if dazed. "I wanted to surprise you." It's like he can't even fathom this reaction and yet, how could he not have? He knows me, and our finances.

"Let's talk about it inside."

Doug remains planted on the sidewalk. "How can you not be excited, Kat? They match the house. They match our life. It's summer in the AV. Everyone goes out bike riding."

"I haven't ridden a bike since I was eight years old, Doug. We didn't even discuss this." I gesture back toward the house. "Sadie's sleeping. Can we please talk about this inside?"

He ignores my request again. He wants to keep it outside. He probably thinks I'll have to cave, if I'm in full view of the neighborhood. Anyone walking by would take his side and assume I'm some ungrateful bitch.

No, Doug's not manipulative. He just can't believe I don't feel as he does. He's sure he can convince me with the force of his vision.

He smiles at me in a way that normally makes me melt. "I told the guy at the store that you had limited experience riding a bike. He said this is a great starter bike. It's called the urban cruiser. Try it. Just get on and go."

"Sadie's sleeping inside."

"I'll wait in the doorway. Get on. I want to see you take a spin."

"If I ride around, then you can't return them, can you?"

"I can't return them anyway."

I take a deep breath, trying not to lose it. "How much did you spend, Doug?"

"It's an investment. In our happiness."

He'd never even told me that he wanted bikes for us. If he had, I could have asked on GoodNeighbors about ones that were cheap or even free. That trailer could be a few hundred dollars, and someone a block over was just about to discard one, like it's nothing.

Clearly, Doug didn't want the neighbors' hand-me-downs. He wanted bikes that were Crayola-bright and shiny and new. Statement bikes. Calling cards. Announcements that we've arrived, that we belong.

It scares me because prior to this, I'd assumed that we were in agreement. It was unspoken, but it seemed self-evident. Once we got into this neighborhood, we wouldn't have the money to keep up with the Joneses—or the King Spuds, as the case may be—and we wouldn't even try. We'd live within our means and be content with what we had.

He's always been too optimistic, too sure everything will work out. I blame his parents. He's been too pampered and protected from life's realities, and now he's going to have to learn, and I'm going to have to be the one to teach him. It's not fair. But it's better to blame them than to blame Doug himself.

Doug looked so excited and then so deflated, and now he's stubbornly insistent. We're locked in a stalemate. He's urging me to go for a ride, and I'm urging him to just come inside so we can talk about it, so we can figure out some way to get around that no-return policy, or maybe we can just sell these on GoodNeighbors, since they are pretty much new. As I'm imploring, "Put them somewhere, please, and come inside," a Porsche Cayenne pulls into the driveway of the Victorian across the street and a tall, thin man who looks remarkably like the director John Waters steps out and approaches us.

Oliver.

"Oliver," he says, his hand extended. He looks north of fifty, with that same skeletal quality as Waters and the same slightly creepy pencil-thin mustache. His hair is salt-and-pepper.

Doug shakes Oliver's hand. "I'm Doug, and this is Kat. Sadie's inside, taking a nap."

"Great bicycles! I have that one, but in black." That's when I know: Doug went top-of-the-line. I don't even want to know how much he spent, except that I really, really do.

My blood is boiling, but I can't let it show because Oliver is turning to me now. "Gina is really enjoying getting to know you, Kat. And that girl of yours—Gina keeps talking about wanting another one now. Like that's going to happen. We've got the two boys ourselves." He glances back toward his house. "You want to come over for a drink?"

Doug is nodding as I start to say, "We really can't, Sadie's still—" and then, as if she's in collusion with Doug, the truest Daddy's girl, she begins to cry so loudly that Oliver can hear it from the sidewalk. We must have woken her, Doug and me, with our argument. I'd thought we were keeping our voices low, but there was undoubtedly some heat in them, and Sadie's room is closest to the street.

Who else on the block heard us?

"So it's settled, then," Doug says. "We're coming over for a drink."

I don't know if he's just trying to force us over this speed bump and back to our best behavior, our normal behavior. He could want to escape this conversation and he's buying time to amass more arguments about the bikes. Or he's just an extrovert and this is what he does: someone extends an invitation, and he accepts. But he has to know the last thing I feel like doing right at this moment is going to the neighbors' house and leaving something this big, this expensive, unsettled.

Once Oliver's out of earshot, it dawns on me. "Where are you even going to put those?" I say, just above a whisper.

"In the backyard," Doug answers. "It's more than big enough."

"Are you going to lock them up?"

He smacks his forehead. "Right. Bike locks. I need to go back to the store."

I realize he's not kidding. "And what if it rains?"

He looks skyward in an exaggerated and comic fashion. "It hasn't rained in weeks. I think we're in the clear."

"Have you remotely thought this through?"

His affable expression disappears. "How about having a little faith in your husband?"

As he starts to roll the first bike around the house, he jabs, "You think Val and Patrick are planning to steal some bikes tonight?"

Val and Patrick. Those are the names of the fanny-pack-wearing empty nesters with the golden retrievers. This time, I can't let myself forget. It's not Fanny; it's Val, as in validate. Val, as in valuable. Val, as in property values. Yes, that's it. That'll stick.

To Doug's back, I say, "And what about Hope next door, and her friends?"

He doesn't answer, and I know I've scored a point. But I have a feeling I'm not going to win this game. He bought bikes that couldn't be returned. He isn't going to take no for an answer.

I feed Sadie a bottle and get her into fresh clothes. Doug doesn't even set foot inside the house. We don't speak as we cross the street.

Oliver and Gina's Victorian is a dusky blue, all its windows and doorways edged in midnight, so it creates a dramatic effect, like a woman's eyes outlined in charcoal. Gina opens the door and ushers us inside. She says that Lee and Riordan are playing upstairs, and we'll have to meet them another time.

Without further ado, she launches into a well-practiced tour. "This used to be a duplex. We knocked down the walls so we could get nice big rooms. I love Victorians, but I hate small rooms."

Then why do you love Victorians, if you hate one of their principal features?

I'm just being irritable. I don't want to be here, and I resent Doug for making me.

As Andie said, the house is impeccable. The living room is light and airy, white everywhere, including whitewashed wood floors, with built-in bookshelves that are easily fourteen feet high. There's a ladder on rollers against one corner, presumably to reach the highest shelves. Most of the books seem to be about architecture or interior design, and they're as handsome as the room itself.

The dining room beyond is also white, with built-in cabinets and a bar. There's a crystal chandelier above a rustic wooden table that could seat twelve. It looks like it should be in one of those Bay Area farm-to-table restaurants. Three dozen white lilies are in a glass vase at the center.

"The bar's fully stocked," Oliver says. "What can I fix you?"

"Water with lemon for me," I say quickly.

"A glass of your best bourbon, please, sir," Doug says.

Oliver smiles. "Good man."

"A Manhattan for me, please," Gina says. It looks like I'll be the only teetotaler. Again. "I'll show you the kitchen, Kat."

I follow her in, Sadie feeling heavy in my arms. I should have brought the Björn, but I wasn't thinking clearly.

I can hear Doug and Oliver in the next room, already in the throes of energetic manly discourse. Oliver talks like Gina, I realize—with great authority. She has a masculine conversational style, full of strong opinions and proclamations. And she hasn't paid Sadie a bit of mind, which is notable, because everyone pays attention to Sadie. Come to think of it, Oliver didn't, either. Maybe they're not baby people. But didn't Oliver say that Gina was so taken with Sadie she was talking about having another kid?

"Are you sure you only want water?" Gina asks. "I could squeeze you some fresh juice. I remember I was always depleted when I was breastfeeding."

"I'm good," I say. "I'm not depleted."

Then I notice the juicer. It's an insane contraption, something out of Willy Wonka: large and orange with a protruding black metal snout that contains four oranges, loaded up like one of those machines that shoots out tennis balls. It's next to an industrial pasta maker, a bread maker, and some other appliances I can't even identify. Somehow, with all that, it still doesn't seem crowded in here.

Gina starts chopping a lemon right on the countertop—it must be some invincible high-tech material—and Oliver brings in her Manhattan. Doug loiters between the rooms, uncertain how to approach me. He doesn't want a scene, but then, neither do I. I just don't want to have to be fake, either. I preferred having him in the other room.

"What do you think of the kitchen, Kat?" Oliver says.

"It's beautiful. Space-age."

He laughs. "I'm addicted to upgrades. Wherever I am, I look around and I can always see something that could use improving."

We're never inviting them to Crayola, that's for sure.

But Doug is apparently thinking the opposite. "When we have you over, you can give us some ideas." As if we have any money to implement Oliver's ideas. Does Doug know something about our finances that I don't?

"Funny you should say that." Oliver leans against a counter and sips amber liquid from a highball glass. "I was actually one of the bidders on the house."

"On our house? Really?" It shoots out of my mouth like a cannonball. It makes sense, though. At the block party, Gina seemed to know insider information about the bidding war.

"He's a real-estate developer," Gina inserts. "He had a real vision for that house."

Oliver shrugs with something like false modesty. "It wasn't meant to be." Then he seems to switch tracks to a different spiel, as if someone's hit a button on his remote control. "I'm all about customization."

"Oliver is right. The future is all about customization. That's what matters in a trans-urban, trans-suburban world."

"She's always going on about that." Oliver smiles at her affectionately.

Gina never sits down. Even after we all move into the living room with our glasses in hand, she's still constantly in motion, calling up to the boys to make sure they're OK, straightening, aligning, calibrating. I gather that she used to have some sort of high-powered job. Oliver jokes that she transferred all that energy to their home, and that sometimes her need to be hyperorganized means she is *thisclose* to losing it anytime someone fails to use a coaster. I look down quickly to confirm that I did, indeed, use a coaster.

Gina's like me, on steroids. A cautionary tale. A worst-case scenario. No, there are definitely worse scenarios.

Oliver starts doodling on a cocktail napkin with a pen that probably cost more than our month's groceries. "I had all these plans for your house," he says, "and I'm happy to give them to you." He smiles. "Free of charge."

He talks and draws, saying that frankly, our lot is more valuable than the house. "I was debating between razing and renovating," he tells us. "You could expand the kitchen, easily. Turn that utility closet into a half bath. I'll put you in touch with some fantastic contractors."

"That'd be great," Doug says. I stare at him, not sure if he's just humoring Oliver or if he's delusional. I would have assumed the former, until he spent all that money on bikes and a trailer that he'll put Sadie in over my dead body. She can barely hold her head up.

As Oliver continues to pontificate and Gina putters and expounds on his ideas with talk of expensive finishes and upgrades, I start to feel distinctly uncomfortable. They're saying, essentially, that our house is second-rate. We paid everything we had (and much that we didn't) to get into it, as is. That's what it said on our offer: as is. No contingencies. We waived them all, gave ourselves no outs, just so we could make it onto this block and be condescended to by Oliver.

". . . and you can always build up. Another floor, with a guest room and an office, maybe, would increase the value exponentially. I can put you in touch with an architect who's really well connected to the zoning board . . ."

I can't help feeling that there's an edge to Oliver's speech, to this whole evening. He wants to rub our noses in all that he has and all his professional connections, but he didn't get our house. We won, and he lost. Maybe he was even the highest bidder, but Nils and Ilsa chose us. They knew Oliver, and yet, they didn't want their house going to him.

Or maybe he really is just trying to help us improve our house. He doesn't know that we used up all our savings. Gina e-mailed me all her preschool research today, just like she said she would. They're well-intentioned know-it-alls.

I'm not really upset with Gina or Oliver. My problem is with Doug. I can't sit here for another minute, choking on his sycophancy.

I stand up, explaining that Sadie hasn't had her bottle yet, daring Doug to expose the lie. "Stay," I tell him, "for as long as you'd like."

I almost mean it, in that I don't really feel like being in the same room with him, yet I don't actually expect him to remain seated. "I'll be home soon," he says. "Love you."

Back out on their doorstep, I hear the dead bolt sliding into place behind me. I have the distinct and disturbing impression that none of them—not Gina, nor Oliver, nor my own husband—was sorry to see me go.

Session 28.

"It's just so hard for me to trust people."

"Men or women?"

"Everyone. But in a way, it's more women."

"Because of what happened with your best friend?"

"It's not just 'what happened.' It's what she did."

"You can't change the facts of your past. But you can change how they influence your present and your future. You can take back your power."

"I get so angry sometimes. Can you fix that?"

"We need to figure out what's underneath the anger. Hurt, disappointment, sadness. Loss. You've lost a lot."

"I don't think I feel those things."

"Because you cover them up with anger. Because you don't want to be powerless. Anger can make you feel powerful."

"You're wrong. Anger makes me feel out of control."

CHAPTER 10

"Hey!" Andie's in sunglasses and a black sundress that looks like macramé but in a good way. Her strappy wedges are three inches high. She's holding Fisher in her arms, his sleek Eurotrek stroller left at the base of the porch steps. "Are you up for a walk, by any chance?"

I'm torn. All things being equal—all husbands being equal—Andie is the AV woman to whom I feel most connected, the one I'd most want for a confidante.

I'm also not in the best mood. Doug came in after nine last night, and I couldn't help wondering what he, Gina, and Oliver had found to talk about for going on three hours. For the first hour, I'd assumed he was just humoring them, not wanting to race out. But after a few more bourbons, they probably weren't just talking about houses anymore.

Gina isn't having any sex, but she likes talking about it. Did she tell Doug what I said at girls' night about my lack of desire for him? He'd be so humiliated.

No, Gina wouldn't do that. She seems anal-retentive but not mean. Doug was just schmoozing the new neighbors. Maybe he wanted to avoid coming home after the confrontation about the bikes. For us, that was pretty heated. He could have been waiting me out, hoping I'd already be asleep. It's not unheard of for me to doze off before nine.

So I feigned sleep. It seemed easier that way. But today, I've got a pit in my stomach. I just hate having things unresolved between us. I should probably stay home and initiate a big talk with Doug, though honestly, it's the last thing I feel like doing. And he needs to focus on putting together some more furniture, anyway.

Seeing my hesitation, Andie gives me an out. "Do you have other plans? We can hang out another time."

I don't want an out. I want a friend. I want Andie for a friend.

Maybe I can dredge up some strategy that I learned from Dr. Morrison that will allow me to get past Nolan's resemblance to Layton. I'm willing to try. "Now is good," I say.

As Sadie and I cross the threshold, I cast a furtive glance down. Another day without a welcome mat. I let out a sigh of relief.

And then realize I sighed too soon. There's a piece of cardboard on the windshield of the Outback.

Andie hasn't seen it yet. At least, I don't think she has. While she's bent down cooing at Sadie, I grab it and toss it under the car.

You thought we were done here?

Yes, I'd wanted to believe that.

"Are you OK?" Andie asks me. "You just got really white all of a sudden."

I try to smile. "I'm always pretty white."

You thought we were done here?

The note couldn't have come from one of the women at girls' night. They were so nice to me. Not just nice but accepting. Confessional and vulnerable, themselves. They invited Andie just to make me more comfortable. The way they talked to me and looked at me, I felt like part of the gang.

But seemingly overnight, whoever wrote these notes and I have become a *we*, without my consent. I'm locked in something I don't understand, with someone I can't identify. That means she holds all the cards. Whoever it is has the element of surprise. I'm just a sitting duck in my new house.

The wait between notes two and three just underscores it. She wanted me to think it was over, she wanted me to relax, so she could punch me in the gut and remind me who's in charge. We're not done until she says we are.

"Are you sure you're up for a walk?" Andie asks, a concerned expression on her face. "Maybe you could just come to my house and I could make us some tea."

"Fresh air would be good," I say. Deep, cleansing breaths, that's what I need most.

I love the sweet brininess of AV air. I love this neighborhood, and I love our tiny home, and I will not let this bully win.

Andie leads me through the well-maintained residential streets of the AV until we're on an asphalt pedestrian path that winds along the sandy beach. The water is like a hazel eye, fluctuating with the light. Far in the distance, through a hazy fog, I can make out some of the buildings of San Francisco. I'll be commuting there soon enough, but for now, I'm on my own island.

Andie stays quiet until she sees that I'm calmer. Then she asks, "Did you have fun at girls' night?"

I inhale. "I really did." I try to regain the feeling I had that night, the one that the notes are trying like hell to destroy.

"It's hard to hang out with women who know each other so well. You did a great job of fitting in. Better than I have."

"Really?" I can't imagine that's true, given Andie's exceptional social graces, though now that I think of it, the other women were more interested in me than in her. It was something in the way they listened, how they leaned, their eye contact. I was the focus, and Andie was ancillary.

"There's something special about you, Kat," Andie says. "Sometimes it's like your heart is on the outside, you know? Like people can see all you're hoping for, even though you think you're guarding it so well. You're vulnerable in spite of yourself."

I feel flattered but also exposed. When I was a kid, Layton was the first person to tell me I was special. I was a charity case at that school, and I felt it all the time, except when I was with Ellen. And then when I got to fourth grade, I was in Mr. Layton's class. He was the most well-liked teacher in the school, by the kids and by the parents. He was handsome. He was respected.

And he chose me! He relished my company. He bought me poetry books. I stayed after class for a few minutes just to talk to him, and then after school, to talk to him longer. Then he started locking the classroom door behind me and lowering the blinds. Slowly, gradually, we were doing other things. I felt like it was at my pace. I felt like it was what I wanted.

Dr. Morrison said that was all a trick, a manipulation. Ten-year-old girls can't know what they want sexually; they're being taught to want that contact, when what they really want is approval. She said my sexuality was being used and corrupted, subsumed by an adult's desires.

But honestly, that's not how it felt at all. I felt . . . powerful. Being able to please Steve—I mean, Layton—was an experience I enjoyed. The confusion came later.

I did know it had to stay secret, even from Ellen, especially from her, and that was a form of power, too.

I'm almost relieved when Sadie has one of her outbursts. Now I have something to do.

It's a full-scale, pyrotechnic meltdown. We have to pull over to the side of the path and park the strollers in the caramel-colored sand. As it continues for several long minutes, I start to apologize, my face as red as Sadie's. I run through the parent checklist. I sniff at her diaper, no problem there, and offer a bottle, which she refuses as if offended, doing a spastically derisive headshake. I rub ointment on her gums in case it's teething pain. If it's gas, there's nothing I can do except rock and coo, and that's doing nothing at all. So I go to the pacifier, but she spits it out with a type of contemptuous violence I really haven't seen in other kids.

That's what it is; that's what spurs my humiliation. It's not like Sadie cries more than other babies. In fact, she might even cry less. But it's the way she cries.

There's nothing plaintive or forlorn in it. It's angry, right from the first note, a symphony that starts at full crescendo. It makes Sadie sound spoiled. What a terrible word, spoiled, like the baby is old milk, and once milk goes bad, it's rotten. As if Sadie's ruined.

I don't know what I should have done differently, what I can change right now. If I should intentionally make Sadie wait longer for bottles, or for hugs, in order to build up her tolerance, strengthen her muscles. Am I already supposed to be teaching her patience? When she's this little? It seems sadistic. It seems intolerable.

Speaking of intolerable, how many minutes have I been trying in vain to soothe Sadie while Andie stands nearby, alternately talking to Fisher (who is completely fine) or staring out at the glassine water? I just need to put Sadie back in the stroller and head for home, telling Andie we'll catch up some other time. Or we won't. Andie isn't going to want to be friends with a duo like Sadie and me.

See, this is why I'm better off without friends. The humiliation! The self-doubt! The red face and recriminations!

I think of the moms group I tried to join in one of the wealthier Oakland neighborhoods and the perpetual whiff of disapproval. Even when they were sympathetic, it was laced with condescension. The schadenfreude: so she got the bad baby, not me! Or: she *created* the bad baby, not like my little breastfeeding angel.

But then, a miracle occurs. Sadie opens her mouth with a very distinct aperture, and I thrust the pacifier in, and it's over.

"That's so cool," Andie says. "The way you just communicated there. She let you know what she needed, and you got the message."

After all that, Andie is actually complimenting my parenting? That's her takeaway?

This is why people have friends.

I resettle Sadie in her stroller, and we continue our walk, and as if it's the most natural thing in the world, I start confiding in Andie. If she can see through me anyway—if she thinks my best quality is my reluctant transparency—then there's no reason not to. I tell her about the moms group. About the judgment. About my fear of their judgment.

"They were all enthusiastic breastfeeders, of course," I say. "I was so jealous. Motherhood seemed effortless to them."

"That's what they were portraying, anyway," Andie says.

"After seeing three lactation specialists and no latching, I decided enough was enough. I started pumping exclusively. I was telling myself what a good mom I was. Sure, I wasn't successful with latching, but I was successful at breast*feeding*. I was actually sort of proud. And I remember that I took a chance and instead of just nodding and smiling, I told the moms about it. No one said anything for this long minute. They clearly thought I was a quitter. One even said that it's not just about the milk the baby's getting but her problem-solving skills. Like Sadie is going to wind up dumb."

"Fuck her," Andie says passionately. This is definitely why people have friends.

"There are websites with lists of geniuses who were never breastfed. I never breastfed. Not that I'm a genius or anything," I add hastily.

"It's sad that those websites have to exist. Obviously, whoever compiled the list felt like they had to defend their decision to use formula. Isn't the whole point of feminism that we respect each other's choices?"

"I thought so."

"Well, I respect that you tried so hard. You and Sadie obviously have a great bond."

"Really?" It feels so good to hear it. You just don't know what people see when they look at you and your child.

"Really." Andie nods vigorously. "I know what it's like to try to measure yourself, because I really struggled with that at first, too. Like when you tell people you adopted, they make all sorts of assumptions about your fertility, about your womanhood." So she wasn't infertile? I guess I had made that assumption myself. "People can think whatever they want. As long as we know the truth." This funny expression flits across her face, like clouds across the sun, and then she's back to that dimpled smile, as irrepressible and engaging as Doug's.

Thinking of Doug brings back all the anger and hurt from last night. All that's waiting to be settled.

"Anything you want to talk about?" Andie says.

I can feel her good intentions. She's not pushing me; she's just here to listen.

"Doug and I had a fight last night. Nothing ugly," I assure her. "It's just that we spent all our money to get into that house. I know it doesn't look like much to everyone else on the block, but it's our home." Tears prick my eyes. "I thought Doug and I . . . I thought we both felt like that was enough, you know, just being here and living our lives."

Andie's nodding like she really gets it. "It can do a number on you, moving to a new place. The flip side of all that hope is disappointment, you know? We're all afraid to be disappointed."

"I don't feel disappointed in the neighborhood." Well, except for those notes, but I'm not ready to share that with her yet. "But I was really disappointed in Doug last night. He went out and bought these expensive bikes that he knew we can't afford. Then he comes home and says, 'Surprise!'"

I'm laying my cards out on the table, financially speaking. If she doesn't want to have a broke friend, then she can just walk away now, before I get in any deeper.

"Classic male trick." She says it almost fondly. "Do you believe Doug loves you?"

"Of course."

"Do you believe that he values your happiness—and Sadie's happiness—as much as his own?"

I have to think longer on this one. "Yes."

"Is what happened yesterday big enough to divorce him over?"

"Of course not."

"Then it's not big enough to fight over, or hang on to, either. I have it on good authority: dating in your thirties is hell. Ask June."

June's only thirtysomething, with a teenager? She looks youthful, but I just assumed she had a good cosmetic dermatologist.

So June was a teen mom. She's been through some shit, too, then. Just like Raquel, and like me. And maybe like Andie, I don't know. It occurs to me that I don't know anything about Andie's childhood.

But back to the topic at hand. While there may be a flaw in Andie's marital reasoning, it's still so comforting. Let it go. Save myself the aggravation. Better yet, spare myself the confrontation.

"You don't have a problem, really," she concludes. "We're talking about things. Possessions. Never let them get in your way."

She's right, but then, she has way nicer things than I ever will, and no worries about how she'll pay for them.

But they are just bikes, after all. He was trying to make me happy, searching for a fun family activity, something as local as it gets, and maybe it was an error in judgment, but his heart was in the right place. What difference does another few thousand dollars of debt really make, in the grand scheme of things?

We're here, and the sun is shining, and Sadie and Fisher are asleep in their strollers, and I have a new friend. A whole circle of new friends.

"You want to turn inland?" Andie asks. "Wander through the Village?" I'm glad that she'd like to continue on with me after all she's heard, instead of just going back home.

When people say, "the Village," what they really mean is Main Street, though there are a few branching arteries that also feature restaurants, cafés, and shops. On Main Street, there are artisanal bakeries and a market hall full of foodie delights; children's and adult boutiques for clothes, shoes, and glasses (excuse me, "eyewear"); a small bookstore where the wares seem curated by color rather than selected for content; the bike shop; ethnic restaurants from Cambodian to Ukrainian along with California cuisine, pizza, and all the other usual family-friendly suspects; a few bars; and separate shops for ice cream, frozen yogurt, gelato, and bubble tea. Everything is locally sourced and independently owned. It's zoned that way. You drive five minutes to get to the big-box stores, but you stroll on Main Street so you get the best of both worlds, city and suburbia, like Gina said.

We can't go three feet without running into someone Andie knows. She introduces me to at least twenty people, whose names I'll never remember. She's an extrovert for sure.

"I'll text you about the board meeting," Andie tells one hot mama, the kind who's not as good-looking as Tennyson but who likely shops at Le Jardin.

Andie suggests we stop in, though the saleswoman who greets Andie by name says that Tennyson isn't there today. The store smells musky yet botanical, which fits the theme, and many of the clothes are gauzy, barely there, and incredibly expensive. Andie tries on a scarf and looks at some jewelry under glass, unruffled by the prices.

I feel out of place, though the saleswoman is incredibly friendly. She's suggesting outfits that would "look great with my coloring."

"Another time," I tell her. "I really should be getting home." I turn to Andie, who's now perching various hats on her head, pursing her lips, and fluffing the ends of her hair as she stares at her reflection in the mirror. "Sadie could use a bath."

Andie replaces the hat on the stand. "Let's go, then."

"That hat looked great on you. Maybe you should get it." I'm telling the truth, but still, it feels a little phony. If Andie can see through me, she'll know that I'm having a Yolanda-esque moment of insecurity. There was so much competition on that street, tons of women who are already Andie's friends or would like to be and who could afford Le Jardin.

But I'm the one here with her. I want to feel proud, chosen, but instead, my mind returns to the question I had the night she sent me the invitation to GoodNeighbors:

Why would Andie pursue me?

Session 40.

"Honestly, I think there might be some suppression."

"What am I suppressing?"

"I can't answer that."

"But what makes you think it?"

"I've been doing this a long time. It's just a sixth sense I have. There's information that's too painful for you to integrate. That's what denial is."

"I'm not in denial."

"You want to talk a lot about your best friend. That feels safer for you. But you won't talk about him. So I'll help you. I read some articles. I know that there were multiple victims. He had a type. Girls who were looking for a father figure, and that's how he started. That's called grooming, the process of—"

"I've heard of grooming."

"Do you believe that's what he did?"

"I don't want to talk about this."

"We all have certain stories we tell ourselves. Narratives that are comfortable, and even when they're painful, they're tenacious. We're tenacious. We hang on to our narratives."

"I'm not hanging on to a narrative. I'm hanging on to the truth. But you don't seem to believe that I'm telling you the truth. You think I'm in denial."

"I don't know that for sure. I think it's a possibility worth considering. You might have blocked out some memories, the ones that don't fit your narrative."

"I feel like you're trying to trick me. All this talk about narratives and possibilities. You want me to doubt myself."

"No, I want the opposite for you. I want you to learn to trust yourself. But if consciously you believe something, and your subconscious knows it's not true, how can you ever do that?"

CHAPTER 11

DOES YOUR HUSBAND KNOW?

"Can I just tell you," Doug whispers, his palm flat against my cheek as we lie side by side in bed, "how much I love you?"

"Yes," I whisper back. "You can always tell me that." Let it saturate every cell of my body. Let it blot out everything, especially that latest note.

Two notes in one day. No, someone's definitely not finished with me yet.

How can she know that there are things—important things—I haven't told Doug? Is it just a guess, because everyone has secrets, or because it's obvious that I do? If Andie's right, if I'm that transparent despite everything . . .

Then it would mean the writer of the notes is someone who's been looking at me. Someone who's interacted with me. Probably someone from girls' night.

No. It was just a guess. Because every wife has something she keeps from her husband.

Doug snuggles in closer. "I love you more than I ever thought possible. More than I love anyone except Sadie. And I love you even more through her."

"I love you, too."

His face grows serious. "The truth is, I just miss you. It's like, I don't only want to be Sadie's dad. I want to still feel like your husband. I'm not always sure how to do that or where I stand with you."

"What do you mean?"

"You're just so distant sometimes. Will you tell me what I need to know to get close to you? Will you tell me what I should do or what I should stop doing?"

He looks so earnest. He loves me and wants to be close to me, but what I feel is pressure. Like when he's saying he doesn't know how to be my husband, what I hear is that I'm doing a lousy job being his wife.

He inches forward, and I can feel it coming. I don't dread it; I've always liked kissing Doug, but I don't feel up to what's next.

We need this. We have to reconnect. I told Doug that I know he meant well with the bikes and is just trying to make a good life for us and I'm sorry that I get so stressed over money. That's led us here, to his declarations of love, to this precipice. It brings me back years, to before Doug, to when I wondered how I could say no. If I could say no.

I'm grateful for Andie's advice. It's good to just let things go and be happy, admit that I don't have a real problem after all. So we'll have more debt. It'll be OK. We have our family and this house. We'll always have each other.

I kiss Doug back, and I know I could enjoy it if it wasn't for the encroaching awareness that this needs to go somewhere. It has to end in sex because you don't just make out with your husband. He hasn't been inside me in a month, at least. I've put him off long enough, citing the exhaustion of preparing for the move, and the move itself, and being the new kids on the block. All of it true, but they're excuses nonetheless.

I'm a wife. I'm not just a mother. This is what a wife is supposed to do. This is what a sexual being is supposed to do, and I'm not supposed to need three fifteen-dollar cocktails to do it.

I'll enjoy sex again sometime. I'm not asexual, like Gina. I'll start sleeping again, and my hormones will continue to regulate. Like Tennyson said, Sadie's still so little. My sex drive will come back. And once I stop breastfeeding, I'll start drinking again. In the meantime . . .

Fake it till you make it. That's what Dr. Morrison told me. She wasn't talking about sex, but it can apply here, too. You put one foot in front of the other and you smile and eventually, you get where you need to be, and your smile is genuine. She knew what she was talking about. I'm here, aren't I?

Doug's hands migrate to my breasts, which feel more like udders these days, and I just have to hope my nipples will get hard. But instead, they get slippery. Oh no. This is mortifying. I'm leaking milk.

But Doug puts his mouth on them and begins to suck, gently. Is that loving? Or is it gross? I can't even tell.

I grab him, doing the strokes I know he likes. He lets out a moan, with my nipple still clenched between his lips. I can tell he needs this, desperately. He needs me.

That does it. Now I'm a little wet.

I shift so that my breasts are my own again, and I put his hand between my legs. I want him to feel what he's doing to me, and he moans again. I tell myself what I need to hear:

He wants me bad.

He'll die if he can't be inside me.

He's dying for me.

He couldn't want anyone like he wants me.

But behind my closed eyes, I can see them: the women on the block, the regulars. Each face is transposing itself, one after the other. Tennyson to Yolanda to June to Gina (what's she doing here? She doesn't even have sex) to Andie to Raquel, here in this bed, with Doug. I can see what they'd do to him, and for him, and they'd do it better than I can.

My eyes fly open. It's just Doug and me here. Nothing (and no one) to worry about. So what if people were standing a little too close to other people's husbands at the block party. That was, what, five minutes? Ten at most? It was a long party. Everyone had had a lot to drink.

Those women trust each other. That means they're trustworthy, and they want to be my friends. I want to be theirs.

Does your husband know?

No, he doesn't know that the only way I can feel pleasure is through his pleasure. He doesn't know that my desire was co-opted, made approval-based, and I've never found my way out of that.

One of the most shameful parts of my experience with Layton was that I liked seducing him. I was a good student, and I studied him well. Dr. Morrison helped me see that was why he chose little girls, that he was grooming us to be his servants. He wasn't trying to make me happy; he was teaching me to make him happy. He'd turned me into a little fembot, my own desire secondary to the man's, and honestly, I've never been able to find my way out of that. No matter how many times I try to masturbate or rediscover my body or verbalize my own desires, it just doesn't seem to work.

Layton's programming has held, even in my relationship with Doug, where I know I'm loved and that he wants me to be satisfied sexually. He asks me what I like, but I have no good answer. So sometimes, I just have to playact. I have to fake it and hope I'll make it. But afterward, even if I manage to come, I feel sad and alone, because I know that Layton's ruined me.

Doug's rock-hard. Decisions have to be made.

I mount him. It's conventional, but it works. It turns Doug on, which turns me on for at least a little while. I let out the right accompanying noises as we move in tempo. Riding a husband is like riding a bike.

Don't think about bikes.

Does your husband know?

I move deeper and harder. I need to hear Doug. I need to know how he feels about this, and about me.

His noises become louder and more guttural. There've been times when he practically spoke in tongues, but that was long ago.

The only orgasms I ever have are simultaneous ones. When he comes, when I know I've satisfied him completely, that's when I'm most fulfilled. That puts me over the edge. But if you're going to fake an orgasm, that's the time to do it. When he's otherwise occupied.

I just keep seeing them. The women. My competition.

No, my friends.

Doug is starting to explode. "Oh God, Kat, Jesus, I fucking . . . love you . . . Oh fuck . . ." Like a bout of Tourette's.

I want to be right there with him, but those women . . .

I can't let them get in the way. Or am I the one in my own way?

CHAPTER 12

I'm outside, breaking down boxes, preparing for tomorrow's early morning trash pickup. The weather is perfect, and Sadie's lying beside me, burbling in her car seat. She's happy, and that's all that matters.

As I flatten a box, I notice its label, with my name and address on it. And I realize: I left evidence in every neighbor's trash can.

My actions that morning had been so spontaneous that it hadn't occurred to me to rip labels off or even take a marker to them. So no one had to actually see me. They could have gone out in the early morning with some last-minute rubbish and noticed that their cans were fuller than the night before. They pulled out the cardboard for the dining room chairs and the perpetrator's information was right there, in plain sight.

Not that this is about the trash anymore, but maybe that's what got the ball rolling or was the straw that broke the camel's back. Pick your cliché.

Don't worry, people, I feel like broadcasting. *From here on out, my trash and recycling are going in my own can. I'll keep my side of the street clean, literally and figuratively.*

I finish with the boxes. Then I lift Sadie's car seat and carry her up the front steps. She's in a mellow mood, lulled by the sunshine and breezes that can be felt even ten blocks off the water. Inside, I give her a bottle, change her diaper, and lay her in her crib. She goes down easily. I feel like a good mother, an in-control mother. Normal, that's what I am.

Back downstairs in the living room, I sit on the love seat, the laptop on my knees. I try not to stare longingly at the desk that hasn't been built this week. It's a beautiful day, Sadie's content, and Doug and I are back on track.

I check again on Part C for Sadie's dresser. I'm tired of pulling her clothes item by item out of the garbage bags we used for the move. Tired of thinking in terms of garbage.

If Part C arrives tomorrow, then Doug will have the whole weekend to put the dresser together. And if he doesn't work late tonight, I'll ask him to bolt the bookshelf to the wall. It can't take that long, and I'd be able to get rid of five boxes of books and break down the cardboard in time for tomorrow's trash pickup. That'll feel satisfying—a far better climax than our recent sex. I wouldn't be faking my pleasure at unpacking the books.

Oddly, though, the tracking service reports that Part C was delivered this morning, left at the front door.

I was just outside, and there was nothing on the porch. I call Homestore's customer service, and they refer me to the shipping company. I'm getting increasingly angry. I'm sick of waiting and living in chaos.

"The driver left it at the address at 10:38 today," I'm told.

"I was home, and I never heard a knock."

"They don't always knock."

They confirm my address. They put me on hold and come back to report that they spoke with the driver, who insists that the package was left on the doorstep. That's when I get a sinking feeling.

"We can launch a full investigation to try to find it, and the shipper can file a claim . . ."

I'm barely listening. I've had lots of packages delivered to this house, and to our previous address, which was in a neighborhood with much higher crime. Nothing's ever gone missing before.

I'm convinced that the same neighbor who's been leaving notes stole Part C.

How could that person know what Part C means to me, that I've been waiting for it anxiously?

They couldn't. No one would steal my package.

But it's not like it just up and walked away.

I yank the front door open to do one last check, in case I somehow missed it. No Part C. Only cardboard from those same blasted dining room chairs.

YOUR POOR LITTLE GIRL

I feel sick. It's not just about taking Part C but about invoking Sadie. When did someone leave that note? Just since I've been on this phone call? It wasn't there when I took Sadie outside to break down the boxes.

A time line emerges. Someone stole my package between 10:38 and 12:30, since I was in the driveway after lunch, and then left this note sometime in the past fifteen minutes. Whoever is behind the notes is definitely watching my house.

Three warnings in two days, talking about Doug and now about Sadie. If that's not raising the stakes, I don't know what is.

What does it even mean, poor Sadie? What do they know? And what do they want from me?

They know nothing. They're just trying to hit me where it hurts, in my mothering bone. To make me doubt myself. I'm a great mother, or at least I try to be. I certainly work hard enough at it.

Why would someone want to hurt me where it matters most?

You have 10 new messages from your neighbors!

> I never used a home day care, but I researched
> them when I was thinking about it. I'd been con-
> sidering going back to work and then I chickened
> out. I was afraid to have someone else watch my
> daughter. Silly, right? So here's a list of three day
> cares that I heard really good things about a few
> years back. Good luck!

That's from Raquel, sweet and self-effacing. My new friend.

These are good people who just want to help each other and know each other. To know *everything* about each other, isn't that what Fanny—I mean, Val—said?

> Dog walker, with references!

> We're cutting off my daughter's long hair. Should
> we donate to Locks of Love, or is there something
> more local?

> Colitis 5K Walk—all are welcome to bring aware-
> ness to the cause.

> Mountain of Styrofoam. Anyone need it for art proj-
> ects or packing?

So that's how it's done. But then, I didn't even know about GoodNeighbors before last week's trash pickup. What a difference a week makes.

> Free Restoration Hardware dining room table and six chairs. In good condition, two years old.

> Wonderful kitty needs a new home.

> Please join our book club!

> Coed softball game tonight.

See, the AV is full of good people. Welcoming, inclusive people.

I need to tell Doug about the notes, now that someone's brought Sadie into it and is actually stealing from us. It's become a safety issue.

> Steve Johnson's the best general contractor around. Trust me.

Oliver, of course. I see him on the site all the time, always the first to recommend painters, roofers, and contractors of every stripe. I suppose it is very neighborly of him, but it also strokes his ego. I have no idea how Doug could have talked to him for so long. I still haven't asked what they talked about.

An ego like his, getting bested by Doug and me for this house . . . Could it be him?

Does your husband know?

Well, he's about to know about you, you coward. Whether or not Oliver is the psychopath behind the notes, I decide this is one secret I just can't keep anymore.

I call Doug at work. "Hey there," he purrs. It's his I've-gotten-laid-recently voice.

"Hey. I'm freaked out."

"What happened?" His concern is instant.

I take a deep breath and tell him everything. That I've been getting notes but I didn't want to bother him. I wanted to handle it on my own, and I didn't want to prejudice him against his new neighbors. Everyone's been so kind, by and large. I hoped I could just forget about the notes.

"But I can't ignore them anymore," I say. "Whoever's writing them has taken it to the next level."

"What did they do?"

"They stole Part C."

"What do you mean?"

"You know, that part we need for Sadie's dresser. It was delivered this morning, and now it's gone."

"Are you sure it was there, and then it disappeared? Maybe it was never delivered."

"I had the shipping company ask the delivery guy. He confirmed that he left it. Why would he lie?"

A long pause, and then Doug's voice takes on an eerily calm quality, like he's a hostage negotiator or whoever it is who talks suicidal people off ledges. "Because he was covering his ass. He probably delivered it to the wrong house."

Unlikely, but possible, I guess.

"The notes are weird," he says. "I'll give you that. But to think someone's running around stealing packages?"

"If they can leave notes, why wouldn't they steal? They're getting bolder. That's what scares me."

"This is a really safe neighborhood, Kat."

"I want to think so, too."

"It's a really *expensive* neighborhood." Like I can forget that. I make sure our bills get paid on time. "What I mean is, if one of our neighbors is writing the notes, then they might be eccentric, but I doubt they're dangerous." Another pause. "Speaking of eccentric, there's that lady across the street. The one who's obsessed with parking. Did you park in her space?"

"No, I haven't parked in her space. And it's not Gladys."

"How do you know?"

"She's eighty years old. Part C is heavy. It's particleboard."

It's like he didn't even hear me. "Gladys probably watches the street like a hawk. She doesn't have anything else going on in her life, so she's got the time to nurse grudges." I can hear him warming to his argument. "You said yourself that the handwriting is perfect. She probably had to take penmanship classes in her day. No one under fifty even knows how to write anymore. You think you're on the geriatric mob hit list?"

We might laugh about this later, but it's not later. "The last note said, 'Your poor little girl.'"

"I get why you're bothered. I know you're already on edge with the whole move and trying to make a good impression on everyone."

"Do not make this about me."

"I'm trying to say that I understand why you'd be upset."

"But you don't think I have a reason to be?"

I hear him sigh. "I just don't want you to work yourself up. Whoever it is—man, woman, aardvark—don't let them get to you, OK? A bully loves a reaction. We're talking about high school pranks here. Maybe it's that Goth girl next door."

"Maybe." Though I don't really think it's Hope. Somehow, it just feels more adult than that.

"We'll talk when I get home, OK? We'll figure out how to make you feel safe."

"I'm going to call the police."

"Wait until tonight. I'll talk to Wyatt when I get home. I'll see what he thinks we should do."

That implies that Wyatt is someone to be trusted. We have no idea if that's the case. "I don't think that's a good idea."

"You wanted to call the police, and Wyatt's on the force. It just makes sense. I ran into him the other night, and we talked for a half hour. He's a good guy."

I read somewhere that the psychological profiles of cops and criminals are extremely similar. They both think they're above the law. "I don't want him repeating this to the other neighbors."

"I'll tell him it's just between us. He's a cop. He knows how to keep things quiet."

I don't answer.

"Listen," he says, "I'm upset, too. I don't like someone treating you like this. But you know how you can get."

"How do I get, Doug?"

Now he doesn't answer.

"Let me help, OK?" he finally says. "Let me talk to Wyatt."

I know how this will go. He's determined, and he'll wear me down, nicely. Because he's undamaged, so his judgment is above reproach.

But what's that old saying? Just because you're paranoid doesn't mean nobody's after you.

CHAPTER 13

"Maybe you could just put up the spice rack?" I say to Doug with a weary hope. If our house is more in order, literally, everything will feel manageable again. Once the spice rack is affixed to the wall, I'll be able to at least put the spices in their proper place. That's one more box I can break down, albeit a small one, and it'll be easier to start cooking again. Cooking is a baby step toward making a house a home.

The kitchen is small and the oak cabinetry is dated, but it gets good light. Someday, I'd like to add a backsplash in a bright color, something befitting Crayola. But today, I'll settle for the spice rack. And then tomorrow, Doug can build the kitchen cart to house our pots and pans. One foot in front of the other, one box at a time. Everything's going to be fine. Sure, one person doesn't seem to want me in the AV, but I'm wanted by everyone else. I've been invited to my second girls' night out, and not just by one person. They've all texted me to make sure I'm coming. That means I'm going to be a regular at girls' night. Andie never pulled that off.

And sure, Part C is missing. But that could be because the driver made a mistake and then lied to cover it up, like Doug said, or, if it was stolen, that only renders the whole note thing juvenile and harmless. Someone who steals particleboard is not someone to fear. It probably is Hope and her teenage friends. It could be some Goth initiation ritual, for all I know.

Doug is dancing around with Sadie, and she's rewarding him with giggles. This is what I should focus on. This is real life.

"It's the weekend," I say. "Let's make some progress on the house, and then we can go have fun."

Doug does a little soft-shoe. "I've been cooped up all week in a cube. I need a break. I need to get out in the sunshine, pronto."

"We'll get out. But do one thing first." I'm practically begging. "Just the spice rack or the bookshelf."

"I'm the one who watched Sadie while you were out partying with your new friends last week. Doesn't that count for anything? I mean, I did everything for her. You wouldn't believe the size of her poop. I should be nominated for Father of the Year after cleaning that up."

I know he's kidding—he's not one of those guys who's never changed a diaper—but it rankles anyway. He watches Sadie by himself for one night and changes a poopy diaper, and he's Father of the Year?

"Please, Doug," I implore.

He stops moving and cocks his head. "Then we stroll Main Street? And for the rest of the day, not another word about building or installing or, heaven forbid, affixing?"

It's the best deal I'm going to get.

A half hour later, the spice rack is up and we're headed out with Sadie in her stroller. Doug is in high spirits. "I wish there was a boys' night out," he says. "Maybe I should start one myself. Vic seems cool. Oliver. Definitely Nolan."

I wince. It's visceral, my response to that name. Doug might as well be saying Layton. It's a good thing that Andie doesn't bring him up much. Come to think of it, open as she appears, she doesn't actually share that much personal information about her home life at all.

"And Wyatt, for sure," Doug says. "He's awesome."

Doug had been true to his word, knocking on Wyatt's door and disappearing inside for more than an hour. Yet when Doug returned home, he was unusually succinct in describing their talk: yes, Wyatt was going to keep things confidential; no, he didn't have any idea who the writer could be; yes, Wyatt would keep more of an eye on our house; no, there was no need to call the police.

"The thing is," Doug told me, "the department wouldn't do much in a case like this. There's no one to issue a restraining order against, and they're not really going to take a bunch of anonymous notes seriously."

"The notes are threatening."

"There's no explicit threat. You wouldn't believe how overt it has to be before the police will do anything. Wyatt told me some stories—" Seeing my face, he clams up. Then he says, "It's going to be OK. Wyatt says whoever's doing this will get tired. They'll run out of steam."

I hesitate. I want to believe that so badly, but then I remember Note #3: *You thought we were done here?*

"Wyatt knows how these kinds of people operate, Kat. He knows common harassment patterns. And an increased police presence as soon as the new neighbors arrive won't exactly endear us to the block. He's looking out for us, Kat. He's a good person."

"You're sure he's not going to tell anyone?"

"Positive. He said he won't even mention it to Yolanda."

If Wyatt thinks it's no big deal, if the police see far worse all the time, then I should try to accept his assessment.

It suddenly strikes me that Wyatt's wife is the only one who hasn't texted me about girls' night out. Yolanda is the only one who hasn't regularly made it clear that she wants my friendship.

Now, as we stroll past the park en route to Main Street, the first people I see are Wyatt and Yolanda. It's like when you've had a dream about someone and then you open your eyes and there they are. There's a sense of unreality to the whole scene.

But nothing could be more ordinary. Branstone's daughter, Zoe, is playing with Yolanda's twin boys in the sandbox. Wyatt's got his feet submerged beside them. Brandon and Yolanda are sitting on the edge, chattering away like magpies (I remember now that they watch each other's kids a lot. Though right now, Wyatt's doing all the watching). Stone is on a nearby bench, scrolling on his phone.

Doug pushes the stroller over to Wyatt, activates the foot brake, and then claps Wyatt on the back. Wyatt stands up and gives Doug a bear hug like they've known each other for years.

Yolanda is watching our approach, her eyes slightly narrowed, before her expression melts into a smile for me. Brandon leaps up. "Long time no see!" he crows. He clutches me in a hug.

"Hi!" I eke out.

When Brandon releases me, he smacks himself on the forehead. "I've been totally meaning to bring over some hand-me-downs for the little lady, if that's all right. We spend way too much on Zoe's clothes. It'd be great to keep them on the block."

"Thanks," I say with a smile. "But don't worry; we're getting by."

"Of course you are. That baby of yours could be in a potato sack and she'd win first prize at the county fair."

Yolanda laughs. "You can take the boy out of the country, but you can't take the country out of the boy."

"I hope you're wrong about that," Brandon says.

The conversation between Yolanda and Brandon flows around me, a slow-moving current, and I can wade in whenever I feel like it or stand on the banks. It's comfortable, nondemanding. I find myself hoping that neither of them wrote those notes, that neither of them grabbed Part C. They're both around on weekdays, right? For reasons of scheduling, Stone's off the hook. Maybe Wyatt, too, though cops can have irregular hours.

"Hey," Doug calls over to me, "what do you think about having a housewarming party?"

I feel almost like he's testing me, making sure that I'm still prepared to open up despite everything, and in such a public forum. But that's not Doug's way; he's not underhanded like that. He loves a party, that's all.

"We'll talk about it," I say.

"Uh-oh!" Stone laughs from his bench. Other than his initial wave and greeting, I hadn't thought he was listening.

"We just need to get things more in order. Our house is still a mess."

"It's adorable," Yolanda pronounces. "And so colorful."

"It's all Kat's doing." Doug grins at me.

Then he's back talking to Wyatt, and I smile awkwardly at Yolanda and Brandon.

"I know you're not completely settled in," Brandon says, "but I bet you've at least gotten rid of all the bad juju?"

Yolanda smacks him on the shoulder playfully. "There's no bad juju!"

"Nils and Ilsa?" He raises an eyebrow. "There's some bad juju."

"What do you mean?" I ask, my throat tightening just slightly.

"Brandon just likes to gossip." Yolanda gives me a smile. "You have nothing to worry about."

It seems like Wyatt kept his word and she really doesn't know about the notes.

"It's not gossip," Brandon says. "It's personal experience."

"Story for another time." Yolanda regards him fondly. There's true affection between these two. But was there also a tiny hint of warning in her look?

"We should get going," Doug calls to me. "Our girl's getting antsy!"

I'd enjoy Main Street on an ordinary day, but the phrase *bad juju* keeps ringing in my ears. Could Nils and Ilsa be behind the notes? They sold us the house and then regretted it?

I'm tired of speculating, tired of everything all of a sudden. That morphs into irritability, which centers on Doug, perhaps unfairly.

I'm trying not to be bugged that Doug put me on the spot about the party, the same as he forced me into drinks at Oliver and Gina's, which then reminds me of the bikes. I'm also trying to forget that Dad of the Year comment, and how Doug makes me twist his arm to get anything done in the house.

But he's working hard these days, I know. I don't want to resent him, and I do want us to spend more time strolling around the neighborhood, doing what normal people do. I want to get to know the Village. I like gelato as much as the next person.

I find myself trailing Doug, who's using Sadie like a prop, since everywhere we go, she attracts attention. I stand by, doing my best to smile while he makes small talk, seemingly oblivious to my mood. He's probably just chalking it up to introversion, thinking I should push myself out of my comfort zone. It's not like he heard the bad juju remark, after all.

In the bike shop, Doug and the proprietor start gabbing away. He has me trying on helmets. He even picks one out for Sadie. Then there are the bike locks and rainproof covers that are perfectly sized, which also means perfectly expensive. "Couldn't we just buy this stuff at Target?" I ask him when the owner steps away.

"You have to support local businesses!" he says with a cheerful smile.

I bounce Sadie up and down in my arms, smiling stiffly, while he talks to shopkeepers and customers alike. I watch him in his element. He doesn't seem to notice (or care) how I'm feeling. I should probably tell him outright, but isn't he the one who claimed, on our second date, that his skill was reading people and giving them what they want? That skill seems to have abandoned him when it comes to his own wife.

Stop it, Kat.

I don't want to be that wife who stands by silently, awash in resentment. I want to appreciate him for what he's good at, like talking to people, and accept what he's not, which is putting together furniture in a timely manner.

Besides, this isn't really about Doug. This is about the notes, Part C, and bad juju. It's my fear of escalation, of what might be coming next. It's about the shame I feel over a past that I'm afraid is catching up to me right now, that a neighbor somehow knows what I haven't even told my own husband. It's about all that I need to keep boxed up and buried, on a block full of people who claim they can see through me.

"Can we just get a gelato and go home?" I say.

"Sure. The only other thing we have to do is stop by Tennyson's boutique."

"I'm really tired, Doug."

He squints in evaluation. Finally, he says, "OK. A gelato and then home." I give him a big hug and smack a kiss on his cheek, and he laughs.

I knew it would be OK if I just told him what I want and how I feel.

But I can't share it all. For him to know the whole of me would change everything. He'd never look at me the same again, and I've always loved how he looks at me.

He knows about my mother's depression. He knows she could barely function, let alone attend to me emotionally. He knows about the poverty and the neglect.

There's the father I never knew and the mother who didn't give me enough love, but that's it. No more. Layton and Ellen—that's another level.

As it is, Doug thinks that the reason I'm not crazy about his parents is because of my childhood. Imagine how he would consider my thoughts and behaviors, especially ones he didn't like, if he knew the rest. Imagine how easily I could be dismissed. It's OK if Doug pities me, just a little, but if he knew everything, he'd be disgusted. And I couldn't live with that.

CHAPTER 14

Andie's driving again, though I notice she's dressed a lot more conservatively this time. Actually, she's dressed like I was the first night, in jeans and a cute top.

I wind her up and let her go. I ask questions about her favorite restaurants in the AV, the best sangria, a great manicure, a skilled hairstylist. I'm doing a Doug trick: make her feel like a valued authority. But unlike him, I'm not paying attention to her recommendations. I'm just killing time.

Much as I like Andie, the last thing I need is to be around someone who can read me. I want to be in my bed, shades drawn, covers pulled up to my chin, watching a Netflix marathon. I feel like this night is destined to end badly, but I didn't know how to get out of it. Declining the second invitation seemed like terrible form. There might not be a third.

"You seem sort of quiet," Andie says as we're pulling into a parking space across from Hound. "Is everything OK?"

I could tell her about the notes. Then she'd forgive my strange mood, and it would cement our friendship.

"Just tired," I say.

Hound is still cramped, serpentine, and dark, but this time, Andie and I are the last to arrive. June, Yolanda, Raquel, Tennyson, and Gina are assembled around the conjoined table, with shots lined up for all of us, including me. It's an offer that's hard to refuse, in my current fried state. My nerves are crying out for a salve.

"You made it!" Gina seems truly happy to see me. She's in a shapeless T-shirt, her mushroom hair anchored by a headband.

"Hey there!" June looks like she's in good spirits, too, much more coiffed than I've seen her before. Her auburn hair is usually in a ponytail, but tonight she's styled it into spiral curls, and she's in full makeup. I wouldn't have thought it before, but she can be nearly as attractive as Tennyson and Yolanda.

"Tequila," Tennyson says, by way of greeting, pointing at the shot glass intended for me. "We're starting with a classic tonight."

"It's a nice bed for the Golden Revolver," Raquel adds.

Tennyson laughs. "It's not called a Golden Revolver!"

"Whatever." Raquel is looking unusually sexy tonight in a low-cut shirt and push-up bra. Something else is different. It takes me a second, and then I realize she's not wearing her glasses. She and June got the same memo. Andie and I missed it.

"Down the hatch," June says. She lifts her glass in my direction, as if to toast.

"*Salud,*" Yolanda says.

"Mazel tov," from Andie.

I don't know if it's the fact that each woman is tossing her drink back in turn and I'm just susceptible to peer pressure or if it's that earlier I noticed Sadie has way more than enough milk and one pump and dump wouldn't impact her at all. It could be nerves or that the shot glass is just sitting there and I hate to waste anything. It could be a desire for obliteration. Whatever the reason(s), it's *salud* and down the hatch and mazel tov for me, too. The other women congratulate me, like I've done something brave.

"Sometimes you just need to look after yourself," Tennyson says approvingly, as if this is a version of treating myself to a massage.

From there, it doesn't seem like much of a leap to my first Silk Purse. Both go to my head quickly, and I see, with perfect clarity, why alcohol is essential in life. All of a sudden, I'm in the moment and forgetting all the stresses of the past couple of weeks. My inner censor has been muted. I feel verbally limber and loose enough to banter with the best of them. I'm even feeling, dare I say, a little bit sexy. If I had a button to undo, I would. If I get the next round, I might even flirt with the bartender.

Then Gina says, "Let's get down to business."

Tennyson does a mock spit take. "Gina, seriously?"

"The guest of honor is already liquored up," Gina answers.

I look around, wondering who she's talking about. Then I realize they're all looking at me.

Gina leans toward me just slightly, her mushroom hair especially voluminous tonight, her eyes intent on mine. It occurs to me that Tennyson could just be a figurehead, and Gina might be the true power. She's certainly coming off like the ringleader tonight. "Let me ask you something crucial. Why are you monogamous?"

Now I want to do a spit take. "What—what do you mean?" I stammer.

"You've probably never even thought about it before, right? You're monogamous because that's what marriage is. Because you think it's the only way to do it."

"Listen," Tennyson drawls, "marriage is an evolving institution. I mean, women used to be property."

"Now men and women make each other property," Raquel says. "Controlling each other. You know, 'You love me because you won't have sex with anyone else, even though it's totally normal to want to.'"

"Have you read Esther Perel?" Gina asks. I shake my head. I wish I hadn't had that Silk Purse. It's hard to keep up with this conversation.

"Esther Perel talks about how sexual desire is activated by novelty, while traditional marriage says that denying yourself any other partners is a prerequisite. That's a paradox. A double bind."

"No wonder there are so many affairs." Tennyson raises her hand. "I mean, guilty! Vic and I decided that we were going to do it differently this time around. No one owns anybody, and we can accept ourselves and each other as sexual beings. That's why we're so happy."

"Why are you so happy?" I ask stupidly. I'm not quite following.

"Here's the deal," Tennyson says. "Normally, you're monogamous because you think the only other options are eternal dating or being in a relationship and cheating."

"Or you're monogamous because you only want to be with your husband," I say. "And he only wants to be with you."

But I already outed myself at the last girl's night. They know I don't exactly want to be with Doug. I *want* to want to be with Doug. That's a big difference.

A part of me has always known, deep down, that the AV was too good to be true. I've been waiting for the bottom to drop out . . .

Tennyson is giving me a slightly dubious look, a smile playing at her lips. Can every one of them really see through me? This is a nightmare. "If that's the case—if you and Doug only want to be with each other—then you opt out."

"Opt out of what?" I say.

"The spreadsheet."

I look at Andie, and I see that she knows exactly what the spreadsheet is. Of course she does. I feel blindsided by my new friend. She couldn't have given me some sort of heads up? I would have prepared something to say. Or at the very least, I wouldn't have had a shot plus a Silk Purse after a year of abstinence.

"The spreadsheet is where everyone states their preferences," Andie tells me quietly. "There are couples who are primarily monogamous, with an occasional hall pass. And some who have ongoing relationships outside of their marriages."

"Each couple comes up with their own rules," Yolanda says. "It might be that same-sex is OK but opposite isn't. Or they can only be with the third party together. You can only be with someone if I am. We get to veto each other's potential partners. No sex in our house or in our bed. No sleepovers. Don't ask, don't tell." I see her really warming to this. Where Yolanda is concerned, the more rules the better.

"Some couples opt in for a while and then opt out," Andie says.

"And then some," June says, her eyes dancing, "opt back in."

Is June involved in this? She's not even part of a couple. She just gets to sample everyone's husbands without any complications at all? It doesn't seem quite fair.

"The spreadsheet is really dynamic." Tennyson polishes off the rest of her drink. "Each couple has to decide together what they really want. It leads to all kinds of really intimate, revealing conversations. You'll know Doug better than you ever imagined you could just by talking about all this stuff. About your truest desires." My stomach plummets just as Tennyson stands up. "Anyone want another?"

Raquel tosses hers back and then rattles the ice in her now-empty glass. Everyone else, including me, says they're OK.

A hush falls over the table once she's gone. "I don't really know what to say," I tell them.

"You're not expected to answer tonight," Raquel says. "It's a lot to think about. Obviously, you need to talk to Doug."

He'll dismiss it out of hand, I'm sure.

We'll dismiss it together.

"People are so jealous and paranoid because they're afraid to lose," Gina says. "Think how liberating it would be to set your marriage free."

Raquel reads my expression because she says, "No, really. You go off and you're with someone else, and you get that euphoria, right? You get the initial infatuation. Then you go home in a great mood, and everything's lustier. But we all have our eyes open. We all know exactly what that is, and we don't fool ourselves into thinking the grass is greener on the other side. In the end, we're all going home to our husbands and wives. There are no affairs here. It's all out in the open."

"That's the key," Yolanda says. "We're open here. And there are no divorces. Families stay together."

I glance at Tennyson. She's on her second marriage, right? But maybe her first marriage didn't have the spreadsheet.

"Families are stronger because they're headed by two people who know they're not just stuck with each other, you know?" Raquel's eyes are bright, even in the dim. "We all *want* to go home to our husbands."

She really means what she's saying, but a part of me just can't imagine wanting to go home to someone who looks at me the way Bart was looking at her that day at the block party. Like he wanted to rip her limb from limb. Or was that just the intensity of his sexual desire? Because he'd just been with, say, Tennyson, and now he was hot for Raquel?

It doesn't compute, and yet, these are smart women. Vital, interesting women. And they're telling me that this works. They want me to be a part of their community. I mean, *really* a part of their community. I'd wondered if I'd be accepted; now it's much more than that. I'm actually desired.

Or Doug is.

"This probably sounds kind of insane, right?" June says. "Every one of us thought so, once upon a time. But it actually works."

If it works so well, what happened to her husband?

"We've never asked someone to join this fast," Raquel says. "Usually, it takes a while of getting to know someone. But with you, it was unanimous after the last girls' night. We were like, 'Why wait?'"

I'm slightly flattered, warped as this whole scenario is.

"There's something about you," Yolanda says. "We all felt it. It's like, we knew we could trust you."

"Don't take this the wrong way." Raquel goes to push her glasses up her nose and then realizes she's not wearing them. "But you've got this kind of awkwardness, like you're wrestling with yourself. You're all earnest and hopeful, but it's like you know better than that; you don't want to get crushed. And I don't know, we just all really responded to that and wanted you around."

"Because it's not just about sex," Gina says. Then she laughs self-deprecatingly. I didn't know she had self-deprecation in her. "I mean, obviously, with me, it's not about sex. We're really good friends. We lean on each other. We can share anything."

It seems like Gina has been doing the hardest sell. Maybe she's the mastermind behind the spreadsheet. Her marriage needed an arrangement, and she's the definition of an overachiever. She found Oliver a neighborhood full of women to do what she doesn't want to.

Tennyson returns with two drinks in her hands and plants one in front of Raquel. Then, feeling no need to catch up on the conversation, she says, "Affairs are rampant. It's not sleeping with other people that kills marriages. It's the secrecy. Secret fantasies and longings. Self-denial. And eventually, betrayal. It doesn't need to be that way."

"It's an experiment," Andie says. "You can try it, and if you don't like it, you just forget all about it."

I study her, trying to gauge what she has and hasn't done, and whether what's done can really be undone. If Doug has sex with one of these women, I'll always know that. If I have sex with one of their men, I'd always know that, and so would they.

Is that part of the allure? How incestuous it all is? That they're all bonded by intrigue and drama?

"You have a favorite meal, right?" Gina looks at me, and I nod. "You don't want to eat it every day for the rest of your life. You want to switch it up. Your taste buds want a different experience, and everyone gets that. Well, sexual appetites are the same way. Why do we accept our appetites around food but not sex? No one insists on gastronomic monogamy. On gastronogamy." She and the others laugh.

"Let's go around the table," June says, "and everyone can say the biggest advantage to the spreadsheet."

"You don't have to stifle your true nature," Tennyson says immediately. "I want a life partner, but I still like variety. Vic is great in bed, but he can't be every man, you know?"

"You don't have to wonder if the grass is greener," Andie says. Does she mean that she was with someone else, and it made her realize her own grass was just fine? That she and Nolan tried and then decided to opt out? I'm assuming she's not part of the spreadsheet now or she would be a girls' night regular.

"Well, you know my grass isn't greener," Raquel quips, and everyone laughs. I assume she means her actual brown grass and not Bart.

"It's affair prevention," Yolanda says quietly. "He'll have his experiences, but he'll never leave."

"You have someone else to do the dirty work," Gina says. "You know, to have the sex you don't feel like having. It takes the pressure off."

"Sometimes you're more sexually compatible with someone other than your husband," June says.

"It's always good to get some new inspiration," Raquel says.

It occurs to me how incredibly confident they all are (with the exception of maybe Yolanda). Are they that way because of—what should I call it—swinging? Swapping? Orgies? Polyamory?

Gina says, "This isn't all about sex. It's not even primarily about sex. It's about freedom and openness. It's about accepting one another's choices and accepting yourself. I wasn't always so comfortable being asexual. I used to feel like I had to pretend, but now I can just be who I am. It's a legitimate choice, to choose not to have sex, and since Oliver can meet his needs elsewhere, I know my value to him is about much more than sex. It's a true partnership. Society tells women they have to be sexy, and sexual. Fuck that. It's freeing not to want sex. I feel so in control."

"And Oliver is really OK with that?" I'm thinking it, but Andie asks it, like an act of ventriloquism.

Gina nods. "He likes clarity in all things. This way, he knows exactly what he's getting and when. He knows the bottom line. It's like all the best business deals: it's clean and everyone profits."

"What do you even call this kind of arrangement?" I say.

"Openness." Tennyson smiles.

"Neighbors with benefits," Yolanda adds.

"Don't you get jealous?" I ask, and they all laugh. Jealousy is clearly well-covered territory.

"Of course!" Raquel says. "We help each other through it. We've all been there."

"Jealousy is human nature." Tennyson finishes another drink ahead of the rest of us. "But I don't want to control my jealousy by chaining up my husband and keeping him in a cage."

"Unless that's what he's into," Raquel says. More laughter. "This isn't an arrangement that just benefits men, Kat. In my experience, it benefits women more. Men have always known who they are and what they want—they're encouraged to from childhood—but women? We're supposed to make everyone else happy." I feel myself flush. She can't know, and yet . . . "So we have a lot to figure out about what we really want. It's more complicated for us, and society is more judgmental. We're prudes or we're whores or we're just old married ladies. But think about this: If no one had to know, if you could shed your inhibitions just for a day, or a week, what would you want to do most? What would you want to try?"

I realize it's not just rhetorical; she's actually waiting on an answer.

Andie comes to my rescue. "Whatever it is, you can try it with Doug."

"Truly," Raquel says, "my communication and my relationship with Bart have never been better. And my self-image has never been higher."

"We accept you even if you don't want to be a part of this," June says. "It's not mandatory. It's a perk."

"Just think about it, and talk to Doug." Tennyson finishes her drink. "If you guys opt out, we totally respect that. But consider it first, OK? And ask us any questions you have."

"Everyone says no at first, and then we get worn down." Raquel smiles. "Well, it's not exactly like that, but at first, everyone is bound by convention. It just seems so abnormal, you know? And so terrifying. But then you think on it some more, and you look around, and it becomes a version of normal."

"Pleasure is normal," June says.

"Attraction to people other than your spouse is normal," Tennyson says. "And embracing that while still loving your spouse can be normal, too."

"I think I was the most resistant to the idea," June says. "I held out for more than a year, and meanwhile, my marriage was going down the toilet. I'm seeing all these other people indulging, happily, and they're staying married, happily. They're not letting society tell them what to do. But I was, and my husband was, and we were miserable."

"Don't be afraid, Kat," Tennyson says. "Fear is the real killer in life, you know?"

"You've just got to know you're beautiful, Kat, and worth coming home to," Raquel says.

"We all are," Yolanda says.

It seems eerie and cultlike, but also so seductive. A siren song.

They're telling me I'll want to resist but I won't be able to. And neither will Doug.

"There's a fifty percent divorce rate, right?" June says. "But not on our block. On our block, I'm the only one."

"We're all in this together," Tennyson says. "Think of us like a big support group."

Then they get down to brass tacks. Gina says, "The people at this table aren't the only ones participating. But we're the organizers. The welcome wagon, so to speak. We control the spreadsheet. We know who's opted in and who's opted out, who's currently looking and available, what everyone is looking for, and the rules for each particular couple."

"If you're into someone but they're not available right now, I'll make a note," Tennyson says. "Then I'll let you know when they're back up for grabs."

It's like an out-of-stock item on the Internet. This is the craziest thing I've ever heard, but no one seems to think so except me. They all seem so sane and so happy. And they obviously like each other. I saw that at the block party. This is the happiest group of people I've ever encountered.

The truth is, I've never been a particularly happy person. I've tried to be, mightily, but with my background, it doesn't come easily.

"It's all about informed consent," Tennyson tells me. "You and Doug need to know this exists, and then you can decide whether you consent, as a couple. You're either opting in as a couple or out as a couple."

"If one of you is participating and the other isn't, the nonparticipant has to consent as well." This is, naturally, from Gina. "It's a marital decision."

"Those are the block rules." Tennyson is trying to get the last tiny droplets of alcohol out of her glass. "But you need to develop your own rules, too, as a couple. And whatever you decide, you follow religiously. The biggest problems arise when a couple starts to break their own rules. That's a betrayal of trust and a violation. That's an affair, basically."

"Why are we talking about such heavy stuff?" Raquel says. "You don't start there. You start by looking around and seeing who catches your eye."

Tennyson runs her finger lightly around the rim of her glass. "You flirt, and then you fantasize. You let your mind wander. It's amazing what's possible. *Who's* possible."

They've clearly misjudged their audience. I do everything I can to keep my mind under control.

Then we adjourn. The business is over, and it's time to have fun. There's general talk and laughter, but I'm too preoccupied with what I've heard to join in.

"I'll get the next round," I say, casting a quick glance at Andie, hoping she can read me as well as she claimed she could.

"I'll help you carry them," she says.

As we dodge people, I'm light-headed from the alcohol and the pitch I'm trying to digest. We belly up to the bar, and I hiss, "What the fuck was that?"

She laughs, and I can see the tension she's releasing. "I figured this was coming at some point. I just never thought it would be this soon!"

"Did you think about telling me?"

"I felt like it wasn't my secret to tell. Even though it's kind of an open secret."

"You and Nolan have opted out?" I ask, holding my breath for the answer and exhaling at her nod.

"They've refined their presentation since I first heard it. But when Gina said they were going to get to business, I knew what was coming."

The bartender notices us and starts to walk over. I wave a hand to tell him he can take other people first, no rush here. "I'm definitely going to say no. It's just a question of timing."

"Don't you want to talk to Doug first?"

"I'm not sure I need to. If one of us is opting out, we both are. That's how it works, right?"

"You just might want to give it a little time. You've had a lot to drink, and it's all sorts of overwhelming at first."

Whose side is she on? Didn't she just tell me she opted out?

"You need to do what's right for you. And I'll be here as a sounding board. Someone neutral. Because all the women are great, they really are, but they have an agenda." She must see the alarm in my face because she adds, "Not a scary agenda or anything. I mean, they really will respect if you opt out, but they're obviously hoping you'll opt in."

Does the person who's writing the notes want me to opt in or out?

"The arrangement thrives on new blood, that's all," Andie says. "When someone new enters the mix, it shakes up the dynamics. There's all this interest and rivalries. Block parties feel a little more exciting. It spices things up." Again, she catches my expression. "In a harmless way, of course. They really are all good people. They truly are close, and they do take care of each other through any drama."

"I don't think I need any drama."

"A little drama can be fun." She smiles. Then she grows more serious. "I'm here for you, Kat. Opt in or out, it makes no difference to me."

"I can't believe they're hitting me with this the second time we hang out."

"Well, someone obviously took a quick liking to you and Doug."

Of course. Doug.

The women find me trustworthy, and what they want is fresh meat. They want Doug. At the first girls' night, they were feeling me out, talking about their sex lives to bait me, to see if Doug is available. Stupid me, I basically told them he was, seeing as I have no physical desire for my imminently desirable husband.

Some part of me must have known. That's why I saw their faces when Doug and I were having sex. I knew they were competition then. Community of women, my ass. The spreadsheet needs fresh meat.

I feel my face heating up. I signal the bartender.

"So, you ready for a little dirt?" Andie asks.

"Tell me."

She says that Oliver has been with men and women (I knew it!). Vic and Raquel were hot and heavy for a little while, and there were some threesomes with Tennyson. Bart's always had a thing for Yolanda, but she turned him down. It's a big secret who Yolanda has been with, but everyone knows that she and Wyatt have the most restrictions.

"Did you opt out from the beginning," I ask, "or did you try it for a while?"

"For a very short while." She's clearly reticent to talk about her and Nolan, and I'm good with that. I don't like thinking about Nolan in any sort of sexual context.

"I can't imagine sharing Doug."

"There are some open marriages that really work. Vic and Tennyson are incredibly happy and stable. But what I can say is, don't do it to fix a broken marriage."

"Doug and I aren't broken."

"I didn't think you were. You guys seem great." The operative word is *seem*, and it hangs there between us. "I'm just saying, you need to be rock solid to introduce something like this."

After the first girls' night, I was so hopeful. I thought maybe I'd found a group of women who truly liked me, who would accept me, and now I'm outside the circle already. Not that I want to be inside, not anymore, knowing all the strings that are attached and the price I'd have to pay.

So I hadn't just imagined that sex was in the air at the block party. They've set it up so that within every interaction, there's always possibility. It creates an energy that permeates everything.

They have what I want—not the sex but the confidence. Comfort in their own skins. Freedom. Nothing could be more seductive than that.

Everyone opts out at first. Then they get worn down.

The rest of the night is a blur.

I feel depressed, and then angry at how it's all played out, how they invited me here and gave me their spiel. But maybe I did it to myself.

I removed myself from the equation. I can't be a part of their sexual round robin.

I'm staring down into my fourth empty Silk Purse when this incredibly powerful force comes over me. Suddenly, I feel happy, so ridiculously happy. And so tactile. These are my neighbors, and I feel love for all of them. I talk and flirt and dance with everyone, men and women. The whole floor twines together, as if it's one organism with a hundred limbs, and it's amazing to feel this type of connection. Sensuality without sex. It's beautiful and harmless. Tonight, I'm just having good, clean fun. Tomorrow, I'll opt out.

Then the first thing that changes is the smell. Someone's perfume has become rancid.

I look into the crowd by the bar, all dark and menacing figures, and I could swear I see Layton. He's not in prison; he's right over there. He begins to turn, and I want to run, but I'm frozen in place. My muscles will not obey my command. Terror sets in, while all around me, my neighbors are oblivious.

Except for Andie. Thank God for Andie.

"I need the bathroom," I tell her. I can't get there without her, and somehow, she figures that out—or maybe I tell her; I can't be sure of what's being thought and what's being said—and she gets me there, my arm around her neck.

The bathroom is gray, filthy, and windowless, like what I'd imagine in a prison. The smell is abominable. It's bleach and feces and, perhaps more disturbingly, cotton candy and popcorn, like a county fair run by Satan. There are cockroaches. There are rats. I try again not to scream. Fortunately, Andie is a good friend and waits outside the stall. She won't let anyone hurt me.

"Are you OK?" she asks. "Are you crying?"

That's the last thing I remember.

Session 57.

"He wasn't only a teacher. He was a pillar of the community. He was on all these different boards, had his hand in everything. A model family: one son, one daughter, a stay-at-home mother. As a teacher, he was one of the most well loved. He'd won awards from the district. Parents wanted their kids in his class."

"But what was he really like, behind closed doors?"

"I've already told you that."

"You haven't told me much. But tell me more about you."

"I was kind of nerdy. I always got good grades. I had a best friend I really loved but no other friends. I tried to be a good girl."

"What was your relationship with him like?"

"I tried to please him. I don't think there's anything wrong with that. At the trial, the district attorneys painted this picture of someone who was calculated and diabolical, always scheming, choosing kids whose parents didn't give a rat's ass about them. Kids who weren't likely to speak up. Kids who weren't popular. Who didn't have a lot of friends."

"That sounds like you."

"No comment."

"What was the trial like for you?"

"I think we should just stop now."

"OK."

"That's it? Just 'OK'?"

"I told you that you're in control in here."

"But you still think I'm in denial."

"I shouldn't have said that."

"You mean you're admitting you made a mistake?"

"Of course. I make mistakes all the time. Sometimes I think I see an opening and I charge in, and then I realize I should have taken it slower."

"I've made a lot of mistakes."

"I think you confuse your mistakes with his. You're still protecting him. But he should have been the one protecting you. He was in a position of authority."

"You don't really understand the situation."

"Help me understand."

"You said I could pump the brakes whenever I want. Well, I'm pumping them."

CHAPTER 15

I'm fumbling, flailing, and emitting strangled cries. I'm harpooned here in the dark, suffocating. I've been swallowed. I'm in the belly of a whale, like that book I should have read in high school.

I scream. I don't know if anyone can hear me, but I have to try. I want to live. Sadie. I have to get back to her. I need to live, for her.

I hear heavy footsteps, someone running. To save me or to hurt me? I don't know. I should have stayed quiet. Maybe they didn't even know I was here, whoever they are, wherever here is.

Then I'm free. My bindings are lifted, and the room is flooded with light. It's my bathroom, with the gray-blue tiles, like I'm being tossed on stormy seas. I'm breathing heavily, and I realize that I'd been under a blanket made by my mother-in-law, the kind of loose knit pattern that seems like a net. I'd never actually been trapped, but sometimes the illusion is enough. It's like how people can drown in water a foot deep.

"You scared the shit out of me," Doug says accusingly. He's breathing heavily, too, though I don't know why. It's a tiny house. Maybe we really do need to start riding our bikes. We're in terrible shape.

Well, I am, currently. My head is pounding; my stomach is roiling. I have to close my eyes against the fluorescent light.

"Sorry," I tell Doug. "First time drinking in a year. Regrets."

"Yeah." His tone is bitter. "I bet."

I try to remember what I could have done to make him mad. Even at the height of my partying days, I never felt like this. This sick, with a cratered memory. I remember the spreadsheet, though; there's no way I could forget that.

"You were throwing up a lot," Doug says, disapproving.

"I'm sorry. I shouldn't have drunk that much."

"Andie had to knock on the door and wake me up at one a.m. She needed me to come out and carry you out of her car, caveman-style. You were completely out. Like, unconscious but mumbling."

My chest tightens. "What was I mumbling?"

"I couldn't make it out. Neither could Andie. She said that it had taken four of the women to get you into her car."

I throw the blanket back over my head. "I am so mortified."

"Andie tried to make excuses for you. She said those drinks were hard-core. She only had one herself."

So Andie had stayed sober. Great. She'd remember everything.

Doug squats down beside me. "Andie really likes you. She said she knows you're going to be great friends." His tone is scathing, like there are air quotes around "great friends." I'm keeping the blanket over my head. I don't want to see him right now. Don't want to see his disgust.

"Did you guys talk long?" I ask him.

"She came in for a drink."

They used to call those late-night drinks "nightcaps." It seems a little weird that Andie was having a nightcap with Doug while I was somewhere passed out. But Andie's not someone I need to worry about. She opted out; I definitely remember that.

146

He says defensively, "I needed to stay up for a while to make sure you were OK. I couldn't let you choke on your own vomit, could I? She offered to keep me company."

"I should have had one drink at most. I probably shouldn't have even had that." My breasts are heavy and leaking, or have already leaked. The front of my shirt is damp. I never did the pump and dump. I need to do it now.

I throw off the blanket and stagger to my feet. I'm not drunk, not in my brain, but in my body.

I'm still in last night's clothes, so my phone is in the front pocket of my jeans. I hear an incoming text and I see that it's one of many from Andie, including one that reads, I've never seen anyone that drunk!

As if my face could grow any hotter.

Thanks for getting me home last night, I text back. I'm so sorry about that. Did I do or say anything I'll want to forget?

No. You were a blast. Don't worry at all. What are friends for? Then quick on the heels of that one, she writes, The whole point of girls' night is to let your hair down. You partied like a rock star!!!

No, the whole point of girls' night is to get fresh meat for the spreadsheet.

Well, I won't be a regular, not once I tell them I'm opting out, but I'll still have Andie.

I hate not knowing exactly what happened last night. It's part of why I stopped drinking entirely for a period in my twenties. I don't want to have to ask other people what I did. I haven't had this experience since I started seeing Dr. Morrison. Back then, I was trying to forget. Now, my life is entirely different. I have so much that I want to remember. Like Sadie.

I feel like crying, I miss her so badly. I'm such a mess. We didn't move here so she could have a wretch of a mother. Quite the opposite. "Is Sadie sleeping?"

"Yes. But don't worry about her. I fed her in the night. I was Father of the Year." There's no humor in the reference this time.

"Thank you. I never worry when she's with you."

He ignores my comment. "Do you need anything?" He's in the bedroom doorway, watching me, waiting to be dismissed. "Tea or toast?"

It's like he can't *not* ask me; it would go against his ethos. But he obviously doesn't want me to say yes. His anger is palpable, and I don't really get it. He's the one who insisted I go out last night. So I overdid it. I don't know my limits anymore. So he had to do a night feeding. It doesn't seem like a reason to seethe.

After I do my pump, I hesitate over the bathroom sink. I've never had to discard my milk before. It's a precious thing, a gift for my daughter, and I've contaminated it. For what? To please my new friends? What am I, sixteen?

I take some aspirin and get into the shower. With Doug this angry, there's no way he's building me a desk today. I hear him moving around the kitchen, making eggs and bacon, based on the smells. I feel a wave of nausea.

I'm so tired that I go upstairs and pull the covers over my head. That's where I am when I hear Sadie wake up. I force myself out of bed, but my joints feel creaky. It's like I've aged fifty years in one night. Never again, I swear.

"Don't bother!" I hear Doug yell, and not kindly, either.

"I want to see her!" I yell back. If he's this upset after one night of my going out, I can't imagine how he would react to my pitching the idea of an open marriage.

I can hear him talking to her, his voice light and teasing, and then they appear. She's in a fresh diaper and a short-sleeve onesie, and I reach out my arms, tears in my eyes. There's nothing greater than this joy.

I drink her in—wrong word choice after last night—I breathe her in, that's it, and let the sweet smell of her envelop me. Oh, I love this girl. In this moment, I love nothing more than being her mommy.

Doug has stepped away, and he's watching from the doorway again. I want us to get past whatever this is. We're family. I hold out my hand, inviting him into the circle for a cuddle, but he just shakes his head.

I nuzzle Sadie, my wet hair plastered to her beautiful cheek. I close my eyes and just let time pass, savoring like a rich and delicious meal. Then I hear Doug's voice, loud and startling, right next to the bed: "We should get moving."

He looks like a glowering giant standing there at my side. He'd moved so silently and stealthily that I hadn't even heard him cross the floorboards.

"Where do we have to go?" I ask him.

"You know my theory about hangovers." He's unsmiling.

I remember him pulling me from the bed early in our relationship after we'd both tied one on the night before. I'd groaned theatrically, and he laughingly said, "Hangovers are a sports injury. You get beaned by a baseball and what do you do?" I'd never played a sport in my life, never been a part of any team, so he answered his own question: "You walk it off."

I've never been part of any team, that is, until this one. I wish he'd stop glaring at me like that, like Bart did to Raquel the day of the block party.

"What do you do?" he asks me now, like it's a pop quiz.

"You walk it off." I know it's the right answer, and I hope it'll have an open sesame–type effect where his broad, handsome face breaks into a smile, but he turns from me and begins to tickle Sadie.

She melts for him. "See," he says, "Sadie knows the remedy."

"Well," I say, "let's hope she doesn't need it."

"Someday, she'll need it. Let's not kid ourselves."

I gaze at a laughing Sadie and say softly, "I want to kid myself."

"I need to get out of the house. I've been cooped up all night. Are you with us or not?" It's an invitation, at least, though it's tinged with that same anger.

"Can we walk slow?" I say.

"We could take the bikes."

He's not kidding. He's needling.

I remind myself that the bikes are not a divorceable offense. Ditto his behavior right now. He'll get over whatever's bothering him, and I'll get over the way he's acting. This will all blow over.

Doug pushes the stroller, and I trudge along beside them, sunglasses on.

"We're headed that way," Doug says.

I give him a quick reproving glance. I agreed to a walk; I never agreed to a destination. I certainly never agreed to a Sunday stroll on Main Street where we'd see everyone out and about. It feels like he's punishing me. But my own body is already doing the work for him. I can't ever remember a hangover like this.

No matter how much I drank back in the day—and sometimes I drank a lot—I never felt that peculiar sequence from last night: the extreme highs and lows, the paranoia, the hallucinations, the near-paralysis, and finally, the blackout. Back when I was craving a dose of true oblivion, I took whatever people handed me. LSD. Ecstasy. One time, something called Special K. That was the closest to what I experienced last night.

I've stopped in the middle of the pavement, and Doug is asking me, with more irritation than concern, what's going on. I tell him that I have to go home. "I feel sick," I say, and his face darkens.

"Of course you do," he says shortly. "Well, Sadie's going to Main Street with me."

I don't feel like I can really argue, when clearly he's in better shape to take care of Sadie than I am, but I'm sorry to see them go. Doug doesn't so much as cast a glance over his shoulder to make sure I'm OK.

We haven't even done a full revolution around the block, so I get home quickly.

Inside, I open my laptop. Special K is also known as ketamine. It can be used as a roofie. A date-rape drug.

Andie and I were standing at the bar for a while, talking. Could a stranger have slipped me something?

It's all crazy. Every bit of it. The notes, the openness, the neighborhood, the roofie. None of it seems real. None of it seems possible. And yet, I know that the spreadsheet is real. So it's possible that I was drugged, by a stranger or a neighbor, maybe by whoever's been writing me notes.

I'm sweating. My fingers tremble as I scroll down. Just reading the list of side effects jars my memory a little. Not all the way. That's because one of the major side effects is amnesia.

The other side effects are hallucinations, agitation before euphoria, and confusion. Muscle rigidity, that was the telltale one. Andie had to help me to the bathroom because I couldn't move. And finally, sedation. Doug had to carry me inside. Vomiting. Lots of vomiting, apparently.

I feel faint. Not one of the symptoms.

Please come home, I text Doug.

He ignores it for several minutes. Then, Why?

I need you. Please. I'm begging you to come home.

Another long minute passes. Fine.

It's fifteen minutes before he's pushing open the front door, and I can't help feeling that he took the longest way back. He takes his time settling Sadie on her activity mat, tickling and cooing at her, before he sits down on the love seat next to me.

Wordlessly, I show him the website.

He reads and then peers back up at me skeptically. "You think someone *drugged* you?"

I give him the evidence for each side effect. "I felt something like this once before, when I took Special K."

"When you took *Special K*?" He looks at me incredulously. "You're jumping to conclusions. You don't know how your body reacts to alcohol after a long period of abstinence. You don't know how it metabolizes alcohol after having a baby. And let's face it, you're not the most reliable reporter lately."

Not being believed by someone you love. This is all so terribly familiar. *Don't abandon me, Doug. Believe me.* "What does that mean?"

"With how much stress you've been under, between the move and the notes. It can make you perceive things differently than they actually are. Plus, Andie said those were incredibly strong drinks, and you had, what, three of them? Four? Plus a shot. After more than a year of—"

"More than a year of not drinking, I know!" I'm shouting, even though we don't shout in this marriage. Sadie looks over in surprise but not fear.

Even so, Doug snatches her up off the mat, like he doesn't want her near me, like I might be contagious. He's taking her upstairs, taking her away.

"What about muscle rigidity?" I say, trying to make my voice reasonable. Our house is so small that you don't really need to raise your voice to be heard. "You don't get muscle rigidity from alcohol."

He turns around at the top of our steps. "Do you think you might have imagined the muscle rigidity once you saw the list? It's the power of suggestion."

"No! I felt it! I couldn't move last night, Doug."

"The mind can invent things after the fact. There's a term for it, something like confabulation."

"That's for Alzheimer's patients!" But my protest has lost a bit of its conviction. I'm remembering my Layton hallucination.

"Not only. It happens to people who are a little compromised mentally." Now he doesn't seem angry exactly. There's some mix of pity and fear, like he's afraid for me. Sadie is watching the two of us; she's looking to us for cues as to how to feel. Doug and I need to stop this conversation, for her sake. For all of our sakes. "You have to admit you haven't been yourself lately. Not since becoming a mother."

It's the first time he's said it like that, so bluntly, and I feel too hurt to say anything back.

"I'm sorry, Kat, I don't mean it in a bad way, but . . ." He indicates Sadie. "I need to take care of her now, OK? We'll talk later."

He's already said more than enough.

CHAPTER 16

100% CONFIDENTIAL

CHECK AS MANY BOXES AS APPLY:

- WOULD YOU AND/OR YOUR PARTNER ALLOW KISSING WITH A NEIGHBOR?
- TOUCHING ABOVE THE WAIST?
- DIGITAL PENETRATION?
- ORAL SEX?
- INTERCOURSE?
- ANAL SEX?
- THREESOMES?
- FOURSOMES?
- MORE-SOMES?
- DO YOU WANT TO WATCH WHILE YOUR PARTNER HAS SEX?
- DO YOU WANT HIM/HER TO WATCH YOU?
- ARE YOU BISEXUAL OR BICURIOUS?

- DO YOU LIKE (OR WANT TO TRY) ROLE-PLAYING?
- WOULD YOU PARTICIPATE IN BDSM? DOM OR SUB?
- IF YOU'VE NEVER TRIED IT, WOULD YOU LIKE TO, WITH AN EXPERIENCED, RESPECTFUL PARTNER? OR WITH A FELLOW NOVICE?
- DO YOU HAVE ANY QUIRKS OR FETISHES? (PLEASE DESCRIBE)
- HOW IMPORTANT ARE ORGASMS? (NOT AT ALL, SOMEWHAT, VERY, OR ESSENTIAL)
- WOULD YOU WANT TO ALLOW PEOPLE INTO YOUR HOME AND BED?
- WOULD YOU NEED TO MEET ELSEWHERE?
- ARE YOU OK WITH YOUR TRYSTS AND LOVERS BEING PUBLIC KNOWLEDGE, OR SPREADSHEET ONLY?

I can't let myself think about the spreadsheet. Or about Tennyson's preferences e-mail, or about my conduct at girls' night. It's all just noise. I need to focus on what's real, on Sadie.

Mondays are already a challenge. Usually I'm like a drug addict in withdrawal, I miss Doug that potently. (Don't think about drugs, either.) On Mondays, I bump up hardest against the reality that as much as I love Sadie, I don't always like being with her. Not alone. She's different when Doug is here. It could be that I'm different when Doug is here. I have someone to spot me, like when a gymnast attempts a tricky dismount, and knowing that relieves the tightness in my chest.

When Sadie and I are alone, I'm a little bit afraid of her, with her moods and caprices. She fusses when she's bored or displeased, when she doesn't have enough attention or the right kind. She's like a tiny empress: off with my head. Sometimes it escalates to a red-faced, screaming tantrum. My love makes me a hostage to her moods.

Right now, she's sitting in her car seat outside the shower. She can see me through the glass, though I hope that she'll play with the toy in her lap instead. No such luck today. I turn the water on, and she begins to whimper almost immediately, a warning whistle before the full-force gale.

I keep up a running monologue. It's our thing. Usually, I tell her happy things we're going to do. I tell stories about a little girl named Sadie and all the adventures she's going to have, the people she'll meet. Oh, the places she'll go.

"We're going to Mommy and Me soon," I say, in that upward lilting voice that she likes. "Just as soon as your mommy can get herself together. Not today, but soon. There will be musical instruments. You'll have your own tambourine, maybe . . ."

Sadie calms a little, long enough for me to get my hair washed. Then she's fussing again. Screw the conditioner.

I soap up quickly and decide not to shave my legs. I'm not going anywhere today. There's always tomorrow. "There's always tomorrow," I tell her.

I feel another bout of nausea. By now, it's not a hangover. It's that Tennyson's e-mail brought back my flirtatious behavior at the last girls' night. I vaguely remember the dancing, the crush and the brush of bodies around me. I'm so embarrassed to have cast myself in that light, even if it is the very behavior the women were encouraging. They must think I'm going to opt in, after that display.

It might have been the power of suggestion, that we'd just been talking about freedom and indulging your fantasies, or if I was dosed with ketamine, that has a sexualizing effect. Or it might have been something that lives inside me all the time being unleashed, and that scares me the most. No matter what Dr. Morrison wanted to believe and wanted me to believe, I liked being seductive with Layton. Once, I told her I felt I'd seduced him, and it was the sharpest she ever sounded with me when she said, "No! Children are not capable of seduction. That is an adult skill." Is it awful to admit that I felt in that moment that she was the one taking my power away, not Layton? If he's entirely responsible, if I'm nothing but a victim . . .

Stay busy, that's all I can do.

The regulars have bombarded me with texts. With the exception of Yolanda, they all want to know if I've talked to Doug, which way I'm leaning, if they can answer any questions for me. But at least I haven't had any new notes today.

As I comb out my hair in front of the mirror, I continue, determined to stave off further displeasure. "So we can't go anywhere today, but tomorrow, in the morning, on a beautiful sunshiny morning, we'll go to the library for story hour. They'll read Mother Goose or *Frozen* or, if I'm lucky, *The Giving Tree* . . ." Sadie punctuates my sentences with gurgles and various happy noises. The empress is pleased, for the moment.

Doug could never have me on a string like this. Sadie's helplessness, her dependency, her potential to make me look (and feel) thoroughly incompetent—they grant her control.

Is that what Doug meant when he said I'm so different since having Sadie? It clearly wasn't a compliment. But then, he'd been angry that whole day.

I can't talk to Doug about openness, not when he already finds me so—what was his word?—unreliable. I've considered not telling him about openness at all, just going straight to Tennyson and opting out, but he'll find out at some point. Someone will let it slip, and that would be yet another wedge between us.

There's already so much that I can never let slip because I need to stay unblemished, untainted, in Doug's eyes. If he knew about the past, he'd draw all sorts of conclusions about our sex life, and everything else.

So I can't face Doug, and I'm not ready to face the women, either. I just want to retract my head like a turtle's and let a day or two go by. Then I'll be ready to leave the house again. I can figure out the least rejecting way to decline, so there's the least social fallout. Maybe Andie can help me with that.

I can feel that Sadie's getting antsy. Something's not right. I run through the checklist, and it's nothing I can detect. I thought I'd somehow diverted it, that the winds had died down, but no, the hurricane is coming.

I stoop down and pick her up, the towel wrapped around me, the moisturizer forgotten, but Sadie's too far gone. My tolerance is nil. I could dissolve into tears at any moment, which isn't something I want to do in front of my child. It could give her the impression the world is a scary place and yes, that's true sometimes, but it's too soon for her to know it. My job is to keep that information from her for as long as possible. That's what this house was supposed to be about, this neighborhood. The AV was supposed to make me—and us—conventional in the best sense.

I've utterly screwed up. My life is a disaster and, by extension, Sadie's will be, too. We live among people who have sex with each other's mates, who might even roofie the newcomer. We're in deep, deep shit.

I can't hold it back. I'm crying. Dancing around with Sadie and crying, while she releases that angry wail of hers. *I know, baby.* We could have just found another house, another neighborhood, one within our means, but no, it had to be the AV.

I'm still in my towel and Sadie's still in the throes of an inconsolable tantrum when the doorbell rings. I'm worried about how long Sadie's face has been red, afraid that she'll burst a blood vessel at this rate. There's nothing I can do. She's never wanted my boobs, and she doesn't want the bottle with my milk, either. Not even the pacifier will do.

This is the problem with trying to avoid your neighbors. They see the car out front; they know I'm home. No, they know I'm home because you can hear Sadie crying a block away.

"You're blowing my cover," I say into Sadie's hair as we bob some more. I should just put her down. It's not like she's deriving any comfort from being in my arms. But putting her in the crib seems like a form of abandonment in her hour of need. Think how much worse she'd be if I weren't holding her.

I actually can't imagine how her cries could get any louder. She is royally pissed off at me. Maybe a little space would do us good. She'll start to miss me.

Now the knocking has started, a syncopation that's making me batty. I don't even understand the mind-set of someone who wouldn't just leave. Clearly, I've got my hands full. Do the women need fresh meat that badly?

I place her in the crib and wipe at my eyes. I yell, "I'll be right there!" Then I take my sweet time putting on a bra and some clothes. If they need to see me that desperately, they can wait. If it's my tormentor finally ready to go mano a mano, a part of me welcomes that. Let's just get it over with. Say what you need to say. I'll apologize. I'll kiss ass, whatever it takes to get a clean slate on this block. I can't live this way.

When I open the door, I see Brandon, and over his shoulder is a large bag made out of bamboo or some other expensive natural fabric. He's holding Zoe's hand, and she's peering up at me politely, his perfect child an unintentional rebuke, a study in contrasts with my own fire-breathing spawn.

"Hi," he says, his voice raised to be heard over Sadie, his eyes full of sympathy. "I would have gone away, but I thought maybe I could help. I brought over every colic remedy I could think of. Zoe had some problems when she was younger, and we tried *everything*. Sound machines, homeopathic remedies, belly massages, probiotics . . ."

I burst into tears.

He drops Zoe's hand and pulls me to him for a hug. "Oh, I get it," he tells me. "Knowing she's suffering and not being able to help is the worst. It's water torture. But it'll get better, I promise you. Look at Zoe now. We all survived."

"It's not just that," I sob, but I can't tell him the rest.

"What do you think about my taking Sadie for a walk? I can wear her around me in a sling. That used to work sometimes for Zoe. The thing is, nothing works all the time. That's part of what makes it all so maddening. But breaks help. No offense, but you look like you're at the end of your tether."

He's just so good. I cry harder.

"What can I do to help?" Brandon asks. "Just name it. Put me to work. Really, I need something to do. I'm going crazy."

He's going crazy? He doesn't know the half of it. Improbably enough, I start to laugh.

"Oh, my poor mental health amuses you? What am I, some kind of clown?" He's doing the worst *Goodfellas* accent I've ever heard, and my laugh turns more genuine and less maniacal. "Listen, you'd do me a favor to let me take your squalling kid. I need to get my mind off some things."

I hesitate, wondering if it's safe to hand over your child to someone you don't know well. I would have thought so, given that he's a neighbor, but that isn't exactly the most reassuring thing a person could be right now. Still, he's Brandon.

"Are you sure you don't mind taking her for a walk?" I ask.

"Of course not. I've got the swaddle I used for Zoe. Let's see if I remember how to tie it around me. It's a memory exercise, and at my age, I can always use one of those." He fumbles in the bamboo bag and removes half a yard of fabric. I never got the hang of those myself.

"If you're sure, I'll run upstairs and get her."

"Oh, wait!" he says. I spin back, heart sinking already. There's always a catch. "Take this." He gives me the bag full of colic remedies. "And don't start crying again."

"Thank you," I tell him with great feeling. "Can you have her back soon, like in ten minutes?"

"Absolutely," he says.

I shoot upstairs to where Sadie is on her back, limbs flailing, face a devastating shade of tomato. I sniff her diaper—clean and dry, just like it was the last time I checked—and despite her impotent waving arms, despite her rage, I get the sunbonnet tied under her chin. It's sort of sad how she can be so angry and yet so powerless.

I lift her up and carry her downstairs. "Sadie," I say, "do you remember Brandon? And this is Zoe. They're going to take you on a walk. A sightseeing tour of the neighborhood."

"Sweet Sadie," Brandon croons, taking her from me. "Even when she's cross, she's beautiful, Kat." She already sounds calmer in his arms. Her cries are more piteous than angry. What am I doing wrong? Why is she so mad at me?

Because she can be. That's what Dr. Morrison would say. I'd been a perfect child for my mother because I had no choice. I was trying to win her over. Sadie knows she's got me, completely, and that's what I want for her. Absolute security.

After Brandon does some impressive jujitsu moves with the fabric, she's fastened to his chest, gazing up at him, the sobs on her lips replaced by curiosity.

"It's just the newness," Brandon says. "I'm an unknown quantity."

This whole neighborhood is. At the thought, my gratitude becomes mixed with unease.

"Speaking of newness and unknown quantities, how are you doing after the other night?"

"Girls' night, you mean?"

"I know they talked to you about becoming open. Don't worry, they expect you to be kind of freaked out."

"Good. Because I am." That's not all I'm freaked out about, though. I don't know what to believe—whether I really just drank too much and blacked out like Doug thinks or if I was the victim of foul play.

He laughs. "I was the only person who wasn't freaked the first time I learned about it. I was like, 'Bring it on! New experiences in suburbia!' Though I won't let Gina catch me calling it suburbia." He turns more serious. "Openness works for certain kinds of marriages. Not every marriage is cut out for it."

"You and Stone are cut out for it?"

"I thought we were."

"What happened?"

"There was a little stalking incident. That can happen with the closeted types."

I stare at him, trying to unravel what he's said. "So one of the husbands was stalking you?"

"As it turned out, I'm really more of a cuddler anyway!" He grins, trying to make light.

Who did the stalking? Oliver, maybe? Andie said Oliver had been with both men and women. "I'm more of a cuddler these days, too."

"Could I give you a little piece of advice?"

"Absolutely."

"Sometimes people say yes who should say no. Like . . ." He looks behind him. "Yolanda and Wyatt. She doesn't feel like she can say no, and she's so afraid of losing him that she said yes. Now she's stuck. All she can do is layer on more and more rules."

"I could tell sometimes she feels kind of insecure. But he seems to really love her."

"He does, but . . ." He glances toward the street again. "She's gotten herself in this bad position. She gets together with men she doesn't want, because what she really wants is for Wyatt to stop her at the door. She wants him to grab her arm and say, 'Don't go.' She never would again. But he never does."

It's obvious this isn't just idle gossip. Brandon is truly sad for Yolanda and the state of her marriage. For whatever reason, though, I can tell that he really wants me to have this information. It could even be the real reason he came over this morning.

"Poor Yolanda," I say. "Thanks for warning me."

He looks down at Sadie, who is calm as a lake now, and I assume he's going to unwrap her and hand her back. Instead, he says, "I'll have her back in a jiff."

Before I can respond, Zoe gives me a wave, and the three of them are off down the street.

If someone like Brandon lives happily on this block, then it could be a good place after all. I really want that to be true. We just got here, and to sell the house and start all over somewhere else, to have to admit to Doug's parents that we made a mistake . . .

I'm not going to sell my house and move away, so I need to follow Andie's marital advice to its logical conclusion. I need to let all this go. Accept Doug's explanation. Three (or four or more) strong drinks and a shot after a year of abstinence could very well mimic the effects of ketamine. People have hallucinations with too much alcohol, and I could have imagined the muscle rigidity. It's not like I've never had a blackout before.

Brandon is a kind and genuine person, and he loves this neighborhood. He loves these neighbors. The same neighbors who took care of me in my blacked-out state and brought me home safely and texted me again and again about how much they like me. The ones who want me to join their club, strange as it may be. And then there's Andie.

I'm lucky.

I think it again, making the thought bigger, louder, more vivid, like Dr. Morrison taught me to do. It's like it's written in the sky.

I

AM

LUCKY

Doug texts me, checking on how I'm feeling. He tells me not to worry about making dinner. It's not lovey-dovey, but it shows that he's not happy with how yesterday went, either. He's also prepared to let things go.

When he arrives home, he holds up a bag. "Your favorite," he says. "Sushi."

I try not to think about how expensive sushi is. Instead, I appreciate his effort. I thank him and lay out the plates and chopsticks on the kitchen table. He sits opposite me, feeding Sadie a bottle as he gazes at her adoringly. "Don't wait for me," he says. "Dive in."

I also try to ignore the fact that he hasn't touched me or made eye contact.

He likes the rolls, while I like the sashimi, which means I can tell easily what's mine. Slowly, I eat the ahi, yellowtail, salmon, and mackerel, allowing myself unfettered pleasure with each bite. I savor.

He shouldn't have splurged, but I decide not to care. I chew languorously. I luxuriate. When Doug and I used to go out to dinner, before Sadie, eating could be a sensual experience, not simply a refueling. This is the woman I used to be, and perhaps that's who Doug is trying to conjure. He didn't call me crazy, I remind myself, not exactly. He just said I was different. Well, I can be that person again.

Sensual. That makes me think of girls' night. I'm pretty sure there was flirting and dancing. But with whom? All I can remember is the heat of bodies pressing in on me, and that I liked the feeling.

Does Doug need to know how I acted? If I don't tell him, will one of the neighbors? I wouldn't blame him for feeling hurt. He hasn't seen that side of me in a long time.

"I have another surprise for you," he says. "I'm going to build the kitchen cart tonight."

"Thank you. That means a lot to me."

I take Sadie, and he starts in on his maki. He doesn't look up as he says, "What do you think about my going out to a sports bar on Main tonight to watch the game with all the guys? After I've finished the cart."

So the cart is just a ploy so he can go watch the game. Not that I would have stopped him from going, even without the cart. Doesn't he know me better than that?

"Which guys?" I ask.

"Bart, Oliver, Nolan, Vic. Wyatt begged off."

It's all his new friends, the husbands of the women from girls' night out. What if they want to get together so they can warm Doug up to the idea of the openness?

"Go," I say. "Have fun." Maybe Doug can be the one to bring it up to me, the one to say no.

He nods slowly. Then, out of nowhere, he says, "You know you can tell me anything."

I nod slowly back and lie, "I do know that."

Session 68.

"What did it mean to you, that there were so many?"

"It wasn't that many."

"From what I read, eight victims came forward, though they didn't all testify."

"What does that say to you? It says to me that at least some of them were lying. They probably misinterpreted him. They wanted to feel special, and they misunderstood his kindness."

"Like—"

"I'm just saying, people like to blame other people. They don't like to take responsibility. That's the whole problem with society."

"I feel like you're deflecting a bit. Let's not talk about them. Let's talk about you."

"We've already talked about me, ad nauseum. I'm sick of talking about me and about feelings. It doesn't really get us anywhere. I'm still stuck being who I am. I'm stuck being part of this terrible story, betrayed and alone.

I just want to run away. I wish I could change my name or my face. I'm afraid this is going to follow me everywhere."

"Do people recognize you?"

"Not often, but enough. The newspaper can't show photographs of minors, but once in a great while, it happens. And in Haines, people talk. I never go back there. It's unfair. None of this is my fault."

"No, it's not. But you do have to make sense of it."

"I have to come out of my denial, is what you mean."

"Possibly."

"How about you just say it? Just tell me what you really think of me."

"I'm not here to sit in judgment."

"Everyone passes judgment. That's why I need to stop talking and just escape. Find myself a nice guy and marry him and have a baby or two and stop being me."

"Wherever you go, there you are."

"Yeah, well, we'll see."

CHAPTER 17

I'm trying to think positive, to silence all the niggling doubts, to forget. It's exhausting. But I'm making progress. I force myself out of the house, and Sadie and I take limited trips to the park and around town. I'm afraid to run into any of the women except Andie, afraid they'll ask me again if I've spoken to Doug, afraid to disappoint them with my answer.

Andie's the one I want to see, but she seems to be avoiding me. Her texts are friendly but brief, and she's too busy to go on walks or to lunch. She offered to be my sounding board, but now she won't let me take her up on it.

Maybe she's just flaky. She could make overtures to lots of people and never follow through. Better to have found out sooner rather than later, before I get in too deep or share too much. Still, it hurts to have misjudged her. It hurts just to miss her.

I go where I need to; I take care of my responsibilities. While at the grocery store, Sadie has an epic meltdown and my face is aflame, yet I forge ahead. Two different women, obviously mothers themselves, tell me, "Hang in there, Mom!" and I do.

Doug comes home with a bunch of new clothes he bought. He says that the AV is hotter than our neighborhood in Oakland, which is patently untrue. Here, we have breezes off the water. The clothes are from a men's store on Main Street that he says Tennyson recommended, and I gape at the price tags. But I say nothing. Since I'm not going to divorce him over some linen pants, I have to let it go. He's going to iron them himself, though.

We haven't had a conversation of any depth in days. I don't think any of the men spilled the beans about openness while they were watching the game. If they had, Doug would have said something.

The next morning, I run into Andie at Mommy and Me class. She knew that I'd been meaning to go; why didn't she call me? We sit next to each other, shaking our maracas and singing, making exaggerated expressions so our babies will smile. It feels awkward to me, but nothing in her bearing suggests she feels the same. Afterward, she rushes off immediately, saying she has an appointment but that we'll "definitely talk soon. Maybe we could all have dinner again?" She doesn't wait for my response.

Briefly, I had the promise of a whole social life. Now I feel like it's receding. I'm an island within an island. Yes, the women are texting me, but they're not inviting me anywhere. I can imagine all the fun they're having without me: boat rides, shopping trips, jogs along the beach, bunco games. But I can't partake of it unless I let them partake of Doug. Can I?

Maybe I can. They told me how much they like me, immediately. Not only Doug but me, too. They said that even if I opt out, we'll still be friends. And at the block party, everyone did seem to be friends. I can't imagine that all those people are on the spreadsheet.

I just don't want it to be weird when Doug and I opt out. We should have everyone over. A cocktail party, maybe? No, we can't really fit everyone in our house. Our yard is big, though. Maybe a barbecue? Doug would love that, even though it would mean that he has to mow the grass and pull some weeds. We'd also have to buy a grill, which means more debt, but that wouldn't trouble Doug. Then we can announce that we're opting out. I'll have to talk to Doug before then, which will give me a much-needed deadline, since I'm quaking at the thought of that conversation.

Doug comes home, and I tell him about wanting to throw a barbecue. He grabs my face and kisses me. I bask in the spontaneous show of affection. We're going to be OK after all. The walls between us will come down.

"Awesome! Yes! Absolutely!" He's nearly dancing around the room. "We have to go to my parents for July Fourth, but how about that next weekend? Who should we invite?" He's giddy, like a girl about to have her first sleepover. His excitement is infectious, and we plan the guest list together. It'll be all the usual suspects, and they text back their RSVPs quickly.

On the one hand, I feel extreme relief. Everyone is coming. On the other hand, I'm terrified. Everyone is coming.

I've read a lot of Agatha Christie. When the whole cast of characters is in one place, that one place could very well become the scene of the crime.

No, we're talking about a barbecue. How bad could it be?

Before I know it, it's July Fourth weekend, and I still haven't talked to Doug. But I will. I'm going to do it. I can't chicken out forever.

"Do you think we forgot anything?" I ask Doug, the hatch of the Outback still yawning open, our suitcases inside.

"If we did, we can just buy it there."

I never like to go to Scott and Melody's house in Fort Bragg, yet this holiday, I'm actually OK with it. Some time away from the AV might do me good. It's a palate cleanser.

"Oh, you know what?" I say. "I lost Sadie's sun hat, and I forgot to buy her a new one. I don't think we'll be able to find that in Fort Bragg. Isn't it basically a retirement community?" I glance across the street. Brandon and Stone keep forgetting to bring over Zoe's old clothes, which might include a sun hat, so now's a good time to get them. "I'll be right back."

No one answers when I knock on their door. I know Doug and I could just stop at Target on our way, yet I want some reassurance from our neighbors that everything's OK. I see that Andie's car is gone. I look up and down the street, my eyes catching on the brownest lawn.

Raquel seems like the safest bet. We had a really good time at the park that one day, and she was the one knocking on my door then.

I ring the doorbell. Then I knock, waiting a long minute. Her car is in the driveway, so she's likely home. One more ring, then one more knock—that's not too stalkerlike.

I'm just about to turn around and retreat down the steps when Raquel opens the door narrowly. Really narrowly, like barely wider than her head. She doesn't want me to go inside. Or she doesn't want me to see inside.

Her smile, by contrast, is exceptionally warm and friendly, which could mean she's genuinely happy to see me. It could also mean that she's afraid I've caught her in some sort of compromising position.

I already know her marriage is open. What's she worried about?

"Hi!" I give Raquel a big smile back. "We're headed out of town for the weekend."

"Really? Cool! Where are you going?"

"Fort Bragg, up north near Mendocino. That's where Doug's parents live."

"Well, have fun!" She seems eager to shut the door, to get back to whatever or whomever.

"Could I just ask a quick favor?" I read somewhere about the Ben Franklin effect: that someone who's done you a favor will actually like you more as a result. Time to try it out. I need to build up some good-will for when I opt out. "I was wondering if Meadow has an extra sun hat we could borrow?" Creepily, Meadow's head isn't much bigger than Sadie's.

Raquel shakes her head. Does the Ben Franklin effect work if you ask for a favor but the person doesn't do it for you?

"But have fun," she says with another smile. "Bart and I can't wait for your barbecue next weekend. Maybe by then, you and Doug will have an answer for all of us?"

I'm so stupid. It hadn't even occurred to me that they all RSVPed yes so quickly because they're expecting a big announcement. Barbecue = fresh meat. They might think we were telegraphing our intentions.

But someone in this neighborhood is targeting me. It could even be Raquel, because it could be any one of them. Really, everyone coming to my barbecue is a suspect. There's no way I can let them have access to my inner world—my marriage, my husband, my body. His body. That's the one they really want, isn't it?

"I'll have an answer for you," I say.

"Great. Have fun on your trip!" Before I can get out a response, she's shutting the door on me, obviously so eager to get back to what—or whom—she was doing that I'm not sure why she even answered it to begin with.

I'm about to cross back over to our side of the street when I see Yolanda and Wyatt exiting their house with the twins. I think of approaching them—maybe I'll still get to test out the Ben Franklin effect after all—but Yolanda sees me and her face, which had been neutral, is transformed. Her expression becomes one of pure hate. It stops me in my tracks.

Wyatt sees where she's looking, and his face changes, too. He looks afraid. He raises his hand in the most perfunctory wave and then hurries after her. She's immersing herself fully in the twins, and I know that trick. Kids are the most acceptable diversion, the best way to be instantly and entirely busy.

I have no idea what I could have done to make Yolanda so angry. It's been radio silence from her since girls' night out when all the other women were texting me.

Then why did she RSVP for the barbecue? Just one curt word, but still. She said yes.

Doug already has Sadie set up in her car seat, sucking away at her pacifier. As he and I get in, he fixes me with a stare and says, "What do you think that was about?"

I buckle my seat belt and try to keep my voice level. "They must have been in a rush."

Once we're on the road, Sadie falls asleep quickly. I feel like this is our chance to talk, without having to look each other in the eyes.

"Are you mad at me about getting drunk at girls' night?" I blurt artlessly.

"No." Flat, inflectionless, devoid of information.

"Are you mad at me for something else?"

"What else could there be?" It's amazing how that same flat tone can suddenly feel so challenging.

I glance back at Sadie, not wanting to corrupt her virgin ears even though I know all she'll be aware of at this age is tone, not words.

"Did someone already tell you about openness?" I say softly. I can't put it off any longer, not with the barbecue looming. We'll need to opt out before then, and if people still show up, I'll know they really meant it about being friends.

"I don't know what you're talking about."

So I tell him, making it sound as patently absurd as possible.

By the end, Doug's mouth is hanging open, a great big cartoon *O*. "Everyone on the block," he finally gets out, "they're all sleeping with each other?"

"Not everyone. Some people opt out. Andie and Nolan opted out, for example."

"Do you know everyone who's in and everyone who's out?"

I want to believe his interest is more academic than prurient. I want to believe that he's going to dismiss the possibility out of hand. Because he loves me. Because he can't stomach the idea of another man ever touching me or another woman touching him. Because we belong only to each other. We're not monogamous because we saw no alternatives. We're monogamous because it suits our love for one another.

"Wyatt and Yolanda?" he asks. "They're part of it?" I nod.

"He probably hasn't mentioned it because it seems like the women talk to each other first. They're touting it like it's some sort of feminist movement." I hope he'll roll his eyes with me, though truthfully, it may very well be feminism. This is grrrrrrl power. I'm just not that kind of grrrrrrl.

"Wyatt and Yolanda," he repeats, like something's becoming clear.

Is Doug harping on it because he thought he and Wyatt were better friends than that or because he's just happened to notice that Yolanda is beautiful? Sure, she's an aging beauty, a bit zaftig maybe, but she's a certified beauty. She used to be in pageants, as she found it important to note.

Or maybe Tennyson is more his type. She actually looks like the girlfriend he had just before me, the one who intimidated me even in pictures, making me wonder how he could be slumming with me.

Not that he's ever given off that impression. Not at all.

My self-esteem was so low when we met. All my confidence came from doing well in school and then at work. I was terrified of relationships, terrified of being truly seen for what I thought I was. I didn't just have a fear of intimacy; I had a terror. It wasn't only because of what had happened with Layton, but with Ellen, too. Doug broke through all that with patience and kindness. He was the first person who thought I was worth it. Thought I was worth something.

And now, here he is, hesitating when he should be saying hell no.

It's just that he's in shock. Of course he's going to say no.

"What would your parents think?" I ask. I know it's kind of a low blow. But they were entirely behind the idea of us moving to this neighborhood. They were willing to put up a whole lot of money to make it happen. His dad's ex-military; his mom's a Suzy Homemaker. It's about as apple pie traditional as a marriage can be, and Doug reveres them both.

"I don't ask about their sex lives, and they've never asked about mine."

Don't ask, don't tell. That's one of the arrangements that was mentioned at girls' night. Doug and I wouldn't need to know the specifics of each other's dalliances.

The air is charged, and not in a good way. Just talking about this is a threat.

I'd presented openness like it was cockamamie, a quirk of our neighbors that we can laugh about, but that's not how he's taking it.

"People can get jealous," I say. "They can get obsessed. It's hard for a breakup to be truly mutual. There can be gossip and lies. Why subject ourselves to all that? Do we need an orgasm that badly?" I mean the last part as a joke. He doesn't laugh. And it occurs to me: he might need an orgasm that badly. I haven't been stepping up in that department.

"Some people must be happy with the arrangement," Doug says. He pauses a beat, but I'm too upset to answer. "You said people do it all different ways. You make up your own rules. Like, it doesn't just have to be a license to screw around." Do I detect an imploring note? Is he actually trying to convince me to give this a shot?

"Do you already know who you'd pick?" I ask, knowing that I'm treading on dangerous ground, but I can't help myself. Some part of me always thought it would come to this, that he would realize I'm not good enough.

"No." I'm hoping that he'll reach for my hand, tell me I'm the only one for him, that he never even thinks of other women. But it would have to be a lie. I mean, he's a man. He has eyes. Tennyson, Yolanda, even June when she's done up right—they're all incredibly attractive women. He might have already had fantasies about them.

"But you like thinking about who you'd pick," I say.

"That's not what I'm thinking about. I'm thinking about open marriages. I've heard that sometimes they work."

"What do you mean by 'work'?"

He stiffens, and again, not in a good way. "I'm just trying to talk to you. We're adults, right? We can talk about things even if we don't decide to do them."

"But you want to do it."

"I'm not saying that. Most likely, we'll opt out. But can't we just think about it first? There's no rush to say yes or no."

I know in my heart I'm not strong enough for an arrangement like this. Even before learning about openness, I'd imagined Doug with the other AV women.

"I love you, Doug. I don't want to share you. I don't want to be with anyone else but you."

He nods, keeping his eyes on the road. His face doesn't soften.

I'm so afraid of not being special anymore in his eyes. Of being replaced. Because whatever I do, even if I force myself to step up my game sexually, I can't be new for him. I can't be someone else. But how can I explain that when he won't even look at me? When he's barely looked at me for days?

"Fine," he says. "We'll say no."

"You wanted to think about it."

"But you want to say no. So do it."

I didn't want to say no like this.

Pandora's box is already open, no matter what we do now. The idea of other people is alive in our marriage. We can opt out, but it doesn't change that there's an option.

"Are you being honest with me?" he asks.

"About what?"

After a pregnant pause, he says, "Listen, monogamy's all we've known together. Sometimes, when someone's so familiar . . ."

"It's not so exciting anymore," I finish for him. "You're not that excited by me."

"Or maybe it's you who's not excited by me. You used to initiate sex all the time. Now you never do."

I initiated sex because seducing him was the only way I could get turned on. Because that was what I'd been taught. But I just don't have the energy lately or the need to perform. I'm a mother now.

Is that why he's seemed so angry lately? Because I haven't been initiating? Or because someone told him what I said about not wanting him? He stayed at Gina and Oliver's without me. He's been talking to the guys. And he and Andie had that drink together, late at night, while I was passed out.

"We can work on our sex life, if that's what you want," I say. "But we can't bring anyone else in."

He nods slowly. He doesn't look happy.

Of course he doesn't. I've just told him that the AV is where you can have your cake and eat it, too. Only he doesn't get to sample. He's just got pound cake for the rest of his life.

Everyone starts out saying no, and then they get worn down. I'd assumed that the neighbors were the ones who did the wearing down, but now I see that it's probably the spouses. One person says no, and then the fantasies grow for the other person. Just because Doug is telling me I can opt out, that doesn't mean he can't pressure me to opt in later.

Fantasies can be deadlier than reality. Because maybe Doug would have been sexually incompatible with, say, Tennyson, or maybe she's actually a total dud in bed, but that would never be true in his imagination. Is that why some of the women, like Yolanda, agree to openness? While Raquel was extolling the virtues of self-confidence and empowerment, Yolanda called it affair prevention.

All that cake, parading around. Surely Doug's mouth will start to water.

CHAPTER 18

"You're here!" Melody runs out to the car. "Sadie's gotten so big!" She's practically clawing the window to get at her grandchild.

Melody power walks every day for hours to maintain her trim frame. Her short hair is dyed blonde, identical to her natural color before she went gray, and it's thinned in recent years until it's almost diaphanous, revealing a hint of scalp beneath.

Scott is hanging back, framed by the front door. He's tall and equally trim. Bald on top, gray hair trimmed neatly along the sides, his head is shaped like a football helmet. He's in a polo shirt and khakis, same as he wore to work every day as an engineer. He's a creature of habit, not prone to sudden moves and disapproving of them in others.

Now that I've got all those cake images dancing in my head—Tennyson as red velvet, Yolanda as lemon meringue, June as carrot—for the first time, I'm thinking we might just want to get the hell out of Dodge. The notes are scary, in their way, but it's not the same way. Because with the notes, Doug is still standing beside me. We're still a solid team. The openness is a threat of an entirely different magnitude.

It occurs to me that even if I convinced Doug to sell Crayola, his parents could prevent us. After all, Scott, Melody, and Doug are the only names on the deed. They told me it was better that way, since my student loan debt would have led to a higher interest rate. I don't know what would happen if Doug and his parents disagreed on something so huge. It's hard to imagine Doug really taking Scott on.

I was such an idiot. I never even read through all the loan paperwork, let alone consulted my own attorney. I just let Doug and his family cut me out of Crayola. But trusting Doug so fully, so blindly, had felt like progress. I thought Dr. Morrison would have been proud.

Crayola can still work out for us, if Doug and I stick together. We can opt out and find a different, nonswinging group of friends, and over time, the spreadsheet will just become a funny story.

As usual, Scott and Melody's house instantly makes me feel confined. Trapped. It's an "authentic Victorian reproduction" (Melody doesn't realize the oxymoronic nature of that statement). Because it's mimicking the past, the rooms are all tiny and overstuffed. Heavy valances adorn every window, while small lamps and knickknacks clutter every surface. The walls and furniture are all in somber shades like dark green and wine. Oil paintings depict dour-faced people in starched, suffocating collars from the turn of the century, except for the cherubs dancing in the master bedroom.

The exterior is white with a gray-shingled roof and a latticed porch and gate. A gardener comes once a week to do the prissy English gardening that comprises the small front and back yards. There's a carriage house to the side (Melody's taxonomy, not mine) that is basically a small studio apartment without a kitchen, and that's where Doug, Sadie, and I stay. The carriage house has an A-frame shape, but the wide double doors make it look like a barn. I like that we have our own place, which is essentially one open room, since the main house feels so claustrophobic.

Melody has Sadie out of her car seat now and is clutching her tightly, like Sadie is more doll than human. Doug has our suitcase, I have my breast pump tote, and we all caravan toward the house. Scott pinches one of Sadie's cheeks perfunctorily before slapping Doug on the back in a way that seems more fraternal than paternal.

We're close enough to the coast, to Route 1, to be able to smell the ocean tang if we just open the windows. But Melody and Scott never do. The windows are shut and the curtains drawn in the living room.

Doug and I sit on the couch, which is uncomfortable and covered in some sort of dark-green velour or velvet upholstery. Whatever it is, it always feels slightly dusty to my fingertips, despite the vigorous cleaning I'm sure it had recently, courtesy of Melody or a cleaning woman. I don't think Melody would ever admit to paying someone to clean the house. All those years as what she called a "homemaker" have made her proprietary about all things domestic. That includes her monopolization of Sadie, which has already started. Melody has Sadie in her lap, turned around so they're nose to nose. It'll be three days of cootchie-cootchie-coo.

"You're looking well, Katrina," Melody says, though she's not actually looking at me.

"I've been telling her that," Doug says. "She might believe it from an unbiased source."

Oh, his mother is plenty biased. Now from his dad, I'd believe it. That's a man who doesn't dish out compliments lightly. It's funny how I used to like Melody so much more than Scott. I thought she had a sweet, gentle nature and got run over by Scott's alpha maleness. I've actually come to prefer Scott. He can be an asshole at times, but he is genuine. I think Melody manipulates Scott, lets him be the bad guy and do her dirty work so she appears pure and sweet. Scott can be obnoxious, but Melody is wily. And Scott adores Melody. He never wants to see her upset in the slightest. If he feels we've done something, we'll face his wrath, which is formidable, and with Crayola at stake, it's a whole new level of walking on eggshells.

Melody leans in to Sadie and does a loud sniff. "Someone made a wee-wee in her diaper!" She looks over at Doug and me. "Shall I change her? It would be my pleasure."

"Of course," I say. "Thank you."

I keep seeing Yolanda's guarded face. No, not just guarded. Angry. I don't know what could have made her look like that. Maybe she and the others are lulling me into a false sense of security, and they'll roast me on a spit at my own barbecue. They've all been writing the notes together, a team-building exercise for the block.

How ironic that by wanting security for my family, I am the most insecure I've ever been in my life. Well, in my adult life, that is.

Melody swans back into the room, Sadie in her arms. "Ta-da! All fresh and clean." Sadie's beside herself, loving the undivided attention.

I'm overdue for a pump. I whisper that to Doug. "We're going to get set up in the carriage house," he announces.

"Can the little one stay with us?" Melody asks. She bounces Sadie. "Go on, tell them. Say, 'I want to stay with Grandma!'" Sadie laughs.

There's no refusing. I plant a kiss on Sadie's head as I follow Doug out to the carriage house. Melody stands in the doorway, waving Sadie's arm. "Come back soon! We'll miss you!"

The carriage house has pine floors, a closet with a moth-fighting cedar floor, and a brass bed in the center of the room. That's it. I find the minimalism refreshing in contrast with the main house. I get my breast pump set up and turn the dial. Doug putters around, hanging our clothes in the closet.

"Mom said she's hoping to have some time just the two of you," he says.

It jars me a little when he calls her Mom, like she's my mom, too, like Doug and I are suddenly siblings. Melody asked me to call her Mom at the rehearsal dinner, the day before Doug and I got married.

"You're my daughter now," she said, holding me in a long embrace that smelled of powdery perfume. I hadn't yet realized her MO. I thought she'd helped me plan the wedding; I didn't realize until afterward that she'd hijacked it. Everything was to her taste and specifications. While smothering me in words of support and love, she'd undermined me at every turn. She'd caused me to second-guess anything I liked, with comments like, "Your parents never had a wedding, did they?" or "The nicest place in Haines is a Sheraton." In the end, she rendered me incapable of making a decision. Then she swooped in and made them for me.

"She's hoping the two of you can get closer," Doug adds.

I crane my neck to look at him. "Why?"

"What do you mean, why? You're her daughter-in-law. She loves you."

She loves Sadie, he means. She wants us up here every other weekend instead of once a month, but she hasn't yet laid down the law. Until now, it's been only hints. They like us on their turf, which was why I think they never argued for a guest room. That, and we were already way over budget just to get Crayola. Melody was the one who went to bat for the neighborhood, saying she'd never seen a better place to raise children. If she only knew.

"Stop tensing up around my parents," Doug says, irritated. "They're not doing anything to you. My mother couldn't be nicer."

There's nothing I can say. He'll never allow for the possibility that his mother's niceness is a veneer, that it's part of how she manipulates me.

It occurs to me that Melody and I actually have more in common than either of us would care to admit. When it comes to Doug, we're both putting on acts.

CHAPTER 19

Showering in the carriage house's claw-foot tub is no easy feat. The circumference of the tub is such that two thin white shower curtains are encircling and overlapping, and one always seems to be blowing in on me, wrapping itself around my leg like a cold, wet hand.

I poke my head out to check on Sadie in her car seat. "You OK, little one?" Arghh. I must have heard that term of endearment from Melody fifteen times yesterday before escaping to the privacy of the carriage house.

Sadie smiles up at me. She's drunk on all the attention she's been receiving, not to mention a whopping six ounces of breast milk this morning. Being in Fort Bragg has increased her appetite. Must be the bracing sea air.

She's still in her fleece sleep bag, her arms free to wave but her legs zipped up soundly inside. As I watch her, she spits up a small bit of milk. She punctuates this with another smile, not remotely fazed by the unpredictability and mess of her bodily functions. I duck back behind the curtain.

"I thought it would be good for me to get out of the AV, try to gain some perspective, but I just don't know." I keep the singsong lilt in my voice, and I'm sure she's kicking her legs inside the sleep bag responsively. "I can't stop thinking about Yolanda and the notes and the openness, wondering how we can make the best of things." It might help to talk out my feelings, and I can't do it with Doug, who's up in the main house. Besides, running monologues are our thing—Sadie's and mine.

"I'm glad you like it here, though. Your dad likes it, too. I'm the one who's out of step." I push the shower curtain back as it crowds me once more.

"You probably don't know what I mean. I hope you never do. I hope you belong wherever you go. Not that you'll be a follower. That's no good, either. But it's easier if you happen to feel the way the majority does. Like your daddy. He's the kind of person who's in step wherever he goes. Somehow, what he feels and what he does fit." If he had it his way, we'd be doing what everyone else is doing in the AV. We might even be on that spreadsheet.

"No, we don't see everything the same way. Take your grandmother, for example. He thinks she's this incredibly sweet, giving person. But really, being seen that way gives her power. It lets her control the people around her, and no one suspects." Sadie makes a delighted noise. "Exactly! Good girl! You just hold it together out there while Mommy finishes her shower, OK?" That happy noise can be the precursor to terrible things, a sign that she's close to an emotional edge. My heart speeds up a little, and I start conditioning madly. "Daddy thinks that I'm resisting his mother because I've got mommy baggage from my childhood. But the thing is, Sadie, your grandmother pretends she wants to be my mom because then she has license to run my life. Meanwhile, she's judging me all the time. She wants me to do things her way."

Since Sadie hasn't made another peep, I decide to risk it. I apply shaving cream to my legs, striping them with the razor. "Like last night. Every time I held you, her eyes were on me. Appraising me, wanting me to hand you over to her again. She thinks I'm not good enough. But when she caught my eye, she'd give me this simpering smile, as if you and I were just the cutest things ever together. And when you started crying and I walked you around and sang to you, she was at the ready, like I needed backup."

As I rinse my legs, I continue. "I know it's better for you to believe the best about your grandmother. I just can't. Sometimes life is harder when you see things clearly."

I turn the knobs to off and squeeze the excess water from my hair. A towel intrudes, attached to a hairy forearm. "Doug," I say. I drop the towel in the tub, and my heart drops along with it. He storms from the room.

Naked, exposed in more ways than one, I race after him, pleading for him to understand. "Sadie won't remember anything. I was just thinking out loud, that's all. I don't even believe what I was saying."

Sadie is wailing at being left behind. Doug stops and stands dead-still in the center of the room, his eyes cold. He's waiting for me. He wants me to see that look in his eyes, a look that says he could hate me. First the women of the AV. Now Doug.

Then he walks out, and I crumple to the floor.

Vows aside, any couple's love is conditional. In a marriage, what's tied can be untied. My pretty life can be lost, just as I've always half feared.

No, one look can't say all that. He was angry. There's no way he could mean that. He's my family, the only one I've got. Him and Sadie. He knows that.

Maybe it's why he chose me. Maybe Melody isn't the only one whose seeming sweetness is actually power in disguise. Doug picked me because I was isolated, because I was malleable. Just like Layton.

That's only my past and the AV paranoia talking. Doug and I love each other. We both love Sadie. We're a family. Recent events aside, I know these things to be true.

I steady myself enough to return to the bathroom. Sadie's eyes are wet, red, and accusing. She's asking how I could have left her. "I'm sorry, baby."

I wrap the discarded towel around myself, tucking it in, and lift her into my arms. "I'm sorry," I tell her again. She bleats an extra few times and then drops her head against me, spent. I carry her into the other room and climb into bed. Her body is so limp, so trusting. I wonder if I ever trusted my own mother this much, if she ever held me like this or she just let me cry alone. "I'm not going anywhere," I say into the top of her sweet-smelling head. "I'll hold you as long as you need me. Longer." Within a few minutes, she's fast asleep, overdue for her morning nap.

Doug will come back soon, and I'll apologize. I'll tell him I didn't mean a word of it, that it was temporary insanity brought on by stress, and we'll be fine.

He's always been convinced that my resistance to Melody is because of what I never got. Where Melody was supposedly buoyant and thrilled to parent Doug, my mother was perpetually sad and beaten down, paralyzed by depression. My grandmother probably should have raised me herself, but she didn't want to admit how bad off my mother was. So Grandma just covered for her. We scraped by on public assistance and my grandmother's handouts. My mother was unfit to be alive, let alone to parent. Doug thinks I don't know how to be a daughter because I didn't really have a mother.

He might not be entirely wrong, but I'll tell him he's completely right. Melody is wonderful, and I'm the one with problems. I'll work hard to fix them and to accept Melody's love.

I'll tell him whatever he needs to hear, because I can't lose him. I can't lose my family.

I carefully lay Sadie down in the bed, surrounding her with pillows on either side so that she can't roll off. Not that she can roll yet anyway, but you never know when a new skill will kick in. Better safe than sorry.

Still in just my towel, I locate my phone. As I go to push the text icon, planning to beg Doug's forgiveness and tell him we can come to Fort Bragg every weekend if that's what it takes, I accidentally touch the camera instead. Then I freeze.

There on the screen is a picture of Wyatt and me. More specifically, it's Wyatt and me, kissing passionately.

I want to think it was doctored, but despite the darkness, the image remains clear. It would have to be the most perfect photoshopping ever, done on a very tight time line.

Who took that picture?

Has Doug seen it?

And what else could I have done that night to destroy my life that I have no recollection of?

CHAPTER 20

"Absolutely," I tell Melody. "You push the stroller." I glance at Doug, hoping he'll notice how magnanimous I'm being toward his mother, praying he'll forgive me.

"It's two of my favorite things: the three of you and the gardens. Or are those four of my favorite things? Scott's the math wiz." Melody smiles, the fault lines of her face crinkling. She adjusts the brim of her enormous hat, its own solar system, though it's a mostly cloudy day. Practically every day is, this far north along the coast at this time of year.

Doug smiles at her. Since he stared me down in the carriage house, he's ignored me. He blew off my repeated attempts to apologize. But being Doug, he ignores me in a way that escapes his parents' attention and thereby makes only me uncomfortable. He manages to be perpetually occupied elsewhere. For example, he's currently making sure Sadie's stroller is at the right height for Melody.

In the time I've known him, I've never been this close to a breakdown. I'm using every trick Dr. Morrison ever taught me. I even tried to call her, but the number was disconnected, and when I searched for her online, all I found was old practice information. Dr. Morrison has gone out of business. Two therapy sessions for the price of one! Everything must go! Even the couch is for sale, and the soothing pictures of hydrangeas! Anyone need a lifetime's supply of tissues?

I've deleted the photo, but that doesn't mean I'm in the clear. Whoever took the picture knows, and if that's the same person who wrote the notes, then I have no reason to believe they'd be discreet. Someone could tell Doug. He's been so angry lately. Is that because someone already told him?

Of all the people to kiss in the alley behind Hound, somehow I picked Wyatt, Doug's best AV friend and the husband of its most insecure woman. Or did Wyatt pick me? I just don't understand how it could have happened. I don't even remember Wyatt being at Hound. I thought it was girls' night.

Ketamine, that's the only explanation. I would never have done that otherwise. I know that much.

But would Doug understand if I revealed everything? Would he consider me a victim or think I brought this upon myself? For so many years, I blamed myself for inviting the monsters under my bed, like I deserved it. I've tried so hard to believe that I deserve better, and Doug's a part of that. But if I would betray Doug with Wyatt so casually, maybe I was right all along.

Doug's eyes are on Melody, who's in her element on this particular outing. She likes leading us around and seems to feel a pride of ownership in the gardens. She takes charge, striding ahead with Sadie. "You're going to love the rhododendrons!" she says in a singsong voice. I prefer to think her singsong is more annoying than mine, but Sadie likes hers just as much.

Because of Sadie's stroller, we have to keep to the main path. There's a formal lawn, but the vast swaths of rhododendron bushes along the rim have an untended vibe. Multiple blooms adorn each stem, often with prominent stamens, but the overall impression is still feminine. So conservative Melody loves a hermaphroditic flower. I'd laugh under other circumstances. The bushes of varying hues and heights seem anarchic, like they're threatening to come forward; they'll overtake that lawn someday, dammit. They'll defy the odds. I want to believe in the underdog right about now.

"I just love the colors," Melody says. "Don't you?"

"I really do." I try to infuse it with maximum feeling. *I'll be your daughter now, Melody, because my family depends on it.*

Doug refuses to notice. He's pretending to admire the flowers.

"Doug, which color do you like best?" I ask. He'll have to answer me. Engage or risk exposing our dirty laundry.

"Which do you like, Mom?" He punts it to Melody, his eyes on her. He's tricky, that one. Like mother, like son. I'm beginning to despair.

"The deep purple. Right there." She points and then walks in that direction, pushing the stroller onto the lawn, off-roading. She stumbles.

"You OK, Mel?" Scott asks, instantly at her side. See, that's what love looks like, Douglas. Sometimes you have to hold each other up.

"I'm fine." She wipes at her white pants, as if she'd fallen, and laughs.

I take the opportunity to walk over to Doug and weave my arm through his. He can't shrug me off in front of his parents. "I'm sorry," I whisper. "For everything." Might as well cover my bases. "I shouldn't have said those things to Sadie. You were the one who said I haven't been myself—"

"I'm not going to talk about this," he whispers back. His expression is thunderous as he steps away from me.

Should I just be up-front about Wyatt and go ahead and confess? I could say I found the picture and have no memory of that part of the night, which is completely true. I just don't know if he'd believe me.

He's so brutally cold right now. I can't imagine throwing myself on his mercy because he doesn't appear to have any. For all Melody's domesticity and supposed sweetness, I don't think she has any, either. She's so full of judgment: toward my mother, toward me.

Oh God, what if he tells his parents what I said? They'll want him to divorce me for sure. They can congratulate themselves for having kept me off the Crayola deed. Another woman—a stronger woman, from a good family—would never have let them run the show like I did.

I stride ahead to where Melody has parked Sadie in front of the deep-purple rhododendrons. I need to continue my kill-her-with-kindness routine. "Let me get Sadie out of the stroller," I tell Melody. "Then you can walk her around and let her touch things. She loves that."

Melody smiles at me. Doug's not falling for my act, but maybe she is. "That's a great idea," she says.

Sadie was just beginning to drowse, and she erupts when I unfasten and then lift her. "It's OK." I toggle her up and down, feeling the rising panic that signals a tactical mistake on my part. "You're OK, honey. Nothing to worry about." She disagrees heartily, and she wants everyone in the vicinity to know it. I feel my cheeks flushing.

"Put her back in the stroller," Doug commands. "She was happy there."

"Now that she's out, she won't be happy to go back in," I counter. I spend nearly every waking minute with her; I'm the one who'd know.

"Can I take her?" Melody asks. I know that was the reason I removed Sadie from the stroller to begin with, but now it feels like handing her over would only confirm my inadequacy at comforting my own daughter. I have to pull this off. I just have to.

"I've got this," I say, treating it like an offer that can be refused.

"Maybe she's hungry," Scott says, loud enough to be heard over Sadie. It's his answer to everything.

"She just ate," I nearly shout back. I walk her away from everyone, toward a spot in the center of the grass. I pat her back and hum. She's not letting me off the hook for this one, no chance. Her cries intensify. Doug and his parents watch and then whisper, like they're conferring on me, evaluating my fitness as a mother. I want to tell them it's not normally like this, that Sadie loves dancing cheek to cheek with me. Even Andie commented on just how bonded Sadie and I are. But we get around Doug's parents and I become the picture of fumbling ineptitude.

How long has it been—three minutes, an hour?

I hold her high up on my shoulder, supporting her with one arm, groping in the diaper bag with the other. Pay dirt! Her pacifier. I see Melody approaching me, and I think I've just got to get this pacifier in Sadie's mouth and shut her up. I've got a few more seconds.

Furious, Sadie spits out the pacifier. It lands on top of the world's neatest grass, just propped up there like a diamond ring in a velvet box. Sadie is tantruming like a baby twice her age, older, even. She's precocious. She's a prodigy.

"You seem very stressed," Melody says to me.

"I'm stressed because she's screaming. People are staring." I don't really mean the strangers, though a few are. I mean Melody and Scott and Doug, all three of them, conducting their referendum of me. I don't particularly care that Sadie is disturbing the tranquility of the surroundings. It's not like I brought her into a movie theater or to a meditation retreat. We're in nature, sort of. Nature's loud sometimes.

"I think you've been stressed for a while," Melody says with exaggerated delicacy. "Babies pick up on that."

It seems like she is implying that Sadie's tantrum is my fault, that it was brought on by my stress. She's actually blaming me. And a part of me thinks she's right.

Melody has her sweet grandmotherly expression on. "This might be a good time for me to hold her."

"I can comfort my own child."

She raises an eyebrow. Then she smiles and holds out her arms. I stare at her for a long minute, but she doesn't drop her arms. It's a Mexican standoff, and she's going to win. We both know it.

Doug comes over, goes into the diaper bag, and removes a bottle of milk. Without a word, he snatches Sadie out of my arms, as if to say I've had my time, my chance, and I've failed. How easily he takes her from me. It shouldn't be that easy.

He pops the bottle in Sadie's mouth, and she sucks gratefully. "She's not hungry yet," I say, despite the evidence to the contrary. "It hasn't been long enough."

"Tell that to her," he says frostily.

He knows how I feel in front of his parents, how I worry about their scrutiny. I can't believe he'd show me up like this. He's punishing me. For what he overheard me saying about his mother? Or for something else?

Scott is standing by the rhododendron bush, like he's not with us. He hates a scene. Melody moves over to Doug and begins to stroke Sadie's hair. I've been blocked out, displaced.

Before I can even think, I find myself fleeing across the lawn, back to the path. I hear Melody calling to me, a note of bewilderment in her voice. I'm making it too easy for her, too easy for all of them. I look like a mother who fails to comfort her own child and then abandons her. But if I stay there, I will absolutely lose it. What would Melody say about me weeping in front of my baby?

I fly past the heathers and the succulents and flowers flowers flowers, and the end of the path is like the end of everything. I'm high above the Pacific Ocean, overlooking the craggy bluffs, the sky gray and the water grayer. Its swirls are beautiful and menacing. Other visitors with their perfect children look at me with alarm or concern. A few seem like they're about to approach, because an obviously distraught woman on top of a bluff isn't to be taken lightly. I should step back.

Then there's a hand on my arm, and at the surprise, I feel myself stumble forward. Just a little, but enough to be frightening, and then that hand is yanking me back from the edge.

It's Doug. I look at his face, and I don't see any anger there, only my own fear mirrored back to me.

Then I'm sobbing, and his arms are around me. "I'm so sorry," I say, "for everything."

Please know what everything means. "Please, Doug. Just forgive me."

When he speaks, his voice is clogged with tears. "I'll try."

CHAPTER 21

YOU'RE GOING TO SNAP ONE OF THESE DAYS. ANYONE CAN SEE THAT.

I wish I could say I was even a little surprised to see the latest welcome mat when Doug and I arrive home.

Doug says, "Let me take that," and he goes to put the cardboard into the recycling. "Don't even dignify it."

"We can't just ignore this."

"Wyatt said—"

"Wyatt doesn't even know who's doing it!"

Doug shuts his mouth, with effort. I know that in Doug's world, nothing goes too wrong; he has faith that nothing really ever will. That's why he can be so dismissive of this. But I know how cruel, how down-right evil, some people can be.

"I'm saving them," I say. "In the back of the closet. It might be evidence."

"OK." He hands it over and turns away. He wants to say more, but he doesn't dare. He's been treating me with kid gloves since that moment on the bluff.

I keep thinking about what he said. When I begged forgiveness, he didn't say there was nothing to forgive. He said he'd try.

Doug really thought I might have been contemplating a jump. I would disabuse him of the notion, but then he might just go back to his silent fury. So I'm playing along, being his fragile little invalid. I'm not entirely sure it's an act.

Inside the house, there's no sign of an intruder. The rooms appear undisturbed. But then, I'm disturbed enough for all of us.

I don't know what's worse: having kissed Wyatt or not being able to remember kissing him. Because it means I could have done other things I don't remember.

What's strange is that only Yolanda seems outwardly standoffish toward me. At girls' night, they all emphasized the community of women, how they look after each other. It was a betrayal to kiss Wyatt before I'd opted into the spreadsheet. So is it possible the other women don't know? Or do they think it's OK for me to have a trial period, to sample the wares?

Then there's that conversation with Brandon. He didn't just talk about the spreadsheet in general; he specifically brought up Yolanda. So Yolanda must have confided in him, even if she didn't tell the others. I don't know if she sent him or if he came on his own, but now that I think about it, he was definitely trying to evoke my compassion for her. It makes me think of that song "Jolene," one woman begging another not to take her man. Brandon might think I really want Wyatt, when honestly, Wyatt had never even crossed my mind before. So why did I kiss him? I recall the next line of the song, about not taking him just because she can. Brandon and Yolanda might think I'm the kind of person who would be with Wyatt just for sport.

It seems crazy that I could take anyone from Yolanda. She's so much prettier than I am. But from what everyone said at my recruitment, it's not about pretty; it's about new. New is the great equalizer. New is how we're all, as Raquel said, beautiful.

At least Andie has resurfaced. She left a voice mail apologizing. "I really did mean it when I said I'd be your sounding board. I want to be there for you, Kat. It's just been a truly crazy week."

Join the club, Andie. I haven't called her back yet. I don't know who I can trust right now. I would have said I could trust Andie, but she was the person who talked to Doug alone and then disappeared.

You're going to snap one of these days. Anyone can see that.

For all I know, Andie wrote the notes. She's as likely as any of the others. Or as unlikely. I can't even tell anymore. But someone took that picture with my phone. Who would have done that except the writer of the notes, the person who wants me to snap? That means the writer was there that night, either one of the women or one of their husbands.

But I don't have a clue which one, and trying to parse a night that's only half-remembered is exhausting. Not to mention that Doug and I are pretending things are normal. The charade wears on both of us. And, give me strength, we've got a barbecue to plan for next weekend. I want to cancel for myriad unspeakable reasons, but when I mentioned that possibility to Doug, he just stared at me, then rolled over and went to sleep without a word. It wasn't even eight o'clock.

Now he's at work, and I'm on my own with Sadie. She's whining so consistently in my ear that it's like tinnitus. I have to remind myself that love is sometimes a gauntlet to be run. Plastering a smile on my face, I elevate my voice an octave and declare, "It's bath time!" I hold her against my shoulder as I fill the blue plastic tub. She usually likes that part, watching the water that will soon submerge her, but not today. She stares at me, eyes wide with recrimination. Is she doubting my credibility, too?

As I remove her onesie and then her diaper, she screws up her face and begins to scream. "See," I tell her as she writhes on the bathroom floor, "there's the water. You're about to have your bath. You love your bath."

But she knows better. She does not love her bath. She has never loved her bath. I am a fool to believe otherwise.

Shut up, shut up, shut up, I implore her. No, I order her. You will appreciate that I spend my entire life catering to your needs, real and imagined. You will recognize that I have placed my life on hold for you, that I have given up all vestiges of the woman I have known myself to be in order to invest in your present and future happiness. But she is enraged with me. It's bewildering and galling. I'm trying to both wash her hair and keep her head from banging into the tub through her spasms of anger. I swear, I hear her telling me that she hates the bath; in fact, she hates me. "You're a phony," she tells me. "You try and try, but you never get it right. You'll never be right. You'll always be tainted."

I find myself actually screaming, "Shut up!" She's yelling too loud herself to hear me. It's taking on operatic proportions, both of us unglued, each infuriated by the other, inflamed by our private injustices. I snatch her out of the tub, half-sudsed, half-washed, soaking the front of my T-shirt. I stomp down the hall and lay her on the changing table, dripping. She stopped crying somewhere along the way, and her eyes are full of something unfamiliar. Fear. She's afraid of me. I wish I could say that stops me, that my own anger whooshes out like the air from a popped balloon, but no.

I put a diaper on Sadie's wet ass and lay her in her crib. Then I go to my own room and close the door. I need a time-out.

Her protests start immediately. She wants me back. She says, "I don't care how you treat me, just don't leave me," and that's when all my anger dissipates. I start shaking and crying. We're twins, Sadie and me. No, we're two molecules who act on each other. Sometimes we make a beautiful compound; today, we're spontaneously combusting.

I'm so sorry, so mortified. I know that my movements were brusque, but they couldn't have hurt her. The damage is occurring now, making her think she was bad and that she'll be left. These seconds are hours to her. They might not be memories, but somewhere inside her, they're imprints.

Sadie's cries are desperately plaintive. She needs her mommy, pathetically so. I needed my mommy just that way, and she let me down. I remember my mother's emotional absence, the vacuum where a person should have been, the shell; I don't recall an angry presence. I didn't even register that much. I had no molecular influence on my mother.

I rush to Sadie's room and lift her from the crib. I'll have to change her sheet. There's a damp, Sadie-shaped spot in the middle, which makes me cry harder. I'm a terrible mother, despite all my efforts, or maybe because of them. Because I stretch myself like a rubber band until I snap, just like that note said.

I keep apologizing, but it doesn't matter. Sadie's body feels boneless as she falls against me. She covers me, from my shoulder to my pelvis. I rub her back. Why does her skin feel so hot when she's in just a diaper?

I put my lips to her forehead, and I'm filled with terror. I'm the worst mother in the world, tragically stupid. All the time she's been fussing, somehow it never occurred to me that she could be sick. I ran through the list of possibilities (hungry, tired, bored . . .) and never once thought "sick." She's been remarkably, staggeringly healthy since the day she was born. I've never heard a real cough, even, only the occasional sneeze.

Now her body is an inferno, and I never even suspected. Where was my maternal instinct? Melody's right about me.

I go to the bathroom to grab the never-before-used rectal thermometer. Shit, I realize we don't have Vaseline. I look around frantically, and my eyes fall on Doug's nightstand, on the optimistically placed Astroglide.

I undo the tape on the sides of Sadie's diaper and lay her across my knee, as illustrated in the diagram. "It's OK, pretty girl," I tell her. She doesn't make a sound, not even when I slide the thermometer in.

I can't believe how much I want to hear her cry. She's turned lumpish so quickly.

I reattach her diaper and place her on my shoulder, patting her as I call the pediatrician. She's barely conscious. "Her temperature is 104.7, but I don't know how long she's had a fever," I say. I field all the doctor's questions, and at the end, he says to take her to the ER at the children's hospital. "I'll call ahead," he adds. "They'll be ready for you."

We're an emergency. I call Doug. "You need to meet us at the ER," I say. I'm crying again.

"I'll be there soon," Doug answers. "Don't panic, OK? She'll be fine. Kids get sick."

I'd swear Sadie's getting hotter by the second, and not just her forehead. It's her whole body. I find myself talking loudly to keep her awake, like they do in movies when someone has a concussion. "Don't fall asleep!" I sing out through my tears.

She's not going to die. Kids get sick, that's all. Very few of them die.

I strap Sadie into her car seat. She is still frighteningly inactive. "Get mad," I instruct her. "Just really let me have it." Her eyes are uncomprehending. They flicker shut.

When we reach a stop sign, I push back the canopy of the car seat. She stares up at me. I've never before seen eyes that are truly glassy, like a doll's.

In front of the ER, there's a circular drive, and I leave the car parked there. I don't care if it's ticketed or towed; I need to get Sadie inside ASAP.

I'm panting, holding Sadie against me, feeling her terrible heat. There's a line in front of the check-in window and a ton of people sitting around with their children, but everyone parts for me. "It's a *baby*," says one little girl excitedly.

The woman behind the window is in scrubs, and I say that our doctor called ahead. She didn't get any call, but she immediately lets me into a fluorescent-lit room with a gurney in the center, wreathed by machines on standby. I must look that frantic, or Sadie looks that dire, or that's the protocol with a baby this small. She's just so small.

Suddenly, everything is moving very fast. Once Sadie's temperature is taken, the hospital personnel seem to multiply. I think I hear "105.6," and I assume that's her temperature, the reason why Sadie is surrounded and I'm shunted aside. They need access to her veins, to her blood. Tests. They're going to run tests. And cultures. They need to figure out what's made Sadie so sick so fast.

That's what a nurse has just explained to me. I nod convulsively. "Can I get you a chair?" she asks. "Can I get you tissues?" There's liquid all over my face. I don't know if it's from my eyes or my nose. Sadie is in just her diaper, and she's no longer inert. She's screaming. I step in closer and see her head rolling from side to side. She's looking for me.

"I'm here," I say, surging forward, into a gap behind the gurney, near the beeping machines.

The nurse pursues me. She's pretty, Indian, with a soothing accent. Her scrubs have some sort of cartoon character on them that I don't recognize. "You can touch her. You can give her the pacifier." She hands it to me.

"Sadie doesn't like this kind." I stare down at my baby girl helplessly. Wires snake through her nose, providing oxygen. Her head lolls; her screams continue. She wasn't looking for me after all. She needs someone who can make all this stop. That's not me.

"This will help," the nurse says. She hands me small plastic tubes and shows me how to open them. "Sugar water. Squeeze it into her mouth."

I do, and Sadie calms for a few seconds. She's able to see me through her tears. I stroke her hair. She's still so hot.

"We've given her Tylenol," the nurse says, as if she could hear my thoughts. Or did I speak out loud? I suppose they'd be anyone's thoughts with a baby in this situation. She must see this all the time. She sees worse. "She'll start to respond soon."

What if she doesn't?

"We've also started antibiotics," the nurse continues. "They're taking cultures, some of which won't come back until tomorrow. It might turn out to be viral. But we can't take any chances, so we start the antibiotics immediately. Just in case it's a bacterial infection."

"Why are there so many people?" I choke out. "Is that normal?"

"They're taking good care of her. The doctor will talk to you soon."

The doctor—an older woman wearing a lab coat over a blouse and slacks—is on the phone in the corner. I assume she's talking about Sadie.

"Give me a hint," I say. "Please."

The nurse casts a glance around. Everyone else is occupied by Sadie's tiny body and even tinier veins. She whispers, "Her blood pressure was unstable at first." She points to one of the monitors. I can't look.

"What does that mean?" I whisper back.

"They don't know yet. But she won't be going home for a little while."

I burst into noisy tears. "She has to stay here?"

The nurse nods. I lean down and sing into Sadie's ear. I stroke her hair madly. I squirt more sugar into her mouth, and it runs out the corners. She chases it with her tongue. Her eyes droop. I think the crying has exhausted her. I don't know what to hope for, crying or no crying. Which will mean she's getting better?

The doctor hangs up the phone. She appears at my side and leads me away. She introduces herself, and I forget her name immediately. ". . . so she'll be in the PICU overnight, at least . . ."

"The PICU?" I say through a fog.

"The pediatric intensive care unit."

I experience a fresh burst of sobs. "That sounds bad."

"No, it's very good. It's where she'll get the most attentive care. Right now, she's getting oxygen, antibiotics, and fluids."

"What's wrong with her?"

The doctor glances back at Sadie with something like fondness. I'm glad. I want Sadie to be liked by the people we need to save her life. "We don't know what's wrong yet. We need the cultures to come back. She'll be here at least two or three days, maybe more."

I need Doug to get here. I'm splintering apart. No, I'm snapping. Just like the note said.

Like the note said.

It was a prophecy, and it's coming true. Someone made it come true.

"Her temp is 104.1," a nurse reports. The doctor gives me a big smile.

"That's a good sign," she says. "She's responding to the Tylenol."

"And her blood pressure?" I ask.

"It's stabilized for the moment, but we need to keep a close eye. We don't yet know why it was unstable. But let me ask you something: Has she ever had jaundice? It's most common in newborns, but it looks like she has some signs of it now." I shake my head no.

They don't know what's wrong, why a child who's been healthy her whole life suddenly gets jaundice and needs intensive care. But I'm afraid that I do. It looked like no one had been in our house, but someone could have been.

If someone hurt my daughter, it's all my fault.

Session 80.

"It's hard for me to come here."

"We talk about hard things."

"I mean that it's hard for me to sit across from you. I'm really mad at you."

"Let's unpack that."

"See? That's the kind of thing that makes me mad. The way you talk."

"What else are you angry about?"

"That you call the truth a narrative. That you don't believe me."

"I do believe you. I believe that you're being honest in the way you see things."

"But you don't believe the things themselves! Admit it. You think it's a narrative. You think it's a lie I tell myself."

"Your whole life was ripped apart. You had to tape it all back together somehow."

"I see the way you look at me."

"How do you think I look at you?"

"It's not what I think. I know how you look at me. You think I lie to myself. You think I'm in denial."

"We've been cutting too close to the bone lately. You've been confronting some uncomfortable truths about what might really have happened and who's truly responsible. Sometimes it's easier to get angry than to confront all the pain that's underneath."

"You want him to be a monster, but I don't."

"That's not what I want. I want to help you process—"

"Fuck processing. Listen to me. Eight children. That's what they say. That there had been eight victims, but only two took the stand. What does that tell you?"

"The trial must have been devastating for you."

"We're not talking about me; we're talking about you! About you sitting there judging me."

"Let's slow down and figure out where your anger is coming from."

"I'm an angry person, don't you get that by now? Besides, aren't all emotions permissible in this room? Isn't that what you told me in the very beginning?"

"Is it really me you're upset with? It's OK if it is. I just want to make sure."

"It's partly you. It's partly . . . I went to see him. In prison."

"Oh."

"That's it, 'oh'?"

"I'm surprised."

"Surprised I went or surprised I didn't ask your permission first?"

"Just surprised you took that step. What happened?"

"She was my best friend since we were six years old, and she betrayed me."

"I'm not following you."

"No, you can't. No one can."

"Let me try."

"You know what? I think I'm good now."

"Good in what way?"

"I mean, I think I'm done."

"With therapy?"

"Yeah."

"Let's just slow down. We need to unpack this—"

"No, we don't. This decision has nothing to do with you."

"What does it have to do with?"

"You've helped me a lot. But I'm done here."

"Don't walk away, Ellen. Not now."

"I got everything I needed from that prison visit. I know what I have to do."

CHAPTER 22

ELLEN

It seems hard to believe now, but when I first heard about the new neighbors, I was happy. Nils and Ilsa hadn't been any picnic, and I love babies. As far as I'm concerned, the block can always use a newborn. I didn't recognize the name. I mean, there's more than one Katrina in the world, and when she got married, I'm sure she couldn't ditch her maiden name fast enough. So she was well camouflaged.

Besides, she's not Katrina anymore; she's Kat, like some sassy little sprite. Ha! She looks just the same, though. I'd know her anywhere.

She hasn't recognized me, which is both an insult and a blessing.

It's also my life plan. New name, new hair color, cosmetic surgery, some colored contacts, and voilà.

Now I have a new plan: Operation Get Katrina the Hell Out of My Neighborhood. It's not going to be derailed by her daughter being in the hospital, though I do feel bad about that. No one wants to see a baby suffer. But she'll recover. The vast majority of us make it to adult-hood, scars and all.

Oh, and I have a motto, too: don't kick Katrina when she's down; kick her out when she's down. There's no better moment, really. Katrina couldn't be any more vulnerable than she is right now, subject to dis-orientation and rash decision-making. Sadie will be fine, but she'll be raised somewhere else, so I don't have to look at her mother's face ever again.

It won't be easy, though. I was lucky enough to never have an emer-gency situation on my hands with my own child, and seeing Sadie in any kind of pain, seeing all those other kids . . . But the thing is, Katrina's misery is only fair. There was a time when I was consumed by the idea of vengeance. I let that go, with difficulty, but I still believe in justice.

Word traveled fast about Sadie's illness. I volunteered to go to the hospital first and find out what the family needs. If we all went together, I said, we'd overwhelm them. Instead, I'd do reconnaissance and return with a full report. They agreed that was the best way.

Now, I just need to make sure I keep Katrina isolated.

The PICU is one large room segmented by curtains, and Sadie's in quarantine. That means that yellow-and-black hazard tape has been laid down on the floor around her curtained area, and everyone who comes into Sadie's sphere has to wear latex gloves and a gown over their clothes. There are face masks, too, but when I draw back the curtain, I see that Katrina and Doug aren't wearing theirs. See, what kind of par-ents are those? I've never trusted Doug. For one thing, he married her. Also, there's just something sketchy about him. You can tell he's used to being liked all the time, he needs it like air, and I never trust those people. He can tell I don't buy his act, and that makes him nervous. Good.

"Hi," I whisper through my mask. "The neighbors sent me to check on you guys."

"Hey!" Doug says, too loud. "Thank you for coming!" Like he's throwing a party. We're already assuming the weekend barbecue is canceled. *Down, dog. Down, Doug.*

His only concern should be Sadie, not pleasing me. He doesn't have to be a good host by his daughter's ICU bed.

But Sadie, that poor kid. She's in what looks like a small Plexiglas box, raised on a platform, wearing a baby-size hospital gown. A tangle of wires, lines, and tubes runs from her to the hissing, beeping machines. A light is taped to her finger, and plastic tips are inserted in each tiny nostril to deliver oxygen. There are round, flesh-colored patches affixed to her chest and upper leg and stents in her hands that are attached to boards; I assume it's so she won't remove the IVs, similar to how dogs wear cones around their necks so they won't pull out stitches. She's just so restricted. She's also eerily quiet, motionless. Her skin has a decidedly yellow cast to it.

Katrina follows my eyes. She must like what she sees in them, and she must trust my tears, which are genuine. I never wanted this to happen. Sadie's so innocent. I want to think she's dreaming of being somewhere else, sucking from some giant boob in the sky.

"The nurses say it's good for her to sleep," Katrina says softly. "Her body's working so hard to fight the infection." Her voice is hoarse. I can tell she's been crying a lot. Doug's hair is disheveled, but other than that, you wouldn't be able to guess he has a sick baby.

"I'm sure she's a fighter," I say. Katrina gives me a sharp look, while Doug smiles, like he appreciates my intent.

As if he has any idea of my intent.

Katrina starts to speak in this weird spacey voice. "Sometimes I think about who has a better prognosis, the screamer or the sleeper. Do you hear her?" I shake my head. "There's this little baby even younger than Sadie who's been crying the whole time we've been here."

"She's not crying now," I say.

"Oh. She's not?" Katrina looks confused.

She's cracking up so easily. I thought that's what I wanted, but it's hard to see anyone go through this.

"I'm hoping both babies will be OK," she says, "but I worry there's a quota. Like, a certain number of people in here have to die to make room for others."

I look to Doug. It seems like he isn't even listening to her. There's no outward acknowledgment of how peculiar she sounds. Maybe he's heard it before and he's just tuning her out at this point. I can't exactly tell what's transpiring between them.

"Like there's a quota from God. A big cosmic ledger. I don't want Sadie to be pitted against the others like that. I don't want to compete with the other parents to see who can pray the hardest."

You can't compete with other parents, Katrina. With what you've done, they'll win. In a great big gladiatorial arena, with God pointing his scepter to decide who lives and who dies, Sadie's a goner.

But I hope not. She's just a little baby. She doesn't deserve to pay for the sins of her mother. The problem is, it doesn't work that way. The innocent feel the pain, and evil walks free all the time.

There are only two chairs. One is hard-backed, and the other is the upholstered type that converts into a bed, albeit a pretty uncomfortable one. Doug jumps up from the hard-backed chair, realizing that he's forgotten his manners, but there's something phony in his gentlemanly gesture.

"Why don't you sit down?" he says to me. "Stay awhile, since you came all the way down."

"It's not far."

"Well, it was really nice of you anyway."

"I'm supposed to report back," I say. "Tell the others what you need, so we can organize. How long is she going to be here, do you know?"

Katrina shakes her head sorrowfully.

"Could we start bringing some meals?" I offer.

"We don't need anything." Her voice has gone cold. It's unnerving, how she flits between spacey and penetrating. I'm not sure if it's that she doesn't trust me, specifically, or that she doesn't trust an emissary of the AV. I can understand that. The notes have gotten a little more menacing. At this point, I have to speed things up. I can't take this much longer. That's why I had to come here.

"Some food would be nice," Doug says. Katrina turns to glare at him. "Well, you need to eat, and I need to eat." Doug's tone is defensive. Something's going on between them, clearly. They haven't really looked at each other the whole time I've been here.

"I don't want anyone coming here." Her tone is absolute.

"Kat—" Doug begins.

"I said no."

Now they're looking at each other, all right. I'm curious to see which one of them will back down, and when it's Doug, I have the strangest reaction. I actually think, *Good girl, Katrina.* Like I'm rooting for her. How insane is that?

"Just think about it," I say. "After I leave, you can text me. I'll make myself available every day."

"That's really kind of you," Doug says.

Katrina says nothing. She's looking at Sadie, her eyes brimming with tears.

"I'll leave you two alone." Doug is on the balls of his feet, all nervous energy. "I need a walk anyway." Turning his head—but not his eyes—in Katrina's direction, he says, "Remember, my parents will be here soon." There's a strange warning in it. Then he slips out.

"You said you don't want anyone here," I say. "I totally respect that. Should I clear out?" I need to get her permission. That's critical. She needs to think my presence is, on some level, her idea.

It's kind of handy, wearing the mask and gown. I won't have to do that much acting. Plus, it makes it much less likely that she'll (finally) recognize me.

"Do you want me to go?" I ask again.

CHAPTER 23

KAT

I can't believe I'm hesitating. She really should go. I can't trust her; I can't trust any of them.

But I can see that she's really hurting for Sadie. And I'm just so fucking alone here.

Crisis supposedly brings some couples together. That's not how it is for Doug and me. We're sitting together behind the hospital curtain with no privacy, so I can't ask him why he's acting this way. So distant. If I didn't know better, I'd think he blames me for Sadie's illness.

I blame myself. I should have gotten her to a doctor sooner. I should have known she was sick. More time could have made a difference.

They don't even know what the infection is. They're still waiting for more cultures to come back, and while it could ostensibly be good news that the ones so far have been negative, it means we're currently in the unknown. She's had vomiting and diarrhea, symptoms of jaundice and anemia, but they can't treat the source. They can just make her more comfortable and give her fluids.

The rule is that only one parent can sleep by her side, and since I'm pumping milk, I'm the obvious choice. Doug slept in the waiting room last night. I was left alone here with Sadie and the industrial-strength pump that takes half the time. I couldn't even hear it over all the other hospital machines. I cried the whole time. She's not drinking it. The bottles are going in the floor refrigerator while fluids enter her little body intravenously.

I haven't mustered an answer yet when a new doctor comes by. He's short, wiry, and hairy. He could be my savior, Sadie's savior, so I pump his hand and tell him just how happy I am to see him.

"My husband just stepped out," I say. "I can get him back really quickly. Can you wait? Or can you come back?"

"This will only take a minute," he responds. It's true, his physical exam is incredibly brief, and Sadie sleeps right through it. I can hardly watch. It's like she's unconscious, like she's dead.

Please, please, let us be on the right side of the ledger.

The doctor smiles and says, "She's looking better." I don't see what he sees, though I wish I could. He tells me that her last blood pressure reading was normal, and her fever is well controlled. "All good signs." He looks like he wants to wrap this up quickly, like he wishes he were doing wind sprints rather than practicing medicine.

That's when I remember that she's still here, that I didn't tell her to leave. She's hearing everything. I don't want her knowing my business, reporting it back to anyone. But how can I kick her out now, in front of the doctor? He'd think I'm nuts.

"What about the jaundice?" I say.

"That's about the same."

"And the anemia?"

"The anemia is mild. It might have even been present before the illness and went undetected."

"So you're not treating her for it?"

"Not at present, no." He looks like he really wants to bolt. I was just supposed to take his "all good signs" at face value and let him get on with his day. "We're monitoring her symptoms very closely. We don't want to overtreat."

"Or undertreat?" she pipes up, and I can't help it, I look at her gratefully. It's like she's on my team, more than Doug has seemed. He's too busy sucking up to the doctors to pin them down on specifics. He just trusts way too easily.

"But what's wrong?" I ask. "Do you know if it's viral or bacterial yet?"

"Not just yet. Some of the cultures will be ready tomorrow. She's already getting fluids and antibiotics. We're controlling her fever. Believe me, she's getting the best care." He pats my arm. "We've got this, Mom. Don't you worry."

As he leaves, I feel deflated. I fall into the chair, and again, I can't help it, I'm glad she's here. I'm just glad not to be alone.

"That was good news, right?" she says. "About her blood pressure and temperature?"

"No one was in here for more than an hour. No nurse and no doctor. I think that means she's doing better, but maybe it means they're giving up on her."

"I don't think it works that way."

I don't know why, but I'm talking. I'm telling her the theory I just came up with, just since being here, about the circles of luck, which are also the circles of hell.

"In the outer circle," I tell her, "there are all the people with healthy children. Their kids get common colds, but they never need to visit the ER. That's most people. That was me, until now. And then one circle in, it's Doug, Sadie, and me. The ones who are lucky because they have health insurance and access to good medical care, and when they realize something's wrong, they can bring her to a place like this. It could be worse, I know that."

She's listening attentively. She's just so present. I've been missing that with Doug for a while, I realize. And this might sound crazy, but when I look into her eyes, I get this feeling like I've known her forever.

I really must be losing it.

But I keep talking, because I need to.

"There's a boy next to us," I continue. "He whines sometimes, and the nurses go in and out constantly. His mom seems to know them really well. I overheard them talking about him. He's three, and he's got some kind of brain tumor. This is his fifth surgery.

"The curtain was open one time, and I could see inside. His head is in this weird vise, like in the Hannibal Lecter movie. And I think, that's a circle worse than mine. Because Sadie will probably be fine, but he and his parents have to keep going through this, time and time again."

"Or maybe he'll be cured. Maybe the fifth time is the charm."

"Or maybe he'll die. Or maybe Sadie will. That's the inner circle."

"But it's also the smallest, right?"

Our eyes meet, and that earlier gratitude returns. I want her here. I need a friend so badly.

"I can imagine with all the free time you have in here," she says, "your mind goes all sorts of places."

"My mind does that anyway. Even when I'm not at the hospital."

"Mine too," she says. "The thing about having kids is that there's such a small chance of something really awful happening. Like a one percent chance, maybe. But you have to keep dodging it. In the womb, you're dodging. They say up to fifty percent of pregnancies end in miscarriages. Then they're out in the world." We both look at Sadie; both of our eyes fill with tears. "There's a slim possibility of any one terrible thing happening to them, but you have to keep dodging. It's like this juggernaut you spend your whole life running from. But you wouldn't have it any other way, right? You can't imagine going back to your life before they arrived."

"No," I say, "I can't imagine going back."

CHAPTER 24

ELLEN

"So, how is she?" Brandon stands on my doorstep, his eyes worried but something else, too. He's hungry for the update. He likes to be in the loop more than any human I've ever known.

"She's still in the ICU," I say. "The ICU for kids. It's called the PICU. She's barely conscious, and the doctors don't know what's wrong with her."

"I can't even imagine. A baby that young, in a big, scary hospital. So full of germs. I get freaked out just visiting a place like that. I want to take a Purell shower afterward."

"Well, that's why I went instead of you."

His eyes narrow just slightly. "I didn't really expect you to be the one to volunteer, honestly."

"I didn't expect to, either. But when someone's in need, you go to them."

I can tell he thinks there's more to the story, and boy, is he right. But I'm not about to divulge it, especially since my plan is working.

Katrina needs a confidante, and right now, it's clearly not her husband. As much as she might want to push me away, she doesn't have the strength right now.

"I'd like to do something, though," he says. "I can start organizing meals. Oh, and I can put together a visiting schedule, since she probably can't have a ton of people converging all at once."

"There can only be two people at the bedside at a time. Katrina really only wants me there right now."

"Really? Just you?" At my nod, he adds, "Doesn't she prefer to be called Kat?"

Everyone loves Brandon, thinks he's so kind and good-hearted, and I used to think that, too. But after what went on with my husband . . . We all knew the rules. They were right there on the spreadsheet in black and white.

I ignore his question. "Her in-laws are there, too. Doug's parents. I don't think she has family of her own." In fact, I know she doesn't.

"I'll work on the meals, then," Brandon says, with just the slightest touch of obstinacy.

"She doesn't want anything from anyone."

"Does Doug want anything?" So he's setting his sights on Doug now?

I shrug. Take it up with them. Oh wait, I just told you that you can't. I want to smile at the handcuffs I've placed on Brandon, kind of like the ones he once placed on my husband.

"So they really want *nothing* from us?" He looks distressed. "This is what community is for! This is why you move to the AV. We band together for support. Everyone's stronger with the Village behind them. What are they thinking?"

"She's thinking about Sadie. She's going to what she knows."

"Which is?"

"Handling things on her own."

He shakes his head. "So sad. But I guess people do return to what they know in times of crisis." His tone isn't barbed, but I feel a chill anyway. I've always wondered what my husband told him. What you discover is that the scariest part of openness isn't the sex; it's the pillow talk. You can never be entirely sure what other people know. What slips out after they've slipped it in.

"I should go," I say, moving to shut the door.

"Let me know if anything changes."

"You'll be the first." Really, he's the only one who needs to know. He's better than a megaphone. Our entire block will be feeling the sting of Katrina's rejection within the hour.

"Sorry," I say. I'm in my gown and mask, having vigorously scrubbed up to my elbows, but I don't recognize the two senior citizens in the cordoned-off area behind the yellow-and-black tape. I start to withdraw, but then I see that Sadie's inhabiting the raised dais.

Oh, Sadie. The air in here smells residually noxious, like she had another recent bout of diarrhea. She appears as lifeless as she did yesterday, and her skin still has the tinge of urine. It hurts to look at her.

"Are you here for Doug and Katrina?" the man says. There's something military about him, though he's dressed casually in khakis and a polo shirt.

"Yes. I'm a friend. Well, a new neighbor."

"Oh, that's so lovely!" the woman exclaims. I dislike her immediately. There's just something false about her. Like mother, like son.

"I'm Scott, and this is Melody," the man says.

"Nice to meet you."

"Likewise!" Melody beams. "Doug and Katrina are in the cafeteria. They'll be back soon. The waiting room is right down the hall."

"OK. Thanks." It's interesting that Scott and Melody are calling Katrina by her full name. I guess they're not Kat people, either.

"Who should I say stopped by?" Melody pesters.

"I'll go find them. Thanks."

The cafeteria is spacious and purple, like Barney exploded. There's plenty of noise and bustle, but Katrina is sitting alone, picking at a croissant, her eyes glazed. Seeing her there brings me back to a place I never go, when I was in elementary school and she was the new girl who nobody really wanted to talk to or sit with. I took her under my wing and looked after her. We were so close.

But she betrayed me. It took me so many years to recover, and the AV was a big part of that. So I can't have those kinds of memories or any twinges of conscience. I have to remember she brought this on herself.

I take the seat across from her. "Hey," I say. I'm a little nervous, since I've removed my mask and the lighting is nearly fluorescent. Much starker than daylight, and a hell of a lot brighter than Hound. We're looking at each other more intensely than we ever have before. I don't want her to notice the slant of my eyes or the curve of my jawline. "I met Scott and Melody. They told me where to find you."

Fortunately, she just keeps playing with the croissant. "Hi."

"How are you?"

"Her temperature spiked, and she had more diarrhea. They say it's 'back under control' now." Tears fill her eyes. "But for how long?"

"They're taking good care of her. It just takes some time for the antibiotics to work."

"They'll only work if it's bacterial. The nurses and the doctors are supposed to be more attentive on the PICU than on the regular floors, but even so, they left the leads on her chest for two whole shifts. There were red marks!" The table next to us looks over briefly, then turns away, realizing that you can't judge here. "They're supposed to change those every shift. I don't know what to do. I don't know how to help her. I just have to depend on these people. I just have to hope . . ." She puts her head in her hands, and I think she's going to start sobbing.

I remind myself that no matter what, I will not feel for her. I can't. It would be so much easier if I were some kind of monster. But she fucked up my family; I have every right to fuck up hers.

Besides, Sadie's going to get better. I can't miss my opportunity; I might not get another this good. Katrina cannot stay in my neighborhood. I wouldn't be able to survive.

This is my moment. I have to seize it, monstrous as it might seem.

She looks up, and her eyes are dry. That helps me a little. "Why are you here?" she asks, none too friendly. That helps, too.

"I've been through this before," I say. "I've had a sick child, too."

"In this hospital?"

I nod. "I remember being in this very cafeteria."

It's a gamble, what I'm about to do. I read this book once about going undercover, and it said you should always use your real name and lie as little as possible. That way, you won't have so much to remember, and you're less likely to trip yourself up.

The book also said that you should find something to like in even the vilest people. Find an area of common ground. See if they love their families like you love yours, if you're into the same sports team, even. You want to like them, at least a little, in order to make them like you.

Fat chance of that.

So lying isn't recommended when you're undercover, but I need to build trust quickly. Besides, it doubles as kindness. She wants to know about another child who went through this and survived.

"What happened?" she asks.

"Same thing. Some weird virus at maybe six or seven months old. Eight days in the hospital and then a full recovery. The staff here is amazing. They know what they're doing."

"Some seem to care. Others just seem so rushed."

"That's because they have to be everywhere at once. It's because they're working so hard. And how could anyone not care about Sadie? They'd have to be total monsters."

"Sometimes," she whispers, "I think this wasn't an accident."

"What do you mean?"

"That someone tried to hurt her. Is that crazy?"

If she's telling me this, then she doesn't think I'm the one who did it. Unless she's telling me *because* she thinks I'm the one who did it. She could be baiting me.

I keep my face as composed and empathetic as I can. "When your child is sick, you have all kinds of crazy thoughts. Believe me, I know. I remember."

She's got her fingers back in the croissant in a manner that's oddly proctologic. "You're going to tell them, aren't you?"

"Tell whom?" She doesn't answer. "What happens in the hospital stays in the hospital. I'm the one who wanted to be here with you." She stares at me. "I mean, a bunch of the neighbors wanted to be here. We thought I'd be the best choice because I've been through it."

I see from her face that she's not quite ready to buy what I'm selling.

Speaking of buying and selling, I wonder if before all this happened, she was going to opt in or out, which way she was leaning. I was the one who pushed the hardest to make her a regular so quickly. Sure, the others liked her, and sure, the spreadsheet could use some new possibilities, but I thought a proposition like that, so soon, would send her running for the hills. Instead, she was supposedly still thinking about it, and then we all got invitations to a barbecue. Maybe Katrina really has changed. Or maybe I'm just really bad at this.

"You've got enough to worry about," I tell her. "Don't stress at all about my repeating anything we say. Everything is off the record."

Eyes down again. "You met Scott and Melody?"

"Yes."

"What were your initial impressions?"

It's clearly a test. If I say they seemed great but she hates them, or if I say they seem like pieces of work and she adores them, or if I give some milquetoast answer . . . With abuse survivors, you might not get that many chances. You can lose credibility in an instant, and the relationship will never recover.

So I've got to go with my gut. "Scott seemed OK, but I'd watch out for her."

Her eyes widen. "That's what I think, too! Doug says I'm totally off base."

"I'm into people who are kind, not nice. You can't trust nice. And she's got nice written all over her."

Katrina smiles. "You hit the nail on the head." Then the smile dissolves. "Doug and I can't even talk about her right now. That's why he's not here. He stormed off after I said something neutral. He thought I was insulting her. I wouldn't do that. Not now."

Huh. Not now. That means something happened recently. So it wasn't just generic or stress-related tension I observed; there was an inciting event and a history underpinning it.

"That's rough," I say. "Marriages can be minefields." Kind of like these conversations.

"I get scared sometimes, since Doug and his mom are so close."

"Scared of what?"

She hesitates, but just for a second. She's dying to tell someone. "I was so stupid. I trusted them, and now they've got all the power."

"In what way?"

"My credit's bad, so Scott, Melody, and Doug are the only names on the deed."

I'll have to file away that little nugget, see if it could be useful. It certainly won't hurt to feed her paranoia and get her to dig her own grave with the in-laws. It also gives me a backup angle: maybe I can get Doug to kick her out, if that's his house, not hers. Or let something slip to the in-laws . . . ?

"Just watch your back," I say, "that's all."

If she's busy watching her back, she won't even see me coming.

CHAPTER 25

KAT

I'm alone the next time she shows up. I'm alone a lot. Doug has made it very clear he doesn't want to be with me right now. What's unclear is why. Did he see that photo before I deleted it? Did he hear a rumor? Is this still about what I said to Sadie about Melody while I was in the shower? Or is it that he thinks another mother would have taken better care of Sadie? All of the above?

I'm afraid to ask. I don't even want to know.

But it means I'm left with my own terrified thoughts. I don't sleep. I can barely think. And I know I should stop telling her things, but a part of me feels like I'm already in so deep, and I can't just be in my head all the time. And for some reason I can't put my finger on, I trust her. Layton made it hard for me to trust myself, but Dr. Morrison always said I'm supposed to go with my instincts. My instincts say that this woman in front of me is a good person who wants to be here for me.

Just because she happens to live in the AV, alongside a certain nasty note writer, shouldn't automatically disqualify her.

Sadie's still attached to all her machines, but I'm cradling her.

"I didn't know you were allowed to take her out," she says.

"Didn't you hold your baby sometimes?"

"The rules must have changed."

"Wow, that would be awful, to never be able to pick her up." But even so, I don't take Sadie out much. I don't want to disturb her. She needs her sleep so she can fight the infection, whatever it is.

She looks like she's sleeping right now. I don't know if it's sleep or some other loss of consciousness. I just know that I'm desperate for her to come back, for good. She doesn't have the energy to be her feisty self.

There's been no diarrhea today, but her iron count is even lower. It's like one thing gets better and something else gets worse. They still don't know what's wrong. And she won't drink my milk; it's still all intravenous fluids. I pump out rivers, and the nurses label the bottles and put them away for me like we might need them later.

She'll never catch up with all that milk. I should just dump it, but I can't. It would be like saying she's not going to get better.

"Sadie's going to get better," she says. It's jarring, as if she could read my thoughts. Maybe it's that they're such obvious thoughts. Any mother would have them.

"In the night, she had chills along with her fever. It was so terrible. She was just lying there, vibrating, and it took a while for the medicine to work. All I could do was watch. I was afraid to touch her, afraid I'd make it worse." I pull Sadie closer to me, but gently. "She'll be here a few more days at least." I carefully put Sadie back inside the cube, realizing she hasn't stirred during this entire conversation. Would someone tell me if she were comatose? Would a mother know? Maybe not this mother.

I let my hands hang, limp and useless, at my sides. "I smell! I haven't changed my clothes! I've been pretending we're going home any hour now, any day. Doug's gone home to shower."

"Is he bringing you some clothes back? They probably have a shower you can use here at the hospital—"

"I don't care! I don't care how I look or how I smell! I deserve to stink!"

Before Doug, I didn't think I had what it took to be a mother. Maybe I was right. Another mother would have gotten her help sooner. Another mother wouldn't have engendered such bad will in her new neighborhood that . . .

I wanted so much to have a community, and look what happened.

I don't even know what I'm thinking anymore.

I crumple into the chair.

A nurse comes in at just that moment. She's young and perky, pretty but for an astonishing overbite. "Hi," she says with a slight Southern twang. "I'm Kendall."

"Hi," I say listlessly.

There's a sweetness to Kendall, an innocence, but I wish Sadie had someone a little more seasoned.

Kendall checks Sadie's vitals. She's bad at the baby blood pressure cuff and has to redo it. Sadie wakes with an earsplitting cry.

I look up, almost happy. "That's Sadie's cry," I say. "The angry cry. Distinctive as a fingerprint."

I move behind the Plexiglas cube and put my hands flat against Sadie's cheeks. I tell her it'll be OK. The cries continue, louder, if that's possible, and still, this is the happiest I've been since I brought Sadie to the ER. "You tell 'em, girl!" I say.

We listen to the symphony of Sadie's machines, in concert with the machines behind all the other curtains. My joy fades. Doug should have been back at the hospital a while ago; it doesn't take two hours to shower. Should I text him and tell him that Sadie did her angry cry? He hasn't answered my other messages.

"Could you maybe go find Doug for me?" It might seem like a strange request, but it's not like she's a threat. She's not going to seduce Doug in a hospital.

"Where do you think he is?"

"I don't know. The cafeteria, maybe? Somewhere with his parents? He hasn't answered my texts." I'm a little embarrassed to say it. But I can't leave Sadie alone while I try to find her wayward father. "He's having trouble with this whole thing."

"It's hard having a baby in the hospital, no doubt."

"I feel like maybe he blames me, because I was the one home with her when she got sick."

"I'm sure he doesn't blame you."

"I didn't have much of a mother. Melody, Doug's mother, was apparently the perfect mom."

An inscrutable expression crosses her face. "No one gets the perfect mom."

"Melody thinks that I can't possibly be expected to know what I'm doing because of my own mother. She condescends to me all the time." What I'm really afraid of is that she's fueling Doug's negativity about me. She's always thought I'd be a disappointment as a mother, and now he does, too. "But maybe Melody's right. Maybe she would have known her baby was sick much earlier than I did. Maybe I didn't take care of Sadie the way I should have."

"You did the best you could, Katrina."

My head snaps up, and my stomach drops. No one in the AV calls me Katrina.

Seeing my reaction, she explains, "That's what Melody and Scott called you, when I ran into them in the hospital room."

It makes sense. But still. "I go by Kat. You know that."

"You're a great mom, Kat. You are. The whole block can see it."

What else can the whole block see, I wonder? Not for the first time.

CHAPTER 26

ELLEN

The anger keeps coming back to me, little aftershocks. I try to stop thinking about what Katrina said about perfect mothers.

I had a perfect mother, and Katrina killed her.

Technically, it was cancer, but it wasn't even a year after our world came crashing down. I know what really caused her death. It was humiliation. I almost died of it, too.

But I managed to get through, and I became a mother, and that allowed me to let go of so much of the anger. My transformation—both physical and emotional—was complete with that baby in my arms.

The AV helped, too. To come from where I did, with all the losses and pain and the infamy, to a place of initial anonymity and, later, full acceptance and love . . . it brought me back to life. And now Katrina wants to take it away. She wants to co-opt it and make it hers.

I will not let her destroy this new family of mine, the AV family, like she did the last.

Speaking of home, I've been neglecting my duties because I've been so consumed with Katrina. There's barely any food in the house, so I have to stop off at Trader Joe's, where I immediately run into Val and Patrick. It's the one downside of my new life: when I want to be anonymous again, I can't really pull it off.

Val asks immediately about Sadie, and she and Patrick both look shaken up when I tell them that there's been no change.

"I can't imagine," Val murmurs.

"Our kids were always so healthy," Patrick says. While he seems genuinely sad, he can't keep his eyes from grazing my chest. Maybe what he's saddest about is that he never got the chance to try and seduce Katrina. Kat—I have to remember to start using that name in my head, otherwise "Katrina" is going to slip out again. I had to do a lot of trust building and damage control to come back from that.

I can never see Val without thinking of the stripper pole she installed in their walk-in closet and the private lessons she took on how to use it. All that, and Patrick still strays. You just can't keep some people on their leash. Of course, he has permission, but everyone knows—and Patrick must realize—that Val doesn't want an open marriage. She knows it's either give permission or he'll just do it anyway behind her back. Not on the block, we'd respect their opt-out, but there's a whole world out there.

For a while, the spreadsheet said Val was available for casual flings, no overnights, never in her own bed. According to Brandon, there were no takers, so she changed it to say she was off-limits. Maybe that was for pride's sake, or maybe she thought that men would want what they couldn't have and it would create some interest. As far as I know, that never happened.

Even with the supposed feminism of openness, a sixty-three-year-old man does better than a fifty-five-year-old woman. Patrick's been with a surprising number of the spreadsheet's women. His reputation does a lot of the heavy lifting: he'll give and give, and he gets off on that so fully that he never needs to receive. That tongue of his is legendary. It knows just where to go, it never gets tired, and the beauty of it is, since you don't have to see his face, you can just fantasize about whoever you want, for hours.

The other good thing about Patrick is that he takes rejection well. He just backs away, hands in the air to show he's harmless, no pressure, no hard feelings. Some others on the block should take notes.

Revenge fucking, trophy scoring, saying "I love you" only to be dumped immediately, sexual obsession . . . Not to mention, there's never enough time for balancing/juggling the spouse and the kids with an outside person; something has to give; it's a scheduling and logistical nightmare. The spouse feels neglected, the household chores are neglected, and sexual needs go unfulfilled because one person is already fulfilled on the outside, so then the other might have to go seeking, causing the same scenarios but in reverse. And while the husband can try to satisfy his wife with his hand or mouth, his lover is often getting the dick. So there's loneliness, resentment, and loss, but somehow, no one wants to stop, because the carousel ride itself is addictive, because everyone else is doing it, and who said peer pressure stops at a certain age? It doesn't; it goes on and on and on . . .

Would I live anywhere else, though? No, I wouldn't. These are my best friends, and we're in it together, no matter what. The system we've crafted is complex and, at times, downright ugly, but there's love and beauty in it, too. And sex, of course. Lots of that. It beats all the alternatives. Families are messy. Maybe that was the problem with my family growing up. It was too good to be true.

No, it wasn't too good. It just seemed that way to other people, so they wanted to tear it down. They envied us, Katrina most of all. That's the only explanation I've ever been able to come up with for how she could do what she did.

But enough about Katrina—Kat—for one day. I need to think happy thoughts. Funny thoughts.

I remember when Brandon first told me about the stripper pole and the lessons, and we couldn't stop giggling over the image of Val suspended from it, naked but for the fanny pack, while Patrick texted other women on the block madly to see who was available for some quickie cunnilingus. Brandon and I used to laugh together and then say how bad we were being, and that we needed to stop, poor Val, and then we'd laugh some more. Because sometimes it's just good to be bad.

Ilsa didn't agree. That's why she and Nils had to go.

"I've texted Kat, but she hasn't responded," Val says. "I don't have Doug's number. Could you just let them know we're thinking of them? As soon as they're comfortable having more visitors, we'd love to see them. You're sure we can't bring them a lasagna or something?"

"I'm sure. They just want space."

"Of course," Patrick says, his eyes again stopping at my breasts. I don't even mind. It's just a quirk of his, a tic.

Val sees it, and she clearly does mind.

"I should buy this stuff." I indicate the contents of my cart. "And get back to the hospital."

Later that day, when I arrive, Doug and Kat are whispering heatedly. I try to loiter outside the curtain to make out their words, but Kendall calls out a greeting to me and when I answer, the voices cease.

"Hey," I say, drawing back the curtain.

"Hey!" Doug is too hearty, as usual. Kat looks upset as she squeezes out a hi.

"Is it a bad time?"

"Not at all," Doug answers as Kat says, "Yes." She adds, "Doug was just headed out to the waiting room. You can walk with him." She won't look at him as she tells him to send in his mom or dad, whoever. The implication is clear: she'll take anyone over him at the moment.

Doug and I head out into the hall, removing our gowns on the way.

I put my hand on Doug's arm, stalling his progress. He's in jeans and a T-shirt with a tiny hole at the collar, wearing way too much cologne. The bags under his eyes aren't nearly as pronounced as Kat's. "Are you OK?" I ask him. It wouldn't hurt to buddy up to him, try to get some information or give some, depending on what's most advantageous to me. His rift with Kat could pay dividends, especially since he and his parents own the house that I want Kat to vacate.

I sense his uncertainty. He's not sure how to play this. His veil is different, yet in his way, he's guarded, too. He hides behind layers of joviality.

"I'm holding my own," he says. "I just need to support Kat. She can be kind of fragile."

Yeah, dude, you really seemed to be supporting her back behind that curtain. "Were you mad at each other? It was kind of intense in there."

His eyes darken. "It can be intense having a sick baby. You should know, right?"

So Kat told him my lie. But from his tone, I'm not sure he believes it. "Yes," I say, "I know."

"It seems like you and Kat have gotten pretty close, pretty quickly."

"We understand each other."

He colors. He's wondering what I know that he doesn't. "Is there a reason you're the AV's representative?"

"I was the first to volunteer, and now Kat doesn't want anyone else just showing up. She trusts me."

"And what about what I want? Who I trust?"

"They're assuming Kat speaks for both of you. Doesn't she?"

"I like people!" he nearly yells. A nurse walking by casts him a quick reproving glance, and he gives her a reflexive smile. That's his tic. "I like people," he says softly. "We moved to the AV to have them around, and now she's making the executive decision to only have you here."

"Well," I say finally, "talk to your wife about it."

He turns and stalks away, leaving me to follow him.

In the waiting room, I see someone he'd apparently prefer. It's Andie, in a halter dress and high-heeled sandals. Doug seems happy to see her, yet not surprised. Did he call her? Or did she call him? The block knows to go through me, but Andie's not exactly on the block.

She's sitting beside Doug's parents, and they're all talking like old friends. Andie's good at forging connections with people immediately. It's crossed my mind before that it's an act, just a really good one, but Nolan assures me that Andie is 100 percent real. And I have to admit, the vast majority of the time I'm as captivated by Andie as everyone else. She's like the cheerleader that you just can't manage to hate, because she's rooting for you, too. She has a star quality that somehow only burns brighter because she reveals just enough of her foibles—her messy car, her shyness at girls' night, the bitten nails with the hundred-dollar manicure.

Scott has his finger in a paperback spy thriller, holding his place, while Andie and Melody talk with great animation. At Doug's entrance, Andie leaps to her feet and embraces him, rubbing his back in a way that seems far too intimate. But Andie is a truly friendly person, and an empathetic one, so perhaps I'm misreading the situation. Andie's the one who wanted to opt out of the spreadsheet. No one questions her love for Nolan.

When she sees me behind Doug, she releases him immediately. She greets me with an equally giant hug, sans the back rub, almost like she's trying to illustrate just how normal her previous one had been. But then, Andie is a touchy-feely sort of person.

"You met Andie?" Doug asks his parents.

"She introduced herself," Melody says approvingly.

"Sadie's vitals were stable all last night and today," Doug reports. "No diarrhea, no fever." Doug grins. "The tests and cultures have all come back, and they're negative. If everything stays normal through tomorrow, this could be her last night in the PICU."

"That's great news," Melody says.

"Damn straight," Scott seconds.

"You must be so relieved." Andie gives Doug one of her sweet smiles.

"I'm feeling pretty good," Doug says. Then why did it look so awful between him and Kat just a few minutes ago? You'd think Sadie's recovery would have brought them together. "If all goes well, Sadie'll move to a regular hospital room for observation, and then she comes home."

My emotions are a complicated brew. I'm happy that Sadie's turned a corner. I'd love to see her acting like a normal baby again—squirming and squalling and laughing. But it means that I have a lot of work left and not much time. At the hospital, I can just keep stopping by, but once Kat's home, I'll need to be invited in. She could freeze me out so easily. She could connect with the other women, who'll greet her like a returning hero. This is a very loving neighborhood, after all. A forgiving one, too.

That's why I moved here. Unlike the other couples, I already knew about openness, and I was trying to get in. Not just to the AV but to that very block.

Really, I was recruited. No, that's too strong a word. Lured. No, still wrong. It's more like I was convinced, told that it would help my marriage, and I believed that it would.

Through years of experience and observation, here's what I've learned: when openness works, it works because it's temporary. People can talk differently and flirt differently because they don't have to look each other in the eyes for the rest of their lives. They avoid the routine. They don't have to do the boring stuff, like getting the kids ready for school. They'll never depend on each other. They can fuck without giving a fuck.

Sex slows down in marriage because it's hard to really share yourself with someone, tell them everything about yourself, and then still want them sexually. Openness tries to give people a way around that, and sometimes it works, and sometimes it doesn't. But I love that the AV lets you try.

"Well, let's go celebrate," Scott says, getting to his feet. "Should we take a trip to the cafeteria?"

"I've barely been eating, but all of a sudden, I'm ravenous," Doug says. He asks Andie if she wants to go with them. I'm conspicuously left out.

Melody and Scott probably wish Kat was more like Andie—poised, expensively dressed, with impeccable social graces. Kat probably wishes that herself.

I hate when I start feeling sorry for Katrina.

Melody has wound her arm through Scott's, and they're about to head to the cafeteria. I'm hoping Andie will go with them, and then I can get some alone time with Kat.

But instead, Andie turns to Doug and then to me, asking, "Could I be the one to go in next? I haven't seen Kat or Sadie in days."

"Sure." Doug smiles at her like she's a real gem. He continues to ignore me.

"I'll go in afterward," I say quickly.

Andie picks up a bulging canvas bag from one of the chairs. "I brought Kat some things." She holds up items one at a time, brandishing them like a spokesmodel. There's pricey shampoo, conditioner, and body wash; a travel-size blow-dryer; and layers of clothes (T-shirts, a lightweight cardigan, and yoga pants, all of them expensive with the tags still on). So Kat can smell—and dress—like Andie.

The way Andie's looking at Doug, and that bag for Kat . . . If I didn't know Andie better, if I wasn't so sure of her love for Nolan, I'd think something strange was going on. But what I know and what I'll tell Kat are two very different things.

"I also brought energy drinks and snacks, and some books and toys for Sadie," Andie continues.

"Looks like you thought of everything!" Doug says admiringly.

He's not talking about me, but he should have been.

CHAPTER 27

KAT

"Could I hold her?" she asks.

I'm surprised by my reaction, which is nearly feral. I clutch Sadie in an involuntary spasm, a protective instinct. No, a maternal instinct.

She takes it in stride. "Now that she's finally better, I can understand you not wanting to let go of her," she says.

We're both wearing our masks, which serves to intensify our eye contact. I just feel like I know her. She's here for me, and I need that. Especially after Andie's visit, which was unsettling to say the least. All those questions about how Doug's holding up, how our marriage is holding up, but nothing about how I'm holding up. And that mini-me bag. It all felt off.

But the woman in front of me right now, the woman who's been coming here every day to support me, she's truly my friend. She doesn't blink, doesn't look away. She's got nothing to hide.

"There's something I need to tell you," I say. I peer down at Sadie, who has fallen asleep. Slowly and carefully, I transfer her back to the Plexiglas cube. "She drank my milk this morning."

"Awesome!"

"It really was. It's like, she's becoming herself again. For a while there, she just disappeared. She was just a body. But now it's like her spirit has flown back in. Her soul. Not that I'm religious or anything."

"I get what you mean."

I feel like she does, that's the thing.

I should be in a great mood. Sadie's getting better. Soon, she should be coming home. Only I know, in my heart, that the AV should not be our home.

Doug feels differently, and we had an argument behind the curtain, conducted entirely in heated whispers. He told me we shouldn't make any rash decisions, that lots of people would kill to be where we are. I told him that maybe someone tried to—that maybe it's not a coincidence that Sadie got so sick, after we've been getting all those notes. That's when he told me I was being crazy. And that's when I told him that he might want to stay there for more than the school system, that maybe he wants to stay for the women. He stormed out.

But is it really so crazy? I have someone here who might know.

"There's something I need to get off my chest," I say. "Ever since the block party, I've been getting these notes."

"What kind of notes?"

"The first one said, 'That wasn't very neighborly of you.'"

"Do you know what they were talking about?"

I shake my head. "They just kept coming. They were more antagonistic and personal and threatening. Like someone had a vendetta against me. Doug wants to believe they're harmless, like a prank or something."

She's nodding slowly. I can't tell if she's surprised.

"Do you know anything about the letters? Who might have written them?"

She shakes her head.

"Have you heard anything? Anyone who has a problem with me?"
Another headshake.

"I saved the notes," I say. "I can show you if you want."

"No, I believe you. I'm just thinking . . ."

"What are you thinking?"

"I'm just thinking how incredibly awful that must have been for you. You're a new mom, in your new neighborhood, and someone's targeting you."

My eyes tear up. She gets it, when my own husband doesn't. "It has been awful."

"And scary. I mean, you don't know what they're capable of."

"Do you have any reason to think that any of our neighbors are dangerous or violent?"

"No. No reason."

But she doesn't sound as sure as I would have hoped. She's taking me seriously, and that's actually even scarier.

"Sadie's a lot better," I say, looking around, wanting to knock on wood but realizing we're surrounded by metal, "but they still don't know what landed her here. By process of elimination, they're assuming it's a virus, but they don't know which one or how she picked it up."

"The world's a germy place."

"Sadie had never been sick before. Then we go away for a few nights and when we come back, bam."

"What do you think happened?"

"Maybe someone snuck into our house while we were away and did something. Like they contaminated her crib sheet or her changing table, something like that." I pause. "I know how it sounds, but it's not just notes. A package went missing, and something got slipped in my drink at girls' night; I'm sure of it. And now this. We're dealing with a psychopath here."

The more I say it out loud, the more plausible it seems. Maybe that's in part because of her expression. She's really considering the possibility. And she's a denizen of the AV. She knows those people way better than I do.

"What would you do if it were your daughter?" I say.

"I don't know . . ."

"I can see that you do know."

She meets my eyes. "I wouldn't go back to that house."

"Because Sadie's life is worth more than a house, right? How can Doug not see that?"

"He must not believe that Sadie's in danger."

"What does he know that I don't?"

"Or what do you know that he doesn't?" She gives me a meaningful look. "About the world we live in. Maybe he's the naive one."

"Maybe he is."

I'm getting an eerie feeling. Like she gets me a little too much.

"Listen," she says, "you're a mother. If you need to protect your daughter, you'll find a way."

Leave my husband, is that what she's saying? Give up on the only family I've known?

"Can I tell you something, and I think in your heart, you'll know it's true?"

I take a deep breath and nod.

"There might be another reason Doug doesn't want to move. I think there's something going on between him and Andie."

"What makes you think that?" I ask. She's echoing my own suspicions from earlier, when I saw Andie and had this feeling like something wasn't right. The question I'd been posing for weeks—why is she pursuing me?—now has an answer. She was pursuing Doug.

"It started on girls' night out."

"The first one? Or the second?" But I can answer my own question. "The second, while I was passed out."

"Yes."

"Andie's more his type," I say.

"More his family's type, you mean?"

"Why, what did you see?"

"They were getting on like gangbusters in the waiting room. They practically adopted her."

He's got all the money. His name's on the deed. He's in control. I'm in debt, and I haven't even returned to work yet. I'm not getting paid while I'm on leave.

I'm trapped.

But I can't leap to conclusions. Just because Andie came in here and brought me body wash and body lotion that made me smell like her . . . just because she talked like she knew my husband's emotions better than I did . . . just because my alarm bells were ringing, telling me that this woman could even be the one writing the notes because she wants me out of the picture and she wants my husband . . .

I can't jump to conclusions. I have to talk to Doug. But he's been avoiding me, like a man with something to hide.

"I thought I was giving Sadie such a good family," I say. "But maybe I never really knew what a family was."

CHAPTER 28

ELLEN

On my drive home, I pass by the park. I've always liked that place, even before it got so ridiculously over-the-top fancy. I liked when it was just swings, a slide, and a climbing structure on top of concrete rather than wood chips and mats, back before everyone was so afraid of lawsuits and children's boredom. It makes me remember the early days of motherhood, when it was all promise and expectation.

Really, it couldn't have gone better today. Kat seemed to just take my word that Doug was having an affair. She might never come back to that house of hers. Who names their house Crayola, anyway? She'll be better off without that guy. I've done her a favor.

But I'm not happy, not at all.

She used the word *psychopath*, and I can't stop thinking about it. I have crossed lines no normal person would cross, because she crossed all sorts of lines. She caused me so much pain. But what if she's right, and I really am a psychopath?

I'm just stressed out, that's all. Operation Kat has taken over my life. Maybe it's that I've been missing so much of my own family. I know I can be a better mother than I've been lately—so consumed by my own history, with the latent hatred of Katrina roaring back to life. Since she moved in, I've been fighting the memories. The nightmares have returned. Then there's the anger I'd tried so hard to extinguish. That's why I know I need to get Kat out of the AV. I need to be the best mother I can. But sometimes I feel like I'm just using Kat as a reason to avoid things at home, that she's a convenient excuse for the mess I've made of my own life.

Soon, this will all be over. I'll be free of Katrina, and my past will be back where it belongs. I'm doing this for my family, for their future as much as my own.

The ketamine wasn't my idea or my preference, but it has worked in my favor. It's primed her to believe something as preposterous as someone poisoning her daughter. I don't think she's even suspected that it might be more than one person, that multiple people are trying to drive her out.

Kat might not have been with Wyatt under normal circumstances, but it was shockingly easy to get her to compromise herself, given how compromised she was. All we had to do was get her and Wyatt outside and move out of the way. She practically pounced on him. No sex drive, my ass. She just isn't driven toward Doug. And Wyatt showing up that night, already drunk, and he and Yolanda were clearly having words that ended with her yanking her arm away . . . that was all too easy, too. Everyone knows that when Wyatt gets tired of dealing with Yolanda, he rushes into other women's arms temporarily, even though he's going to get an earful when he gets home. Wyatt seems to have taken the idea that it's better to seek forgiveness than permission to heart.

While the ketamine wasn't my idea, the pictures were. And sending them to Yolanda from Kat's phone had, I thought, been a stroke of genius. That way, it would look like Kat had opted in the second she had the chance, and that she wanted to rub Yolanda's nose in it.

It had been my insurance policy: if the openness didn't freak Kat out enough to make her want to leave, then Yolanda telling everyone what Kat had done and the resulting ostracism would. Kat would watch her shiny new future go up in smoke.

Instead, I never heard a peep. Everyone could tell that Yolanda didn't like the new girl anymore, but she wouldn't say why. My suspicion is that she didn't want the humiliation, and that she has something else in mind for those pictures, like keeping Wyatt right where she wants him, doing penance. Maybe it'll even give her the leverage she needs to finally opt out.

I'm not the biggest fan of Yolanda, with her myriad insecurities, but I do care about Wyatt, and I'm sorry that he's become collateral damage.

Lately, I'm just feeling so alone. When this started, I felt like I had support, but it's been dwindling. It could be an attack of conscience or a loss of faith. All I know is, there's been more distance since Sadie got sick.

Or he might have problems of his own, but I can't be sure. He doesn't burden me with things like that.

I've just got this feeling like things are spiraling and soon it might be beyond any of our control.

CHAPTER 29

KAT

I just keep picturing them together. Andie and Doug.
Thinking how much better she is than me, in all ways. I
can't compete.

It's late at night, and Doug is out in the waiting room. I'm practically delirious from the days of sleep deprivation and the stress and
strain of trying to figure out what's really happening in the AV, who's
after me, who's after him. I still haven't confronted him, though my
imagination is running wild.

It's like texting is a direct link to my subconscious.

Maybe we should opt in, I write. Maybe that would solve all our
problems. Then Doug can sow his oats and my family stays intact.

She texts back, Are those really all your problems?

There's the notes. There's the ketamine. There's the possible poisoning of my child. But if Doug and I were just stronger, if we were back

to being ourselves, we could survive anything. We could figure this out together. Maybe leaving Crayola isn't the only way. Together, we could find the culprit and make it all stop.

We've always been a team. I can't let the AV tear us apart. That's just what whoever wrote those notes wants. They want me to doubt my husband, my marriage, and my sanity.

How do you know that Doug and Andie are together? Who told you?

It's all over the block. Everyone knows. It started the same night you kissed Wyatt.

So that's all over the block, too?

Yes.

Does Doug know everything? I mean, does he know I kissed Wyatt?

That I don't know. But if I had to venture a guess, I'd say yes.

So we cheated the same night. But I was drugged. What's his excuse? Was it revenge, because Andie told him about Wyatt? Or was that just how he gave himself permission to do what he already wanted? Who he already wanted.

Kat, are you still up?

Kat, are you OK?

I'm always up, but nothing's OK.

CHAPTER 30

ELLEN

Sadie's in a regular room, and I'm dying to see her.

Poor choice of words, perhaps.

But I just want to verify with my own eyes that she's on the mend, that no babies have been harmed in the making of this revenge tale.

Also, I have to remind Kat of what she has to do to save that precious little girl of hers. Last night, I felt her wavering. She even mentioned opting in. That would be the worst-case scenario for me: not only does Kat stay in the neighborhood, she invades the spreadsheet. She gets into the AV even deeper.

Doug's talking on his cell phone outside the room, and when he sees me approaching, he ends the call and stands directly in my path.

"I want you to leave my family alone," he says. He's not angry, exactly, more like grave.

"I'm Kat's friend."

"I'll bet you are." It's like he knows that I can't be trusted, like he's actually looking after his wife for once, the way a husband is supposed to.

What did Kat tell him? Or could it have been Andie?

It would be so like Katrina to tell him about our conversation and make it sound like I'm at fault, like I'm the bad influence. I know she's capable of lying, no matter who gets hurt.

I force myself to stay calm. "I'm Kat's closest friend," I say. "I'm the one who's helped her through all this when you were MIA."

"MIA?" He scoffs. "I've been here the whole time."

"There've been some unexplained absences."

He glowers. "I think you should leave now."

"I want to see Kat and Sadie. I want to make sure they're all right."

"Everyone's doing great. Sadie's going to be discharged tomorrow. The last thing we need is stress."

"I don't stress Kat out; I alleviate her stress. Can you say the same?"

I start to walk around him, and he grips my arm.

"Do you want this getting around the neighborhood?" I ask. "That you manhandle women?"

Of course that does the trick. Gotta protect his image. He lets go and steps to the side. "I'm sorry," he says. "All of this does a number on your head." He sounds sincere, but whatever.

Inside the room, Andie is chatting up Scott and Melody, while Kat plays with Sadie. I can't believe Kat would allow Doug's presumed mistress entrance into her private life. It's like she's got no self-respect at all.

The room has two cribs, one at each end, but Sadie's the only child there, so the family's commandeered the entire space. There's an actual door and a window. Even though it's antiseptically white and the view is of the busy boulevard below, it feels lavish compared to Sadie's previous accommodations.

Sadie is responding to Kat with smiles and giggles. When Kat sees me, she looks pleased, and I cast a triumphant look in Doug's direction.

He doesn't notice. He's already too engaged in the conversation with Andie and his parents. I can't tell if Kat is isolating herself or being frozen out, but there are two camps: Kat and me versus the rest of them. It's like there's one of those invisible electric fences down the center of the room. It looks to me like Kat's in-laws are embracing the mistress.

"So, how are you?" I ask Kat. As in love with Sadie as she looks, she also appears entirely exhausted, on the verge of collapse.

"They think it must have been a virus," Kat says. "They're still not really sure. I just need to focus on the most important thing, which is that everything's under control and she's being discharged tomorrow."

"Where are you taking her?"

"I'm taking her home." Do I detect a note of defiance, like Kat's telling me my plan isn't working? Or maybe she just thinks she has no other choice but to go home, so she might as well act like it's what she would have chosen anyway. I know a little something about denial. Or at least, my therapist said I do.

"I'm feeling a little tired," I hear Melody say. She looks lovingly across the room at Sadie, and then she crosses the line. "Could I hold her before I go?" she asks Kat with exaggerated deference.

Kat nods and gives Sadie up. Then she goes and stands by the window, like she can't bear to look at Sadie in anyone else's arms. Scott and Doug encircle Melody and Sadie, a perfect little family tableau.

"We're going to drive home now," Scott announces. "I think Melody and I could use a night in our own bed."

Melody is making a great show of her reluctance as she hands Sadie to Doug. Then she gives Kat a pro forma kiss on the cheek, while Scott doesn't even bother. They close the door softly on their way out.

Then there were three. Well, four, counting Sadie, but three is so much more Agatha Christie. I loved those books. Kat and I loved them together. We spent an entire summer in the library, reading through the shelf.

Sadie is still in Doug's arms, and now Andie's standing way too close to them, alternately cooing at Sadie and looking up into Doug's face. I don't know if she's trying to put on a show and make Kat feel awful or she's so into Doug as to be completely oblivious. I've never doubted her love and devotion to Nolan before, but now . . .

Speak of the devil. I notice Nolan is standing in the doorway, his hands clenched around Fisher's stroller. I don't know how long he's been watching Andie and Doug, but there's a darkness in his face that I've only seen a few times before. Then he's saying, "Hello! Room for two more?" in a compensatory, jolly tone.

Doug leaps up, replacing Sadie unceremoniously in her crib. She emits a protest cry that he doesn't even dignify. He radiates guilt. "So great to see you, Nolan!"

"I didn't know you were coming," Andie tells him. She gives him that same smile she gave me just a moment ago. Either she's not guilty or she's much better at concealing it than Doug is.

"I wanted to surprise you." Still in that same jovial tone, but Nolan's eyes are hard. He rolls Fisher forward. "You've been spending so much time here. I thought you might be missing your son."

Nolan and I trade greetings. Then he bends down to release Fisher from the stroller's bindings and, without another word, thrusts Fisher into her arms. She's clearly startled but recovers well, smiling and cooing at Fisher.

Nolan is watching her and Fisher with that same granite expression. For a second, I think that he could be capable of anything. He's that angry with her. He's not the type to allow himself to be cuckolded, not after all he's overcome in his life.

Nolan approaches Kat and pecks her on the cheek. "I'm so glad that Sadie's better," he says. I realize that he hasn't looked at Doug at all, which seems more intense than if they'd been locked in a stare-down. He reaches into the area beneath the stroller seat and brings out a grocery bag. "I brought dinner for everyone. Are you hungry?"

"I forgot to eat lunch," Kat says, as if she's just become aware of the existence of this thing we call food. "We were waiting for them to come and move Sadie, and then we waited some more, and now . . ." It's four thirty. "So yes, I'm hungry. Thank you."

Doug approaches Nolan and claps him on the shoulder in manly appreciation. "You're awesome, thanks."

Nolan just starts laying out the food like Doug hasn't even spoken.

Taking in Nolan's demeanor, it's clear that he believes something really is going on under his nose. I want Kat to think it's true; I don't want it to actually be true. Nolan loves Andie so much. He'd be destroyed.

Doug fixes a plate and then brings it over to Kat in an attempt to prove he's a nice guy. Well, wrong room, buddy. Neither Nolan nor I are buying it. But Andie might be, and she could be his actual target audience.

Kat takes the plate without a word. That's a good sign, from where I'm sitting. She's picking up on what's going on between Nolan and Andie, too, which validates my story. I had to tell a few lies in the texts about how everyone knows about Kat and Wyatt and about Andie and Doug, but it's for a good cause.

Nolan says to Andie gruffly, "Who's eating first?" Then, to no one in particular, "Eating in shifts. You know how it is."

"You eat first," Andie says. She's on her feet, dancing with Fisher, moving him toward Sadie's crib. "See, it's Sadie. You know Sadie. She's starting to feel better." Fisher stares down at Sadie, and his fussing ceases. It occurs to me that it's not very wise to bring their baby into a hospital. The place is a giant petri dish. Either Nolan is oblivious to that or too angry with Andie to care.

Nolan sits with his plate on his lap, watching Andie and Fisher with little expression. "This is good," I tell him, the mashed potatoes melting away on my tongue, and he registers it with the briefest of smiles.

Andie gives him a sudden sharp look, at odds with the sweetly maternal tone she's been using on Fisher. "Hurry up and eat," she says. "I'm starving."

"Then why didn't you tell me to take Fisher first?" Nolan stands up and storms over to her. I flinch. I feel like I'm watching the homecoming queen and the captain of the football team devolve into domestic violence. Doug must have the same thought because he half rises, like he's going to intercede if anything dicey happens. So chivalry is not dead; it's just displaced, onto the other woman.

Nolan maneuvers so that he takes Fisher from her and simultaneously thrusts his plate into her hand. "Here. Eat," he commands over Fisher's crying.

"Give him back to me," Andie says. "He's calm with me."

"But you're starving, remember?"

Andie glares at him and then takes a seat, rapidly shoveling forkfuls into her mouth. I've never seen anything like this between them.

So it must be true. Andie really is sleeping with Doug.

I'm angry on Nolan's behalf. There are men who deserve that, but he's not one of them.

Nolan is normally a good dad, but right then, he's terrible at soothing Fisher. He's rocking him and patting him on the back, talking in a higher register, repeating a lot of the same things Andie said but to the opposite effect. He's getting increasingly frustrated, and then it seems like the rocking is a little too much like shaking and I'm afraid, because who doesn't realize that you never shake a baby? Even though I'm definitely on Team Nolan rather than Team Andie, I'm glad when Andie takes Fisher back.

I can't take the tension another second. "Let's get out of here," I say to Kat, who's also shoveled in all her food.

"But . . ." Kat looks around, like she shouldn't leave Nolan, Andie, and Doug alone, and then it seems like she gets my meaning: We should absolutely leave them alone. Let Nolan take care of whatever's going on between Andie and Doug.

She follows me up the hall. There's an alcove with some seats in it, the walls painted in a woodsy nature scene, bright birds in the boughs.

"I can't leave Sadie for long," Kat says. "She needs me." A sudden smile. "She's been drinking my milk like crazy today. I thought for sure all that milk would go to waste, but no, she drank, like, eight bottles."

"That's great."

"That's why I've decided that no matter what, I'm preserving her family." She smiles again, like she's happy about this decision. She's not fooling either of us.

"You saw what was happening in that hospital room, right?" I just need to make sure she hasn't lost her faculties entirely, in the wrong direction. I mean, it's OK if her lunacy causes her to flee the neighborhood but not if it makes her determined to stay. No matter what. You should never utter that phrase in your life, because you never know what's going to matter.

"Doug and I just need to get home and get back to normal."

"The way he and Andie were acting . . . it's like they're throwing their affair in your face."

"They're friends."

"But the whole neighborhood—"

"The whole neighborhood could be wrong. I need to get Doug's side of the story."

"You mean you haven't even talked to him yet?" Annoyance crosses her face. As in, she's annoyed with me, not Doug. I lean in, infusing what I'm about to say with maximum meaning. "*I'm* your friend, and I'm telling you, you can't let him treat you like this. You can't go back to a house where you're getting threatening letters, where you don't know what's going to happen next. You don't know what someone's willing to do."

She looks at me with mistrust, and I realize that I might have made a fatal error. I've pitted myself against her husband, leveraging a friendship that she doesn't remember. She doesn't know who I really am.

"I'm in a glass house," she says, "and I shouldn't throw stones."

It takes me a few seconds to know that she's alluding to her and Wyatt, to what I helped orchestrate. That's part of how she's going to justify staying with her asshole husband? I can't even speak. This is all blowing up in my face. Every rotten thing I've done has been in vain.

No way. I'm going to finish the job, one way or another.

CHAPTER 31

KAT

DON'T COME BACK.

THIS IS A FRIENDLY WARNING.

The e-mail address is a bunch of numbers at Gmail. Untraceable, to me. But maybe it's time to get the police involved, instead of just taking the word of a neighbor who might have his own secrets to protect.

That neighbor was the only man I've kissed other than my husband in the past eight years. And I can't even remember it. Not sure if that makes it better or worse.

Is there any way that warning is really friendly?

I glance over at Sadie. She's in her hospital crib instead of that Plexiglas cube, and her sleep is that of a normal baby. She's just a few hours from discharge. Whoever wrote this e-mail must know that.

No, it certainly isn't friendly.

Doug's not here. He said that since Sadie's doing better, he needed to go to work today and start catching up. I still haven't asked him about Andie; it's just not the time or the place. We should be home for that.

I am afraid to be back in the AV, but I spoke to one of the doctors about the potential poisoning, and it was clear from his reaction that that's just impossible. So really, it all comes down to a bunch of notes and this e-mail. It's all the work of a bully, plain and simple. A coward who has never dared show her (or his) face. Meanwhile, I've been tearing my hair out, which must be the point. That's what the bully wants, right?

The vast majority of the AV is filled with good people, and no one is going to run me out of town (especially since I have nowhere to go, not if I want to save my marriage and my family. And I very much do).

The prevailing wisdom is that if you stand up to bullies, they cave. I've never tried that. The person who wrote those notes hasn't heard back from me at all. It's time to issue a threat of my own. They might think they've reduced me to a terrified wreck, but they need to know that I'm more of a cornered animal. A mama bear. I can strike back.

I try to respond to the e-mail, but it bounces back, undeliverable. So I log in to GoodNeighbors and write a friendly warning of my own.

It could just be the realization that my daughter is nearly healthy and I get to take her home; it could be post-stress euphoria. But I feel empowered for the first time in I don't know how long. I feel like I'm the mother Sadie needs, like we've survived the worst and we're only going to get stronger.

They were just some notes and an e-mail. OK, and some ketamine. But what's any of that compared to Sadie's life, which I will protect with my own? I will fight to the death for that little girl over there.

I look at the post with satisfaction, and then I curl up in the recliner, and finally, I sleep.

I awake to Dr. Vreeland, the cold fish who I met yesterday and didn't much like, though he did serve his purpose. He let me know that the idea of poisoning is nothing more than paranoia.

"Sorry to wake you," he says without a hint of a smile. But there is something odd in his manner, and it takes me a second to place it. It's remorse. He rolls a stool over to sit beside me and lowers his voice. "I'm also sorry for how I treated you."

I blink at him. Am I dreaming this? A doctor actually apologizing?

"I know I was dismissive of your earlier questions. But I've been thinking more about you, and about Sadie, and about her unusual presentation. When we spoke, I was in a rush, and I thought you were one of those people who just couldn't take good news at face value. Sadie is on her way to a full recovery, all the usual tests and cultures came back negative, but you were still so bent on figuring out the cause. It even sounded like you thought someone might have tried to harm her."

"It crossed my mind, but really, I just don't like unanswered questions."

"And honestly, I don't, either. So I gave her case more thought and more analysis. A lot of Sadie's symptoms actually correspond to a very rare bacteria called leptospirosis. But leptospirosis has a lot of symptoms, and like I said, it's rare. So rare that to make an absolute determination, we have to send Sadie's samples to the CDC in Atlanta. What I can say is that, based on her clinical presentation and by using microscopy to identify the spirochetes in her urine, leptospirosis may have been present."

I'm not exactly following him. "Does that mean she's not OK? That she's not being discharged?"

"No, her prognosis is very good, fortunately. But leptospirosis is found in the urine of cattle, pigs, horses, wild animals, and, rarely, in that of dogs. You notice how frequently the word *rare* is appearing in this conversation."

I nod, feeling like I might be dreaming after all. Nightmaring, actually.

"Humans can become contaminated through contact with the bodily fluids of an infected animal, or with water, soil, or food that's been contaminated by an infected animal. You don't have a dog, correct?"

"No."

"You don't live on a farm."

"No."

"Nor do your family members in Fort Bragg?"

"No."

"The people at highest risk for this very rare bacterial infection are farmers or those who work in sewers, mines, or slaughterhouses. That's why no one suspected leptospirosis in Sadie's case. That, and the infection mimics many other more common viruses."

"So you're saying that if it was leptospirosis, then Sadie was poisoned?"

"I've sent the sample to the CDC for more conclusive results, and what I'm telling you is preliminary; it wouldn't hold up in a court of law, but . . . if it were my daughter, I'd want to know."

I feel like I might have a panic attack, but Dr. Vreeland seems oblivious. He's still talking. "I should mention for the purposes of a time line, of sorts, that the incubation period is typically seven to twenty-one days, though it can be as long as thirty days. And it's rarely—there's that word again—fatal, if you get medical attention promptly, but sometimes it can cause permanent damage to the kidneys, lungs, and other major organs. In Sadie's case, we've ruled all that out. But permanent damage was a possibility, is what I'm saying. Sadie is one lucky girl."

Luck is a relative term. "Thank you, Dr. Vreeland."

He stands up. "The nurse will be in with the paperwork in a few minutes."

Oh God. When I wrote that post on GoodNeighbors, I hadn't known Sadie really was poisoned. I've gone and fired a warning shot at whoever tried to hurt her.

With that incubation period, it could be anyone. Practically the whole neighborhood's been through our home. I don't know the method of transmission, but it feels like they all had their opportunities. They created them.

I text Doug frantically. I need you.

Come to the hospital now.

We can't go home.

Fifteen awful minutes pass. This is inexcusable. He knows that I'm alone at the hospital with our sick baby. Yes, she's on the mend, but people can take turns for the worse. He's supposed to be making himself available to me. I didn't tell him that when he left, because it seemed too obvious.

Where's the nurse? Not that I want her bringing me that paperwork. Then we're supposed to vacate the room, and I don't know where to go.

I call Doug's cell. He doesn't answer. I call his work line. No answer. I go to his company website and look up his colleagues. I call every one of their numbers until someone answers, and then I say it's an emergency, that I need Doug to call me immediately.

"Doug's not in. He hasn't been in since your daughter got sick. It sounds like maybe you misunderstood . . . ?" The woman trails off, with obvious sympathy. She thinks what anyone would think in this situation. That he lied to me. That I'm a fool.

The neighborhood rumors must be true. He is with Andie.

I wanted him to talk to Dr. Vreeland and figure out what questions I'd forgotten to ask. I wanted us to call the police together. Then we could sell the house, and if we lose some money, so be it. It's only money; it's not Sadie's life.

But I can't reach him, because he doesn't want to be reached. He wants his privacy. He wants Andie.

All those unexplained absences. The fights he picked so he could storm off.

He's been having an affair while his baby's life was in danger. This is not the man I thought I knew. This is not a man I can trust.

If we'd never moved here, would he have just found a different woman in another neighborhood, or is it really something about the AV? Has this block destroyed us or just exposed us?

We're safe here, at the hospital. I don't know how we can be safe at home, but I also don't know where else we can go. To a hotel, maybe, just the two of us. We'd have to tell Doug where we were or it might be considered kidnapping. Whatever it takes, I will keep her safe.

CHAPTER 32

ELLEN

I've seen Nils driving down the street really slowly on two separate occasions. Casing the joint, that's what they would say in old movies. It weirded me out, even though I've never been of much interest to him. I'm sure Ilsa doesn't know.

They look more like brother and sister than most actual siblings—both so towheaded they're practically albino, both so tall that they've developed the habit of stooping so they won't intimidate. But that's not why Nils was riding so low in the seat. He seemed, absurdly enough, like he was trying to appear inconspicuous. It might have helped if he wasn't driving a Hummer.

It's just one more sign of the apocalypse—the walking dead returning to haunt the living.

Here's another sign: I barely sleep anymore, so this morning I saw (and heard) Gina and Oliver fighting in the street at the crack of dawn.

"I was back before the kids woke up!" he was protesting. She grabbed his collar and screamed in his face, *"That wasn't the rule!"*

I've never seen that side of Gina before. Sure, tightly wound people can spring open, but I never thought Gina would be one of those. And as a couple, Gina and Oliver have always seemed rock solid. I'd assumed that being asexual had some sort of protective aspect to it, like an amulet that would shield her from jealousy. But maybe Tennyson getting it on with Oliver is just too much for her.

I want to go outside and tell Gina it's casual. I mean, she knows this. Everything with Tennyson is casual. She's not much for intimate conversation. It'll be short-lived, too. Tennyson and Vic are the best advertisement for why (and how) openness works. If they're out in the street fighting tomorrow, it really will be Armageddon.

Then there's Andie and Nolan. If she's not actually having an affair with Doug, she's doing a pretty good job of faking one. I feel like I should do something, help Nolan somehow, but it's not like he's any good at talking about feelings. He doesn't like to admit he has any. But I know how he reveres Andie, and I always thought she felt the same way. If Doug and Andie are together, it will truly be cataclysmic.

Then there's Wyatt, who seems so distraught every time I see him on the street. I know Yolanda is putting him through the wringer. I set him up, with no conscience. I was just so single-mindedly focused on getting rid of Kat that I never thought twice about sending Yolanda that picture from Kat's phone. I didn't care what happened to him. I was that obsessed.

I'm afraid this whole neighborhood is falling apart, that it's been some gigantic house of cards, and that Kat and Doug were the wind to blow it all down. Or maybe I'm the one who flicked my finger and set it all in motion. My vendetta against Kat, my need to drive her out, is destroying what I love.

All that, and I've failed. She's coming back here anyway. It's the only home she has, and that's the only family she knows, and unless I can get Doug to boot her out, I'm stuck with her as my neighbor.

I can't talk to anyone, can't get a fresh perspective. My secrets have segregated me from these women whom I've come to love. But do they really know me? They don't even know I'm from Haines. They have no idea who my father is.

Katrina knows me best, if she'd just open her eyes. It's like she's blocked me out, pushed me down into the most subterranean part of her subconscious. I feel like even if she changed every feature in her face, I'd still recognize her. I couldn't help it.

We were best friends for eleven years, from ages six to seventeen. Then there was the accusation about my father, and I went to her, crying my eyes out, not knowing that she would turn around and go to the police and claim he'd done it to her, too.

There weren't that many victims, and most of them dropped out, until only two remained. One of those was Katrina. She testified against my father, who had treated her like his own daughter for years. She had no dad, she had nothing, and my family took her in. She ate dinner at our house practically every night. All those Saturday night sleepovers. All that compassion we had for her, and she turned around and lied. She destroyed us.

That's what it was all about: I had the best of everything, and she had so little. I tried to share with her, but that wasn't enough. She wanted to make sure that I was left with nothing.

My father insisted upon his innocence, but the town was happy to bring him low. He told me that Haines was full of envious people, and I could see it in their bloodthirst. They practically came out with pitchforks. The jury was rigged. That was the only way they could have convicted him.

Having the last name Layton had always been a badge of honor and a source of pride. I'd been from the best family, and now I was a pariah. People looked at me with pity, or with contempt, or disgust, treating me like I was contaminated. The whispers. The ostracism. The loneliness of trying to defend someone who everyone said was indefensible. But he wasn't! He was my dad. He was a good man, and I couldn't say that out loud anymore. No one wanted to hear it.

Katrina had gotten her wish. She'd turned me into an undesirable. Just like she was.

I was so angry. All the therapy in the world couldn't stop the anger.

Really, the therapy made it worse. Being told I was in denial, having to hear the lies from the newspaper about how he groomed all those kids, and sometimes, I have to admit, she even got me to doubt him. There were times I thought that eight was a lot of victims, and that they were all telling versions of the same story, and that one of those victims was a girl I had loved. There were times in therapy when I started to wonder if it could have happened, and times since. I know my father. My heart knows him.

But I can't see him anymore. He's still in prison. I can't visit because the last time I did, I sat across from him and—I would never admit this out loud—I had the feeling that maybe he really was capable of what they'd said. I've gone back over that again and again, and I honestly don't know what changed. It wasn't like he confessed. But after he was out of my sight, I revisited all my childhood memories, the way he was with me and the way he was with Katrina, and I knew the truth again: that Katrina and the others had set him up, for their own bizarre reasons.

I got so furious. It was like I really could have gone on a murderous rampage. I wanted to track her down and kill her with my bare hands.

What stopped me was believing in karma, that she'd get hers, that she'd live a terrible and miserable and lonely life. I told myself that I'd live out that old saying about how the best revenge is living well. I found a husband and I had my baby and I was accepted into a community, which felt so good after the ostracism my family suffered. But then Katrina showed up in the AV with this husband everyone liked and the most beautiful baby. All the fury came back. I would do whatever it took to get her out of my neighborhood. An eye for an eye. A family for a family.

I don't care what some therapist thought. Katrina is the villain, and that's not a narrative. That's the truth.

I log in to my e-mail, and there's the usual digest from GoodNeighbors. Twelve new messages from my neighbors! I scan, my eyes widening as I read the third post:

> I got your e-mail, and I've had enough of your notes. And I know you're behind the rest of it, too. You know exactly what I'm talking about. I was afraid, but I'm not anymore. I don't even care who else reads this. I can't worry about what anyone thinks of me. Not now. It's gone too far. I just care that you're reading. You're somewhere on this site, and you're on my block, and I'm going to find you. I'll do whatever it takes to stop you. ANYTHING.

So instead of Kat leaving the AV, she's putting us all on notice. She's so unhinged that she's going vigilante, and she wants us to know it.

I can't tell if she's bluffing.

What I do know is, I never wrote any e-mail, and he wouldn't have, either. Which means that either Kat's truly batshit and is conjuring phantom e-mails, or this has officially gotten out of control.

CHAPTER 33

KAT

Doug and Sadie are both asleep, and I wish I could join them. But I can't stop thinking about who might be behind the notes and now the e-mail, who roofied me, who poisoned my child. All that, and I'm still in this house. Because it occurred to me that running might not end it. If someone hates me that much, they could follow me anywhere. So I'll stay, embedded in this neighborhood, where I can find the clues and the proof. Then they'll pay for what they've done. They'll be locked up like Layton, and I'll be truly free. Sadie and I will be safe.

Though if I'm honest with myself, having Layton behind bars hasn't released me from my own prison of shame. Dr. Morrison talked about how brave it was of me to testify against Layton, how I protected all the other little girls he might have gone on to victimize. But when I testified, I was only seventeen, and I wasn't thinking of the little girls in the future; I was thinking of the little girls in Layton's past.

Learning that I wasn't actually special, that there had been others, devastated me. Ellen came to my house to tell me that her father had been falsely accused, and my first thought was, *It's all true*. And I wasn't the only one. I was such a fool.

Layton and I had been together from when I was ten until when I was thirteen—until I started to look more like a woman and less like a girl. But what he told me at the time was that he needed to end our relationship because it was wrong. As much as he loved me, I was his daughter's best friend, and even though his marriage was nothing but an empty facade, he needed to rededicate himself to it for his children. He made it sound like a terrible sacrifice, like losing me was practically killing him.

But it was bullshit. He was moving on to other prepubescents. He'd lied to me.

I'd been so hurt and so angry, and I didn't know what to do about it. I thought that Ellen deserved to know who her father really was, and before I went to the district attorney, I told her. She didn't believe me, but I was sure she'd come around.

Then there were all these other victims coming forward, and I found out just how not special I was. We were all just so horribly similar, all duped in the same exact ways. One by one, they dropped out—their parents changed their minds or they had emotional breakdowns—until it was just the original accuser and me.

Ellen stood by her father. She even manipulated for him, begging me not to testify. She didn't stop me, but she made me feel guilty. It was terrible, being on the stand, having to look at Layton, the only man I'd ever loved (I didn't have a father, after all), and looking out at Layton's wife, who'd treated me so kindly and who resembled Ellen. I was tearing apart their family and for what? For vengeance. I was punishing him for the fact that I wasn't special at all. I was just stupid.

But I'd loved him. I didn't love all the sexual things, not on their own, but I loved making him happy. He tried to end our relationship a bunch of times, and I seduced him back. I was ten and eleven and twelve and thirteen, feeling powerful. Feeling irresistible. Then I hit puberty, and he could resist me, all right. Intellectually, I know that makes him a pedophile. But sometimes I still don't know what it makes me.

Here I am, with a husband who's supposed to love me, who's supposed to have chosen me above all others, forsaken all others, and I'm still so stupid. I don't know where he was when he was supposed to be at work, not for sure, but I have a pretty good idea.

What I do know is that I was terrified when I brought Sadie home by myself, letting myself back into Crayola, i.e. the scene of the crime. I know that I disinfected every surface twice over. I know that I was afraid to put Sadie down anywhere, that I just kept her clutched to me. I know that this is not what home should feel like.

I know that Doug continued to ignore me for hours, until he walked inside at six p.m., pretending it had been a long day at the office. He was obviously genuinely thrilled that Sadie was back with us, and he asked questions about how she was. As an afterthought, he asked about me.

What I didn't tell him was that I'd called the police. That two officers came out and took my statement. They also took all the cardboard notes, except for "Does your husband know?" I hid that one, wanting to retain some evidence of my own and not wanting them to wonder what it was that my husband doesn't know. I can't afford to lose any credibility, with such an incredible story.

I've already forgotten the officers' names, though I wrote them down. I thought of them as Big and Little, for obvious reasons. They seemed sympathetic about Sadie's recent hospitalization, but Big raised an eyebrow about Dr. Vreeland's intimation of poisoning, like he thought maybe the doctor was some kind of quack. "Do you know Dr. Vreeland?" I asked, and they shook their heads. "He's very professional," I told them.

"He has no reason to make anything up." Another slight eyebrow lift from Big.

Little assured me that they'd speak with Dr. Vreeland, and Big said that they'd start talking to my neighbors, see if anyone suspicious had been hanging around. Big wanted to know whether anyone had directly made a threat against Sadie or me, if I'd had any negative run-ins, and I said no, everyone had seemed lovely—to my face. "It's a great neighborhood," Little said, with the most feeling either of them had shown, and I had a sinking sensation. Even though I stressed again that the bacteria was rare, that the virus showed up most often in people working with livestock, Big asked, "Do any of your neighbors have dogs?" and I knew I was fighting a losing battle.

They clearly didn't believe anyone in the AV would do something like this. I had the sense that their investigation would be cursory at best. Though they were unfailingly polite, I was pretty sure they'd laugh at me later. Maybe they'd even call Wyatt to let him in on the joke.

I decided not to even fill Doug in when he got home. He'd just find a way to dismiss me, too, to downplay everything. I'm on my own.

I can't sleep in the bed with him, not after everything, so I'm lying on the love seat, staring up at the ceiling; my mind is spinning like Sadie's mobile. I go back to Big's final question: "Is there anyone you've wronged? Anyone who could be holding a grudge against you?"

I hear a noise outside, and there's Yolanda, pushing her double stroller. It's definitely odd, since it's ten at night. Shouldn't her kids be in their beds sleeping? Though the ground is flat, she seems to be huffing. I think she's put on more weight since I last saw her, or it could just be the unflattering shorts she's wearing.

Without thinking, I dash outside. I plant myself directly in her path. Her hair is pulled back severely in a bun, and she's not wearing any makeup. She looks aged.

"Oh," she says without a smile. "You're back."

"Sadie was discharged."

"Congratulations." She starts to push the stroller around me.

Her kids are asleep. I might not get a more perfect moment. If Yolanda's behind all this, then I need to call a cease-fire. Even though she hates me now, the notes started way before whatever it was that happened with Wyatt, the day of the block party. I have to start somewhere.

"I'm glad I ran into you," I say. I take a deep breath.

"I wanted to say I'm truly sorry. For what happened at girls' night, with Wyatt." Her face goes from stony to stormy. "I didn't know what I was doing. I didn't even remember it. I only found out when I saw a picture on my phone."

"You expect me to believe that?"

"I was blacked out that night. Someone slipped me a roofie. I'm positive. Someone in this neighborhood has had it out for me since I moved here. They leave me hateful notes."

She shakes her head angrily. "This is the story you're going with?"

"It was a kiss," I say. "Nothing else."

"How do I know that?"

"Well, what did Wyatt tell you?"

She looks away. "He doesn't remember what happened that night, either. But he's pretty sure it was just a kiss."

"Wyatt doesn't want me, and I don't want him. Doug and I aren't going to be open."

She snorts. "You could have fooled me."

Is that a reference to Doug and Andie? "I'm not going to be a regular. I'm not going to put myself in that position ever again. You have nothing to worry about."

She looks directly at me, trying to figure out if she should keep hating me. I can tell she's vilified me in her own mind in order to be able to live with Wyatt. I get that. All the compromises, all the rationalizations, all the little mental tricks we do just to get through the day and have what we thought we'd always wanted.

"I am so sorry," I say again. "There was never anything between Wyatt and me, I swear to you. We never even flirted. Someone put ketamine in my drink. That makes people overly sexual."

She's dubious, but then I see her dawning realization that this could work in her favor. "Do you think someone could have drugged Wyatt, too?"

"I don't know. Maybe."

"Unbelievable," she says. But I can tell she's a little relieved. Like maybe there's another way to let Wyatt off the hook.

"Thanks for hearing me out."

She starts to push the stroller away and then says, "You're better off."

"What do you mean?"

"Opting out."

What she doesn't know is that I'm the one opting out; I'm just not sure if my husband is.

CHAPTER 34

I creep outside at four a.m., while Doug sleeps on peacefully, down the hall from Sadie.

He should be tossing and turning, his slumber fitful and disturbed. Even if he's not an adulterer, he must know that he's appearing to be an adulterer, with his disappearances and his emotional distance.

I will deal with my marriage at some point; I have to. We're Sadie's parents, and what we do will inevitably affect her.

But right now, I have to stay focused. There was an attempt on Sadie's life, and the perpetrator is still out there, needing to be stopped.

Many of the couples on this block are wealthy. Wealth buys access. It can also buy secrecy. Vic and Tennyson, Oliver and Gina, Nolan and Andie, Brandon and Stone—they could all afford to do it and to cover their tracks afterward. Yolanda and Wyatt don't seem nearly as rich, but Wyatt might have contacts through the police force. Obtaining leptospirosis is not out of the realm of possibility for my neighbors, if they wanted it badly enough.

But the motives . . . that's where it's murky. I've barely seen Vic, and I imagine he has his hands full with the spreadsheet. The idea of my being a threat to Tennyson is fairly laughable. Oliver and Gina—that they hate to lose, and that Doug and I got Crayola? Brandon and Stone—no way. Just, no way. Nolan and Andie.

Andie. She wants my husband.

I'm standing in the street, and now it's 4:12 a.m., and I'm quaking. I'm dealing with an attempted murderer here. If I get caught, what will he (or she) do next? Whoever it is must be on alert. I basically announced on GoodNeighbors that I was planning to strike back.

How I wish I hadn't written that, and I still had the element of surprise. But I am where I am.

The police won't do much without hard evidence, and they're not going to look very hard *for* evidence. That much was clear. So as frightened as I am, I need to be just as determined as my enemy.

This is for Sadie.

I start with the cans across the street. I'm wearing a pair of bright-yellow kitchen gloves, the kind you'd normally use to wash dishes, and I quickly develop a method for searching. Raquel and Bart, Oliver and Gina, Brandon and Stone, Wyatt and Yolanda, Vic and Tennyson, one after the other. Just for good measure, I check inside the can of the old crone Gladys. There's not even one trash bag in there. Huh?

She's not really on my suspect list, and the rest are, for lack of a better word, clean. It's just the ordinary paper trail and detritus of life. I don't care about the processed foods my neighbors hide or their brand of personal lubricant. I don't care about their fungus cream, their stool softener, their Viagra, their probiotic pills, their Rogaine, their facial lotions and potions. Brandon takes Ativan; Yolanda takes Prozac. They see the same psychiatrist. But that hardly seems like a smoking gun.

I don't have time for garden-variety snooping. I'm looking for something very specific, though I can't say precisely what it is. Like porn, I'll know it when I see it.

Gina and Oliver's papers are shredded; everyone else has their bills, paycheck stubs, canceled checks, and other financial documents right out there for anyone to see. The numbers are, often, astounding. I'm amazed that anything legal can yield that kind of return. But it's confirmation that my neighbors have the means to obtain anything, including that virus. Not that that'll convince the police to do their jobs.

I mean, wouldn't it have made the most sense for them to start questioning my neighbors yesterday, since they were already on the block? Instead, they just got in their cruiser and drove away, and I'm not sure when they'll be back. Despite what they heard about the poisoning of a baby, they clearly feel no urgency. I need to create that urgency.

I cross the street and visit Andie and Nolan's house. When I open their trash can, the stench of dirty diapers assaults my nostrils and almost prohibits me from going further. Almost.

I steel myself and paw through. No bills or financial documents, no embarrassing Twinkies. It's like they want to make sure their garbage is of the highest quality. Everything organic, quinoa, spelt, high-fiber bread, sugar-free and low-salt marinara sauce . . . their nutritionist must be proud. No cheating on their diets here. There are some Q-tips and cotton balls but no old jars of moisturizer or other products. Diapers notwithstanding, they're keeping it classy, those two. Well, three, counting Fisher.

I close the lid. I move back toward home and stop at Val and Patrick's, leaving no stone unturned. If Val's garbage is any indication, it seems like there's nothing she won't try to keep her weight low and the wrinkles at bay. Empty containers from detoxing fasts, supplements, and shakes, plus creams and supposed miracle products from QVC abound. Meanwhile, Patrick just has a can of old-style shaving cream from Gillette. The double standard of men's and women's aging is on full display.

I glance toward June's house. I don't want to snoop on my new best friend, the one person I've come to count on, since I can't seem to count on Doug these days. But I need to be thorough, for Sadie's sake.

At first, it's going well. There's nothing incriminating in the garbage. It's just Goth makeup (Hope stuff) and auburn hair extensions (June) and food wrappers and sundries. I'm about to turn back toward my own house, satisfied, when some sixth sense tells me to look in the recycling. That's where I see the dining room chair cardboard, what's left of it.

I try to think of any other explanation for it being here weeks later, anything besides June being the author of the notes. When I told her about them, she acted surprised. Now she's getting rid of the evidence, a day after the police were here. Their squad car was right in front of my house, so either she saw it or someone told her, with the AV being what it is.

If she was scared of getting caught, does that mean it's over, or will she just move on to some new way of terrorizing me? Or could she have had a change of heart after all this time?

None of it makes any sense. She's been the only thing keeping me going, besides Sadie herself. She took care of me. I cried in her arms. She understood because she went through it with Hope all those years ago. She volunteered to be with me, day after day. She was by my side, on my side, I could feel it. She hated that Sadie was in pain. I know she did. I felt it.

Could someone else have put the cardboard in her recycling to frame her? They all told me how transparent I was, like it was an endearing quality. Maybe I telegraphed my next move in that GoodNeighbors message. The real perpetrator is one step ahead of me.

My first AV best friend is probably sleeping with my husband; my second AV best friend may very well have poisoned my daughter.

It can't be true. It can't.

I go back over each conversation June and I had, as best I can remember it, and yes, she asked a lot of questions, but I thought she was just trying to understand me better.

Or she wanted to find out things she could use against me. But why? How could someone I'd never met before hate me so much?

She's sent me only one text since I've been home, asking how Sadie was; I told her, and then she didn't respond. I'd thought, just for a second, how strange it was that June would spend all that time with me at the hospital only to disappear once Sadie was out of the woods.

She was there when I was at my most vulnerable. By design. Because it served her somehow.

Some part of me just can't believe it, though. June? I felt like I'd known her forever, like I could trust her with my life and Sadie's life. How could I have been so wrong?

That last day at the hospital, there was something about the glow in her eyes when I talked about Crayola, the way she wanted me to leave Doug rather than fight for my marriage. That glow didn't care. It just wanted me gone.

But I saw how she looked at Sadie. I saw the tears in her eyes. Could anyone possibly be that good of an actress?

Maybe she meant to hurt me, not Sadie. The leptospirosis was meant for me, and when she saw Sadie there . . . those were tears of guilt.

I could call the police and tell them that the cardboard's in June's recycling, but they're not going to make it here before the recycling truck does. It's already less than a block away.

I could take a picture or take the cardboard out of June's recycling, but it'll really just be my word against hers. She'll deny it, of course. I know she's an excellent liar. The neighborhood will take her side. She'll have a block full of character witnesses, one of them a cop, and I'll have nobody. Maybe not even my own husband.

I need to turn the tables somehow. I just can't let her, or anyone else, know that I'm onto her.

The AV is where people know everything about their neighbors, where there are no secrets. So somewhere on this block, someone must have the goods on June. They have what I need. I'll just have to get it out of them.

CHAPTER 35

Doug told me that his manager gave him the day off today, after seeing yesterday just what a toll everything has taken on him. Another lie, but I'm not going to call him on it right now. I don't have the energy for a come-to-Jesus conversation about our marriage.

What matters right now is protecting Sadie, and the fact that he's inside, sleeping, with her down the hall means I can start my mission. I'm going to level the playing field. June thinks she knows me; well, I'm about to get to know the real her. And why she's after me.

At seven a.m., I start going door to door with my petition. Ostensibly, it's to increase funding for children's hospitals; really, it's to get samples for a handwriting analysis. The notes are my only real clue. I imagine that no one will check whether Proposition 29 is for real; no one reads fine print.

I figure it's early enough that everyone's up and getting ready. I plan to knock as insistently as everyone else does in the AV.

Raquel steps outside in a robe, closing the door behind her. I go into my spiel, explaining what great care Sadie received and how everyone should be able to get the same care, regardless of their economic means. Raquel doesn't listen or ask for any particulars, and she signs without hesitation, telling me how happy she is that Sadie's all right. "I was so worried!" Then she grabs me in an impromptu hug. I thank her and extricate myself quickly, asking if Bart is home and would be willing to sign.

"Of course he'd sign! But are you OK? Like, really OK?" She's studying me with concern.

"Sure, I'm fine." I try to assemble my face into the appropriate expression.

"Because I saw your post."

Shit. The GoodNeighbors post. I hadn't exactly forgotten about it, but I have no prepared response.

Seeing how tongue-tied I am, Raquel says softly, "I know how it is. When you see your child sick, it can play tricks on your mind."

"That's what it was." I agree immediately. "Everything with Sadie was so stressful, and I think I just misread some things. Read into them, I mean."

"I have the best therapist. Do you want her name?"

I can just imagine the GoodNeighbors post about that, all the folks in the neighborhood recommending their own therapists. Who does June see? Is baby poisoning confidential? "Maybe," I say.

"Well, you'll let me know." She smiles at me with something like affection. Then she tells me she'll get Bart so he can sign, too. I'd almost forgotten I was holding the clipboard.

She goes back into the house, and when she emerges, Bart is with her.

"So sorry you went through that," he says, "but happy to hear your little one is all right." It's the most I've ever heard him speak. His cadence is polite and formal, almost like a military man on leave.

"Make sure you print on this line"—I point—"and sign on this one." All the notes were printed.

I figure it doesn't hurt to get handwriting samples from the whole block, in case I'm wrong about June. In case someone else, say, put the dining room chairs in her bin to frame her. It's a long shot, but I've always been cursed with hope.

"June was such a help while I was at the hospital," I say. "I want to get her a thank-you gift. Do you know what kinds of things she likes?"

Raquel and Bart look at each other, with identical thinking expressions. Then they start to laugh, at I don't know what. They actually seem, bizarrely enough, like a good couple.

"I'm not sure," Bart says. "Sweetie, what do you think?"

"She's got so much Hope drama. Maybe a massage?"

"That's a great idea," I say. "Do you know if her ex-husband helps at all?"

Raquel shakes her head. "Total loser."

"Really? That's too bad."

"Yeah, it is. I love June. She deserved better than that guy."

Bart casts her a sideways glance. "He was all right. He was more blue collar than the other guys around here." So blue-collar guys stick together.

Raquel exclaims, "He was *all right*? June let him have everyone on the block, and then he still went and had an affair with someone he worked with! Then he left her with Hope, with no emotional or financial support! And he cancels half the weekends he's supposed to take her!"

Bart chuckles. "OK, OK. You win." His eyes stray across the street. "I don't know how she gets by. I never got how they afforded that house to begin with, and she hasn't gone back to work. It's like she has a sugar daddy or something."

At that, I notice that something in Raquel's face closes off, like Bart said too much.

"We should get back to breakfast," Raquel says. "So glad Sadie's better and that you're home. You just need to catch up on your sleep. That'll make a world of difference. Hey, maybe you and June can get massages together."

"Maybe," I say.

Gina and Oliver are pleasant, brisk, and efficient. They sign with little fanfare, like people with nothing to hide. "We've got to get the kids ready," Gina says. Then, before she turns away, "Do you want to come out for girls' night tomorrow? Same time, usual place."

Didn't she see what I posted on GoodNeighbors? If she didn't, someone must have told her. So the invitation is pretty weird. It's like she wants fireworks; she wants a powder keg of crazy in their midst.

"You probably haven't even had a chance to consider," she says, "with everything that's been going on."

Consider? Then I realize: she means the openness. I still haven't officially opted out.

"We'd still love to have you as a regular. Come out tomorrow night, OK?"

"I don't know," I say. "I'll have to talk to Doug. We haven't really had a chance to think about much other than Sadie."

She smiles briefly. I see how sad her eyes are. Oliver puts his arm around her in a perfunctory way, and then that door is swinging shut, too.

Stone and Brandon are up next. Brandon is his usual voluble self. "I wish I could have done more for you while you were in the hospital," he tells me as he scrawls his name. "I felt like the worst neighbor in the world."

"I appreciate how you respected my wishes. We just needed to be together as a family."

"I can understand that," Stone says, taking the petition from me. "See you around, I hope?"

It's an odd question. I'm right across the street. But maybe not that odd, given the GoodNeighbors post. I smile back at him, and then he withdraws into the house. Brandon stays where he is. Perfect.

"Did someone really leave you notes?" he asks.

"They really did. But I probably blew them out of proportion. They were just like, 'Don't park your car in my spot.'"

"But they were anonymous?"

I nod.

"Must have been Gladys, then."

"With Sadie being sick and with Oliver next to Stone, I just started to dabble in some conspiracy theories."

He lets out a delighted laugh. "That must be it!" Then he lowers his voice and leans in. "No one else could have done it except for Gladys. I know everything that goes on around here. No one can keep a secret. Not from me, anyway." He sounds a little bit territorial and a little bit proud. "We're good people on this block. Flawed, sure. And quirky, what with the openness and all, but good."

"I kind of wish you'd been the one to come to the hospital instead of June," I say. "You would have made me laugh." I have the sense that his currency is flattery.

"I wish I could have gone, too. But honestly, I can't stand those places. I smell that disinfectant, and I'm reminded of the super-germs they're trying to kill. So when June volunteered, I was relieved." There's a funny quality to him, like guilt with some additive I can't quite place.

"She did a good job, though," I say.

He nods, and that's all.

In my admittedly limited interactions with him, Brandon never just nods.

"You don't like June?" I ask.

"It's not that. It's just . . ." He leans in and lowers his voice again. "I think her husband told her some things about me that weren't true, and she believed them, and it's never been the same between us."

"What kind of things?"

He looks left and right exaggeratedly, like the shifty eyes of a picture in an old episode of Scooby-Doo. "He wanted to be dominated, but only by a man. He was into it, but he made it sound to her like I was somehow *forcing* myself on him." Brandon makes a face. "Some people just don't want to own what they're into. It doesn't fit with their image of themselves. Sexuality can be a messy, ugly thing, and I'm OK with that. But he definitely wasn't."

"I hear he wasn't such a great guy."

"Really? June said that?"

"No. Raquel said it."

"I was hoping June was finally ready to admit it and file for divorce. They've been separated for years now. She deserves better." It's clearly the party line. He looks over my shoulder, and then he does this theatrical sort of ducking down, like he's hiding behind me. "Nils again," he explains.

"What?"

"Nils drives around just to get a look at me. He's like this lovesick puppy. I should never have gotten involved with him. I had a suspicion he was closeted."

"Nils? As in, Nils and Ilsa?"

"As in, the people who used to live in your house. I was so glad when Ilsa insisted they move away. At least now it takes him some work to stalk me. Before, it was way too easy. He'd just walk out his front door and *ta-da!*"

I'm trying to think how to get the conversation back on track, back to June, when he says he really needs to go.

"Don't tell June I said anything about her husband, OK?" he says.

"I won't. Thanks for signing the petition."

"Anytime. Love to Sadie!"

So June had a bad marriage, to a bad man, who she tries to believe is good. She may have a sugar daddy, and I know she has a daughter who's out of control. But what does any of that have to do with me?

Tennyson answers her door next, her hair unkempt, in a robe loosely belted over a black satin negligee. "Vic goes to the gym at the ass-crack of dawn every day, but I know he'd want to sign this," she says. "Come back in an hour?" She writes her name and scribbles an absolutely unreadable signature beside it. Then she hands me the clipboard with a huge smile. "Now that we've got that out of the way, let's get down to business." I look at her nervously. "Is Sadie really and totally better? Please say yes!"

I relax and smile. "Yes. She just needs to drink lots of milk and get lots of sleep, but it's a full recovery."

"I can't wait to see her. Can you take her out of the house yet? Like, could you bring her over to the park today? It'd be great to catch up."

"Not quite yet, but I'll let you know."

"So someone's harassing you?" she says conversationally. "Who do you think it is?"

Of the three neighbor reactions to my post, this one seems strangest. Raquel assumed I was having some sort of a breakdown, Brandon assumed it was Gladys, but Tennyson seems to find it not only plausible but a general topic for conjecture. It's like she was completely oblivious to the panicked tone of the post—a woman with her back against the wall, coming out swinging.

For the first time, it occurs to me: Tennyson is sort of narcissistic. She doesn't seem to feel what other people feel. She's not malicious; she's simply unaware. She's got her spreadsheet, and the block orbits around her, and she's perfectly happy.

"I don't know who it is," I say. "That's why I put the post up. Do you have any ideas?"

She cocks her head and gives me a coy smile. "Depends. Who've you been sleeping with?" Then she lets out a big laugh. "Just kidding!

We're still waiting for you to give us an answer. Are you in or are you out?"

"Doug and I have been kind of busy. We haven't really made a decision."

"Which way are you leaning? No, wait, don't tell me. Just give us another chance to convince you. Tomorrow night we're going back to Hound for another girls' night."

"I'll think about it."

She winks. "That's right, play hard to get!"

I start to head down her front steps, looking up and down the street, debating my next destination.

I don't see Yolanda's car, but Wyatt's is there. The last thing I want is for word to get back to her that I was interacting with Wyatt alone. I feel like Yolanda and I are at a détente after our talk last night, and I don't want to jeopardize it.

I also want to avoid Andie's house, but I can't anymore. I need to get that handwriting sample and rule her out. Or in.

I knock on the door of their immense Tudor, remembering how intimidated I once was by her, for an entirely different reason. I recall that first dinner, and her awe-inspiring kitchen ceiling, and her breathtaking dining room, and all that talk about Fisher's adoption that felt both spontaneous and intimate. Did she know then that she wanted Doug? Did she already know she was going to betray me?

"Here," I say coldly. I shove the petition at her. "It's for Children's Hospital. Print and sign."

"How is Sadie adjusting to being home?" Her tone is sweet, like she won't even dignify my rudeness. She takes the clipboard and signs quickly, like she has nothing to hide. "You must be in heaven having her back!"

I can't make pleasantries with her after everything. "Is Nolan here? I need all the signatures I can get."

"He is, but he's upstairs in his office, in the middle of a conference call." She signed, but she doesn't seem very eager for him to do the same.

"I'll wait and catch him on his way out. What time does he leave for work?"

"He's working from home today."

I stare her down. She needs to know I'm not just some pushover. I'm Sadie's mother and Doug's wife, and both of those mean something. "I'm passionate about this, Andie. I'm going to get that signature. So when will he be available? I'll keep coming back."

She splits my eardrums with a sudden yell. "Nolan! Come here!"

He appears relatively quickly, a piece of half-eaten toast in his hand. She lied. He wasn't upstairs on a conference call; he was in the kitchen.

"How are you, Kat?" I realize that he's the first person who led with that, rather than asking about Sadie. He seems like he genuinely wants to know. If our spouses are sleeping with each other, that's got to be a certain kind of bond.

"Just happy to be home and to have Sadie home."

"What do you have here?"

I hand him the clipboard, and he's the first one to read it. He hesitates, the pen in hand, and then he looks at me curiously. I get the funny feeling he knows it's a bunch of hooey. I gaze back at him, like a woman with nothing to hide. He prints and signs, then returns the clipboard. "Seems like a worthwhile measure," he says. "I hope it makes the ballot."

Andie is standing a little bit behind him. She seems subdued. Chastened, I hope.

"Thanks," I say.

"No, thank you," Nolan says, and I don't know what he means, but he sounds friendly and sincere, so I'll take it. And run.

I've saved June for last. Her car is there, and so is her daughter's. Yet I bang and bang, and ring and ring, and no one answers. Strange that she'd avoid me, since as far as she knows, I think she's my AV soul mate. That's what I told her, back when I meant it.

Maybe they're just heavy sleepers. I'll go back later.

Inside my own home, Doug and Sadie are still asleep. I linger an extra minute in Sadie's room, stroking her hair with the lightest of touches, like a present I'm giving myself. Then I force myself to leave. I can't risk disturbing her. She needs her rest.

I go back downstairs. Since I can't get the most likely suspect's handwriting sample yet, I might as well inspect what I do have. I lay the one remaining note out in front of me and hold the petition in my lap.

At first glance, none of their handwriting matches. No one's printing is neat enough. But the notes are block letters, and no one printed their name that way. Also, they could be writing in a different style to throw me off.

I Google forensic handwriting analysis and try again. I'm looking for differences first, at the amount and degree of slant, at the spacing between letters and words, and at the shapes.

Still nothing.

That could just mean, by process of elimination, that June wrote all the notes.

She acted alone, that's all. Everyone else is in the clear, which is good news. It's just one bad apple.

But somehow I don't think so.

Because she didn't even check who was at her door. I know she's an early riser because she told me that during our very first conversation, when she mentioned how early the trash pickup is, and because she welcomed me to GoodNeighbors before sunrise. She's up; I know she is.

Someone must have texted her and told her not to answer the door. They might have told her I'm onto her, that I'm coming for her just like I posted on GoodNeighbors. Because normal people don't ignore someone that insistent. Normal people are, at least, curious as to who needs to see them that badly at 7:40 a.m.

I go to the window and look out at the street, hoping for some inspiration, willing the next step to come to me, and that's when I see Hope heading for her car.

I don't like the idea of manipulating someone's child, but June may have poisoned mine. Besides, Hope's a teenager. A rebellious one, I've heard, and I've got to try to use that to my advantage.

"Hi," I say as Hope's hand is on the driver's door of her Audi. "We've never officially met. I'm Kat, your neighbor."

"I know. I'm Hope." She doesn't make eye contact or smile. Her hand's still on the door, but she hasn't opened it. So that's something.

"Good to meet you. Your mother's told me all about you." Actually, June's said practically nothing about Hope in all our time together, and next to nothing about herself. I didn't even realize how solipsistic all our conversations had been. "She said when you were little, you were in the same hospital as Sadie."

Hope makes a noise of obvious contempt. "What doesn't she lie about?"

"You were never in a hospital?" I glance up at the house to see if June's by a window, watching us. We seem to be in the clear, but I still have to act fast.

Hope shakes her head, disgust splashed across her features.

Those features. They're strangely familiar. I've never seen Hope up close before, and I peer at her, trying to see beyond the mime-white face paint, and the heavy eyeliner, and the red lipstick. I know this girl, don't I?

I stare at her, and she stares back, with bold annoyance. It's the first time I've really looked into her eyes, and now there's no mistaking it. I looked into those eyes a million times when I was growing up. Those are Ellen's eyes.

Then I'm seeing June's face in my mind, despite all the times she shifted so that her hair was partially covering it. I can see Ellen's face—with some sort of time-lapse photography like she's on a milk carton—and I superimpose and cross-reference and, yes, there's been some surgery (definitely her nose and probably her chin, and could they have done something to her cheekbones, or is her face just that much thinner?) and colored contacts, but some essential Ellen-ness remains. I was just too self-obsessed, and too Sadie-obsessed, to see it.

Yet I must have sensed it. Because when I sat with June at the hospital, there was this feeling of comfort right away. We were capable of companionable silence of a sort that usually takes years to achieve. And I opened up to her so easily, in a way I never would have ordinarily. I thought it was just the circumstances, but it was something else, something more. Some part of me felt like the woman in front of me was someone I'd known forever. Because I had.

After all these years, Ellen and I found each other.

"Are you, like, having a seizure or something?" Hope asks. She looks like she really wants to get the hell away from me, but she's making sure I'm OK first. So there's some decency in her. She might be wayward, but June raised her better than everyone thinks.

"Sorry. It's just . . . I was knocking on your door a little while ago. Did you hear it?"

"Yeah. Mom said not to answer it. She said it was someone trying to sell us something. But then, she's always ridiculously nervous about things like that. Stranger danger!" Hope is clearly mocking her mother. Does she know anything about Ellen's history? Does she know her mother's real name? Who her grandfather is?

"I wanted your mom to sign a petition for funding for Children's Hospital. They took such good care of Sadie."

"So Sadie's OK now?" Hope's concern proves she's not a bad kid at heart.

I smile. "She's better than OK." I can't forget my purpose here. "When I was your age, I was really good at forging my mother's signature. For when I got a bad grade or something. Are you, by any chance, good at that?"

She gives me an honest-to-God smile. "I'm excellent."

"I'm only asking because I have to get the petition in later this morning, and I want to have as many signatures as possible. I'm sure it's something your mom would support."

"Why don't you just text her? Tell her you were the one at the door."

I'm trying to think of some other way to trick Hope, which feels kind of wrong and dirty but unavoidable, and that's when she says, "Have you already tried my uncle?"

CHAPTER 36

It's not easy, biding your time, nerves jangling, everyone drinking except you. Inhibitions being lowered, laughter becoming more bawdy and raucous, and you're just waiting. Just hoping you can finish this, tonight.

Watch your back. No, watch your front. Someone
just might stab you in the heart.

It was a new e-mail address, another series of numbers. I forwarded it to the police, but they said it was untraceable. Big promised that he and Little would start interviewing my neighbors tomorrow and that a squad car would drive by my house several times a day. So the threat is getting a little more real, from their perspective.

Then there are the other AV threats: Andie and openness. I'm upset with Doug for lying to me about where he was when he should have been at work, but I realize I haven't yet given him the chance to explain himself. It's not like I haven't kept secrets from him, after all. The reality is, people have affairs. They get caught up in things they shouldn't. It doesn't mean the relationship is irreparable. In Europe, they keep the family together and turn a blind eye.

No, I don't think I could do that. But we could go to therapy. All the love we've had for each other doesn't just vanish in a puff of smoke. Marriage is not a magic trick. It's about putting in the time and the effort when things are hard. It's about tough conversations and forgiveness. Isn't it?

I want a drink so badly right now.

Yet I have to be stone-cold sober if there's going to be any chance of turning the tables on them tonight.

It's a smaller group than the last time. Yolanda won't be here. Andie's running late. June is dealing with some Hope-related emergency but will arrive shortly.

Now that I've met Hope, I wonder if all the stories about her are exaggerated or even made up entirely, if June just likes to have a ready-made excuse to rush off, maybe to be with her sugar daddy. I mean, obviously lying is in June's wheelhouse. Even her own daughter thinks so.

That leaves Raquel, Gina, Tennyson, and me. None of them questioned my decision to stick with club soda, and they've suspended the ban on talking about kids, just for tonight, for me.

"It must be hard for you to be away from Sadie," Raquel says. "I remember Meadow got really sick one time—not sick enough to need the hospital, but we were on the fence about that; we almost took her to the ER—and when it was all over, I just wanted to hold her tight. Like, for days and days."

"You think how it can all vanish in an instant," Gina says, succinctly, unemotionally. She wants to get on to the next conversation, you can tell. Back to the fun. Even fun has to keep to a strict timetable.

I tell them I don't mean to be a killjoy, and I'm sorry that I'm not myself, not that they actually know me. They assure me it's absolutely fine. "You can't always be the life of the party," Tennyson says.

Then June/Ellen breezes in. She says, "It's always so dark in here; it took me forever to find you guys!" She kisses everyone on the cheek, including me. She takes the farthest seat and avoids looking at me.

Her energy is off. She's already got a drink—a rum and Coke, from the looks of it—and as she sits down, she knocks it over. She's a bundle of nerves, clearly.

I study her face for the first time since learning who she really is. It's amazing that I could ever have missed it. The changes now seem shockingly superficial—just her nose and chin and a thinner face and auburn hair instead of dark brown and bright-blue contact lenses over her nutmeg irises. No one could blame her for wanting a new face and a new name. But once you really look, she's so fundamentally Ellen.

Now I can see it in her mannerisms. It's unmistakable. And watching her, even knowing all I know, all she's capable of, something inside me gives way. This is Ellen, my best friend. I loved her deeply. She loved me, too. I know she did. Her father is the one who ruined everything. He brainwashed her, got her to think I was a liar, that all the kids were, and she thought I'd betrayed her family after they took me in and treated me like one of their own.

Of all the awful parts—having to share every terrible detail on the stand chief among them—losing her was the worst. I didn't have a confidante through it all. But more than that, I didn't have anyone to take my mind off things and make me laugh. I didn't have anyone to just plain get me.

But it never occurred to me that she'd become my enemy. A small part of me thought that one day, she'd have to realize who her father really was: a wolf in sheep's clothing, the worst bogeyman of all because he was disguised as everyone's favorite teacher. But he also disguised himself as the best father. He stole my best friend from me, and he stole me from his own daughter.

He told me he loved me. And I believed him. I didn't even think the things he was doing were wrong, not for the longest time, but I knew that it was a secret I was supposed to keep from everyone, including Ellen. "She'd be jealous," he said.

I'm hit by a wave of nausea. Layton brought us here, pitted us against each other. We were just children. Damaged children who became damaged adults. We both feel like we have to fight for what's ours, fight for the families we've created. He made us loyal to him over each other. Now we're adversaries when we should be best friends. When we understand each other better than anyone. We're both victims.

When she talked to me at the hospital, did she feel it, too? That I'm still me, Katrina. Did she feel a connection? Did she ever waver in what she was trying to do? I feel like she had to.

I want to believe her brother is her accomplice, and that he's the one who poisoned Sadie, and that Ellen didn't know, not until it was too late. There's just no way she's a good enough actress to have pulled off those tears at the hospital. She hated seeing Sadie in that state. I know she did.

Or had Ellen actually tried to poison me? Could she really be her father's daughter, after all?

The conversation has been flowing all around us, bubbles on a champagne sea, but Ellen and I aren't a part of it. She's nursing her new drink, stirring it slowly. Her eyes are faraway and full of pain. I'm probably her mirror image.

Whatever I'm feeling, though, I'm going to finish this tonight.

The boys show up together: Oliver, Nolan, Vic, and (to everyone's surprise) Wyatt, who's looking grim. Bringing up the rear is Andie. Impossible as it seems, somehow, I'd forgotten about her, just for a little while.

The women protest flirtatiously. Nolan says, "We thought it would be fun to crash!" but there's nothing fun in his delivery. His being here is intentional. It's deadly serious, and I have the feeling that it's about me.

So I won't be confronting Ellen/June alone. She called for reinforcements.

I never really knew Ellen's brother, Mark. He was years older and always off playing sports. Back then, I didn't think he looked like his father, but he must, a little. I mean, that first night at Andie and Nolan's house, I saw some resemblance. Sensed something. So Mark became Nolan, Ellen became June, and they both tried to start over in the AV where no one knew about their family's disgrace. Then I showed up.

There are greetings all around. The boys are finding another table that they can carry over and put next to ours, and Andie is doing her rounds, her lips lightly grazing my cheek.

That's what does it, what pulls me out of my grief-stricken inertia. Whatever's happening between her and Doug, she thinks she's untouchable. I need to take care of this and get out of here. This ends now.

I'm on my feet, everyone looking up at me in surprise. Except for two people, who came prepared. Good thing I am, too. They don't know my secret weapon. "Could I talk to you outside?" I say, looking at June and Nolan.

I'm so anxious that I can barely walk, but I can hear their steps behind me. I keep going, because this is for Sadie. If I don't take care of it, I'll live in fear, and that'll infect her. It'll be a poison that runs through our home. She's been poisoned enough for one lifetime.

I don't remember the alley, but I must have retained some sense memory about where it is because my legs are carrying me toward the back of the bar and through an unmarked door. It's like I'm seeing it for the first time, though it's familiar enough from the picture. It's long and narrow, with a giant Dumpster not quite ten feet away. The night is breezy, and some garbage swirls by our feet, straw wrappers like snowflakes.

Someone just might stab you in the heart.

But not tonight. Not when everyone knows where I am and who I'm with. These two people have a lot to lose, and they're not stupid.

Then why are they still sending e-mails when they know the police are investigating?

Because they think they can get away with anything. Because they have loyalty to each other. Because whatever happens, they'll tell the same story.

Someone once mentioned a safety net. Well, I've got one of my own. There's no backing out now.

"Hi, Ellen. Long time no see," I say. She registers no surprise. She doesn't speak. "Let's start with why you put the ketamine in my drink," I dare her.

Again, nothing.

"Or was it you, Mark?" I ask, turning to Nolan. "I mean, I get it. I get why you wouldn't want me living next door to her and why you would want to protect your sister. It makes sense. But did you have to be so brutal?"

"No one's done anything brutal," Ellen says. Nolan—Mark—gives her a quick look, from an older brother to a younger sister. He's telling her to keep quiet.

"We don't know what you're talking about," Nolan says.

"Deep in your heart," I say, "you know the truth." I'm talking to Ellen, to my friend, the one who knows me.

"*You* know the truth," she says hotly. Nolan steps forward and puts his arm around her, both support and restraint.

"I told the truth on the stand. I kept your father from victimizing anyone else."

"He didn't victimize anyone!" she says.

Nolan tries to intercede. "Listen, now you know who we are. We know who you are. Let's try to work this out like adults, not children. It's true; we don't want you in the neighborhood. It's very painful for June."

"What about you?" Ellen asks him. "Isn't it painful for you, too? She ruined our family."

"You buy a new house somewhere else," Nolan tells me, "and I'll compensate you for the time and trouble."

"You'll buy me off, you mean," I say. This, I wasn't prepared for. They drug me, they poison my child, they terrorize me, and then we're just supposed to exchange some money and I'm on my way? There's no justice in that. And suddenly, I realize that's part of what I'm looking for. Justice. And acknowledgment. I told the truth. None of this was my fault. It never has been.

"She doesn't deserve your money," Ellen says.

"You need to hear this," I say. "Both of you. You need to hear that your father seduced me, and I spent years believing I was complicit in it. That I was the one seducing him. Because he taught me how to please him, and that's all I wanted to do."

"Stop talking," Ellen says, breathing heavily.

"No! You need to hear me. I even felt guilty for testifying. I felt disloyal. Isn't that how you felt, too?" I'm talking to both of them but looking at Ellen. She's looking back at me, desperate. Desperate not to believe me, but I can see the knowledge is dawning. "He nearly destroyed me, but he made you think I was the one doing it to him. Doing it to your family. And hasn't he nearly destroyed you, too? He's the reason you were terrorizing me. That's not who you really are. You're a good person, Ellen. For you to do what you've been doing to me, even poisoning my child—"

"I would never poison a child!" Ellen turns to Nolan triumphantly. "See? She's a liar!"

I notice he hasn't said a word, but he has gone pale.

"Someone poisoned Sadie," I say. "Dr. Vreeland at Children's Hospital told me so. I can prove it to you. Please, Ellen. Stop ignoring so much evidence. It's time to see the truth."

Suddenly, the door opens, and it's Andie. "I thought maybe I should be a part of this conversation."

"It doesn't have anything to do with you," Ellen says.

"El," Nolan says gently, "she already knows."

Ellen looks back and forth between them. "She knows what?"

"Who Katrina is. What's been going on."

Ellen looks between them, disbelieving. She thought her brother had kept secrets from his own wife?

"I'm his partner in every way," Andie says.

"If you're his partner, why are you off fucking my husband?" I ask.

"Doug and I are friends, that's all."

I see that Nolan's lips are still pursed. He doesn't believe her any more than I do.

Wyatt pushes the door open and steps outside. He looks us all over. "Hi," Nolan says casually, as if we're all just taking a breather from the fun inside.

"Everything OK out here?" Wyatt asks, like he's in his official capacity.

"Everything's fine," Andie says, cool as ever.

"It's good you're here," I say. "You can make the arrest."

"Arrest?" Andie laughs. "No one's getting arrested."

"These three," I gesture, "are the ones who left the notes. They're also the ones who slipped ketamine in my drink and who tried to kill Sadie."

It occurs to me that Andie should look shocked at what I've just said, that she should be saying no one poisoned anyone, that's crazy. Instead, she says, "Nolan and I had nothing to do with that. June tried to get us caught up in her vendetta."

Nolan turns to Andie. Turns on her. "Don't talk about my sister like that. She would never harm a child, and you know it."

"It was you," I say to Andie.

"No." She shakes her head.

I look at Nolan. He's gone even whiter. "You know it was Andie. Deep down, you know. Same as you knew about your father."

He doesn't speak, and I can see I'm right. Ellen turns to him, and she's starting to shake. Somewhere inside, she's known, too. But instead she says, "Dad didn't do anything wrong. His whole life was ruined for nothing."

Nolan's still silent.

"Tell her," Ellen exhorts him.

Finally, he says, "I can't."

"This is bullshit!" Ellen explodes. "Katrina's a liar. She was jealous of our family. You know that as well as I do. We lost a lifetime with our father—with both our parents—because of her."

"I know that you've believed it a long time," Nolan says quietly. "I did, too. I've wanted to, but since everything started with Katrina moving here, and since things have gotten so out of hand, I've started reading the court transcripts. I read Katrina's testimony, and the other girl's, too, and they're almost identical."

"That's because they were prepped by the DA. They were coached to lie."

"I don't think so. Look at her and listen to her. You know what's true."

My eyes meet Ellen's. She can't resist knowing anymore. She sags against her brother. I see something I'm very familiar with: shame. "I'm sorry," she whispers.

Tears are flowing down my cheeks. I feel like I've finally shed this awful weight I've carried for so long. I know now that Layton was the dirty one, not me.

"This is bullshit!" Andie snaps. "Family is family, and Kat is no one to you. You put family above everything, no matter what."

No one speaks for a long minute. Then I say, "You did it, Andie. You poisoned Sadie. Was it because you were putting family above everything or because you wanted my husband for yourself?"

Andie turns to Wyatt. "She's clearly unstable. I hope you're not actually believing any of this."

"No," Ellen says. "That wasn't for family at all. That was all for herself."

"I don't know what you're talking about," Andie says.

"You met Doug before he and Katrina moved in," Ellen says. "Doug came out a few weeks before to measure inside the house. Andie offered to help. They were inside for a few hours, at least. When you came outside with Doug that day, after all the 'measuring,' the two of you were laughing like old friends. You gave him a big hug before he got into his car. You told me how good it would be to have him in the neighborhood. You said, 'He's the kind of guy who could make me rethink my closed marriage.'"

"That was a joke!" Andie protests.

Nolan is staring at Andie, and even though he's known for a while—he couldn't avoid knowing when he saw them in the hospital room—the devastation looks fresh. Ellen is piecing things together, connecting the dots for him.

"The vasectomy," she says. "So you wouldn't reproduce the Layton genes. That wasn't really your idea, was it? It was Andie's." He's too anguished to answer. "She was always leaving an escape hatch." Ellen spits out her next words at Andie. "How long has it been going on, Andie? You and Doug?"

Nolan can't even look at Andie as he says, "You're the one who came up with the ketamine. You talked about how Ellen needed an insurance policy when it came to getting Kat to move. You said the threatening letters weren't enough. You did what you always do. You made me think it was my idea, but it was what you wanted all along."

"You're all crazy! It must be contagious." Andie tries to laugh.

"You want Doug, but he's mine," I say. "And I'm going to fight for him."

"Like you can win!" Now Andie is laughing, but it's ugly and harsh. Has she forgotten her own husband is standing there?

But she hasn't won yet, or she wouldn't be so insecure. "Doug told me he doesn't have feelings for you," I say. I want to inflame her, get her to show her colors all the more. I need Nolan and Ellen to turn on her for good, to turn her in to the police, because I know that she's behind the poisoning. Nolan and Ellen are done terrorizing me, but Andie still needs to be stopped.

"He's lying! You're nothing! Just a fucking victim." She sneers at me, infusing the word *victim* with loathing.

"He's been using you," I say, hoping it's true. "You're a placeholder. He loves me, and you know it."

It's a direct hit. She flies at me, knocking me against the brick wall. I'm so startled that it takes a second to react, and by then I'm down on the ground. She's smacking my head against the concrete, and someone's trying to pull her off, but she's curiously strong, feral.

I hear a loud, authoritative voice. "Freeze! Get off her now!" It's Wyatt, bellowing, and I look up to see a gun trained on Andie.

Andie listens, standing up and stepping away. I'm dazed, from the shock of the attack and from the blow to the head.

Ellen squats down next to me. "Are you OK?" she asks. Wyatt is looking down, waiting for my answer, and maybe that's why Nolan grabs the gun away from him so easily.

"Hey, Nolan. Hey, man," Wyatt says. "You don't want to do this."

Nolan gestures for him to get back, and Wyatt complies.

"So you did sleep with Doug," Nolan says. "Even though you spent all last night convincing me that I was wrong about what I saw in the hospital room. And it almost worked. I came so close to believing you."

"We haven't slept together," Andie says. "He has feelings for me, yes, but that's because I wanted him to. I wanted that insurance policy we talked about. If he fell in love with me, if his marriage ended, then he and Kat would move away. See, it was for the family."

Nolan continues as if she hasn't spoken. "You talked about killing Kat. In that last e-mail you sent her. Stabbing her in the heart."

"You know I wasn't serious about that," Andie says. "I was trying to help you. You and June. That's what this has all been about."

"You made that comment one time." Nolan is seeing Andie as if for the first time. "You said that if something happened to Kat, you would hate for Ellen to take the fall. But she would be the most likely suspect, the one with the grudge, who'd written all those notes." He levels the gun. "Katrina wasn't getting out of the picture fast enough. Doug hadn't chosen you. You were going to murder her and frame my sister."

"No, no." She waves her hands frantically. "I would never do that!"

"You poisoned someone. Maybe it was meant for Kat; maybe it was meant for Sadie. But I don't want to know what else you're capable of."

Andie is talking to Ellen now, probably calculating that it'd bring Nolan back to his senses. "Ellen, you know me. I love your brother. Tell him."

"She's not worth it," Ellen says to Nolan. "Give the gun back to Wyatt."

"I'm Fisher's mother," Andie says. "He needs me."

"You're not Fisher's mother anymore," Nolan says. "You're a monster. And I've known monsters before."

He shoots, and Andie crumples. It really is like slow motion, like a movie, and the sound is still ringing in my ears, and I don't know who goes to whom, but my arms are around Ellen and hers are around me.

Nolan is doubled over on the ground. It's like he's the one who's been shot. Wyatt, meanwhile, is springing into action.

"Call 911," he tells me. "And remember this, all of you: she was reaching for the gun. Andie reached for the gun, and with all that we'd just learned about her, Nolan had no choice."

"It was self-defense," Ellen says, robotic with shock.

"Exactly." Wyatt is pure kinetic energy. I think of all those stories you hear about the thin blue line, the way the officers pull together, how they plant guns in the hands of people they've shot.

"Call 911," he says, "now."

I take out my phone, which has been recording since we came out here. I didn't get a confession exactly; I don't know why Andie did what she did. But I told the truth, and I got more than I could have hoped for. Acknowledgment. Vindication. Ellen's arms around me. Ellen and Nolan don't need to be punished by the law. They've suffered plenty—in different ways than I have, but still.

I look over at Andie. Is she breathing? Do I want her to be?

Maybe justice has been achieved after all.

CHAPTER 37

Doug is on the love seat. The room is dark except for one dim lamp. He's slumped, wrapped in blankets, a portrait in misery. I've never seen him look like that.

Is it because he knows? Word spreads fast in the AV about the most minor things; it's hard to imagine it hasn't spread about something as big as this.

"It's after two a.m.," he says hoarsely. "We need to talk. I've been waiting up for hours. Where've you been?" There's no anger in it, only fear.

So word hasn't spread to Doug. He's that out of the loop.

"Just girls' night," I say. "You know how those nights can go."

"Kat, I have to ask. Were you with Wyatt tonight?"

"No."

"But I know you've been with him before."

"I was dosed with ketamine, Doug. Just like I told you. You may not believe me about that, or anything else, but I'm not crazy. This neighborhood is."

"I'm sorry I didn't believe you."

I stare at him. "Why the change of heart?"

He sighs. "Let's just put it all out on the table. I've been spending time with Andie, as friends, but tonight, after you left, she came over to tell me she loves me and that she wants us to be together. She just wants to wait until after her tenth wedding anniversary to Nolan so she can get his money. What kind of person is that?" He looks amazed, and he doesn't even know all that came to light earlier. That's the least of her crimes. "I told her she was crazy and that I love you." No wonder it was so easy for me to push Andie over the edge. Doug had just rejected her. He'd chosen a nothing like me over her. So what I told her actually turned out to be true.

"You're saying you aren't sleeping with her? You've never slept with her?"

"No. I swear to you. But I know I made a mistake spending time with her at all, when I should have been on your side and by your side. She was in my ear this whole time. She showed me your phone and said that you'd been with Wyatt. I should have confronted you then, but I was just so hurt. And angry, too. Maybe I wanted you to see me hanging out with Andie. I wanted you to see that someone else was interested in me, since you haven't been lately."

I almost laugh. So it was true. He really was using Andie.

"I flirted with her, which I know was wrong, but I felt like I needed the escape. From us, and from Sadie being sick. That day I went in to work, I couldn't focus, and she texted me. I told her how bad I was feeling, and she said we could take a drive together. We went to Point Reyes and ate some oysters, but that was it. Still, it was enough. I lied to you. I was weak, and I was running away."

"You didn't sleep with her, but do you have feelings for her?"

"I didn't even like her much, once I got to know her. She's so full of herself."

Not anymore, she's not.

"I love you. I love our family. I just didn't know where your head was and how you could kiss Wyatt. Andie made it sound like you'd done a lot more than that. Then she told me about the openness, and she said you were supposed to tell me about it, and you didn't, so I felt like you were keeping it all to yourself. You know, like you didn't want me to be with other people but you were doing it behind my back, with my new friend."

I can understand his point, but after the night I've had, I don't know what to think or feel.

"You've been through so much in your life, Kat, and you always deserved better than me. I'm just this spoiled kid, and the first time things didn't go my way, I started spending time with another woman."

So much that he doesn't know about, but he needs to.

"Are you still seeing Wyatt?" he asks.

"I was never seeing him. I kissed him once because Andie tried to frame me. I'm not interested in Wyatt or anyone else."

"I should have talked to you about everything. Is it too late for us? Can you forgive me?" he asks.

Layton was a monster. Doug's my husband, a flawed person, who loves me. And I still love him.

Andie's a monster, too. Well, she was.

"It's not too late," I say. His eyes fill with tears. "But I have to tell you something. The reason that I know Sadie's safe is because the person who poisoned her is dead." His eyes widen. "That person is Andie."

He visibly startles. "Is that a joke?"

"No. She was shot tonight."

I'd learned of her death from the police as they were questioning me. It took a long time for the police to take everyone's statements, including Wyatt's, which was the one that gave all the others credibility. The officers obviously had a great deal of respect for him. Enough to sweep any discrepancies under the rug? I have to hope so.

"Escalation of force," Wyatt said grimly. "Nolan had no choice but to shoot her when she tried to grab the gun." The rest of us told that same story.

Nolan hasn't been arrested. Not yet, anyway. He was by Andie's side when she died. I can't even imagine what he was feeling. All I know is, it's over, for all of us.

Despite all Andie's done and how Doug told me he didn't even like her, there he is, looking shattered. I feel myself shattering, too. He shouldn't look like that.

Then he says, "What can I do? I'll tell the police whatever you want."

It dawns on me: he thinks I killed Andie. That's why he looks like that. He's not thinking of her; he's thinking of me. He looks shattered because he thinks I might be guilty of murder, and he's offering to tell whatever lie will protect me.

"I didn't kill her. Nolan did."

He exhales, his relief palpable in the room. "But why would Nolan . . . Because of . . . ?"

"No, it's not because he thinks you slept with Andie." There's so much I need to tell him, including who Ellen is. Who Layton is. Who I am.

I can't keep secrets anymore, for my own sanity. I want to live clean for Sadie, and for me.

I'm too exhausted to think, but I know this: we need to get out of this house that we never should have bought—not only because of Ellen but because we can't afford it. We should never have taken something we didn't earn, especially when it came with so many strings attached.

The AV is Ellen's, and she can have it back.

"We need to get out of this house," I say. "Have your parents buy you out, and then we'll move into an apartment somewhere. We'll do our best to get past what's happened, and then we'll buy a house within our means."

Silence.

"You're right," he finally says. "We can't stay here. I've been stupid, and I've been cruel, and I've tried to keep up with the Joneses, and in the process, I've hurt you and shattered your trust. But I promise you, we'll get it back."

I reach out my hand. "Let's go to bed," I say.

In the morning, I'll tell him everything. Because he needs to know if we're going to get the trust back. Because he deserves to know, as my husband. But most of all, because I deserve to be able to tell, without shame. I didn't do anything wrong, and now Ellen knows it, too, and that makes all the difference.

CHAPTER 38

Moving out of the AV is pretty different from moving in. There's no block party this time. The neighbors come by, two by two like on Noah's ark: Raquel and Bart, Gina and Oliver, Tennyson and Vic. They tell me they understand and they hope we'll stay in touch. I don't know what it is they could possibly understand, but I hug them back anyway.

Brandon has a big bag of clothes and toys for me, and he asks if he can bring the next batch to wherever I'm living. I tell him absolutely.

I'm touched that Yolanda and Wyatt show up, and while there are no hugs from either of them, I appreciate that they wish me well. "I'm glad Wyatt got to be a hero," Yolanda allows. They can spin it however they want. All I know is, I'm walking out of this neighborhood a free woman, an accessory to nothing.

I have no hard feelings, really, toward any of them. They're just regular people struggling through, and they want a community that will make it easier. They want something egalitarian and democratic; their aspirations are noble. The AV is no throwback to a kinder, gentler time like I first thought. It's incestuous and it's fraught, but they're all genuinely trying for their own strange kind of utopia. Trans-urban indeed.

They want to know each other's secrets, sure, but they also truly want to know each other. There's love between these people. Ties that bind (and gag—sometimes literally). It's complicated, like family. I think they love June, though I don't know how many of them know about Ellen.

It was never too good to be true. It was always exactly good enough (and bad enough) to be true.

Doug's starting therapy, too. In a strange way, it's nice to realize I'm not the only one with issues.

For Doug and me, openness was never going to work. I'd kept so much of my past from him that we couldn't start from a place of transparency, which seems to be the prerequisite. Plus, I have so many issues I still need to figure out that there was no way I could give Doug, or myself, permission to be with anyone else.

The real surprise is that Doug is finally admitting he has issues, too. Now, whether they can be fixed, or whether they'll fit together with mine—that's an open question. But the fact that we're about to wrestle with it makes me hopeful.

Neighbors-with-benefits is not the reason my marriage is in tumult. I don't think it would have mattered if we'd opted in or opted out. It would all have come to light eventually. It seems like openness is just amplification. If you were happy, you're happier; if you were unhappy, you're unhappier. It doesn't save you or destroy you. You do that yourselves. Cracks in the foundation will eventually be exposed, and openness is no quick fix. Relationships are work, however you play them.

The AV proves that generally, people are not good or bad; they're simply warring with their own impulses, good and bad. I just need to surround myself with people who win that battle most of the time. And I have to engage in that fight myself, so that I can embody not just the mother I want to be but the person: kind and loving and open, when it's warranted. My neighborhood will be a reflection of me, and vice versa.

Someday, I'm going to tell Sadie about my past. It'll be an expurgated version, but enough for her to get the gist. I need her to learn that her body is her own and that any sex she has needs to be sex she truly wants. When it isn't, she needs to be able to speak up and say that. I want her to discover her body herself first, in her own time, and make sure anyone who enters it is worthy. She'll be the girl, and the woman, I never was but still hope to be.

The truck is loaded up, and Doug is chatting with the movers. Ellen is the last to show up. I hoped I'd see her. She wrote a letter and slid it under my door a week ago expressing, in great detail, her remorse and regret about not believing me all those years ago. It was a relief to see her handwriting on something other than a piece of cardboard. She also told me more about what she's gone through all these years and why her denial was so powerful. She just wasn't ready to lose her family or even the idea of her family; she was too scared to stop being angry, scared of what she'd feel and what she'd do.

"Can I apologize again," she says, "in person?"

"You don't need to. You were driven mad trying to protect your family."

"The wrong family."

"It was the only one you knew for a long time."

She nods, with a small smile. "I can't believe how forgiving you are. I don't know that I could do it."

"None of us is innocent." Sadie is in my arms, and she reaches out for Ellen. "Well, almost none of us."

Ellen smiles at Sadie. "Such a beautiful girl. I hope she grows up safe and happy."

"I'm going to do my best." I tear my eyes from Sadie. "How's Nolan?"

"He's a mess. He's actually been in a psychiatric hospital. I've had Fisher with me ever since . . . well, you know. He's inside with Hope now. She's actually really good with him."

"I can believe that."

"It's good to see this side of her. But it's terrible, how it came about." She looks right at me. "Thank you for protecting Nolan. You didn't owe him that. What you told the police, I mean. They're not going to charge him."

"Charging him wouldn't help anyone."

Ellen averts her eyes back to Sadie. "I'm still in shock. I can't believe how out of control everything got, how far I was willing to go." ·

"You thought I was the enemy. That's what your dad wanted you to think."

She takes a deep breath and finally looks at me. "So where do we go from here?"

"I have no idea. But I feel like something inside me has been exorcised, if that makes sense."

"I feel that way, too." She looks toward the now-empty house.

Then we turn to each other with uncertain smiles. There's nothing and everything left to say. So much that no one else could ever understand, a bond deeper than perhaps any other I could ever make, forged in the trauma of misplaced loyalty, stronger than steel.

Layton tried to pull us apart, but it didn't work. Somehow, we found our way back together.

Love is like that.

ACKNOWLEDGMENTS

To start at the top: I want to thank my husband for his unwavering support, encouragement, and belief. And while I'm not Kat, I was able to summon up the experience of having a newborn—the terror that comes with loving a tiny being so very much—because of my own beautiful daughter, now six years old. So glad you're you, kid.

Gratitude goes to Mary Jane Weatherbee, Natalie Kiff, and Tara Yudenfreund for being my beta readers, though there's nothing beta about any of you. You're all generous and astute, and I'm very appreciative of your contributions.

To the Lake Union team: What a godsend! Danielle Marshall, you're a fount of enthusiasm and knowledge, and I'm so pleased that you chose me, and *Neighborly*. Alicia Clancy, when you said you were excited about the new book, you backed it up. What editor reads your draft overnight (when there's no deadline in sight)? Alicia, that's who. So glad to continue the journey with you. And Sarah Murphy, I'd never heard of a developmental editor until you came along, but you made me an absolute believer. You brought out the best in my manuscript. Thank you, thank you, thank you!

And finally, to my sterling agent, Elisabeth Weed. You're a champion of each book and a fierce guardian of my career. What would I do without you? Please, let me never find out the answer to that question. To many more!

ABOUT THE AUTHOR

Photo © 2013 Yanina Gotsulsky

Ellie Monago is the pen name of an acclaimed novelist and practicing therapist. She's also a wife and mother, and when you add it all up, she doesn't wind up with much time for hobbies. But she's an avid tennis fan, a passionate reader of both fiction and nonfiction—especially memoir (nothing's as juicy as the truth!)—and she relishes a good craft cocktail.